The Luna Queen Awakens

THE QUEEN'S COURT SERIES
BOOK ONE

AUTUMN MARIE

Copyright © 2021 Read Autumn Marie LLC.
All rights reserved.
The Luna Queen Awakens Second Edition 2022

Cover Designer: Ctrl Alt Publish
Content Editor: Cassandra Higgins
Formatting: Ctrl Alt Publish

No part of this book may be reproduced in any form or by any electronic or mechanical means, including information storage and retrieval systems, without written permission from the author, except for the use of brief quotations in a book review or social media post.

WARNING

This book contains violence, sexually explicit scenes and adult language. This book is intended for adults over the age of 18. For more detailed warnings please visit my website via code above.

For all event details and book signings please check my website for details.

For my husband:
Thank you, for believing in me even in my darkest of days. I will love you till my last breath.

For my children:
Please never give up on your dreams. Even when life throws you a curveball, make sure to grab your bat and swing.

For my parents:
Thank you for helping me to understand how important dreams really are.

For my 5th grade teacher:
You told me I would never amount to anything worthwhile in my life. Here's my chance to say, "Fuck You."

Autumn Marie
www.readautumnmarie.com

"I'M JUST ROLLING THROUGH LIFE WITH
A CUP OF TEA AND MY NEXT
BOOK BOYFRIEND."
          - AUTUMN MARIE

PAST
MALINDA

    The full moon sits high in the sky tonight. Without a cloud to be seen, the field in front of us is practically glowing. I fear if we don't win tonight, this war will drag on forever. Our warriors can't keep going on like this. It always seems that it takes twice as many people to defeat evil, and I'll be damned if we fucking give up. We've been fighting for the last couple of years, and I can tell many are getting tired, but they refuse to quit.

    This shit is devastating all of the supernatural world. You see, dark witches, rogues, and some vampires want to rule the world of the supernatural.

    To them, they have been controlled for too long by the rules that keep this world running in harmony. Now, they seek the control. Not only of our world but of the human world as well. They have made their goals clear—destroy the light.

    We refuse to give into them though. Light witches, werewolves, fae, and those vampires who love the world as it is, will keep fighting for what is right. We must maintain the balance of the worlds. What kills me the most is to see so many sacrificing everything, but even with everything on the line they keep fighting. Their strength to keep going seems to be kindled from the rogue blood, my mate Alpha Jared continues to spill across the battlefield. His skills are unmatched, our warriors push harder because our alpha leads by example.

Suddenly the energy shifts, you can almost feel how unstable the air has become. As time passes the evil surrounding us seems to be getting stronger. Tonight, the pit in my stomach grows. This has absolutely been the toughest battle we've been in and damnit, I just want to come out of it in one piece. I'm almost twenty years old and this is not how I pictured life was going to be. I need this to end, our world needs this turmoil to end— now.

I'm currently fighting in wolf form, my heavy paws push through the dirt with precision and accuracy as I zone in on my next rogue. My wolf, Sahara, looks majestic in the moonlight; her fur is a mix of blonde and red. Even through the chaos of battle, she doesn't stumble. Her movements are strong and graceful. The adrenaline pumping through my veins is just enough to get me into the air and straight at my target.

Gaining the upper hand on this rogue, I lean in, clamping my jaw around his throat. My teeth pierce his skin and as I jerk my head from side to side. I have every intention of ripping this scum apart, but I lose all the breath in my lungs when I'm slammed hard in the side. With my mouth empty, I fall to the dirt as someone jumps on my back. I'm pissed the fucker got away, but the bastard who crashed into me has gotta be three hundred and fifty pounds of pure muscle. Normally this would be no problem, but I'm pretty sure I just broke a few ribs. Thank god for our ability to heal quickly, cause I need to dish out some fucking pay back for that blow.

Suddenly, I howl in pain when the sting of an injection hits my neck. A cold liquid pierces my insides, but then immediately the sensation turns to fire as it spreads through my body, attacking every muscle. This means only one thing, *"fucking wolfsbane."* Sahara growls in my head, the damn concoction forcing me to immediately shift back to my human form. I can't stop the blood curdling scream that comes straight from my soul. A forced shift like this is excruciating, my body is shutting down fast.

Wait, what the hell is going on?

Wolfsbane doesn't force a shift like this. Shit, this is no ordinary wolfsbane. It's gotta be laced with something. I try to wrack my brain with what it could be, but the pain I'm currently experiencing is indescribable. I've been injected with wolfsbane several times before, and whatever is currently coursing through my veins is a little bit of wolfsbane and a whole lot of something else. I try to call out to Sahara, begging her to help speed up the healing process, but she is quiet. The rapid healing abilities all werewolves experience have not kicked in. My panic goes from zero to sixty in the blink of an eye as someone glides their dirty hand down my leg.

The rogue that tackled me reaches down, grabbing me by my ankles. Roughly, he pulls at the joint, dragging me a few feet in the dirt. Then as if I weighed nothing, he spins around with such force heaving me across the small clearing into a large tree trunk. I knew the second I made contact with the tree, everything changed, and just like a crack of a whip my spine breaks.

With immense glee on his face the rogue stalks over to me. Rearing his foot back, kicking my legs–I feel nothing.

This can't be happening. This can't be fucking happening. Tears stream down my face as I'm hit hard with the realization–I can no longer move the lower half of my body. And now I'm at the mercy of this evil man?

The rogue kneels down to straddle my broken, naked body. He reeks of rotting flesh and disease. Fear sets in as I try to struggle to get him off, but it's no use. Bringing his arm back he punches me relentlessly in the face. My eyes start to swell, and black spots cloud my vision. I taste the blood trickling from my split lip and I'm fighting unconsciousness. The bastard slaps me again, hard. He grips my face with one hand, digging his nails into my flesh.

"I want you to watch bitch," he growls as he violently forces my head to the side. My eyes land on Jared rushing in my direction. I can tell he's frantic... Shit, he felt me through our bond. Ugh, this stupid bond. I try to call out to him, to tell him to stay away, but the bastard holding me down covers my mouth, silencing me.

As if in slow motion, Jared's wolf gets closer and closer to finding me. He pushes off the ground hard to leap over two wolves fighting but is tackled midair. They crash to the ground, in a fury of teeth and claws. Suddenly Jared's howl pierces the night air right before his body goes limp. The rogue that was fighting him jumps up and disappears into the chaos. I see a nearby man toss a knife covered in blood to the ground. A tilt of his head to my captor then vanishes right before my eyes.

The asshole releases my face, and his menacing laugh echoes off the trees. Slowly he backs away, never taking his yellow eyes off my discarded form. An evil smirk creeps on his face just before he turns and runs back into battle.

I slowly roll my broken body over onto my belly as I attempt to crawl toward Jared. *I need to get to him.* Putting one arm in front of the other. I pull my useless limbs closer to my best friend. Any pain I have as a result of my wounds doesn't come close to the torment slashing away at my heart. An eternity later, I'm close enough to assess. I take my hand, caked with blood and mud and try to stop the bleeding, but all of my efforts are failing fast.

"Mal–stop. It's no use." Jared's command is no more than a whisper. The moon glints off of a crimson covered blade laying discarded on the ground. The blade that was used to take the life of my best friend. I reach for it and smell the wolfsbane it's been dipped in. There is no coming back from this.

He's not coming back from this.

I reach over, running my fingers through his hair. My heart shatters when I see a tear run down his face. A war is raging around us and for the first time since it started, I couldn't care less. My best friend is dying. I drag myself as close as possible so I can lay next to him as he struggles to breathe.

"Mal, listen to me," he whispers. "I need you to do something for me." My chest tightens as his tears start to spill over. He pulls in a ragged breath. "I need you to live, okay? I... I need you to find someone who will love you in a way— I couldn't."

"Shhh, don't worry about me," I choke out. The lump in my throat is making it difficult to breathe.

"I don't regret anything we had and would not want... want to fight next to anyone else." He struggles as he leans in to kiss my forehead. His head falls back to the ground with a thud and slowly his eyes meet mine. He tries to smile but starts to cough up blood. I grab his hand and squeeze, resting my other upon his forehead. Desperation must be written all over my face.

"Stop talking and just focus on breathing, focus on staying here...with me." I say, choking on my words. "Please keep breathing. Don't give up on me yet." I grip his hand tighter. His labored breathing begins slow, as a peaceful aura washes over him. He has accepted his fate, but I haven't. "Don't you fuckin die on me, do you hear me." With his eyes still on mine, he lets out one last breath. And just like that–he's gone.

My best friend since I was two years old is dead. I kiss his forehead, close his eyes, just as the pain from our mate bond dying rips through my body. It's so intense that I can't help but scream out in pain. The ground beneath me begins to literally shake. The sound of my scream radiating out of my body is coming from both me and my wolf. The sound is of pure, tortured pain. Even though we weren't in love with our mate, we did love him.

Pressure in my head begins to build and I feel like I'm losing control. My sadness begins to quickly grow to anger, my scream grows to a roar, my roar becomes a heartbreaking howl that is loud and vicious. Out of nowhere, a light— huge, white, and blinding appears over the battlefield. Just like a dying star exploding. A rumbling sound echoes across the battlefield as a deafening boom shakes the ground. A consuming high-powered wind engulfs the battlefield, the magical energy swirling inside of it wipes out our enemy. Killing most and injuring even more. Victory may have been claimed tonight, but there's no joy for me as darkness comes for me.

Chapter 1
Landon

Three years after the great war

    Life is pretty much back to normal and areas that had been decimated by the war have finally been rebuilt. The city of Paisley, which is the New York City of the Midwest, is encircled by several packs and covens. It's been this way since forever, its accessibility to all supernatural creatures is a huge draw. The best part is that humans think it's just a city surrounded by lush forests. The demographic of Paisley is predominantly human, however those that live here are absolutely clueless what is going on around them when it comes to the supernatural world.

    My pack, Full Moon, borders what has been my favorite hangout spot since I was a teen, Wolf It Coffee Co. They make some of my absolute favorite treats and I fully take advantage of my visit whenever I have to attend meetings in the city. Today happens to be one of those days!

    The Annual Alpha Meeting. It's held on the anniversary of the final day of battle. Alpha's from around the country get together in honor and memory of those that fought for our world and as Alpha of Full Moon it's my responsibility to represent our pack.

Walking into the renovated local coffee shop, I'm hit with a delicious aroma of baked goods, causing my stomach to growl. My Beta Sam claps me hard on the back. "Dude, by the sound of your gut, I'm guessing you forgot to feed your wolf this morning?" he laughs as he shakes his head. Sam is a beast. He's not as big as me but he's still fucking intimidating. Sam's a tall guy at 6'4" with brown eyes and blond hair that looks like he just rolled out of bed. The ladies freaking love it though. He is built like a damn tree trunk. The bastard's muscles have muscles.

"I wasn't able to. Dexter had me up till two. I slept like shit. I had to haul ass out of the house this morning so we could get to this meeting on time."

"*Today is a big day. If you would just keep your damn eyes open, I might just be able to figure it out,*" my wolf, Dexter, jests, and I can practically hear the smirk on his face.

"Dex, what's up with you today? You've been in a mood."

"*The moon goddess said that something was going to happen today, but apparently you and I have to figure it out on our own,*" he mumbles a little miffed.

"*Wait, when did you talk to the moon goddess?*" I ask in surprise

"*If you must know, she came to me last night.*"

Did he just say she came to him? Sam pulls me out of my conversation with Dexter with a jab of his elbow in my ribs. "Landon! The servers asked you three times what you want to eat."

After all our orders are placed, we squeeze our way through the crowd to go sit at the end of the counter by the huge window that looks out to the busy city streets. Sam drums his fingers against the countertop as we watch people push past each other on the sidewalk. Big cities provide interesting characters.

"Alpha Greg seemed a little hasty on the phone last night. I know we were scheduled to meet with everyone today anyway, but I can't shake the feeling something is amiss." He states as he looks over to the kitchen door, willing our food to come out. Sam looks back at me with a look that says if he doesn't eat now, he is going to lose it.

I nod, acknowledging his statement. It was an odd conversation with Alpha Greg. He called to request he run the meeting, which was just odd. The annual meeting doesn't normally conduct itself formally, but I could tell by the tone in his voice that whatever he needs to share, must be very important. As we speculate what it could be about, my attention is drawn to the patrons around us. I can't help but people watch. I scan the inside of the restaurant, looking for nothing in particular, but amused by their eclectic styles in front of me. Out of the corner of my eye I see a stunning woman sitting at a table close to the bakery case. She is sipping on a cup of tea. I'm mesmerized as she brings the steaming cup to her lips. Her emerald-green eyes flutter closed as she savors the taste. My cock twitches in my pants as she swipes her tongue along her bottom lip, the action so simple but yet so sexual.

"Sexual? Really, Landon? She's drinking tea for fucks sake. It's been too long since you got any."

Ignoring the mutt in my head, I take in more of her, her long reddish, blonde hair pulled into a high ponytail. Loose pieces haphazardly frame her beautiful face. My line of sight is cut off by our server pushing through the crowd with his arms weighed down by plates full of our breakfast. He balances the large tray on the edge of the counter, then hands us our food. I take a huge bite of my pork roll, egg and cheese sandwich. I can't help but moan as the flavor explodes in my mouth. on a hard roll, but I doubled the pork roll. My mom used to call it a heart attack sandwich. I dig into my food, but I can't help stealing glances of this woman. She looks like an angel.

"My angel."

"Your angel?" I shake my head at Dex.

"I can't get over how busy this place is!" I say as I wipe my mouth. "I'm so happy for Jake that business is booming again." Sam nods his head in agreement as he takes a sip of his coffee. The cafe owner, Jake, comes out of the kitchen. He works his way around the room, mingling and greeting his customers.

"He's definitely in his element," Sam says with a chin lift in Jake's direction. He's like a damn mayor. Slowly he makes his way over to my green-eyed beauty. I'm almost jealous as a big smile graces her face. I want to be the cause of her smiling. *What the hell is with me today?* I observe as they interact. While he speaks to her, he places his hand over his heart and bows to her. *Odd.*

"Sam did you see that?" I question as I lean over to try and get a better look at her, but all I can see is her silky long hair.

"See what?"

"Jake just bowed to that woman. Do you know who she is?"

Sam tilts back and follows my stare. "Hmmm, she looks familiar, but to be honest I can't place her."

The gregarious, gray haired bakery owner makes his way to us. "Alpha, Beta." He whispers. Trying not to draw too much attention from the humans that surround us. "It's an honor that you both still come to eat here. It keeps me young." He says with a laugh.

"*Ask him about the girl,*" Dex insists in my head.

"Jake, who is that woman you just bowed to?"

"Honestly," he pushes his hands into his pockets. "I've never asked her name."

"You, Mr. Social. You never asked her name?" Sam barks.

"I know, I know. But she's very sweet, but very closed off. When you're near her you feel warmth. She just has this aura about her. I'm always compelled to bow. It's almost like I can't control it."

"Does she come often?" I question.

"Actually, like clockwork!"

"Really?"

"Yeah, really. Every Monday, Wednesday, and Friday for the last month or so. I really should ask her what her name is. She's a great customer!" He laughs and awkwardly rubs the back of his head.

We collectively glance over at her as she bites her bottom lip, while peeling off the wrapper to her muffin. I inwardly groan, as she puts a piece in her mouth. My eyes trail down to her throat and watch as she swallows it. Visions of my cock in her mouth fill my mind. A dish crashing to the floor pulls me from my dirty thoughts. Jesus this is what happens when you don't get enough sleep. You start fantasizing about random women.

"Alpha, we need to head out to our meeting. We cannot be late today." Sam states as he gets up, grabbing his garbage and heading toward the door.

I shove my remaining food into my mouth then we head outside. I can't help but steal a glance into the window as we pass. I need to see her one last time. As I spot her through the crowd, her eyes flutter up meeting my gaze and a small smile appears on her beautiful face. I feel a warmth spread throughout my body, and I'm confused by the sensation.

"*I think I'm in love, Landon. If second chance mates were a thing, I would swear she's it.*"

"Dexter thinks he's in love." I chuckle trying to laugh off the pull I'm feeling.

"What, where, who... What do you mean, *you think*?" Sam stops and looks around.

"It's definitely a different feeling from how I felt when I met Tara."

Tara was my mate. We met the day of the final battle of the war. Tara was beautiful and she was mine. Sadly, she was killed *that* night. I don't know if it was because we didn't mate but her death was not as painful as some of my other were-friends who lost their mates during the war. I felt the pain of loss, but I did not feel like I was going to die without her.

"I only made eye contact with that woman from the bakery, and I don't know how to explain it. I almost feel whole again. I mean it could honestly be that I am attracted to her."

"She could be your second chance mate, dude."

"Second chance mates are not a thing anymore. It's more like, Dex is just pissed at our non-existent sex life."

"I heard they're making a comeback."

"What is?"

"Second chance mates. We should ask at the meeting."

"When we get there, I'll ask the elders that are present if they know anything."

"What the hell are you talking about? 'you'll ask?' Man, go get her number or at least talk to her, you dipshit." He laughs at me as realization hits.

I stop myself mid step. *What the fuck am I doing?* Sam's right- there's no way I'm going to tell him this though. No matter how important this meeting is, my possible mate is a thousand times more important. I jog back and look through the window, but she is gone. I quickly search around, but I don't see anyone that looks like her! "Damn it." I groan, as I walk back toward Sam. "She wasn't there."

"At least you know she comes here like clockwork." He says with a wink.

MALINDA

It's been three years but feels like a lifetime. I moved to the amazing city of Paisley a year after the war. I stayed on as Luna to help my best friend and our beta's mate, Stacy, through the transition to her role of luna. It was an emotional day because the title was not being passed on, because of years of hard work, but due to tragedy. The pack buried their alpha, and I stepped down because I was too injured to do the job fully without my alpha. My mate. Then one night I left the pack I have known my whole life and became a rogue.

The morning after I left, I got a phone call from Stacy, she was pissed. She refused to accept me as a rogue and I refused to go back and be considered the weak link. I hung up the phone and never looked back. Over time I got more accustomed to life on my own and have blended in well. Stacy has finally accepted me for my decisions.

I found this adorable coffee/bakery shop when I started seeing a new physical therapist on this side of town. No, I don't mean I'm dating a physical therapist. I mean I'm going to a new PT to see if he can help get me to the next level in my healing journey. My injury from the war caused spinal cord damage and because of the tainted wolfsbane, I've not been able to heal. It's been a little over six months with this new therapy and training and I swear I'm slowly getting sensation in my legs. Could it be wishful thinking? Sure, but a girl can dream, can't she?

"How are you my dear?" Jake, the owner of the establishment asks as he bows to me. I haven't been a luna in a long time, but I guess once you have the luna aura you always have it. I truly thought that the rogue smell of rotting flesh would have overpowered my old aura, but I guess not. It's said that rogues can't smell how badly they truly stink, but here I sit, and no one seems too bothered by my stench.

"I'm well, thank you and yourself?" I smile at the warmth emanating from his sincerity.

"I'm busy! And being busy is good," he shouts as he slips through the crowd of people. This place is always busy. I've been told that a lot of people got together to help get the business up and running again. It took years to rebuild. They had to literally start from the ground up. The building itself is ten stories high with apartments above and retail shops on the first floor. Looking at it now, you would never be able to tell that this place was in ruins after the war. Jack hung photos on the walls of the building and shop from its heyday, right after the war and during the process of the rebuild. The reminders of the past to keep everyone humble.

A strange sensation creeps its way down my spine as I feel someone's eyes on me. I can't help but discreetly look around. Then I catch a glimpse of a man as people shuffle around the shop. There are way too many people in here to grab a scent, but I could tell he was a wolf. A wolf that's built like a damn Greek god. Oh, he's gotta be an alpha, a beta at the very least. One thing I'm absolutely certain of is that he's definitely easy on the eyes.

The sight of him has my body tingling and my panties wet. I even have butterflies. He is definitely taller than his friend. With blue-gray eyes and brown hair that's cut close to his head on the sides. The top is just long enough for me to run my fingers through. Oh god, I need to get laid. No one has made me feel this way— ever. I try not to pay too much attention, but seriously how can I not. He's blatantly staring at me, plus he's hot as hell and I'm pretty sure I'm drooling. The guy he is with is cute and has a similar build but damn he is not as yummy as Mr. Blue Eyes.

"Sweet goddess Mal, I think you've got something on the corner of your mouth. Now, pull yourself together and go talk to that parking ticket because we need that man's number," Sahara, my wolf, says in her most sexy voice.

"Parking ticket?"

"Yeah, that man is FINE."

"Lord, thank god I'm the only one who had to witness that slam dunk. What has gotten into you?"

"Nothing, just thinking of all the dirty things he could do to us."

"Down girl."

"Listen Mal, all joking aside. You know I feel guilty as hell. I want to be able to heal us. I just can't seem to figure out how. It really shouldn't be this hard. But you can't ignore a good-looking man just because you think he will reject you. You're beautiful inside and out, if I do say so myself!"

"Sahara, I get it and I don't blame you for not healing us. Shit happens! I just miss you. I miss running, letting you out and being free."

"The moon goddess keeps saying we must stick to our training and wait a little bit longer. I never doubt the moon goddess Mal, and neither should you. I trust her plan—whatever it is."

I glance up and notice Jake has made his way over to them. I'm trying so hard to keep my eyes trained on the blueberry muffin in front of me, but I can't help stealing a few glances out of my peripheral vision. Jake tries to nonchalantly look over his shoulder at me and I quickly look down at my food as they all turn in my direction. Oh Lord, I can feel them staring at me, and now I can't stop fidgeting with my muffin wrapper. Risking one look I plop a small bite into my mouth and chance a look in their direction. Jack and the friend look to be discussing something, but the Sex on Legs keeps his intense gaze on me. God, what I wouldn't give to have that man buried inside me.

Did I just think that? *"Yeah, ya did,"* Sahara laughs so loudly I almost believe the people next to me heard it. Embarrassed by my own thoughts I rub my hands over my face to try and hide my burning cheeks. Goddess why am I so horny all of a sudden? Honestly, it's not that I am shy, it's just that I'm awkward around men I find attractive. Plus, it's not like I have a ton of experience. Jared and I were only friends. Best friends but that's it. We were never *in* love with each other, it was a familial love. As a sister would love her brother. He was the person I talked to about everything. Growing up we would talk to each other's favorites, our crushes and share our deepest darkest secrets. He was like my brother, and I miss him.

I want to steal another look, but nerves have me examining my muffin like it's the most interesting muffin ever created. Shit, what if they're staring at me because they know I'm a rogue. I take in a deep breath, then exhale, blowing hair out of my face. I catch a glimpse of my watch... I'm late. Shit. Needing to head out, I quickly ask the waitress for a to-go cup of hot water for my tea. Unexpectedly, the two men get up and rush out. The extremely hot guy finds me through the window. Warmth spreads all over me and dare I say my panties are wet.

"Yes Malinda, your panties are definitely wet."
"Oh, shoosh it Sahara!" I scold but can't help but smile. This is a new feeling. I shake my head and try desperately to push all of the thoughts to the back of my mind as I grab my refill and head out to training.

Chapter 2
LANDON

As we stroll into the annual alpha conference, we are greeted by many friendly faces. It feels like it has been too long since I've seen the alphas and betas of North America. We normally get together with the regional alpha's a couple of times a year and then we send a rep to meet with the council. Today is a big day. It's the three-year anniversary of the final battle of the great war.

My pack, Full Moon, suffered greatly. We lost many amazing members, my parents being among our casualties. But even through our darkest of times we came together as a community, as a pack and have rebuilt. Our pack member numbers are up, our homes, buildings and our little town look better than ever. We finally feel complete again.

I walk around the room, shaking some hands and making small talk with our neighboring pack officials while Sam finds our seats. I catch Alpha Greg striding to the front of the room with his sons not far behind. He's a strong man in his mid-fifties, and if I'm not mistaken, he's getting ready to step down in the next year or two. His eldest son Ben's coming of age soon. He's a good kid and will make a damn fine alpha.

Alpha Greg motions for his son to stand next to him. "Gentlemen, I want to thank you so much for accepting my late-night calls with grace. Also, thank you for allowing me to hijack the meeting a bit." Everyone moves about the room and settles into their seats. "What I'm about to tell you is unprecedented and kind of threw us for a loop last night. My son Ben," he claps his son on the shoulder, "celebrated his eighteenth birthday yesterday. The timing is quite special as he has gained his wolf in time for this meeting. Though we are extremely excited for Ben, and the amazing things he will do in his life, we are faced with a situation that I've never seen before. After Ben's first shift last night his wolf requested a meeting with me."

Gasps emit from the crowd, followed by a lot of confused faces. "Just like all of you, I was extremely confused as to why. But I can't lie, I was intrigued. In all my years as a ranked pack member I have never had the wolf side of a man want to talk to me." He chuckles, rubbing the back of his neck, "and this is where it gets even more interesting. His wolf informed us that... well, he is a newborn wolf."

Silence and pure dumbfounded shock comes over the room. It's almost unheard of for an alpha to get linked with a newborn wolf. It's not a bad thing, it's just more common to get a wolf who has years of knowledge behind them. A newborn wolf is just that, a newborn. This means that it's their first time being paired with a human counterpart. This news does not seem to bother Ben. He only has pride etched into his features and standing to his full height and his head is held high.

"Gentlemen, please, quiet down. We have some important things to discuss regarding this. Ben's wolf has informed us that he is a former alpha." Alpha Greg announces, " also, explains why his wolf is so fucking huge," Alpha Greg says to no one in particular.

"Excuse me, but who does your wolf claim to be?" The alpha of Crystal River, questions. Alpha Greg motions for his son, Ben, and he steps forward to address the room.

"My wolf is the late Jared Knight of the Stone Mountain Pack."

"What?" Sam, my beta shouts from beside me. He stands so quickly his chair hits the wall behind us. The whole room is startled by his reaction and all eyes are now on him. Sam was cousins with Jared.

Growing up, they did not get to see each other often. Downfall to being in different packs and the war, but that doesn't mean they weren't close. It killed Sam that we couldn't make it to Jared's mating ceremony. I never had the honor of meeting him in person, but we did correspond during the war. The whirlwind of emotions Sam is feeling right now are so strong, I can almost feel them. Now, I need to be here for my best friend. I stand, placing my hand on his shoulder, and swallow hard past the lump of emotions in my throat as the tears threaten to spill over the edge of Sam's eyes.

"It's okay man, breathe," I whisper to him. Sam nods and takes a cleansing breath.

"Ben–" Sam takes a moment to clear his throat. "Can you bring him forward?" Sam asks with a sniffle, and not one alpha or beta grunts at his weak moment.

Alpha Greg gives a nod toward his son, "We need to tell them."

Ben stands in the front of the room. "Gentleman, I've only had my wolf for twenty-four hours so, please, bear with me." Everyone smiles and nods. Bringing a wolf forward to speak on its own is not easy for a first-time shifter. Shit, it's not easy for anyone.

He shakes out his arms then rolls his neck. Ben takes a couple of deep breaths, then his eyes begin to change color from blue to black. Ben lifts his chin to sniff the air and locks eyes with Sam. At wolf speed Ben jumps over a table and grabs Sam, pulling him into a big bear hug. Sam cries into his shoulder as they hold onto each other tight. We all just take in the moment playing out in front of us. Jared's whole family had been wiped out during the war and after, there are only a few cousins left today. I notice a few men wiping away their own tears. A few luna's that are present silently sob into their alpha's chests, all of us acknowledging that this moment is rare and a gift from the goddess above.

Sam is the first to finally speak. "How is this possible?"

"The moon goddess said, I proved myself during my time on earth and now I must guide Ben. I have informed Alpha Greg of what

Ben's true destiny is. We must protect the queen." Everyone's jaws are on the table. We haven't had a queen in hundreds of years.

"Yes Jared, you mentioned this last night, but who is the queen?" Alpha Greg questions.

Ben walks back to the front of the room so Jared can address everyone.

"The queen is my luna..." he now has the room's full attention. You could practically hear a pin drop. "My Luna was my best friend, but we never mated. It never felt right. We had been best friends since we were pups, but when we found out we were mates we didn't get the same feelings all of you get from your mates. Please don't worry about that though. It's not that important. What we need to worry about is that the moon goddess says that my Luna is in danger, and we must find her." I'm stunned by what I'm hearing. "I asked the moon goddess, what happened to my warrior luna? She told me that she is hurt somewhere, and we need to save her and restore her."

Jared just told the whole room that his mate was not his true mate. I'm legitimately stuck on the fact that he and his mate were bonded to each other but were not true mates. This is totally unheard of, and I've got questions. I stand up to address Jared. "Did the moon goddess say why she paired you two together if you're not each other's true mates?" I don't know why I felt compelled to ask this question, but now everyone is looking from me to Jared and waiting with bated breath.

"The moon goddess said that my true mate had died by accident before her first shift. The goddess said that she could see the war coming and could not interfere. The goddess knew that the obstacles that laid ahead of us were going to prevent her from meeting her fated mate. The goddess panicked that she was not going to stop the war and paired me with my luna so I could protect her. But she did anyway."

"Did? She did what? Did she find her true mate?" A small woman asks from next to me.

"No, ma'am, she stopped the war."

The whispers can be heard around the room. We were all at the last battle of the war. We all experienced what is best described as a huge explosion. It wiped out all of the evil and dark souled creatures that stood on that field that night.

"How did she stop the war? The goddess never interferes." A man from the back of the room calls out.

"My Luna stopped it. She is special."

"Jared, where is she now?" I question.

"That is something the moon goddess cannot interfere with. We must find her on our own, but I can sense her, and she is hu— hurting."

You can see Ben and Jared struggling to focus now. Beads of sweat are rolling down Ben's face. He sways a bit and loses his footing. Alpha Greg catches him before he falls over. "Sorry gentleman, it doesn't matter how strong of a wolf you are, that's just hard in general." Alpha Greg claps his son's back and helps him sit down. Ben wipes his face off and brushes his father's arm off of him so he can stand to face him. As he begins to speak you can sense his aura getting stronger. "Dad, I cannot take over as alpha. I'm meant to protect the queen. Give Lex a year and he will be fully ready. Lex will make an amazing alpha and he will lead Silver Lake with honor and protect our people with his life." Lex, Alpha Greg's youngest son who has been sitting quietly in the corner watching everything going on, stands and the two brother's hug. "Make us proud Lex," Ben says as he ruffles his younger brother's hair.

There's a bit of commotion with everyone talking and speculating on what needs to happen next. "How are we meant to find her?" An older alpha yells over the chatter.

"Let me call Stone Mountain and see if they know where the former Luna is." Alpha Greg states while pulling out his cell phone and starts dialing. "Alpha John, I'm sorry that you couldn't make the meeting. How is the new pup?" Greg nods his head at the unheard response. "Oh, good— that's good. Whelp, let me cut to the chase. We need to know as much info on Alpha Jared's luna." Greg places his hand over the phone and lets us know that we're all dismissed for today and that we will reconvene tomorrow.

Sam looks at me, his emotions on his sleeve. "Shit, I wish I could help but I never even got a chance to meet her. I think I may have at one time seen a picture of her, but I have no idea if I was ever in the same room as her." He pushes himself up from his chair and rubs his face in his hands. "Fuck, Landon let's go to the gym. After all of this shit I need to beat the crap out of something. Want to spar with me?"

Laughing and shaking my head. "Yeah, I'll let you get a few punches in but then I'm going to kick your ass." Sam heads toward the door flipping me off. I look over to Ben who is standing next to his father. "Hey Ben, do you want to join us?" Ben looks up and shakes his head.

"Not today sir, but I will tomorrow, thank you."

"Wait!" I yell out to everyone who is heading out the door. "I need to know about second chance mates."

A tall beta comes walking over. "Alpha, I'm Beta Zack from Half Moon." He says as he extends his hand for me to shake. "So, a second chance mate? Welcome to the club."

"I don't know if I have one. Therein lies my problem."

"I can probably answer a lot of your questions. But I have to warn you it's not the same experience for everyone."

"Great! We are heading over to the gym; do you want to meet up later?"

"Nah, I'll come, I won't have another chance today to get some training in."

"Awesome." I shake his hand and we head out.

MALINDA

Austin, my physical therapist and I have just finished strength training for my legs. Now, we're leaving his office to head to the gym. He has a deal with the gym owner, who allows him to utilize his facility to help get wounded warriors back to tip top shape. He really is good at what he does. When I first met him, I thought he was a bit much, but I have grown to enjoy the days he tortures me. Just because I'm in a wheelchair doesn't mean I still can't hold my own in the ring. Sparring is one of my favorite things. I was the top warrior in my old pack, being the daughter of my pack's beta definitely rubbed off. Being in a wheelchair just means I've got to think outside the box when it comes to fighting.

This will be the first time sparring during the day, in public... in my chair. Normally we do my training after the facility is closed. Austin gets special permission from the owner to use the arena after hours. I hate feeling like a circus attraction. Unfortunately, today and tomorrow we will have to come in the afternoon. While the facility is open to the public. I mean, yes, my old pack has seen what I can do despite my disability, but I just don't like dealing with people staring. The best is one time when a few people stayed after closing at the gym. Five minutes in some asshats could not stop with the comments. "Oh Austin, don't hurt her." It drove me crazy, after that I swore it would only be the two of us after that point. I'm shy, and the cat calling drives me nuts, but I'm not weak. I might not be able to beat an Alpha in a fight but I sure as hell can give one a run for his money!

"*You bet your ass we can.*"

"*Sahara, I am not going to lie... I am a little nervous to spar at the gym. People will be gawking at me; I hate being a spectacle. Our pack never once looked at us and said "awww look at her." They just let us be.*"

"*Of course, they will. They might even pity us... but then you will punch* Austin *in the fucking face and show everyone who's boss.*"

"Damn girl! We are still a luna... well kind of. I can't go around fucking people up to prove a point."

"Oh yes, we can! We are so much more, we're fucking royalty."

"What the hell was in that tea this morning? You're wound a little too tight." I scoff at her insane amount of energy.

Austin holds the door for me, and we head towards the sparring rings. The space is like a huge warehouse. They have five octagon fighting rings set up in this big room and of course today of all days, the place is freaking packed. There are several people working out and fighting, only a few glance our way as we head toward the empty ring that is in the far back corner. I shoot Austin a look that could kill and with a raise of my brow all the bastard can do is laugh. The second Austin reaches up to pull the reserved marker from the rope is when I feel all eyes are on me. "I kind of forgot about the alpha meeting taking place down the street. The annual meeting draws a lot of attention for the area." Austin says with a small smirk.

"Sure, ya did." This whole thing is going to be a shit show. Sahara sensing my unease, pushes her confidence through our bond, giving me a small boost. Taking a deep breath, I roll up to the edge with my head held high, even if I hate drawing attention to myself.

"You listen good, missy pooh pants, do not go easy on him! Do not hide who you are." Sahara demands.

"It's okay Austin, let me get situated and then I'll let you know when I am ready for you to help me in." I give him a tight-lipped smile to let him know I'm a little pissed. I gather my long hair up into a high messy bun, pull my t-shirt over my head leaving myself in my sports bra and leggings.

I still have very tight core muscles, because my injury is lower in my spine. Thankfully, I still have full function of my abs and that allows me to keep in good fighting shape. As I throw my shirt on the bench, I can hear the whispers. I know they are checking out my tattoo. You can't miss it, it's huge. And since the back of my wheelchair only comes up to the swell of my back you can see the whole thing.

"*Breathe Mal.*"

I position my chair close to the edge of the ring. I reach up and grab the middle rope. I see Austin lean in to help me. I snarl at him playfully…

"Dude, I got this."

"I know you do, Mal, but it's literally my job. Just in case you forgot— you know make sure you are safe. Plus, what kind of man doesn't show assistance to a female in front of all of these alphas?" he questions with a smirk trying to act all chivalrous. "I really don't want one of them to kick my ass."

Realization sets in that I'm a rogue surrounded by a gym full of alphas. I nervously look around a little panicked that they will notice I'm a rogue. But as I take in the room, no one is looking at me at all. Trying to let it go, I roll my eyes at him. "By whom? Them or me?" I growl. Anger suddenly ripples off of me. As I apparently crash and burn in the "letting it go" department.

My emotions are all over the place today and I need to pull my shit together. I bite my tongue from saying anything that I'll end up regretting and swallow my frustration. Austin regards me a bit but moves over so I can pull myself up on the ropes. I lift my whole lower half up, wiggling my butt, so it slides onto the canvas floor of the ring. Austin jumps in, bringing my chair with him. I get back into my chair, take the seat belt and strap myself in. Did you know that a lot of wheelchairs have seat belts? Ha! I didn't either until I was in one. It definitely comes in handy when fighting. I strap my legs together and attach the strap to the footrest bars. It prevents them from flying around on their own. That's the last thing I need, my legs flying around while I'm trying to kick his ass. I pull my tank top off, tossing it on the rope. Leaving me in my sports bra and leggings.

Once I'm all settled, we get down to business and after a little pad work, we go to our respective corners and Austin yells, "FIGHT!"

Chapter 3
Landon

We get out of the building and start walking the six blocks to the gym. "First, Zack let me express my sympathy for the loss of your first mate." He nods his head in acknowledgement. "Thank you, Alpha. To you as well. Marie, my first mate, she was wonderful. She was a warrior in our pack, and another amazing soul lost in the last battle." He has a fond look in his eyes as he remembers her.

"Okay, So I'm assuming you met someone and are feeling things?" he asks as if he snaps back into the conversation.

"Yes, but I have only seen her once, and I've never actually spoken to her. When I made eye contact with her earlier, I felt something. Obviously, it would feel different as she would be my second chance. Tara, my first mate, we literally found each other on the battlefield and a few hours later she died in battle."

Zack looks at me like I have lost my damn mind. "You know who she is right?"

I laugh and shake my head. "No, actually, I've got no clue who she is, but I found out she visits the local coffee shop religiously. I was thinking of stopping by on her next scheduled visit."

Zack looks a little nervous with what he was about to say. "Whelp this will sound odd, but in order to really tell with second chance mates you need to do something—intimate." Awesome. "A hot and heavy make out session is what sealed the deal for my wolf. The wolf needs that intimacy to connect for the second chance. It's what reawakens the wolf's heart. I mean don't get me wrong my wolf was still a horny s.o.b. But to open his heart again, to recognize his mate to feel intimacy instead of carnal need, it needs to be deep and meaningful. My mate Sara says the same for her wolf. She still teases me that the kiss was soul consuming."

"Great, how do I just walk up to a perfect stranger and say *hey I think you could be my second chance— can I stick my tongue down your throat?*" Zack and Sam burst out laughing.

Assholes.

"Landon, listen. If you say that cheesy ass pickup line I swear to the goddess, I am going to record it and put your embarrassment on YouTube." Sam booms as tears roll down his face from laughing so hard.

We get to the gym and the she-wolf behind the counter bows her head in respect for our ranks. "Hello gentleman. Please know that the gym is only open to wolves today. So, no need to take it easy when training." She points to the locker rooms and hands us a key to safely store our stuff. We're chatting with a few others that followed us from the meeting when I noticed a large crowd towards the back of the building by the arena. Curiosity has gotten the best of me. I get the guy's attention and we follow the growing crowd.

Our jaws hit the floor when we take in the scene in front of us. There's a woman beating the shit out of her opponent. She is stunning, her movements are so fluid. She's been well trained and with every combination she throws I can feel the blood in my body rush to my cock. This has got to be the sexiest thing I've ever seen in my life. I need to get closer.

As I squeeze through the crowd, I'm blown away. Holy shit, it's the woman from the bakery! Damn. She's fucking beautiful—an angel. After a moment I finally come back down to earth. It's now that I realize she's in a wheelchair.

I had no clue you could move a chair like that. She is powerful and graceful. She seemed so petite in the bakery. Like a summer flower, but here seeing her like this, raw emotion in each move. Her body is perfectly toned. Even the mated alphas are drooling a little. I don't even know, like me, if the men in this room recognize her disability. Because god knows she's fighting as if she didn't have one.

Everything about her is captivating. Especially the huge tattoo that goes up her left arm and covers most of her back. A battle scene stretches up and around her arm toward her back. Once she turns, I get a clear view of a reddish blonde wolf laying down in a meadow looking up at the moon goddess holding a crown. The full moon overhead with a bright star in the distance. I'm in awe.

The timer on the wall says they have fifteen minutes left of their hour. "Let's go Mal." Her partner yells just as she swings and misses. "Come on! You hit like a girl." The man egging her on must have a death wish, but if she's pissed off, she's hiding it well. I wouldn't want to play poker with her—she's got no tell. We all observe with interest as she places herself on the edge of the ring, turns to face her opponent and charges. She's practically flying at him.

He positions himself for a round house and we all brace ourselves for her to get knocked out. BUT out of freaking nowhere she rocks sideways, causing the chair to fall on its side. The momentum she picked up was just enough to have her slide along the ring canvas. She uses that momentum and pushes up on both arms into a handstand. Then swings her lower half that is in the chair like a damn line drive, hitting him square in the jaw and knocking him flat on his ass.

"HOLY SHIT!" Everyone yells in unison.

"Damn straight I hit like a girl." Reaching up, she wipes the sweat from her forehead with the back of her hand. "Ya, fucking asshole." She sasses.

Sam is jumping up and down like his favorite baseball team just won the world series. "Dude, did you see that?! Did you see that? Shit, that was fucking hot."

Her sparring partner slowly gets to his feet, takes a moment to collect himself, then high fives her. "Yes, yes you do," is all he says as he tries to shake the dizziness off. The crowd erupts into cheers, and I can't help but notice the slight blush travel up her sexy neck. The shy smile on her plump lips has my cock twitching. My legs move on their own accord as I walk closer to her, desperately needing to know who she is.

I'm being a total creeper right now, I'm blatantly staring at her, but there's no way I can look away. She has absolutely captivated me. With her back to me, she looks up and slowly turns her chair. As if like magic her eyes find mine in the crowd. They grow big with shock, but gradually her body relaxes. She bites her lower lip, making my wolf growl in pleasure.

I'm pulled out of my trance when I hear someone yell—"LUNA!" She looks up in a panic, as she recognizes the voice calling to her. Everyone in the crowd stops moving, as a kid no more than sixteen comes running toward the ring. Fuck, if she's a luna. That means she's already mated. Fuck I got to get my shit under control, I don't need to start a war with another alpha. But my dick's not getting the hint that she is off limits.

"Brian?"

"Luna!" He jumps into the ring and hugs her. He cries, sobbing in her embrace.

"Brian where have you been? Your mother thought you died in the battle."

The woman embraces the young man again with a teary smile on her face. "Luna, I saw—what happened to you and Alpha. I am so sorry about what happened." They move more to the center of the ring to continue their conversation. With the amount of people in here it's hard to hear the conversation. She continues to talk to the young man a few more minutes before they say their goodbyes.

An alpha steps forward and addresses her. "Excuse me Luna, may I just say you fight like a true warrior." Others nod in agreement.

My heart is practically beating out of my chest as my eyes follow her hand as she tucks a loose strand of hair behind her ear. Crap, why do I have these feelings for another wolf's mate? I've signed my own death warrant. Dex whimpers and quickly removes all of the naughty images he's been flashing through my mind.

"Oh please, you don't need to address me as Luna, I haven't been a Luna for a few years now."

From the back of the room some asshat yells, "If you're not a Luna anymore can you ride me later?" Most of, if not all the alphas in the room let out a low menacing growl. You do not disrespect a woman like that. What happens next shocks the shit out of all of us. She releases her aura and the sound of her voice booms throughout the room.

"Don't you dare ever disrespect me or any woman for that matter, like that again. I'm no longer a luna because my mate died— in battle. So, please get your head out of your ass before you fucking open your mouth again." Her aura ripples through the air. It's so strong that every single person bows their head. You can see she is trying to compose herself.

"Please excuse me everyone, my emotions seem to be all over the place today." She shoots her sparring partner a dirty look, "Austin we're never training in public again."

I exhale my deep breath and now that I know she is widowed too my shoulders relax a bit. Dex on the other hand takes this tidbit of information and brings back all of the dirty images, *"Damn horny wolf."*

"Mal, unfortunately we will be training here again tomorrow." He says as he slaps her on the back. "Toughen up, buttercup."

"Ugh, you can be such a pain in the ass." She says as she rolls her eyes but smiles at the guy, I'm assuming is Austin.

Sam, Zack and I finally make our way up to the ring. I watch as she undoes the seat belt that has kept her strapped into the chair. Every move this woman makes is sexy, and the heat radiating in my body for her is out of control. Bracing my hands on the canvas of the ring, I clear my throat, in hopes to get her attention. "Does that come standard, or did you order the ninja package?" I ask as I lift my chin in the direction of the seat belt. Dex mentally facepalms at the cheesy line, but she giggles and it's like angels singing.

"Um, actually they come standard on most wheelchairs! I was shocked but it comes in handy when fighting."

She transfers from the chair to the floor of the ring then maneuvers herself toward the ropes. Austin jumps down grabbing her chair in the process and has it waiting for her. I lift the rope for her to slide under. She hesitates but lets me help.

"*Landon, I think she is our mate. I need to know, please kiss her.*"

"*Dex I can't just kiss a perfect stranger.*"

Before I know it, Dex pushes me closer, and I've got one of my hands on her waist. Thanking the Goddess that her leggings come up high covering her stomach, because I think I would've died if I got to touch her beautiful skin. Being this close to her is nothing I have ever felt before. I truly feel like I'm in another world and I'm beyond transfixed by her. "Excuse me, can I help you?" She questions with a tilt of her head. She regards me but there is no hiding the light blush that settles on her cheeks. Dex is doing a fucking happy dance in my head.

"I—um, I just wanted to help you *cough* I'm sure you can handle it yourself. I sound like a fucking idiot, and I internally roll my eyes at myself. She ducks her head under the rope to slide down off the mat but stops. I move in closer silently asking permission and with a nod of her head I scoop her up bridal style. Having her in my arms feels so right, she smells of warm apple pie on a cold fall day. I can sense the faintest tingle where we are skin on skin, it's small but it's there. Her eyes show recognition. She can feel it too.

Slowly, she places her arms around my neck. It's so natural as if she has done it a million times. Then I lose all the breath in my lungs as she looks up through her lashes at me. The longer our skin touches, the bigger her eyes get with excitement. A small tear forms in the corners of her beautiful green orbs. She takes a shaky hand, placing it on my cheek. Then she whispers that one word I've only dreamt about.

"Mine."

MALINDA

The guy from the bakery is here. Not only is he here but he is currently holding me in his arms. I can't breathe. His scent of freshly fallen rain on a hot summer day is so strong, it's a heady scent and I can't help but take another whiff. The second I wrapped my arms around his neck I felt a strong surge of electricity. I could feel the tears building in my eyes. Sahara is screaming *Mate* in my head! I take my hand and try to steady the shaking, but it's no use. I place my quivering fingers gently on his cheek. As if afraid this is all a dream, and I'm going to wake up and he will be gone. I take a deep breath. As I exhale, Sahara and I claim him with one word. "Mine."

As the tears freely flow down my cheeks, our eyes are locked on each other. I can see his beautiful eyes changing from blue to black to blue again. It's visible that he's struggling for control with his wolf, but he hasn't responded yet. His stare is so intense. I sense he is asking for permission, but permission for what I do not know.

My head nods of its own accord and in that moment his lips crash onto mine. Overwhelmed by the sensations, I tighten my hold on him to deepen the kiss. He gently bites my lip and I shamefully moan into his mouth. He takes full advantage by plunging his tongue into my mouth, swiping it against mine. He tastes like peppermint candies. Our tongues start to fight for dominance, but I let him win. I'm definitely going to need to change my panties.

He lets out a throaty growl; letting me know he can smell my arousal. He tightens his grip on me, Goddess, I never want him to let go. I hear someone coughing dramatically to draw our attention. That's when I become painfully aware that we are still in the gym, surrounded by a ton of people! I slowly pull away, as he places one last kiss on my lips. He leans his forehead to mine, while taking a shuddered breath. His face is all flushed and it makes me giggle.

"My name is Landon." He breathes out.

"It's nice to meet you, Landon. My name is Malinda."

"Malinda." The way my name rolls off this man's tongue is like a direct line to my pussy. I bite my lip to stifle the moan that is trying to come out. He leans in and kisses the top of my nose. "Please don't do that." He groans.

"Ha, Alpha Landon, when I said you had to kiss her, I thought you would at least introduce yourself first." The man behind Landon laughs as he speaks. Landon gently places me in my chair, and I situate myself.

Wait... woah...did he say *Alpha*! No, no... NO, I can't be mated to another alpha! Shit, this is not happening. What kind of Luna could I possibly be? I feel myself starting to sweat. Panic must be evident in my eyes. I've no choice but to reject him. Second chance or not. The moon goddess must've been drunk to think I could handle being a luna—again.

I peek over at Austin, his face full of questions and dare I say—sympathy. The one look I can't stand, but just as I'm about to say something, Austin's facial features harden as he realizes his mistake. Sympathy Looks fucking drive me nuts and now finding out my new mate is an alpha... I'm just done. "I need to go." I blurt out. Austin and I exchange another look. He knows I have a test to get to at the hospital and I am absolutely going to use that to get the hell out of here.

"Do you want me to cancel the test?" He questions, softly from behind my mate.

"No." I snap. "I need to see if I've made any progress." I release the breaks on my chair and roll past Landon toward Austin. "I will see you tomorrow." I give him a quick fist bump and turn my chair to face the man I'm about to shatter.

"Um, Alpha Landon. I apologize for the kiss. But I need to go. It was nice meeting you." I stick my hand out to shake his. The look on his beautiful face causes my chest to tighten and I desperately try to keep my composure as I prepare to destroy both of our souls. Confusion covers his features. He is not processing what I just said to him. Not knowing what to say or how to handle the situation in front of him, he shakes my hand in a daze.

"Um, I'm confused. What's happening here?" He's trying so hard to keep his composure. His nostrils flare as his aura starts to seep from his pores. It's taking every ounce of my self-control to appear like this means nothing to me. Like he means nothing to me. "I just found you, and I get the feeling that you leaving is more than just a trip to the store." Landon questions with confusion and hurt in his eyes. "You're running away from me." He grits out. His hands clench into tight fists at his side.

"Alpha, I'm so sorry. This might seem harsh, but I'm not fit to be a luna. I've already been a luna and it's not something I'm looking forward to doing again. Plus, how would it look to your pack if you had a rogue as a luna." I take a deep breath and try to push down the screams of my wolf begging me to not do this .. "I— I will have to reject our match." My insides feel like they're being crushed with each word. Sahara' is sobbing in my head and I want to join her. I don't have it in me to live that life again. If only I can scavenge some strength to create distance.

"I will not accept your rejection. You're my second chance mate, I will not accept it." He shouts as anger flashes across his face.

"You need a Luna who is whole and not broken. I carry a lot of demons, it's not fair to your people if I bring them with me." I'm trying so hard to keep my composure, but my tears are starting to build. I fear my usual calm, cool and collected wall is about to crumble. I need to stay strong. This is not what I want. I will not be able to give him what he needs. What all alpha's need... an heir. I start to wheel away, heading for the door. I need to go, don't look back. I try to coach myself, *Mal... just keep moving toward the door.*

"I will take care of you. I will love you no matter what!" He calls out loud enough for everyone to stop what they're doing. A moment ago, they could at least pretend that they weren't eavesdropping. Now everyone is staring, and my skin begins to crawl. "We can have a happy life; we can have a family. You won't have to fight anymore. I will do all your fighting for you. I will never let anyone ever hurt you again." I hear Austin take a sharp inhale. He knows my truth, and now I'm praying he is smart enough to keep his mouth shut. Filling my lungs with air, I slowly turn my chair around to face Landon.

"A family, you want a family?" I question, just above a whisper. I know what the answer is, but I couldn't stop myself.

"Yes, more than anything," Landon's states as he straightens to his full height. His eyes searching mine and looking at me with all of the love he can muster.

"Then accept my rejection and find a she-wolf that can give it to you." I refuse to give him more about myself then I already have. This is hard enough as it is. If I keep going, and share this piece of my soul with the one person who is meant to comfort me... It will shatter me. I can't do it; I can't be the person who he needs me to be.

Slowly backing away, "Please," I almost beg. "Don't make this harder than it needs to be." the look on his face morphs to panicked anger. His friends quickly recognize the switch in their alpha. Hands appear around his arms, and I see his friends are holding him back from chasing me, so I take the advantage and make quick my retreat.

"Mal, why are you doing this... he could make us whole again?"

""m sorry Sahara, I know you want a true mate. But we can't be a true mate to an alpha. Emotionally whole does not make up for the physically broken Luna he would get."

I make it out of the building and as soon as I'm out of sight, I let my tears flow freely. I grip my push rims tightly and I propel myself forward. Toward what? Fuck, I just don't know anymore. I understand the mate bond. It's that one person perfectly picked just for you. Making you feel whole and loved. But I don't think that is possible for me. Look at Jared and me. Two best friends mated to one another. We did not get this magical love bond.

Then why does this moment feel different? Right now, it feels like I'm leaving my entire world standing heart broken in the lobby of a gym. Quickly wiping my tears, I try to refocus myself. I've got to get to the doctor's office. The hospital is only blocks away and I need to make it to this next appointment on time. I need to wipe away these tears and I need to wipe away any thoughts of Alpha Landon. Easy, right?

Yeah sure.

Chapter 4
Landon

"Then accept my rejection and find a she-wolf that can give it to you." My heart feels like it's being ripped straight out of my chest. Sam and Zack snag me by the arms to hold me back as she rolls toward the door. "Please," she begs as her voice cracks. "Don't make this harder than it needs to be." She turns quickly and pushes out the door. Austin gets in front of me, blocking my vision of her.

"Where is she going?" I shove Zack off me, but Sam won't let go.

"I don't understand what the fuck is happening right now. I'm her mate, why is she leaving?" I roar.

"Landon, you need to relax for a minute. I won't let you go near our luna in this condition. You're too emotional."

"Too emotional? Too EMOTIONAL?" I scream. "Of course, I'm fucking emotional! My first mate died before our bond even got a chance to grow. Now my second chance mate wants nothing to do with me because she doesn't think she can be a good Luna because she is in a wheelchair! I don't give a shit that she is in that chair!" I run a palm down my face. "Damnit Sam, I didn't even notice the chair at first. This is fucking bullshit man!" I let out a roar so loud the windows shake.

Austin pushes against my chest, catching me off guard. You never fucking touch a pissed off alpha. Man's got a damn death wish. I quickly grip his throat with my hand and squeeze. "Excuse me Alpha," he chokes out. "But it's got nothing to do with her chair."

Curious to what he means I slowly release his neck. Doubling over, placing his hands on his knees and begins coughing. Desperately trying to drag air into his lungs. "I'm waiting," I grit out. He holds a hand up to, asking for a moment I'm not inclined to give him.

"Please give her a chance, she's been waiting for her mate for a long time." He gruffs with a pissed off look on his face. "Her reasons for not wanting to be a Luna again aren't what you're thinking. The chair's just an easy out for her." Austin walks over to the bench with a bunch of gym bags and pulls out a towel. Wipes the sweat from his face, throws it back into his bag and zips it.

"What do you mean, that's not her reason?" I question, taken back by his statement. I sigh and run a hand through my hair in frustration.

"It's not my story to tell, it's hers. Plus, she would kill me... like, literally kill me for telling anyone. Please don't give up on her, take your time. She's stubborn as hell, but don't let that outer shell fool you. She's broken and hurting." Austin places a hand on my shoulder. "Listen Alpha, we'll be back here tomorrow, same time for training. You know, just in case you wanted to accidentally bump into her again." He says with a half-smile then walks away.

I can't help but stare at the door my mate disappeared through. I rub my chest over my heart, as if I'm trying to keep it from sprouting legs and chasing my angel. Sam moves into my line of sight, his lips in a tight line. He grabs my shoulders and levels me with a hard stare. "Landon, let's stay in the city tonight instead of returning to the pack house. We can grab dinner and come up with a plan for tomorrow. We also have to go back for the alpha meeting in the morning. Maybe Greg was able to get more info on this missing Luna. But I promise you this, we will be back here tomorrow. You will win our Luna over; you will bring her home... I have no doubt about that." He says with conviction while trying to gauge my mood.

"Okay. Yeah, you're right. I need to get rid of some of this energy. Let's spar and then we can make reservations for tonight." I state as I remove my tee-shirt and jump into the ring. It's going to take a while to feel some semblance of calm but if I'm going to find it, the ring is the best place to start. After kicking Sam's ass, we shower and head toward the hotel.

Standing in line to check in, Sam taps me on the shoulder. "Sir, our Luna is about to come into the hotel. At our four o'clock." I snap my head to look and see her out on the sidewalk. She's on the phone with her back to us.

Panic sets in quickly as I realize I don't want her to see me. I truly do not want to upset her. The lobby is crowded, making it easier to blend in. All I can do is pray that my scent is covered by the hundreds of other wolves around us, but I can't help stealing a few glances at her. Watching as she gets in line behind us. "Landon, she's about ten people behind us." A small growl rumbles from his chest, "She looks... stressed." Sam's play by play and his concern for his Luna has me on edge. I know if I turn around, I won't be able to take my eyes off her, I won't be able to stop myself from running to her. The bond is pulling me to her, drawing me in and begging me to comfort her.

"Hello, next in line please." A blonde she-wolf asks from behind the counter. "What can I do for you?"

"Hello, we need two rooms for tonight please." I answer as I reach for my wallet in my back pocket.

"I'm sorry sir but we only have one room available for tonight."

"Really?" I ask, kind of shocked.

"We had most of the guests from the alpha meeting extend their stays." She whispers. "And a local apartment building had their pipes burst causing a lot of the residents to stay here. We're booked up tight."

My eyes shoot up. "Um, by any chance, would one of those residents be the woman in the wheelchair behind me?" The receptionist leans to her left a little to spy down the line of people.

"Why, yes she is."

"Okay, give us whatever room you have." I hand over my credit card, when the idea of all ideas hits me. "Also, could you do me a huge favor?" I tell the woman what I need done and head toward the elevator. From my vantage point I can see faint smudges of fatigue under her eyes, and her skin seems paler than before. Stress is written all over her beautiful features. My instinct to care for her is clawing at me from the inside. I wish she would have just given me a chance, talked to me about her fears instead of just giving up. Tomorrow is another day. It's the day I win my Luna's heart. I step into the elevator, with a newfound determination and steal one last glance at my angel.

SAM

To say that today was one hell of a day is an understatement. I got an opportunity to speak to Jared. I would never have guessed that Landon would find his second chance mate. Our new Luna is broken, but I've this nagging feeling that I know her. I have an overwhelming sense to protect her. Maybe that's what happens when you finally have a luna. Your ultimate job is to protect her. She's the key to make sure the pack thrives, and she will give us an heir.

We get to the room, throw our bags on the floor and I collapse on one of the two queen beds. Landon heads to the bathroom, shortly reemerging with the shirt he was wearing when he was holding Malinda. Her scent must still be strong on it, like a balm for his anxiety. "Do you want to go down for dinner or do you want to call for room service?" I ask.

"I'm not hungry. I know she's here. I can feel the connection calling me to her. It's very unnerving, knowing we're under the same roof yet still so far." He plops down on the bed and puts his face in his hands. "Sam, fuck man." Apparently, Landon didn't get rid of enough energy in the ring because he can't stay still. He sits up and grabs the tv remote, slowly rolling it in his hands. "I can't lose her. The pull is beyond anything I have ever felt before. It is stronger than what I had with Tara, and she was only in my life for one day! Now in even less time my second chance mate wants nothing to do with me. Nothing to do with us."

Landon is a strong alpha, and, in most instances, you can never read his emotions. The man is a beast. But mates— they can bring you to your knees. He stands abruptly and begins pacing the room. His features are hard, and I know he is losing his shit. "Why does she think I can't handle what she has to tell me?" He yells and whips the remote across the room. It explodes against the wall; bits of black plastic and batteries fly everywhere. My best friend's hurting and no matter what I say to him it's not going to change how he feels. I've never seen my best friend hurt like this before, and there's only one person that can help it. Unfortunately, it's not me.

MALINDA

My test at the hospital was uneventful. News is, nothin's changed. I had another electromyogram or better known as an EMG. It tests muscle and nerve conduction. The doctors stick tiny needles into my legs and send electrical waves into the body, kind of like shock therapy. I was hoping to feel something this time or see the meter pick up a signal from my nerves, but nothing. Still no change. I understand it's been years since my injury but I'm still hopeful I can heal.

I left my pack after the induction of the new alpha and luna. I've not asked permission to join another pack, so from that day forward I've technically been a rogue. That's the main reason I train so hard. I need to be able to protect myself. Defending myself in the ring is one thing but trying to maneuver my chair on a dirt road or on the field of battle is totally different.

Throw an alpha mate into the mix, with all his overprotective bravado and ability to rip off the head of his enemy one minute, then hold you like a delicate flower the next. Oh, and those eyes... "AHHHHH" I scream in frustration, as I chuck my water bottle at the wall. The cap falls off as the half empty bottle spills all over the carpet. After letting out an exasperated sigh I clean up the mess, roll up to the edge of the bed and faceplant into the mattress.

I rub my temples in an attempt to forget today, but deep down I know that is impossible. I've waited my whole life for my mate. The one person who's meant to love me unconditionally and now that I've found him, he turns out to be a damn alpha of all things. Trust me when I say, I didn't want to turn away from him. I want to love him, but I cannot give him what he needs.

The mating pull is ridiculously strong. I mean seriously, if I stopped everything right now, I could probably pinpoint where he is. Sahara's not helping the situation at all as she sends me images of him running his hands down my body, kissing me, mounting me—

"Sahara, you're killing me, please stop."

"Nope, I want him just as bad as you do, you just won't let yourself have him."

"We can't give him the one thing he needs."

"You don't know that unless you try!"

All I can do is roll my eyes at her. *"Don't give me that sass of yours. The doctors said it could happen, but you won't know unless you try!"* With that Sahara closes the link with a huff. Could I make him happy, could he truly love me if he finds out the truth? I don't even know his whole name, or what pack he's from.

"Loser."

"Welcome back."

"Well, I thought I should remind you."

"Shoosh it."

A knock on the door pulls my attention from our little spat. I snap the door open a little more aggressively than intended and there stands a hotel worker with a food cart. "Hello miss may I come in?" he asks when I make no move to let him enter.

"I didn't order anything. I think you have the wrong room."

"You're Ms. Malinda? No ma'am, this is the right room." I acquiesce at my name, rolling my chair back. The young twenty something man pushes the cart in and leaves. I look between the cart and the closed door and back to the cart again. The aroma wafting from under the large silver plate lid is mouthwatering. Grasping the knob, I remove the dome and am hit in the face with a cloud of steam.

On the plate in front of me is filet mignon, roasted baby potatoes and a medley of butter coated veggies. I find a slice of apple pie hiding under a smaller dome, yes please! I'm pretty sure whoever was supposed to get this meal is going to be very disappointed when it doesn't show up, but the man was insistent he had the right room. My eyes drift to the beautiful floral arrangement, a dozen stunning sunflowers surrounded by beautiful baby's breath. These are my favorite flowers, and I can't stop myself from leaning in. Just as expected, they smell divine. On the card it only says, *'For My Angel.'*

My cell vibrating snaps me out of my shocked state. Reaching for my phone on the desk, I read the caller ID. It's Stacy. I've already missed six of her calls. I can't keep blowing her off. Taking a deep breath and taking a longing look at the perfect meal on the tray. Food will have to wait as I prepare myself for the verbal lashing, I'm about to receive from avoiding her this long. Taking a deep breath, I hit the green button.

"Hey girl, how are you?"

"Mal! I miss you sooo much." Okay maybe I won't get the verbal lashing I was preparing for.

"I miss you too, how is everything over at Stone Mountain?"

"Everything is great—" I get cut off when I hear a panicked voice in the background.

"Is that Mal? Ask her where she is." I can hear her mate ask on the other end.

"Um, John wants to know where you're at sweetie. I mean we wouldn't have to ask if you called more often or stopped by. Shit, you haven't even mailed a postcard! Christ, I'd settle for a smoke signal or carrier pigeon. Telegraph even. Do telegraphs still exist?" Ah there it is. It really isn't a conversation with this woman if she's not yelling about something. "You have not come to visit us in a while, is what I'm trying to allude to if you are picking up on my very subtle hints."

"I know, I'm so sorry, how is the pup doing?"

"He is wonderful!"

"Luna... ask her where she is." John asks again.

"John, do you want me to have this conversation, or do you want to take over?"

"Fine." He growls.

"Ummm what's up with John?"

"Besides the fact he is trying to pull the alpha card with me... nothing, he just has a lot on his plate." She grits out, I can practically hear her staring him down.

At the word plate. I steal another glance at the tray and my mouth waters.

"If he's that worried about me let him know I'm in Paisley and I'm perfectly safe."

"YOU'RE IN PAISLEY!" They both shout into the phone.

"John shut it; I can't hear her!"

"I guess I'm on speaker?" I can't stop laughing, some things never change. "Yes, guys I'm in Paisley. I'm seeing a new physical therapist here."

"Ohhhh, you found your second chance mate! I'm so happy they are making a comeback."

"Stacy, no I didn't... Yes, I did, but Austin's my physical therapist. I'm going to a new physical therapist. I'm not dating him— he's not my mate. The mate thing... It's a long story for another day."

"You promise to share the details later?"

"Yes, I promise."

"Okay back to the reason I was calling, we are going to be in Paisley tomorrow for a meeting, I was wondering if you want to meet us there. We could go to brunch." I groan, at the thought of meeting up. Every time I do, they both beg me to come back to the pack.

"PLEASEEEEEE say yes! I miss my best friend."

"Wait, you're calling me to go to lunch but you had no clue I was in Paisley?"

"I was calling to see when we can go to lunch… but since we will be in the same city at the same time, we absolutely have to get together." I can't help the small smile that pulls at my lips. "I'm giving the puppy dog eyes… Can you tell I am pouting?" I hear her giggle.

"Alright, you win. I will meet you. Just text me the time and location. And there better be good pork rolls."

"Okay! Love you, BYE!!!" She sing songs.

"Bye Stacy, Bye John."

LANDON

The sun is coming through the window and Sam is snoring a beast. The only reason why I got any sleep is because my mate's scent is still lingering on my shirt. Not gonna lie, I'm most likely going to wear it again today. My dreams were consumed with our kiss and where it could've gone. Just the thought of my hands on her beautiful body has my blood flowing south. I need to refocus; I can't go around all day with a hard on. Adjusting my cock in my boxers, I wonder if she liked her dinner, and flowers. She didn't strike me as a rose's girl. I grab my cell to check the time, *shit* it's getting late.

Grabbing the menu off the nightstand I place a quick breakfast order for Sam and myself. We have to be at the meeting by nine and it's already seven forty-five. If I don't get Sam up now, we'll never get there. He's a bit of a diva and I'm not sure if that's going to be enough time for him to get ready. I'm hoping Greg made some headway last night with Alpha John. The faster we track down their former luna and help her, the faster I can get back to winning my luna's heart. Our breakfast arrives, but Dex's pacing in my head prevents me from eating.

"*What's up man?*"

"*Landon today is going to be a great day; I can feel it.*"

"*Dex, I promise I will try to bring our luna home.*" I feel him nod as he settles down so I can finish eating.

"Sam, are you ready? We need to get going, it's getting late."

"Yup, I'm ready." He walks out of the bathroom and stops short. "Woah, woah, woah... you can't wear the same shirt as yesterday."

"Shut it, Okay? It smells like her." I yell and punch him in the shoulder. He just laughs and rolls his eyes at me. We grab our stuff and head out.

The car is waiting for us outside. As we get in Sam leans toward me. "Hey, do you see that guy on the other side of the street?" I look out the window and find a man decently dressed leaning against a light post. He is watching the hotel door, he's not conspicuous about it, but he is laser focused. People are walking around him. A woman even bumps into him, and he doesn't even flinch. Interesting. "Landon, my wolf picked up on him. I'm getting a bad vibe, man." Taking out my cell, I snap a picture of the guy. The windows are tinted in the SUV but to be honest I wouldn't have cared if he did see me do it. His eyes are locked on the hotel's door, he's waiting for someone, but this is not top priority. It's going to have to wait.

We get to the meeting and the room is buzzing with excitement as we enter. I notice Beta Zack next to, who I assume to be his alpha, at the far end of the room. I smack Sam on the chest and motion for him to follow me over to them.

"Hey Zack, how are you?"

"Alpha Landon, I'm well. This is my Alpha and big brother Zander."

"Alpha Zander, it's a pleasure to meet you." I say as I extend my hand.

"Please, just Zander." Leaning in, he places his hand on my shoulder like we are about to share a secret. "I hear you had quite the day yesterday. I hope everything works out with you and your mate."

"Me too, Zander, me too." I give him a tight-lipped smile and he nods.

"Okay everyone, can I have your attention please." Alpha Greg walks to the front of the room to get everyone's attention. "Please sit down! We have a lot to discuss and absolutely no time to do it." Everyone shuffles to find their seats. "Yesterday afternoon I spoke to Alpha John. Luna Stacy, his mate and the Luna Queen are best friends apparently. Luna Stacy has informed me that when the Luna Queen left their pack, she didn't join another. She left in the middle of the night and made a run for it." The shock of a luna running away fills the room. What the hell was she running from? "Quiet down and hold on to your hats because according to Luna Stacy, the queen considers herself a rogue."

I never knew silence could be so loud until that moment. A hundred people are simply staring- eyes wide in surprise, jaws on the floor. Softly at first the whispers start to spill through until everyone was shouting over each other demanding answers. The loudest being that of harsh criticism.

"How can we have a rogue as queen?" A luna from the back questions.

"I will not follow a rogue." Another alpha shouts as he slams his fist on the table. "How can we trust her if she has no pack?"

"Please everyone— please be quiet. The queen has been through a lot and apparently her injury from the war coupled with losing her mate was a lot to handle. She wanted to get away from the memories. Alpha John has never removed her from the list of pack members so technically she's still a high ranked wolf within Stone Mountain." Alpha Greg motions for two people to stand. "Please welcome Alpha John and his mate Luna Stacy." Everyone nods their head in a respectful, welcoming manner. "After speaking with them yesterday, Luna Stacy took it upon herself to track down the queen and by some miracle she is here—in Paisley."

This can't be that easy, can it? Just one phone call and she was found? This is completely nuts! Here I'm thinking we are going to have some crazy investigation in order to find her. Nope, this Luna just made a phone call.

Luna Stacy coughs to get everyone's attention. "Good morning," she says with a little wave. "Please know that our queen is on her way here now. I'm beyond honored to know that the moon goddess has chosen my best friend to be our queen. I haven't told her about the whole Luna Queen title or that Jared is back as a wolf. I think that would have been too much for her to handle. The only way I was able to get her here was under false pretenses. She believes we are meeting for brunch. Please know that she used to be the most outgoing person. She was one of the strongest warriors in our pack, and she's the daughter of our former beta. She led us into battle head on. Her determination never wavered. She was also totally girlie, and when she walked into a room you held your breath from her beauty. Now.... Now she is closed off. Plus, now she's also going to be pissed that I'm not actually taking her to brunch because to be honest food is life to her." Luna Stacy mumbles the last part almost to herself. Then a soft knock draws everyone's attention toward the door.

"She's here."

Chapter 5
LANDON

    Silence hangs over the room as Alpha John looks around making eye contact with everyone as he heads toward the door. We all heard what Luna Stacy said, this is going to be overwhelming for the queen. Shit, she doesn't even know that she is a queen.

    Placing his hand on the knob, closing his eyes as if he's saying a silent prayer. Suddenly, I'm a bit concerned with who's about to walk through that door. Going rogue changes people. Slowly the door opens... and the most beautiful woman I've ever seen enters the room. She's radiant and breathtaking. Her long hair is gently twisted on each side and pinned back, with the rest of her hair falling down her back in loose curls. She has a baby's breath pinned in her hair making it look like a crown on top of her head. She has on an emerald-green sundress, with a gold cardigan sweater. An obvious homage to Stone Mountains pack colors.

    I'm in a complete trance, until Sam elbows me in the ribs, hard enough to snap me out of it. That's when I realized that this was not the Luna Queen, this was my mate.

    "She's the queen." My eyes practically bug out of my head at Dex's omission.

    "Dex, are you saying our mate is the Luna Queen?"

    "Yup... you want to know what that makes you, loverboy."

    "The... the Alpha King."

"That's right, pretty boy, but we know ours is just a title. She's the special one."

I stand quickly, not sure if it's the bond drawing me in or what but the pull to my mate can no longer be ignored. Sam hesitates but follows my lead. I don't want to make her nervous but she's just so close to me, my body is acting on autopilot. She looks around very confused, and instinctively she pushes herself backward toward the door. I can see sweat forming on her forehead. She's starting to panic; I can hear her heart rate picking up. Her eyes dart around the room like a caged animal, fear evident in those captivating orbs, until they land on mine. My mate's features change, her eyes are asking me to protect her, while her body language is begging to escape this uncomfortable situation. Movement to her right has her releasing me from our trance. Her eyes land on Luna Stacy and narrow.

"Stacy what the hell is going on?" she asks in disbelief and Alpha John just laughs.

"Whelp I see your mouth is as dirty as it was before!"

"Do not start with me John-a-than, what the hell is going on!" You could feel the energy rolling off of her. The panic in her voice gave her true emotions away, so I did what a good mate would do... I walk closer to her and kneel. Leaning in, I whisper in her ear low enough that only she can hear.

"Malinda, I know you want to reject our bond, but at this moment all I want to do is help. With your permission I want to give you a hug. I want you to breathe in deeply, my scent will calm you." Looking into her eyes a small tear forms in the corner. She slowly and cautiously nods her head, refusing to allow those tears to fall in front of all of these people. The warmth of her body engulfs me as I wrap my arms around her. Heaven, I'm in absolute heaven. Her scent invades my senses, and the feel of her soft skin... goddess I'm in love with this woman already. She instinctively slides her arms around me pulling me closer. I shiver as she takes a deep breath against my skin, humming in appreciation. Her body finally starts to relax. She nuzzles her face into the crook of my neck, causing Dex to purr.

"Landon... Ple— please don't leave my side." She whispers, desperately trying to hold on to her composure.

"Baby, you couldn't get rid of me if you tried." I pull back a little to look into her eyes, giving her a little smirk. A small shy smile graces her face. Her eyes glisten from the unfallen tears, and with that I kiss her. I couldn't stop myself even if I tried. She's my mate and instinct has taken over. What surprises the shit out of me is that she's kissing me back. The kiss is simple, sweet and exactly what we both needed after the last twenty-four hours. I wanted nothing more than to take things further but I'm a gentleman. Please... we're surrounded by a bunch of people, I'm not a total horn ball.

"Speak for yourself." Dex playfully growls in my head.

MALINDA

I feel like I'm being set up as I roll into a room filled with high-ranking wolves. All eyes are on me, and my anxiety rises. All I want to do is get the fuck out of here. "Stacy what the hell is going on?" I growl out, and John just laughs at me. I narrow my eyes at him as he comes closer.

"Whelp, I see your mouth is as dirty as it was before!"

"Don't start with me John-a-than, what the hell is going on!"

I see movement out of the corner of my eye. Then I'm hit with a scent that overwhelms my senses. My eyes are locked on Stacy, who's looking at me in a way I can't quite describe. All I know is the smirk on her face is giving off a vibe that tells me I'm about to be really pissed off. My eyes dart around the room trying to grasp why I'm here. The damn stress is triggering my anxiety, and making my vision go blurry. Sensing someone next to me, I turn my head toward them. My vision slowly clears when I hear the husky tone of *his* voice.

"Malinda, I know you want to reject our bond, but at this moment all I want to do is help. With your permission I want to give you a hug. I want you to breathe in deeply, my scent will calm you."

"Mate," Sahara purrs seductively in my head.

He looks me in the eye, causing my stomach to flutter. I nod my head as he gets down on his knees. He leans in, encircling me with his large, strong arms. Subconsciously sliding my arms under his. I have just discovered my safe space, my everything... where I belong. How did I ever do anything, deal with anything before finding him—this?

His scent is like a drug, and I'm addicted. *Mmmm*. What was I thinking trying to run from this man? He's my other half. Even after I treated him like crap yesterday, here he is trying to comfort me. I nuzzle deeper into his neck enjoying the sense of peace that washes over me. He even has Sahara purring like a kitten. "Landon... Ple... please don't leave my side." It takes everything I have not to cry.

"Baby, you could never get rid of me." He pulls away and I already miss the contact. His eyes meet mine, and I swear the man is staring into my soul. I know at this moment I would never and could never leave this man again. I'm barely holding on to my composure and I nearly lose the last thread of it when he brushes his knuckles gently across my cheek. Then he kisses me.

Awakening everything inside of me. My heart is about to free itself from my chest and I forget everything, including my name. Once my brain starts to process what is happening, I do the only thing I can think of... I kiss him back.

"Excuse me, Mal?" Stacy says as she taps me on the shoulder. "Ya, want to introduce us to this hunky, stud muffin of a man?" It's technically a question, but knowing Stacy, it's more of a demand.

"Damnit Stacy!"

"Oh, hush John, you're still my big bad alpha." She says as her fingers walk up the front of his chest. Placing a kiss on his cheek.

I can't help but giggle at them. It's like being in high school all over again with these two. I look at her and smile. "Stacy, I'll introduce you after you tell me why the hell I'm here." I smile up at her a little more animated than necessary. "Am I being punked." I ask her with a raised brow. Landon stands, placing an arm around my shoulder. The whole show causes Stacy to wiggle both eyebrows at me, just before she throws herself at me for a hug.

"I missed you so much, Mal," she whispers with a hint of emotion in her voice.

"I missed you too."

I really do miss her, but sometimes you need to spread your wings and find yourself. That's why I left; I needed time to heal my soul. Stacy lets go, grabs a chair and pulls it up so she's sitting next to me. Taking a deep breath, she reaches for both of my hands. "Okay, so you know me." Crap whatever she's about to say is going to be a doozy. "I'm a rip the band-aid off kind of girl. I'm going to throw some serious shit at ya and you're going to have to take it like the bad bitch I know you are." My body tenses but I know Stacy would never do anything to purposely hurt me.

"Okay, lay it on me."

"First, do you know where you are?" She asks while biting her lower lip.

"I'm assuming this is the alpha meeting that happens every year in memory of the end of the war?" I glance around the room to see some nodding their heads. "But why's it today instead of yesterday?"

Landon meets my eyes. "Yesterday something happened at the meeting," he nods at the few alphas standing near the front of the room. "That as far as we know has never happened before. Ben, come on over here." Landon calls as he removes his touch but immediately reaches for my right hand.

A young man stands up and makes his way over to us. He's tall, definitely built like an alpha. "Luna, my name is Ben. I'm the first-born son of Alpha Greg of the Silver Lake pack." He makes eye contact with whom I believe is his father, who gives him a reassuring nod. "What

I'm about to tell you or let my wolf tell you might make you upset. Please know it's not mine or his intention to do so."

Apprehension, anxiety and fear swirl around my belly but Landon is able to mute the emotions with a mere squeeze of his hand. Ben holds up his palms, signaling me to give him a moment. He must see the confusion in my eyes as I watch him stretch his neck. I glance up at Landon and he gives my hand a reassuring squeeze. I'm startled when my other hand is grasped. "Luna, I'm your Beta Sam, I'm here for support." Exhaling roughly... I'm so fucking confused. That was until I heard a voice call a name...A voice that I thought I would never hear again in my lifetime.

"Mallie..."

My head snaps to the young man named Ben, while both my mate and beta squeeze my hands. "J..J..Jared.... how... How's this possible?" I choke on the lump of emotion.

"Mallie, hey you goober. I would ruffle your hair, but I don't want to piss off your mate." He says with a chuckle. This whole thing— has my head spinning. How am I hearing my best friend's voice come out of this boy? I don't think my heart can handle this.

Landon squeezes my hand, reassuring me he's with me. Facing him, I offer a weak smile and squeeze back. That's when Ben gets down on his knees so he's eye level with me. "Excuse me Alpha and Beta, please know that Mallie and I were never true mates. She was simply my best friend. That being said, may I please hug her?" Sam and Landon let go of my hands and I'm hauled into the biggest bear hug ever!

"God, I've missed you." He pulls back, his tears are almost my undoing. I shove my emotions down deep and choose to cover it with my normal sarcasm.

"You asshole! I hope you don't end up torturing this poor kid! Goddess how did you end up a wolf?"

" I see you still honor our pack colors, but that damn mouth of yours." I roll my eyes, but deep down I know that there has to be more to this reunion than what's been presented.

"Okay so what's this really all about? Am I to assume that you all found out that my first mate and friend is a wolf and you just wanted to set up a reunion?"

"Mallie, the Moon Goddess sent me for a reason. She paired us so I could protect you. You were always destined to be Landon's mate. He's your true mate, but the war was starting and the Goddess… Her only concern was keeping you safe."

"Keep me safe? Safe from what?"

"Mallie, do you want to have the conversation in front of everyone or do you want to do this in private?" Stacy interrupts. *Ummm, do I?* Do I want to have this conversation in front of a ton of high ranked wolves? Something tells me this is going to be personal, but I have a feeling this will affect everyone as well.

"Yes, let's continue." I need to get to the bottom of this. "Okay, so you are now a wolf, and we already knew that you and I were not true mates." I regard Landon. This man was always meant for me. "I'm yours." I intended it as a question, but it came out like a declaration, a truth. but I thought he said I was his second chance? I feel Landon squeeze my hand again pulling me from my thoughts.

"Okay, what I'm lost on is why the Goddess wanted to keep me safe. What is so special about me? "

"Mallie, this is about to get heavy okay." Stacy says as she hands me a bottle of water. Landon snatches it and without pausing, twists the cap off and hands it to me. He's already taking care of me and I'm fairly certain it came as natural to him as breathing.

"The Goddess says you are our Queen. You're the next Luna Queen. Your parents aren't your birth parents. You were given to them." Jared states plain as day.

Landon kneels again, placing one hand on my leg, the other around my shoulder. He begins to rub little circles on my back. I survey his expression "did you know all of this?"

"We found out yesterday that the former Luna of Stone Mountain was to be our Luna Queen, but I had no clue it was you. The part about your parents, I swear I had no idea, baby." He brushes a stray tear away. I look back at Ben or is it Jared at this point? Yeah, I'm so overwhelmed, I don't know who I'm talking to anymore.

"Okay, Jared. If my parents are not my parents, then who are?"

"Mallie, you're the daughter of Selene and her mate. You are the daughter of the Goddess herself."

My chest quickly rises and falls, desperately trying to pull in oxygen but I can't seem to get enough air into my lungs. I can see people trying to grab my attention. I can see their mouths moving but can't hear anything above the ringing in my ears. My vision blurs, as sweat beads down my forehead. My hands begin to tremble as a tingling sensation spreads across my skin. I gasp for breath when tremors shake my body. The room spins out of control, and I'm grateful when the darkness consumes me.

LANDON

She absorbs all of this information. I don't think she realizes how strong she truly

is.

"Mallie, you're the daughter of Selene and her mate. You're the daughter of the Goddess herself."

There's a collective gasp throughout the room. Attendees of today's meeting never expected the conversation to go in this direction. I'm stunned, speechless. My mate is a true goddess– Holy Shit. She tries to catch her breath, Jesus she's really working hard to breathe. Suddenly, her eyes roll into the back of her head, and she starts having a seizure. I catch her before she hit the floor. "Call an ambulance!" I yell in a panic.

"Everyone back up, I'm a doctor." An alpha comes running up from the back of the room and I feel helpless as he works on her.

"What is happening to her?" I question as her body slowly stops shaking. My heart stops when I notice her skin starting to take on a blue hue. "She can't breathe!" I scream.

"Does anyone know of her medical condition?" The doc yells.

"She was injured during the war. Mal was injected with wolfsbane laced with something that has plagued her ever since. Whatever it is... it's been slowly killing her." Stacy grips the front of John's shirt and sobs.

"What?" I roar. My mate is dying in front of me. I have never felt this helpless in my life.

"It's why she left the pack, to try to find doctors who could help her." John supplies squeezing his luna tightly. I don't know what to do with myself as I stand above Mal's prone body. I fist my SHORT HAIR in both of my hands. All I see is red. Visions of revenge is all consuming, making the faceless fucker who hurt my luna beg for mercy. But there will be no mercy for him.

"LANDON! Snap out of it!" The doc yells at me. "We're losing her, and I need your help. I'm going to start chest compressions. When I count to thirty, I'm going to need you to tilt her head back a little, pinch her nose and blow two breaths into her. Got it?" I nod and do exactly what he asks of me. After three rounds the doctor yells out to his beta, "ask the hotel manager for the d-fib machine, they should have one." I feel death's cold grip on my soul. Surely if he takes her from me, I will gladly follow her. The doctor's count closes in on thirty again and I fear that this will be the last kiss I place on her lips while they are still warm.

It takes forever for the beta to come back with the damn machine. Doc rips the green silk to gain further access to her chest, and I try hard not to growl at him. He quickly places the leads on her chest and starts the up machine. The device beeps a few times then talks in a robotic voice. "No electrical activity detected. Continue with chest compressions." My stomachs in my fucking throat.

"Come on baby you can't leave me." I beg after giving her another breath.

Doc frantically continues working on my beautiful mate. When out of nowhere he shouts, "Holy Shit she's not marked."

"No, we only met yesterday."

The look on his face tells me he has a crazy fucking idea, but I will try anything at this point. "Okay this is the plan you're going to mark her."

"What?!" I roar.

"Listen to me. You are going to mark her and when I say let go, release the bite. At that moment I will shock her with the machine. The process of marking sends a current through the body almost like an electric shock but stronger. That mixed with the current from the machine, it should work."

"Do it!" I shout as I extend my canines and wait for the doc's signal.

"NOW!" he shouts.

I bite down— hard. Pouring every ounce of my soul into it. The taste of her blood dances on my tongue and I can't help but play our first kiss in my head in hopes she can feel my love through our connection. Praying that the connection we do have is enough to keep her here with me.

"RELEASE!"

I release the bite, just as he hits the button on the machine. "CLEAR!" He shouts as her body jumps from the voltage. Then the most beautiful sound fills the room as the machine begins to speak.

"Electrical Activity Detected."

Chapter 6
MALINDA

"Baby, please wake up." His voice sounds a million miles away, and no matter how hard I try, I can't seem to get to him.

"Landon, I'm trying." I whisper into the nothingness that surrounds me. I've been stuck in the darkness for what seems like years, just floating in time and space. I can hear Landon's voice every now and then, but he can't hear me. I grab snippets of conversations before I'm sucked back into the darkness.

"Find who did this, NOW!"

Darkness...

"Alpha, we have the tech team checking surveillance cameras at the apartment, hotel and hospital."

Darkness...

"Alpha, we have a lead."

Darkness....

Once I even heard him reading to me, he was reading pack paperwork to me as if it was some magical story. And it was. Any words that fall from his mouth are pure poetry.

"And once upon a time there was an alpha who fixed a dispute between two pack members today. They were fighting over what color to paint the shared fence...."

I could not help but smile. I could hear Stacy singing to me and I am pretty sure she was dancing around the room. I could hear

Sam and Landon reminiscing about all the trouble they got into as pups. I really hope I remember all of this when I wake up, you never know when you may need a little blackmail material!

But lately it has been so quiet. I can't tell if hours have gone by or days. Sahara is silent too. She is the only reason that the last couple of years have been bearable. Fuck, I'm so frustrated. *Hmmm, what is that?* Through the dark clouds of this black abyss, light dapples off of the nothingness. I muster all of my waning strength to chase it. The farther I travel, doubt begins to grow, and I fear that the direction I'm headed won't lead me to *him*. Like shooting stars, millions of little lights swirl around me, and in a flash—consumes me.

Once the light starts to fade away everything around me comes into focus. It's night and the stars appear to be brighter than I've ever seen them before. The moon is so large that I slowly extend my hand to touch it. That's how close it appears. Glancing around I'm overwhelmed by the beauty surrounding me. To my left, sits a huge weeping willow tree. I stare in wonderment as the leaves sparkle like little diamonds, giving it an ethereal glow. *Wow.* A gentle breeze teases the long flowing branches and the secret to the sparkling is revealed as millions of little fireflies take flight.

"Beautiful aren't they."

A feminine voice breaks the silence. Startled by the sound, I can't help but seek out the source. From the corner of my eye, I notice movement through the branches. Slowly, I make my way closer to the majestic tree. With both hands, I reach up, and open the branches up as if they were heavy drapes hanging on large windows. And what it reveals renders me speechless. The most beautiful woman I have ever seen. Her long silvery hair flows down to rest on the exposed roots of the ancient tree, where she sits. Her eyes brighten when she sees me, and she pats the spot next to her. My breath catches in my throat.

It's the moon goddess.

I walk toward her, pushing the swaying limbs to the side. Wait... I walked to her. "My child. Here you are whole." Her voice is as light as the current that is playing with the ends of her hair. She reaches her hand out for me to hold and gently pulls me down to sit next to her.

"It's been some time since I've been able to do that. It felt very natural, as if I never stopped doing it." I say in amazement. A giggle escapes as I slowly wiggle my toes in the damp grass. I forgot what this felt like. She smiles and nods her head, while placing her arm around me.

"So, my darling Malinda. I know you must have a ton of questions for me." Honestly, how can I not have questions? "Let me tell you a little story and see if I can fill in some of the blanks, okay?" I give her a small smile; she pats my thigh and begins.

"Right before you were born, I had a run in with my sister Fate. She feared a war would plague the world and while she loved a little mischief every now and then she has come to love the world as it is." I had no clue that Fate and Moon were related—let alone sisters. "My sister had a vision of you saving the world, which would have been impossible if I had kept you here with me. So, after much discussion I decided to send you to earth. It was the hardest thing I have ever had to do. I wanted to keep my sweet girl here so I could watch you grow up. Help train you to take over for me one day.

After watching the beta family of Stone Mountain struggle to conceive a pup of their own, I knew what I had to do. I gave them the greatest of blessings. I gave them—you. It was the most difficult decision your father and I ever made. But we were always watching over you. And look at you now. You grew up to be one of the strongest warriors. Your father thinks you get your strength from him. I grant him that small delusion." She jests with a wink. The conversation between us flows as if I was talking to my best friend, not someone I just met... let alone this person being my mother.

"We all saw the war brewing, both on earth and here. The gifts and blessings you were born with by simply being a goddess would have been enough to end the bloodshed. But when you got to earth, we had to hide those gifts. You would be the most powerful werewolf in existence. Others would notice that you were exceptional. It would give the council no choice, you would have to ascend the throne.

Evil was still brewing, and they would have sought you out. Wanting to use you as a weapon. We thought if we hid your gifts until your eighteenth birthday you would be safe. You would get your mate and your gifts would come forward. What I did not account for was the fact that you would not meet Landon in time. I could not leave you unprotected. You needed guards, knights if you will.... I had to ensure that you would survive."

"So, you mated me to Jared?"

"Ah yes, Jared, I had already chosen him to be your guard. He was to be your first in command. He was already your best friend and would protect you with his life. As the war grew closer, I needed you to have a mate bond. Activating the bond would allow your mate to feel you so if you were in danger he could detect and find you quickly." She tugs on my arm a bit and guides me to lay my head in her lap. My mother, the freaking moon goddess, starts to play with my hair. Not going to lie kinda fangirling over here.

"What I didn't expect was that since I had originally fated you and Landon for each other, was that the bond would be weaker when I tried to change it to you and Jared. Now, I don't know if it's because you're a goddess or because I mated you to Landon the day, I brought you to earth. Your bond with Jared should have been explosive, but it wasn't. And when you came of age your powers were almost muted. You were still stronger than normal, but it should have been blatantly obvious you were different. Then I got to thinking. You see, I think because you wanted a mate so badly starting at such a young age, that the desire for a mate kickstarted the bond early." I can't pick my jaw up off the floor as I listen to her speak.

"When you both came of age and felt the mate bond pull was not as expected. I could tell you both were devastated, and so confused. Being mated to each other and yet only feeling friendship. Oh, it strengthened your bond, but you became more like siblings. You wanted forever love and all you got was a big brother." She shrugs her shoulders and I giggle. It's true we were so confused when it all went down.

"Why did you send him back as a wolf?" I ask as I look up at her knowing the answer already but selflessly, I don't want this moment to end.

"He was always meant to protect you. Ben, his human counterpart, is like Jared, a strong alpha male."

"But…uh…" I adjust myself to look up at her. "…why did you mate Landon with someone else?"

"Well, my beautiful girl, I heard Tara's prayers. She had prayed for a mate to love. She wanted to feel the magic of the bond before she died. Since she was fated to die during the battle. I granted her dying wish. To be truly and completely loved." This poor girl was fighting and willing to sacrifice herself for the cause. All she wanted was to feel loved and she got it for only one whole day.

"Goddess, will I ever see Landon again?" I question as I push myself up to look her in the eyes.

"It's your choice, my little one. You can stay here with us," she stretches out her hand to point to a large meadow beyond the willow branches. There I see three people standing at the edge where the tall wildflowers meet the grassy area.

"M—mom, dad!" There they stand. The two people who raised me and loved me as their own. They died during the war. It's been so long, and I've missed them so much. Without hesitation I jump to my feet, run to them and crash into their open arms.

"Oh, my sweet little warrior, how we've missed you!" My mom whispers as she squeezes the life out of me.

"Hey kiddo," my dad says as he ruffles my hair. He was always a man of few words, but the stray tear sliding down his face can't be ignored. Once again proving I'll always be his little girl.

The goddess now stands with us with her arm around the third person. He's tall and built like an alpha. This, this must be her mate. "Hi Malinda, I'm..."

"Hi Daddy." I breathe out with a smile across my face. Tears fill his eyes, and he opens his arms to me.

"You were a week old the last time I held you my sweet princess."

"Here I stand with all of my parents, all the people who love me. How can I leave y'all?"

"Oh, we're not the only ones though, my sweet girl." The goddess declares as she tucks some hair behind my ear. I look at her confused. "We're not the only ones who love you. Landon is waiting for you my dear. You can go back and live the life that is fated for you. It will not be an easy road and danger is lurking." I look off toward the direction I came from. "Are you willing to take a chance on destiny—on love?" She tilts her head to look at me with a knowing smile. I let her words settle in my heart.

I'm pulled from my thoughts when I feel a tap on my shoulder. I turn and come face to face with a beautiful woman, and a strikingly handsome man. The woman has beautiful long dirty blond hair, and her skin has been kissed by the sun. The man is tall and built like a mountain, what has me stunned is the color of his eyes. A breathtaking mix of blue-gray.

"You're... you're... Landon's parents?"

"Yes," his mother answers with a gentle smile.

"Can you do us a favor? If you choose to return to our son... Please let him know we are so proud of him and that we love him sooo much." She declares as she gently grasps my hand in her delicate one.

"Could you let him know that he is doing a good job, a great job even." Landon's father raises his hand for me to shake. "Sorry I'm not as mushy as my mate." The old alpha says just before he grabs me and pulls me into a bear hug. "He is beyond lucky to have you." Not mushy—my ass, I see the tears sitting in the corner of his eyes and I give him a knowing smirk. I don't think there is a dry eye anywhere.

I look at all of my parents, all in the embrace of their mates. With the one person that brings them each solace and peace. I want that... I want him. "Malinda, you need to make a decision quickly. Even though your time here was brief it's taking a toll on your physical body. It's failing. I fear if you do not leave now you will die."

A cry pierces the bubble of tranquility that surrounded us, bringing attention to the commotion sounding in the distance. We all turn to face the noise. I'm running out of time. "Will I ever see you all again?"

"We are always watching over you."

"I want to go back to him." They each pull me in for a quick hug, with the Goddess being last.

"Go, my sweet child," with a kiss to my forehead she forcefully shoves me backward. An invisible force quickly pulls my body in the direction in which I came. The light from the moon and stars disappears, while I'm plunged back into darkness. I hear what sounds like crying... then nothing.

LANDON

It's been three weeks Three. Fucking. Weeks. The doctors were able to get her stable once she arrived at the hospital from the hotel. Numerous tests were run, revealing some very disturbing news. This prompted us to double her security. After a week we transferred her to the Full Moon pack hospital. This way I could work on how to protect her, manage my pack, and still be at her side. She's been breathing on her own and stable for the last two weeks, but she hasn't woken up. Sam and I are currently hanging out in her hospital room. Playing poker for the thousandth time, talking to her as if she is just merely hanging out with us. For the first time in weeks, I'm finally able to relax a bit.

A piercing scream from one of Mal's monitors breaks my revelry. The door slams open and an army of doctors and nurses breach the room—as if ready to battle. And in a sense, I suppose they are. "What is happening? She was fine two minutes ago!" I yell, almost in accusation.

"We're losing her," a nurse, studying the monitors, shouts. Dr. Taylor climbs up on her bed and begins chest compressions.

"Alpha, we need you to step back." Dr. Taylor yells.

"NO!" I growl. Tears stream down my face. There is no way I can hold it together. For the second time in three weeks, I watch as a team of people try to save the life of our luna. Even Sam is affected by the scene playing out in front of us. The young woman that's been helping the nursing staff care for Malinda since she arrived at our pack is quietly sobbing in the corner. Even though Mal hasn't woken up... she is already loved by everyone.

I can't take the sight anymore. The pain of experiencing my mate die is ripping through my soul. Storming out of the hospital room door, practically ripping it off of the hinges. Everyone in the hallway stops, then quickly scurries off once they see the anger and anguish on my face. I do nothing to contain my emotions. I feel like a fucking ticking time bomb. Grabbing the first thing in my way, I let out a deafening roar as I throw a plastic chair down the hallway. I get no satisfaction even though it's in a million pieces. Like my heart will be if my Luna dies. My vision blurs with rage and grief. I lift my fist, repeatedly slamming it through the drywall as I try to feel anything over the ache in my chest.

"Alpha... ALPHA! ENOUGH." Doc K, the other attending physician for Malinda yells. She slowly approaches me and places her tiny hand on my forearm. She's got brass balls, that's for sure. No one would dare come this close to a raging alpha. I don't even trust myself right now, but slowly her inaudible words start to break through. "Sir, we got a faint heartbeat." K squeezes my arm tighter and a small injection of hope that spreads across my face, but quickly falls as she shakes her head. "No Alpha. It's faint and I fear it's not going to be there for long. You—you need to calm down and be with your mate. It's time to say goodbye." I can't help the sob that escapes my lips. Bracing my hands against the wall, I place my forehead on my arm. Desperate for air to fill my lungs that does not feel like hot pokers. Fuck, I need to pull it together for her, she needs me to be strong.

"I don't think I can do this. I'm not ready for goodbyes." I slowly amble to her as the nurses readjust her wires and monitors with unseeing eyes. They bow to my beautiful luna one last time. Slowly the door closes behind them, only the sound of their distant sniffling can be heard. Doc K tosses a towel in my direction and points to my hand. Nodding in thanks, I quickly wrap it up as I grasp one of Malinda's hands in mine. I gently brush her hair from her face. Sam quietly comes near and places a comforting hand on my shoulder.

"I wanted to show you the world, my Queen. I wanted you to feel my love in every way possible. I will love you forever Mal. The only happiness I will find is in the blood of those who wronged you. I vow to bring down every person who did this to you." There's no stopping the tears. Placing a hand on her cheek and gently stroking it with my thumb. "My beautiful Luna, until we meet again."

Leaning down, I place a gentle kiss on the tip of her nose, then her cheeks, her lips, and last, I place a kiss on her mark. The most unique mark I have ever seen sits upon her shoulder. But of course, she would have this. She is the most unique person I have ever met. The image of two crowned wolves looking up at six stars stares back at me. I was shocked when it appeared on her neck. Normally you just see a simple bite mark. This... this is so damn beautiful.

It's the mark of my luna, my queen.

I lean into it, smelling her marked skin, wanting to remember everything. I close my eyes as I press my lips there. A last kiss on an image that was supposed to be a portrayal of my Forever. "Luna," Sam gasps loudly, his voice filled with disbelief. Sam's grip on my shoulder is to the point of painful. He pulls on my arm desperately trying to get my attention, but I don't want to look. I'm too afraid to watch the beautiful blush leave her cheeks. Because the last time I looked up she was alive— and now when I look up, she'll be gone. I'm not ready, I squeeze my eyes shut resting my head on her chest as the monitor sounds with one long beep, signaling she's gone.

"Baby I love you."

Chapter 7
LANDON

"I love you too, honey," a sweet voice mingles with the new, constant beat of the heart monitor. I'm afraid to open my eyes. I'm afraid to move. Surely my mind has created this moment to save me from my pain. Fingers, light and gentle touch my hair. Slowly I sit back and make eye contact with the most beautiful set of green eyes I've ever seen.

"Luna? Luna—Oh goddess, thank the moon you're awake! You're alive!!!!" I pull her into my arms and my heart nearly beats out of my chest as her arms wrap around me. "Oh baby, I—I was so scared." I palm her face in my hands. Tears stream down her face and I make sure to kiss each one. I'm rewarded with a delicate giggle as my beard tickles her face. It's music to my ears. She pulls my lips to hers.

"Landon *kiss* I missed you *kiss* so much *kiss* can you ever." Malinda pulls back to look into my eyes. "Can you ever forgive me?" she asks as she worries her lip.

"Forgive you for what?"

"For not accepting the bond right away…"

"Oh sweetheart," I brush my knuckles across her jaw line and feel her shiver beneath my touch. "It's okay, I know you had your reasons. When you're ready to talk about it, I'll be ready to listen."

She tries to sit up but struggles against the wires. Sam and I help her to get her comfortable. "Luna, you have no idea how good it is to see you sitting up and awake. This Alpha, here," Sam claps my back. "I don't know what he was going to do if you didn't wake up." I shoot him a look, wishing he would learn how to read the room, but she reaches out for Sam's hand.

"Sam, I cannot thank you enough for your dedication to our alpha. You're a true friend."

I can't take my eyes off of her, she looks so refreshed, stunning even. She has to be the only one that can go from death's door to waking up looking like you stepped out of heaven. She moves her hand from Sam's and rests it on my cheek. Staring into my eyes, as if she's reaching into my soul. It's then her eyes change from emerald, green, to an almost glow. The initial shock of her glowing eyes fades as I feel mine turn black. Our wolves are acknowledging the match, and the rise of sexual tension between us is building fast. Sam's eyes bounce between me and Malinda, he clears his throat to catch our attention. "Ahem, why thank you Luna, but truly I would do anything for either of you."

The door swings open and the look of disbelief on K and Taylor's faces brings me to stand taller, slightly miffed that I'm being interrupted. Mal is awake and I want no one to interfere with our time. K folds her arms over her chest and shakes her head and approaches the bed. After fifteen minutes and a quick assessment they leave us be.

"Hey, I was about to go, umm get something to eat. Can I get you guys anything?" Sam mentions

"Yes!" Malinda shouts. "May I please have a hot cup of tea and an apple turnover with icing— ohhhh, maybe an apple crumble, oh no just a slice of apple pie."

She asks with the biggest cheesiest smile on her face. "That explains why you smell like apple pie to me!"

Her face turns a lovely shade of pink, "I really love sweets, but apple desserts are my absolute favorite."

"How about I get you a pudding cup. You know, you did just wake up from a three-week coma." She narrows her eyes at him, then scrunches her nose a bit to mull over what he just said. Reluctantly she nods her head in agreement.

"Sam I'll have whatever you're having." I say with a smile as I slap him on the back and gently push him to the door. He bows to us, and I shoot him a quick mind link.

-Sam, can you give us like thirty minutes?
-Thirty that's it?
-Don't be an ass.

He barks with laughter, and I cut the link. I face Malinda as the door clicks shut. She's fumbling with her fingers, then nervously tucks some loose hair behind her ear. Looking up from her lap, she takes a deep breath, seemingly trying to find courage for something. "Landon, I need to tell you something that is very important." At her tone, I lock the door then quickly climb onto the spot she's tapping, right next to her. I snake my arms around her and hold her to my chest, kissing her forehead. Then let my one hand slowly run up and down her arm. Sparks ignite between us, making me hard almost instantly. "Please— Landon, I need to say this before... before anything happens between us. I need to make sure I'm going to be enough."

Enough? How could she not be enough for me? How could she even think that as a possibility? "My Luna, you're everything I need. You're enough to fill a million of my lifetimes."

A small sob escapes her beautiful lips, "Landon, what I have to say is very hard and I want you to have the opportunity to have an out before this goes too far." Taking a shaky breath, she continues. "After I got hurt, the wolfsbane—it was laced with something. I never found out what it was, but it never fully left my system. The last three years have been so stressful. When I got to Paisley my blood work actually got worse. Eventually everything stabilized, not getting better but not getting worse. I couldn't figure it out and neither could the doctors. I went to all the top doctors and still no answers. The only thing they told me for sure was that I will most likely never be able to walk, shift or carry a pup."

My heart breaks for her. She has been carrying this pain with her for years. Blocking herself off from the world. "Landon, I might not be able to give you an heir and I know how badly you want a family," she says barely above a whisper.

I let her words soak in and for a moment my chest tightens. I've always wanted to be a father, but I have always wanted my true mate. I've dreamed of my mate since I was a little kid. I wouldn't trade my mate for anything in the world and that includes having a family the old natural way. I cup her face and tilt her head up to me.

"Baby, I choose you, I choose us, my little Luna, my queen. We can always have fun trying and if not, we can adopt a pup." Leaning in, I kiss her. The taste of her tears on her lips overwhelms me with a desire to take her elsewhere. Pulling her close, as her body molds to mine. Her breath hitches and I can't stop myself from running my tongue along her jawline chasing a tear that fell. Salt dances on my tastebuds. She takes a deep breath and hums in appreciation as she takes in my scent. Now that I have taken a taste, I want more, every part of her. Slowly, my hands roam her body, my lips leave a trail of sparks down her neck. Making my way toward her mark, there's no stopping me from running my tongue along it. Watching her skin prickle from the contact pushes me closer to the edge. Her head falls to the side giving me better access. My wolf is fighting for control. "Landon," she breathlessly moans. She could have been caressing my cock with her tongue with how my name escapes her lips. Fuck, we need to slow down. I pull back a bit trying to catch my breath, not wanting to push too much. She was just on her deathbed for god's sake. My cock will be fine, yup fine. My balls will be blue, but my cock will be fine. But we'll survive.

Chapter 8
MALINDA

Landon's roaming hands and mouth stop abruptly. My eyes flutter open, and I already miss the contact. "Why–why did you stop?" I whisper. Did I do something wrong? Shit, when's the last time I showered? Holy shit I must stink.

"You didn't do anything wrong, and you don't smell bad." My face heats with embarrassment. "You were thinking out loud," he jests, a small smirk pulls at his lips. "But you did just wake up from a three-week coma and I'm not about to fuck you back in one." He says with a chuckle. Looking up at him through my lashes, I pull in a deep breath.

"I feel perfectly fine. If I could run, I'm pretty sure I could run a marathon right now. That's how good I feel," I state passionately. He gives me a skeptical look, but I mean every word I say. I feel perfectly fine. He runs his nose along my collar bone causing a shiver to run through my body. "I refuse to let this moment pass us by," I say breathlessly. Landon freezes, his breaths are coming out harsh. Those blue-gray orbs hold me in place. He's trying to read me, it's like he is staring into my soul. I can feel the space between my thighs heat from the intensity of his gaze. Without any words I let him know that I want him, and the way his nostrils flare tells me I'm affecting him as much as he is affecting me.

A slight growl rumbles through his chest and his lips crash against mine. His sudden action causes me to gasp, and he takes full advantage. His tongue slides into my mouth and sends my body into overdrive. Landon slides one hand under my nightgown, gently caressing the side of my breast. I can't help the giggle that escapes my lips. I've never been touched like this before. It's light and even tickles a bit. He takes my whole breast in his hand and squeezes. The feeling of his hands on me is so erotic and the sensation as he rolls my nipple between his fingers has my juices running down my thighs. My brain is all fuzzy as he takes the rosy peak into his mouth. I moan at the contact.

Arching my back, I desperately try to get closer. My reaction causes him to smirk against my skin at my excitement. He knows exactly what he is doing to me, and he is loving it. Releasing my nipple with a pop, he begins kissing his way down my stomach. The intensifying heat between my legs is becoming unbearable. I rub them together, searching for any kind of reprieve when I realize I've got no underwear on. *Why don't I have underwear on?*

"Focus Mal, our alpha is making us feel good." Sahara purrs, I can almost see the shit eating grin on her face.

"Nice to have ya back bitch."

"Looks like I got here just in time."

Landon's hand gently cups my pussy, as he places delicate kisses on my thighs. "WAIT!!!!" Landon shoots up faster than lightning. His eyes filled with panic.

"What? Are you okay?"

"Landon... I... I... can feel you," I sob. "It's an odd sensation, but I can feel something when you do that."

A megawatt smile consumes his face. He sits up, reaches for my lips and kisses me hard. Pulling away with a smirk, "If you don't mind, I'd like to get back to making my mate blissfully happy."

With that, Landon slides a thick finger along my inner thigh then gently pushes it inside of me. "Oh, sweet baby moon goddess." My alpha chuckled against my lips. He took this opportunity to slide his tongue into my mouth and it is everything. I can barely breathe.

The kiss is so intense. He kisses me with reckless abandon. As if he's trying to make up for the time we lost while I was in a coma. Maybe even for the years before he knew I existed. I love the way his tongue feels against mine.

I pull back for some air and at that moment he slips another finger inside me. I don't think I can get any wetter, but he was going to try to see if I could. "Luna, you are so tight for me." He growls while he uses his thumb to rub my clit. The sensation is so magical that my eyes roll into the back of my head, and I moan— loudly.

"Look at me Luna, eyes on me." I do as he says when he slides a third finger in. I squirm from the pain and pleasure of being stretched, my alpha is trying to get me ready. The thought has a chill run down my spine. Landon pumps in and out of me while flicking my clit with his thumb. The heat rises within as he increases his speed. It's hard to control my breathing with the heights he is bringing me to. I'm going to explode.

"Relax, let your body go."

"Oh, mmmmm oh my...."

"Landon, yes, yes........" I grind onto his hand trying to push him deeper into me. "Oh, please, please don't stop."

"That's it, Beautiful." My eyes flutter shut as he pinches my bundle of nerves. "Open your eyes. I want them on me when you come."

He glides his other hand under my thin, hospital gown. It travels to my breast and ends with a nipple pinch. That's when I come undone and clench around his fingers. The foreign sensation sends my body spasms out of control. I bite my lip, hoping to hold back my scream. Now is not the time for visits from the hospital staff. I've never experienced an orgasm this good in all my life. And now all I can do is wonder how good it will be once I'm riding his cock.

Landon gently flicks my clit to force another small orgasm and I love every second of it. He slowly removes his fingers then places them in his mouth where he sucks them clean. "You taste like heaven."

My mouth drops open when I see his tongue lapping each digit. Ummm, yeah, that was so fucking hot.

Palming my face with his hands, he places his thumb on my lips. "Open" he whispers.

So, I do.

His finger makes contact with my awaiting tongue. "Suck," he orders. Oh god this is so hot. I do as I'm told, tasting myself on him. Caging his hands with mine, I roll my tongue around his thumb. Showing him what my tongue can do. The ache between my legs is growing stronger. Can I get off by just sucking his thumb? Could I have an orgasm just from this erotic act?

"Just like that baby. I can't wait to take you home."

The answer to my questions is yes, yes, I can. I gently pull his thumb from my mouth and tug on his shirt bringing him closer to me. I want his lips on me again. I want his lips everywhere on me. They are so soft and yet demanding. I don't think I will ever get enough of him.

Realization begins to hit. I really did not want my first time to be in a hospital room but I sure as shit couldn't care less if the foreplay happened here. With how good it is, I probably wouldn't care if it happened right in the middle of a damn restaurant. That thought alone gives me an idea and I reach for his jeans button.

"Luna, you do not have to do this, you just woke up. I want to be the one taking care of you." He places his hand on my cheek and caresses my flesh.

I swat it away, a devilish smile on my face. "My Alpha, thank you for thinking of me but since I can't have you where I really want you, I'll settle for having you in my mouth."

LANDON

My heart is in my throat, while my cock swells against the zipper of my jeans. I can't take my eyes off her. Reaching for the zipper, she slowly pulls it down and over my bulge. There is a devilish sparkle in her eye as her delicate fingers glide into my boxers and grasp my cock. Just her touch sends shock waves through my body, I could have come right then and there. I stand up and lower the hospital bed to the perfect height to make it easier on my mate.

Dex is purring in my head *"Lan we need to get a bed like this for the bedroom."*

I smirk at his amazing idea. Mal looks up at me with her beautiful green eyes and slowly takes me into her mouth. The sensation is overwhelming. I lean my head back as she takes me all in and brings me back out. "Watch me Alpha," she demands, then slides me back in and down her throat. I look down at her as she increases her speed. I can't help but start moving my hips matching her eagerness. My hands tangle in her hair and gently pull causing a delicious moan to come from her. It sends a vibration through my body that brings me closer to the edge.

"Yes, just like that." This is so intense; the mate bond has heightened this so much. I want to make this last, but I think I am going to come faster than I want. I don't want to exhaust my Luna but... "HOLY SHIT" I groan as she does something with her tongue I have never felt before and I start thrusting harder.

" I'm going to come." As the words fall from my mouth, so does my seed. She swallows every drop I've given her. Then she proceeds to lick my cock clean.

Pulling her bottom lip between her teeth a beautiful blush graces her features. Sexy as hell. "Why thank you, Alpha. I'm so glad to finally experience that, it's a bonus that you're my mate," she says with a wink. Processing the words that came out of her mouth, did she just admit that she's a virgin?

"Mal, was that your first orgasm?"

"Well, no. I've touched myself before," she says barely above a whisper.

"Baby, you've never had sex before?" He questions dumbfoundedly. "But you were mated to an alpha, how are you still a virgin?"

"Jared was like my big brother. That would've been gross. We only marked each other for the ceremony. But when he died my mark vanished."

"Mal, I ummm.... was that the first time you ever gave a blow job?" The look on her face is priceless. "Because damn, sweetheart that was amazing." She turns red in the face, but you can see the pride in her eyes.

"Yup, Stacy taught me in high school on a banana."

Dex chimes in, *"Remind me to send her a fruit basket."*

"Landon, I figured you weren't a virgin. You had a mate too." She says as she fiddles with her hospital gown. I place my finger under her chin to guide those beautiful eyes to mine. "Plus, you're sexy as hell. Oh, and let's not forget that most alpha's have a ridiculous sex drive. I would be shocked if you told me you're still a virgin." Guilt slowly creeps into my veins. I lost my virginity as a teenager, the thought of waiting for my mate did not even cross my mind. But now that I have her, how could I have been so selfish to not want to wait for this.

"And I'm only still a virgin because, well... who wants to be mated to a broken wolf? No one, I can assure you. So, I haven't even tried dating."

"Mal, I don't care if you have a disability, I love you for you. I'm sorry I did not wait for this—for us. And despite all of my mistakes the goddess herself chose you for me and I for you. It's a complete honor to know that your mother chose me for her daughter."

CHAPTER 9
MALINDA

  It's been a week since I woke up and I need to get out of this hospital room. Now, let me be honest— I feel great. Better than I have in years. I still cannot walk though. I was kinda hoping that the sensation I felt on my legs during mine and Landon's little encounter would have lasted... I guess I need to take things in stride.

  After much discussion, Dr. Taylor and Dr. K have finally agreed to discharge me. They gave me a list of dos and don'ts and at first, I was frustrated as hell. Then I realized that they're just trying to care for their luna. I've gotten to know them well this past week. They are both beyond nice, but K has grown into a friend. She's really funny, and the way Landon, Sam and her bicker cracks me up.

  "You ready Luna? We've already gotten all of your belongings from your apartment while you were *sleeping* and brought them to the pack house. So, we just need your beautiful ass." Landon says as he exits the adjoining bathroom. He's been staying over and showering in the hospital to be closer to me. I mean who am I to argue, I get to see a show every morning. He's currently tugging on a black v neck t-shirt that looks like it may be a tad too small. I can't help but tilt my head to the side as I take more of him in.

  Damn, it's pulling in all of the right places. I think it may be my new favorite shirt. He tosses a hoodie on the bed so he can tuck his shirt in, captivating me with his rippling muscles. I know I'm blatantly staring at him, but I can't help it. Reluctantly, I hand him his hoodie and it's like watching someone spread icing on a damn cake. Everything this man does is smooth. Oh, sweet goddess... he just put on a baseball cap and turned it backwards— yup I am wet.

Landon coughs and I drag my gaze up to his and he arches a brow. Shit, I've been caught ogling. He takes a step closer to me, as a smirk pulls at the corner of his mouth. I slowly roll my chair backwards, creating a little space between us. He bends down, and I can feel the heat rise along my flesh. This man does things to me I didn't think were possible. Grabbing both wheels with his large hands, bringing me to an abrupt stop. I can't take my eyes off of him as he lowers his face to my ear. His hot breath sends tingles all over. I gulp nervously as his husky voice practically sends me over the edge. "Luna, I can smell your arousal."

I pull my lower lip between my teeth in order to stifle my moan. He gently raises his hand and tugs it free. "Baby, if you keep doing that we may never leave." He straightens up and adjusts his very visible bulge. "You're making it very difficult for me to walk. I want to have you in our bed for our first time, not up against a wall in the pack hospital," he says with a wink. Damn him and that sexy smirk that slowly creeps across his face.

"I want to put it on the record that I would like both please." Landon nods his head acknowledging my request. I must be a lovely shade of pink as a result of my bold statement but catching him off guard was totally worth it. Landon trails kisses from my lips down my neck where he settles on my mark.

"Oh, my sweet Luna, don't you worry. One day soon I'm going to push you up against a wall, wrap your legs around me, and I'm going to take you hard and fast. You will be glad our apartment is soundproof because you'll be screaming my name." His words cause me to moan and giggle at the same time, like come on this ridiculously hot man is talking about taking me up against a wall— yeah, I've got to be the luckiest she-wolf in the world.

"Wait, your apartment is soundproof?"

"And thank god it is. Because something tells me once my cock is in that tight little pussy of yours the only sounds, you'll be able to make are screams."

"Oh, my."

LANDON

I can't help the shit eating grin on my face over the fact that I make this woman so freaking crazy. I feel like she is living in a constant state of arousal, which is making it difficult to fit into my jeans. I can't get her out of this hospital fast enough. "We are going to head to the pack house for breakfast. After that is one quick meeting and then you are going to rest in bed, okay?" I want her to rest but we have much to discuss. Top three things on the agenda are her safety, planning her Luna ceremony and formally introducing her to the pack.

I go to push the back of her chair to help her out, but she grabs the wheels to stop me. "Landon, I'm madly in love with you. I never thought I would ever find a second chance mate… but I need to let you know that I can do a lot of things able-bodied wolves can do. I know you mean well, and you think you are helping—" She puts her head down and almost whispers. "But please, I can get myself around and I promise if I need help, I will ask. You gotta remember that I've been on my own for several years, and I don't like people pushing on my chair or thinking I'm weak."

I get down on my haunches so I'm eye level with my queen. "Baby, I truly am sorry. I'm very new to this world— but remember that it's not only yours now. It's ours, and yes, I'm gonna make mistakes and I might piss you off but we are going to do this together." She releases a shaky breath, shaking her head back and forth as if she is having an internal conflict. The idea that she fears people will think she is weak grips at my chest. "Mal, I absolutely respect everything you are saying, and I will do anything you want. But make no mistake. I know you don't need my help. I'm not doing it to help you. I'm doing it because I want to take care of you, whether it's pushing your chair or doing the dishes. Most importantly, I want the world to know you are mine. Being mine means that pretty little ass of yours is going to get pampered—when you let me." She laughs at that but it's not enough to convince me. I can tell she is so conflicted with her emotions, "Mal, look at me." I raise her chin; tears rim her eyes making them look like sparkling emeralds. She's one of the most confident women I know and even though she told me exactly how she feels, I get the feeling that she is holding back. "Why are you being timid with me right now?"

Breaking free I watch as the tear runs along her nose and down her cheek. She tries to wipe it away quickly, but I beat her to it. Kissing it gone, causing her to finally give me a genuinely shy smile. "I've been on my own, with no pack for so long. I've had to rely on myself. I've got no problem putting people in their place when it comes to my limitations. But with you... I am trying not to be so forceful. I'm pretty sure I tend to come off as a bitch." She barks and shakes her head. "Landon, I know what I'm up against and I am uncomfortable. I worry that the pack will not accept me, especially if they know I can be a huge bitch".

"You're not a bitch, the moon goddess threw you a curveball, but you picked that bat up and you've kept on swinging. You're still fighting, now you don't have to do it alone. Let me help you. Let me love you, and let the pack see who you really are." I'm now on my knees in front of her and lean in for a chaste kiss. This simple kiss is more than reassurance of my truth. It's a fucking promise that my woman will never be made to feel weak again.

Chapter 10
MALINDA

Leaving the hospital, we head straight into the pack house. It's a bustling place. People are milling about, and it's very refreshing to see. We approach an open door leading to a very large room. Landon stops to look in, the smile on his face tells me this is special to him. He leans against the door frame and crosses his arms over his chest. "This here is the Rec Room. We also have a building not far from here for events for the pups aged five to eighteen. We have dances for the teens, lock ins and movie nights. We also rent out the space for birthday parties and such. But this," he opens his arms wide toward the inside of the room. "Is a nice hang out for those newly shifted wolves and others that live in the pack house. It was actually my idea as a teen. We wanted a place to hang out that was away from the younger kids."

I look up at him. He looks like a proud papa. "Who are you trying to convince with this whole, 'we wanted a place away from the younger kids?' It sounds less like a place to hang out and more of a convenient place to hook up" I quip with a smirk. Landon laughs, shaking his head, then slowly nods as a blush spreads across his cheeks.

"Ha, yeah snagged there, aren't I." Goddess this man of mine is gorgeous.

We stop off at the kitchen and my jaw drops to the floor. It's absolutely beautiful. What surprises me most is that the omega staff isn't working alone. Landon must've noticed my confusion when he says. "So, my grandmother loved to cook and help out in the kitchen. Over time, it became custom for families to donate time to help the omega staff out as a thank you. Then after my grandmother passed away it continued in memory of her. Now all families help, every rank. It's something that I'm really proud of as Alpha, each rank in the pack has the same respect." He states as a younger omega guides a few young pups on how to wrap some cookies in plastic wrap.

"Hey Mrs. Lane! I would like you to meet our Luna." A woman in her late sixties, maybe early seventies comes toward us. She wipes her hands off on her apron and smiles brightly. She has beautiful blue eyes and blonde hair in a cute pixie cut. This woman is the epitome of Grandma Chic She and I love it!

"Mrs. Lane here is our head chef, and the kitchen," he waves his hands around the room, "is her kingdom." She playfully swats Landon on the arm.

"Luna it's a true honor to finally meet you." She extends her arms and wraps me in a big hug. "I am so happy to see you up and about." She turns and pulls a tray out of the fridge. "Landon told me Apples are your favorite, so I made you a lot of apple crumble last night. I'll have it sent up to your room, unless you are eating dinner down here tonight?" Yup, I've got a serious girl crush on this woman!

I look up at Landon with the biggest puppy dog eyes. "Can we eat down here tonight?"

"As long as you rest after our meeting."

"Mrs. Lane, it looks like I will be enjoying that yummy apple crumble in the dining room tonight!" Thoughts of apple crumble have me doing my happy food dance in my chair. My little wiggle causes Landon to laugh. Then he bends down and kisses the top of my head.

"I love making you happy babe."

Mrs. Lane gives Landon a fake dirty look. "Excuse me, young alpha, but I'm fairly certain her happiness is because of me." Landon places his hand over his heart feigning hurt.

"You wound me Mrs. Lane." He says as he pulls the old woman into his arms for a hug.

"Let's be honest. If you give me any type of apple dessert, you pretty much got me hook, line, and sinker."

"Luna, the pack will be so excited you're eating dinner with us tonight. I also heard that not only do you love dessert but that you love making it. So, Alpha and I got together with the pack contractors, and we're having a custom island put in. Half of the island will be able to be lowered so you can work out of your chair and not have to transfer. But if you want to transfer we will have special stools, put in that can be easy for you to get in and out of and that way you can bake to your heart's content."

I can feel the tears building up once again. "You did that for me? You don't even know me."

Mrs. Lane bends down and brushes them away. "Luna... one day you and I will have tea together and I will remind you that your presence alone is worth all of this." I nod my head and give her a hug. I can feel the love of this pack already.

Landon excuses himself to get ready for the meeting we have in thirty minutes. Meanwhile, I stay with Mrs. Lane while she shows me around the kitchen and cooks up some breakfast sandwiches and snacks for the meeting.

Sam stops by the kitchen as I'm about to find my way to the office.

"Hey Luna, are you heading to the meeting?"

"Yeah, I wanted to head up early so that way I don't stroll in late and start my first meeting off on the wrong foot." I say with a laugh. I hate being late to anything. I consider five minutes early as late.

Sam extends his hand to point behind me and bows his head a bit dramatically. "Let me show you the way."

As we head to Landon's office, Sam and I joke around. I'm balancing the snacks on my lap, as I try to push myself forward. Sam can't stop laughing as I almost roll over his foot for the third time. "Ha, who gave you your license for that thing?" he chuckles. I can't help the glare I shoot in his direction but can't keep a straight face either and we both start laughing. I have come to love Sam like a brother. He is an amazing friend and a fantastic beta.

As we approach Landon's office, I hear his angry voice through the door. "Jessica, I don't know what gave you the impression that I was not going to accept Malinda as my mate, but I've already marked her. I love her and this— this is not going to happen."

A haughty voice belonging to a female replies and my skin crawls at her snotty reply. "Landon, baby. How can she be a luna? And I'm sure she won't be able to keep you happy. I know how you like it."

A foreign feeling vibrates through my body. A vibration so strong that I'm pretty sure I can even feel it in my toes.

So, this is what jealousy feels like. Well, jealousy and anger. Who the hell does she think she is? Sam takes a step toward the door, but I stop him with a hand in the air. He acknowledges my command with a small nod. I straighten my shoulders and silently signal for Sam to move out of the way. He shakes his head and reaches for the knob but I'm all out of fucks to give at this moment. At the same time, he turns the handle I push forward causing the door to slam open into the wall—hard.

Standing in front of a large dark wood desk is both Landon and a beautiful, tall woman. They swing their heads toward me as I cross the threshold. The woman is dressed as if she's going to the beach. Frayed jean shorts reveal long, smooth tanned legs. On top, it looks like she is wearing a bikini, the triangles barely large enough to cover her nipples. She is wearing a sheer black tank top so I guess she can get at least a C for effort. Or a C for cunt. My body bristles at having such a visceral reaction to this woman being so close to my man. I've never used the C Word before in my life but these new feelings I am experiencing have me doing numerous things I have never done before.

Repeating my manta again, I tilt my head like a scientist would do when examining a bug. "Jessica, is it?" I don't wait for her to respond, "I can tell you are the type of woman that needs attention. So, I'm going to give it to you. But let me be clear. After I am done with what I have to say, you will no longer find what you are looking for from either of us. I am the new luna and I am Landon's mate. Frankly I don't really care if you think I am the queen, but I do care if you think you can force your presence upon my mate. Whatever it is that you think you can do for him that I can't, let me guarantee you that there's nothing you can do that I can't do better, all the while not even having to get off my ass." The bitch has the audacity to look stunned. "So, let's refresh shall we. Him," I point to Landon. "MINE." I growl. "If you touch him, or even think of touching him I will end your life without even thinking twice about it."

Scoffing, she narrows her eyes at me, "Baby are you going to let her talk to me like this? She is threatening my life, some luna she is." Jessica places her hands on her hips, looking very pissed off, but yeah, I don't care.

"Call him baby one more time and see what happens." I growl and Sam sucks in a deep breath as he shakes his head, that's right at least he knows I mean business.

"Listen, sweetheart you haven't marked him, and I was in his bed before you, and I can assure you I will be there during and after you."

Yeah—she went there. "Jessica, I've been luna to a pack already. This is not my first rodeo sweet cheeks. I can assure you that hitting on or making advances on a mated alpha will get you the same punishment as a male would if he did so to a mated luna. So yeah, I threatened your life, and I won't think twice about ending it." I smile sweetly and roll myself right next to Landon, grabbing his hand. "Oh, and one more thing, being in this chair does not make me less of a woman. It actually means I am crazy flexible if you get my drift." I cock my eyebrow at her with an evil smirk on my face. I reach up without breaking eye contact with Jessica. I can hear Sam snort as I pull Landon down to me, slamming my lips to his. The kiss is rough and hot. My hands are in his hair as I deepen the kiss. For good measure I bite his lower lip pulling it between my teeth and tug, causing him to growl. *Ha bitch, whatcha gonna do now.*

With a huff, I hear her stomp off slamming the door shut behind her. The sound of breaking glass quickly follows. Sam calls out after her, "and don't let it hit ya where the goddess split ya." I pull away from Landon, and I can feel my face is flush. What started out as a show ended with me getting turned on and him. I try to sneak a peek at the crotch of his jeans and can't help but humm in appreciation. I need this man inside me.

"Mal, you claiming me like that—that was fucking hot."

"I've waited a long time for my fated mate and I am not going to let some rank digger get my man." Sam bursts out laughing, and Landon shakes his head as he sits back in his chair.

"What the hell is a rank digger?" Sam asks as he tries to catch his breath.

"You've never heard of a rank digger?" I ask dumbfounded. They both shake their heads. "Okay so I'm going to assume you know what a gold digger is." They both nod so I continue. "Rank diggers are she-wolf sluts who go after only high ranked wolves."

Sam and Landon both burst out laughing. "Epic" Sam cackles as he begins picking up broken pieces of glass off the floor.

I roll over to a picture that knocked off the wall and start to help clean up. I glance at the image. It's of a mated couple sitting in a meadow. You can feel their love through the picture. "Landon this picture, these are your parents right."

"Yeah, I would've loved for them to meet you. They would've loved you." I glance up at him with a big smile on my face.

"Believe it or not I've met them before, and boy do they miss you."

Chapter 11
LANDON

    I am taken back by what Mal just said to me. She met my parents?! How? When? I am always in awe of this woman of mine. "Okay, although I now have a million questions, they will have to wait. We need to get this meeting started and something tells me whatever you are about to tell me is going to be a good story." I say as a small blush warms her face. Goddess this woman just needs to look at me and I'm hard. Ugh, getting through this meeting is going to be torture, as I discreetly adjust my pants—again.

    Mal's wearing a teal sundress with thin spaghettis straps. Her long hair is thrown haphazardly into a bun on top of her head. I take my seat behind my desk and ask Sam for the bag of food he is holding. I pull everything out and pass Sam and Mal theirs. My mate rolls her chair closer to me and digs in.

    I can't take my eyes off of her as she looks around the room taking everything in. Voices fill the room as they begin talking amongst each other, but I hear nothing. I'm mesmerized by her. The way her mouth moves, how she throws back her head as she laughs at something Sam just said. Fucking everything.

    My eyebrows arch as she slides her hand between her legs. I'm now blatantly staring as her fingers skim across her creamy flesh. I lick my lips as she slides her hand up her thigh and under her dress. My dick twitches as Mal slowly lifts her thigh up with one hand and slides her other hand down to her calf and pulls her right leg over her left... crossing her legs.

Yup, ladies and gentlemen, I've got a raging hard on from watching my mate cross her damn sexy legs. I shake my head clear and notice that Mal is looking at me with a slight blush to her cheeks and her eyes slowly trail to the bulge in my pants. Snagged. I adjust my pants and ignore the snort from Sam.

With five minutes left till the meeting is supposed to begin when everyone starts to finally trickle into the conference room that is attached to my office. Today we are meeting with my top ranked warriors, elders and my top rank staff. Mal has only met Sam, so I know we are going to spend at least thirty minutes on introductions alone.

"Mal you already know Sam, but I'm not sure if he told you that he and Jared are cousins." Her eyes get big as she looks at him. "Oh, my goddess you're Fin and Sara's son. I loved your parents so much." There are tears in her eyes, but they do not fall.

"Yeah, they were the best," he says with a genuine smile on his face. "Luna, it means so much to me that you knew them." Emotion, evident as he clears his throat. Sam is my strongest warrior, but deep down he is very in touch with his feelings.

"Mal, this is Troy, my Gamma. Troy, Sam and I have been best friends since we were pups."

"Luna it's a pleasure to meet you, I'm sorry I could not be there to meet you in Paisley." He reaches down and takes Malinda's hand in his and places a gentle kiss on it. You could hear everyone take in a sharp breath as Dex forces himself to the surface and growls loudly.

"Don't touch MY mate!" Dex spits out, causing my body to tense with anticipation.

Sam and Troy burst out laughing, as Troy passes twenty dollars off to Sam. "I told you he would lose it. Though I didn't think Dex would take over." Sam laughs.

"*Assholes.*" Dex growls in my head.

I clear my throat, "Okay back to business. Now, these three numb nuts are my top warriors. Mal. I would like you to meet Tim, Tom and Tony. The pack's only set of multiples and Troy's younger brothers."

"Talk about confusing the enemy." Mal laughs as she looks at them. The boys are brutes and glad to always have them at my side during a confrontation. Them being identical is a plus. "Have you boys found your mate yet?" Malinda asks as she reaches for a bottle of water. They shake their heads. "Are you excited to share a mate?" She asks, causing everything to crash to a halt. "Oh, did you not know there's a really good chance that you may share a mate."

"Wait, what?" All three ask at the same time. Their heads perk up at this bit of information. You could almost see their wolves wagging their tails.

"Yeah, in my old pack we had a couple sets of twins and triplets, and the identical sets all shared the same mate. You think our Alpha was sought after…" She says while fanning herself off and causing everyone to laugh at the table, while the triplets high five each other. We get through the rest of the room quicker than anticipated. Leaning back in my chair, I reach for her hand and intertwine our fingers.

"Mal, a few things we will discuss are going to be directly related to you. Everyone here's already been briefed on these topics because we started to tackle the issues while you were in a coma. When we were in Paisley and you had the first attack, blood work was taken as soon as we got to the hospital. The doctor who was at the meeting and immediately tended to you came with us. He is also a fellow alpha, and Alpha Rich determined that you're still being poisoned. How, we are still not sure but since we have moved you to the pack hospital, the levels have gone down. The only thing they can't figure out is how we almost lost you the second time." She takes in all of this information and I'm so proud of how she is processing it all.

"Wow, okay. Is that all." She half laughs but gets quiet, getting lost in her thoughts.

"We will get to the bottom of this baby."

She looks back toward me and smiles. "I know you will. But I was thinking, did you go through all of the surveillance photoaged of my apartment complex? That place has more cameras in the parking lot than a state prison. If we come across someone who doesn't live there but is always there... or maybe—"

Giving her hand a good squeeze. "We're already on that I promise. I want you to think hard. Is there anyone that you remember as being suspicious? A figure? A person that never seemed like they belonged?"

Her nose scrunches up in thought, then she shakes her head. "No, but I promise that I will think about it."

A knock sounds and in walks Ben. "Alpha, I'm sorry that I'm late. But I got on the road later than I intended last night. My mom was more emotional than expected." He says in a huff and rolls his eyes.

"It's totally understandable! Your whole life she was expecting you to stay in your pack and take over. Your destiny has changed." I say, as I rise up to meet him. "Now, are you ready to become a member of Full Moon?" We need to do this now because in order to protect my girl he needs our pack bond.

"Yes, Alpha it would be an honor to join our Queen's Pack." It's at this moment that I look over at my mate, her cheeks are a bit pink from being referred to as queen but the smile on her face as she looks at Ben is brighter than the sun. She recognizes that this alpha male is willing to leave his pack to protect her. It's a huge sacrifice already. Shit, even I quickly realized that though I'm an alpha, my mate outranks me. And I'm absolutely okay with that. I would follow her through hell and back.

Ben stands in front of me with pride written all over his face. "I'm ready sir." With a nod of my head, we begin.

"Ben James, do you pledge your life and loyalty to Full Moon?"

"I Do"

"Do you pledge to protect your pack, with your life?"

"I Do"

"And lastly, do you pledge to put our Luna Queen above all others? Do you pledge to keep her safe at all times or die trying?"

"With my last breath."

Chairs creek as the rest of my warriors stand. Emotion is thick in the air. Each man and woman in the room all place their fist over their hearts. "With our last breath."

Malinda's eyes grow wide at everyone's declaration. "Thank you." She whispers, and with our enhanced hearing we hear her clear as day. Nothing can explain the emotion coming from everyone other than true loyalty, and Mal accepts it with pure love in return.

The rest of the meeting is spent going over security measures on keeping her safe and setting the date for her Luna ceremony. Then finally our coronation. The next two weeks are going to be crazy, but I'm excited to start my life with Mal. It just sucks that I can't make her a pack member now so we can all mindlink, but lunas must wait for the Luna ceremony.

"Okay guys let's meet for dinner tonight and we will make all of the announcements." Everyone agrees and heads out, I look at my watch, realizing it's only 9:45am. "Baby are you ready to go home and rest for a bit?"

"I thought you would never ask." She looks up at me with a tired smile and reaches out for my hand. We head out of the office toward the elevator that goes up to our floor. I link our fingers together, enjoying all of the sparks radiating off this woman, she consumes me. Once on our floor Mal looks around, taking it all in. A wave of excitement floods my senses as we approach the door. I take a deep breath as I turn the knob to our home.

MALINDA

    Landon opens the door, and the sight takes my breath away. Sunlight streams in from the large picture windows that overlook an English style courtyard. I roll deeper into the space to see the whole suite is an open concept. The kitchen feels like a beach getaway with light blue with cream-colored cabinets. The backsplash is an array of sea glass tiles. The large center island is topped with a huge piece of gray granite, while the other countertops have white. The floors are hardwood and look brand new. It's a space I can see myself getting lost in as I bake to my heart's content.

    Coming out of the kitchen area I stop and take more of the living room in. A floor to ceiling bookcase with one of those cool rolling ladders covers the left side of the room. Along the other a large comfy couch faces and a huge tv mounted to the wall. The place smells like it's been freshly painted. I'm in awe.

    "The bedrooms and spare bathrooms are down this hallway," he says as he points to his left. "And the other hallway leads to a small gym and a movie room."

    "Landon, this place is beautiful. Did you pick the paint color?" I ask as I slowly roll down the hallway admiring the pale blue walls.

    "Yeah. Stacy said you liked the beachy chic vibes. I passed that along to my contractor and he gave me a few shades to look through." He says as he opens a few of the bedroom doors and I take a peek inside. One is just as beautiful as the next. Landon jogs ahead, only stopping when he reaches beautiful double barn doors.

    "This is our room." he says, wiggling his eyebrows. I reach out to touch the doors, stunning craftsmanship. As I run my fingers along the details carved into it, I pick up the faint smell of stain. I look back to the other doors and notice they are all brand new double doors. That's odd, I have never seen a double door entry to every bedroom in a house before. I look back down the hall toward the living room and notice that the hallways are a bit wider than normal.

I head back down the hall to the living room. I look up toward the ceiling and notice fresh paint in certain spots. Like a wall was removed and holes patched. Looking over my shoulder I don't miss the fact that Landon is blushing and nervously rubbing the back of his neck.

"Baby did you make modifications to the apartment for me?" I'm a little choked up getting the words out. I had always heard that the mate bond was intense, but I didn't experience that with Jared. This is all new to me, and I am loving this.

"Yeah, I measured your chair while you were in the hospital, and I made the doorways all wider and even removed a wall in the living room. The place had wall to wall carpet as well so I put new floors in so it would be easier on you. There are a few other things too."

He did this all for me.

"Of course, he did, Mal, he loves us," Sahara reminds me.

I grab his sweatshirt to pull his face near mine. With a shaky hand I touch his cheek and relish when he moves into my touch. "I love you" I whisper.

A smile teases as Landon's lips. Next thing I know, he scoops me up and carries me bridal style into our bedroom. His eyes are locked on me, he takes a deep breath and then crashes his lips to mine. I slide my hands into his hair deepening the kiss. He gives me a little love bite on my lip, and I gasp giving him the access he is craving. His tongue dives into my mouth and I savor the taste of him. The way Landon's tongue dances with mine causes me to moan. He grips the back of my neck tighter and my heart flutters. He gently places me on the bed as he trails his kiss down my jaw to my neck. Forcing my body to shiver.

Slowly, he pulls my dress up over my head. I lay before him in a green lace bra and panties. Black swirls in his eyes, as he takes in the vision before him. But it's more than that—even more than lust.

It's love.

This man loves me, and it has ignited a fire to blaze within me. I need this man. I can feel my arousal growing, and I'm pretty sure my panties are very wet. He closes his eyes and takes another deep breath. His nostrils flare when he catches my scent. His eyes snap open, a low husky growl escapes his lips as he and his wolf now know that I'm wanting and in need. A need only they can control.

"Mal, right now I am going to make love to you, but tomorrow… Tomorrow I am going to fuck you." My eyes roll into the back of my head, whether it's from his words, or the way he just licked me from my neck to my ear, I don't care. His fingers dance along the lace covering my breast, heat blooming where his fingers traveled. I bite my bottom lip when his other hand maneuvers inside my thin lace panty and he groans in appreciation.

"You are so wet for me." Landon growls in my ear and my eyes flutter shut in anticipation. "Look at me Mal, open your eyes." he commands, and I listen. My green eyes lock with his blue-gray as he slides a finger into my pussy. "You… baby, are beautiful. No one comes before you. You are my life… my reason for living."

His words push me to the precipice of my control. My breathing is becoming more labored, he is bringing me to my edge just from his words. His fingers quicken their pace while his palm rubs along my clit.

"Can you feel how much I want you?" His thrusting pauses long enough for another finger to notch inside of me, hitting just the right spot. An unfamiliar spark of pleasure has me arching my back. "You think that's good? Just wait until I have my cock inside of you."

"Landonnnnn, oh god." I whimper.

"But I need you as wet as possible because there's no way I can be gentle."

My walls tighten as he adds another finger stretching me. I slide my hand down to his holding it in place, helping me fuck myself on his hand. Bringing my breast to his lips, he pulls my rosy bud into his mouth. The sensation has me teetering on the edge. "Landon," I moan breathlessly. I feel his smirk against my skin just before he bites down on my nipple. Not hard enough to break the skin, but just enough to push me into having one of the best orgasms of my life. My body trembles with aftershocks as he holds me in his arms.

Landon brings his eyes to mine. "That was the most beautiful thing to watch. I love you, Mal." He says as he kisses my forehead.

He slides his fingers out and licks them clean, and just like the first time I'm shocked as he enjoys the taste. I can't wait anymore, I want this. I want to mate. I don't know what has come over me, but I frantically reach for his sweatshirt, pulling it over his head.

Wow is really all I can say. He is sculpted by the gods just for me.

I slide my hands to his jeans and pop the button to push them down as far as I can. Landon makes quick work of his pants and boxers. I reach down and run my fingers up and down the silky flesh of his length guiding him to my entrance. "Take me." I breathe out.

Landon takes my lips in his and as our kiss grows, his head starts to enter my soaking core. I want nothing more than to wrap myself around him, and as if hearing my thought, he grabs one of my ankles and pins it to his hip. In one quick motion, he pushes in, till he is fully seated. I breathe in deeply and slowly. Enjoying the pain as he takes my virginity. After a moment I nod giving him the okay to start moving. His thrusts start slow, taking himself all the way out till his tip is barely in and slowly sliding all the way back in. "Fuck, babe you're so tight," he growls.

After what feels like forever, I can't take it anymore. I thrust my hips up as hard as I can. I need more of him. Reading my mind he flips us over, so I am on top of him. With my hands on his chest to hold my balance, I start to ride him and ride him hard. "Holy shit you're going to make me come." He quickly sits up, wrapping his arms around me. My hard nipples glide up and down his chest. We are eye to eye, as he slides one hand on my ass and the other up my back to grip my shoulder. At this angle, his cock is drilling up deep inside me. This overwhelming feeling of lust, love and confidence takes over my body. It runs through me like magic. I have never felt so in control and turned on in my life.

I stare deeply into his eyes, and lick my lips... "Make your Queen come." I demand as I roll my hips on his hard length. He grabs the back of my neck and crashes our lips together. We become frantic. He is holding me tightly on top of him as he pumps into me. Our foreheads now pressed together, my hands wrap around his neck helping me to guide myself up and down on his shaft.

Our moans fill the air, egging on my impending release. "Yes, harder," I scream. I'm so fucking close. "Oooooo, yes harder." I'm buzzing and my ears are ringing. My head rolls back as I move my hips into his thrusts. He buries his face into my neck, licking, kissing, and then he grazes his canines along my sweet spot. A few more hard thrusts, I'm going to go over the edge.

Landon bites my mark causing my walls to spasm around his cock. Slamming me down one last time as he explodes inside me, coating my walls with his life-giving seed. He releases his bite and licks my neck to seal it again.

This moment has been perfect, except for one last thing. I nudge his head to the side and lick his neck searching for his marking spot. He trembles beneath me, and I know that I have found my spot. My canines come forward and I place my open mouth on it. To make him mine. An alarm blares, jarring me from the trance my determination had me in. The annoyance of being interrupted is quickly replaced with fear at Landon's next words.

"Fuck! That's the rogue alarm."

Chapter 12
Malinda

    We throw on our clothes while our eardrums are being assaulted by the blaring alarm. Talk about an interruption, just my freaking luck. The sexiest fucking thing to happen in my life interrupted by damn rogues. Getting dressed first, Landon grabs one of my t-shirts and leggings from the closet-handing them to me as he makes his way for the door.

    I throw my arms into the black tee, "Thanks, I will meet you down there soon."

    Landon twirls around. "Absolutely not!" he roars.

    My jaw drops as anger rises in me and I snap. "I'm a warrior just like you and I never run from a fight." I yell as I struggle to get my pants on, getting angry and frustrated. Finally, I'm dressed and, in my chair, just to see Landon run out of our apartment yelling over his shoulder for me to "stay." Ha, yeah right buddy, I am his mate not his mutt.

    "Wow! Does he think we're weak? I'm going to have to talk to Dex and persuade him to cut the protectiveness...." I can see Sahara smirk in my mind.

    "We can have this argument later."

    I'm frustrated that Landon just left me here. I am definitely going to have the whole "we are a team" talk again. I rush to the elevator and push the down button—repeatedly. I swear it's moving slow on purpose.

AHHHHH.... This is ridiculous! Fuck it! I roll over to the staircase and lean back, popping my front casters into a wheelie. Grabbing the railing with one hand and a firm grip on my push rim with the other. *Okay, okay you totally got this.* I fill my lungs with air, and I launch myself down the stairs!

"Holy SHITTTTTT!!!" I scream while flying down the stairs faster than I originally intended. My hand fucking burns as the rubber from my tire sizzles against my skin. Getting to my destination is all I care about, that and killing rogues. I brace myself as I get closer to the main floor and say a quick prayer.

10.... I'm basically hyperventilating at this point.

9.....

8.....

7....

6.....

5...... Holy Shit here we go, I hold my breath

4

3

2

1

"COMING IN HOTTTTTTTTTTTTT"

I yell as my back wheels hit the tile and I am still rolling fast up in a wheelie. As I get the chair to slow down a bit and lower my front casters to the ground, I have one thing on my mind....and that's getting to the fight as fast as possible. I push myself as fast as I can out the front door of the pack house and down the new ramp Landon put in. "LUNA" I hear someone scream back from the house, but I refuse to go back inside. The sounds of panicked warriors fill the air.

"LUNA PLEASE!"

"Shit where did she go?"

"Fuck, Alpha is going to kick our asses."

"She's not upstairs, damn it."

"She has to be headed—"

I feel the fight ahead of me. "Come on Mal you got this." I yell to pump myself up and push harder.

As I get to the crest of the hill and look down. There before me are a handful of Full Moon's warriors holding their own against thirty rogues. We must not have pulled all of our warriors from their posts for this battle. I assess what is happening as a strong breeze blows my hair in my face. I grab a hair tie off my wrist and pull it up quickly. As I drop my arms, I see the rogues looking up the hill at me. Confused, my warriors look up. They caught my scent. Shit....

Mal you are no longer just a luna, you are the Queen, we are the Queen, and we have this fight. Let's show them that we are to be feared. Sahara roars in my head, pumping me up.

I adjust my chair and push down the hill at full speed. Some rogues break free and head toward me just as fast.

"LUNA NOOOOOOOO!" Someone yells as warriors try to catch up to the rogues headed in my direction, but the rogues are oddly outpacing them.

First one is at three o'clock. I can only partially shift my claws. And as I do I rip its throat out as it tries to leap over me. I come to a stop as five rogues surround me. My body prickles in warning—something's off. I take a deep breath and close my eyes. My body begins to warm, and I feel my eyes start to glow green. I snap my eyes open, and I see the wolves in front of me hesitate for just a second.

"SHIFT!" I roar in a voice that sounds like a mixture of mine and Sahara's. It's loud, booming and most of all, dripping in authority. Painful howls of rogues perforate the air as their bones crack and pop, their bodies forcefully rearranging back into human form. They're writhing on the ground calling out in agony. A forced shift is the worst kind of pain. Unfortunately, I know this from experience.

Warriors quickly encircle me and the rogues. Studying each rogue, I'm shocked at how young they are. Slowly their pain dwindles and breaths even out. My warriors move in to restrain them, but I throw my hand up to stop them. Taking a deep breath, my eyes widen in surprise. I knew it. Something's most definitely off here, because as soon as they had changed back to human form their scents changed.

"You're not rogues." I exclaim.

I'm looking at a group of teenagers and they look scared and confused. There are three girls and two boys, no older than eighteen or nineteen years old.

"What rogues?! No, I'm not a rogue!!!" A young man roars as he pushes himself up off the ground. His defensiveness earns him a loud growl from Landon as he and Sam have the kid restrained faster than lightning. The other young man jumps to aid his friends, but the triplets aren't having that. They have him by the throat and his arms pinned behind his back. Ben is between me and the scene unfolding. I hear crying and I look over to the girls, all of them look so confused and scared as they're trying to cover up their naked forms.

"Troy can you please get these girls something to cover up with."

"Yes, Luna." My gamma responds with a bow before sprinting off to fulfill my request.

"Where are we? Where is Liam? Oh, my goddess, he is not linking me." Panic fills the air, as the young woman looks around at the dead wolves nearby. "I can't feel him... Lara, I can't feel our bond." The young girl sobs cause everyone to flinch.

"Erica, breathe, he has to be here somewhere." The other girl is rubbing small circles on the distraught girl's back. The girl whom I assume is Erica is barely holding on.

A small ripple reverberates through my body. The only way I can explain this sensation is Magic.

Black Magic.

Someone cast a spell using black magic on these teens. However, forcing them to shift is causing its effect to fade. We are all looking at each other, a mixture of shock and confusion blanketing our surroundings. These kids have no clue what just happened, and now I fear this young lady's mate is dead.

"Someone link Dr. Taylor or Dr. K, these kids need medical attention." Landon nods his head at my command, as three of our warriors go check for more survivors. Turning to my alpha with a soft, but troubled smile, "Landon, release them please."

Landon reluctantly let's go and comes to stand by my side and address the newcomers. "I am Alpha Landon, and this is my Luna, Malinda, of Full Moon." The confused look these kids had a minute just morphed to panic as Landon continued. "When you came on to our territory and attacked my border patrols. You wreaked of rogue stench. What else were we supposed to assume?"

"Full Moon?" The tallest of the boys' askes, disbelief hanging heavy in the air. He is built like an Alpha, has the total bad boy look going for him too. "Your pack is ten hours away from ours." He looks at the other four of his friends with fear in his eyes and stutters out an introduction "I am Future Alpha Caden of Gold Moon, this is Tristan my future Beta and his three sisters Erica, Lara, and Tara."

Landon looks at me with concern. I aim my chair in Caden's direction, but Landon stops me by putting his large hand atop mine. "Caden, I'm Malinda but you can call me Mal. Can you please tell me the last thing you remember? Do you remember anything before I forced you to shift?"

"Ummmm…" He starts, eyes hard in concentration. "The six of us got invited to a bonfire. Liam, my future Gamma and Erica's mate, was with us." I peek at the girls who are now drowning in too large shirts and sweatpants. Tristan is handing Caden a pair of shorts. "A bunch of wolves we didn't know were there, but it was a big party. Everyone was drinking, having a good time, but it was pretty low key considering the amount of people that were there- nothing crazy.

A form in the distance catches my attention. It's the pack doctor being followed by several nurses. They're running down the hill, headed our way.

"Luna, I said take it easy today!" Dr. K gasps as he reaches us.

"Don't worry about me." I wave my hand in dismissal of her concern. "Please follow those warriors. We need to see if there are any wounded." I point over to the guys checking the bodies. Dr. K nods and heads in that direction.

"Babe, we have a bit of a problem." Landon whispers in my ear.

"You mean another problem; we might have killed this poor girl's mate." I say only loud enough for him to hear.

"Yeah, there is that too but Sam... Sam's mate is here." Lifting his chin in the direction of the girls. "The one named Lara."

My eyes go wide as I see Sam struggling with his composure. The girl is still so confused about what is going on that she hasn't made the connection yet. I take a deep breath. That shouldn't be though, she should have scented him. The bond would have pulled her in and calmed her. *What the hell is going on?*

"We have two alive," Dr. K yells from across the field. The kids take off to see if it's their friend, but Landon stops them.

"Caden, we are going to assess the injured. I understand that you are an alpha, but I need you to stay here with my warriors. I need to fully understand what is happening here before I trust you or anyone." Landon's voice is stern and laced with undeniable authority.

"Are you... are you going to throw us in the cells?" Caden questions as calmly as he can, but this just causes the girls to start sobbing again.

"No, I'm not. But something has happened here, and you attacked my warriors and then you all openly tried to attack my Luna. If this was the other way around, you or your father would do the same thing. I need you to stay here."

Caden nods his acceptance with a look of defeat. Landon asks the remaining warriors to stay with the group of teens, while we make our way to the doctor and nurses who are working on stabilizing the two survivors. One is definitely a teenager and does not smell like a rogue at all. The other is a middle-aged rogue, who needs a bath.

"Why do they always have to stink?" Sahara scoffs, sticking her nose up in the air.

"These two will be fine but let's get them up to the hospital and hooked up to IV's." Dr. K says as she stuffs her supplies back into a black bag.

"Doc, I don't want that rogue in our hospital." Landon spits out.

"No, me neither." She does not wait for him to respond. "But let's get him healthy, see if he will talk. If not, then I give you full permission to drag him to the cell and beat the crap out of him." She sasses. K's got spunk and I love her.

"You will give *me* permission?" Landon asks, eyebrows cocked.

"Benefit of being your cousin." She smiles and punches him in the arm.

Warriors are in the process of carrying the teen and rogue to the hospital. As we approach the others, the young girl Erica screams and sprints toward us. One of the triplets grabs her, while she cries and struggles in his arms.

"Please! That's Liam!" Her shriek pierces the air like a knife. I nod to Tony to let her go. She runs up to Liam, brushing his unruly brown hair out of his face. "Why can't I feel our bond? He's breathing so it should be there." I take in the teens; they look so lost.

"Guys try to focus on your wolves, let me know if you can feel or hear them." I gently prod. Silence takes root as the teens' eyes flicker in concentration. Then panic and even more confusion sets in.

"I can't hear my wolf!" Caden's alarm at his discovery is undeniable. You can feel the anguish in his voice, he's a future Alpha with a lost connection.

"Sahara... can you try to reach out to their wolves? Is that even possible?"

"*Yeah, I think I should be able to. We're a direct descendent of the Goddess. So, my pure awesomeness should be enough. Give me a moment.*"

Landon allows the young girl to follow her mate to the hospital and he sends four warriors to guard the rogue. "Let's head up to my office. We can call your pack and get some more info. Sam, can you hold up a second?"

Sam's large body is visibly tense. He's really struggling with wanting to pull his mate into his arms. "Sam, you need to get yourself together. You aren't going to be any good to anyone in your condition." Landon states putting a reassuring hand on his shoulder.

I look up at Sam. "Sam... Sahara is trying to reach out to the kids' wolves. I'm hoping she can reach them, and they can tell us what's going on."

"Do you really think she can reach them?" He asks, looking broken.

"She *did* mention something about being pure awesomeness." I give him a wink. "Let's have a little faith and see what she can do."

Chapter 13
LANDON

This day started out perfectly. Mal got released from the hospital. She met more of our pack, and everyone got along so well. Then I was able to finally make love with my mate. But then right as Mal was about to claim me, all hell broke loose.

Now we're all seated in my office eyeing up these kids. I seriously get the feeling that these kids are just victims. Shit, I know they are. We need to figure this out.

I start the inquisition. "Okay Caden, do you know who threw the party?"

"No, but there's usually a bonfire in the woods just outside our pack border. It's held there almost every weekend. There is a small lake near Forage Woods, so we get together on the beach and hang out."

Taking in this information, I continue. "Nothing seemed out of the ordinary, maybe someone or something that would have stood out as odd?"

The kids are looking at each other, trying to pinpoint something. A girl nervously raises her hand, as if we are in school. Mal reaches out and gently clasps it in hers, trying to bring her some comfort. "There were a couple of guys, maybe two or three of them. They seemed much older than the high school crowd, I thought maybe they were college guys. I honestly thought they were humans, they had no scent, but now that I think about it, they had no scent at all. I mean.... they should have smelt like something."

I am writing this all down, so I do not forget a word. We continue our discussion, trying to jar any and all info from them. After 45 minutes, the lot of them seems to have pretty much calmed down, however Sam looks like he is about to jump out of his damn skin. I link him to see if I can cut the tension.

-Dude you are staring, try not to creep her out.

-Landon I'm losing my damn mind. The second I saw her I wanted to scream: "Mate!" Even when I thought she was a damn rogue who was just trying to kill my Luna! Once Mal realized that it was magic, and we were not going to have to imprison my mate... I wanted to wrap her in my arms. BUT she has not even noticed me or felt the pull of the bond. Jax keeps trying to sense her wolf and coming up empty handed. He runs his hands through his hair in frustration.

-Who said she has not noticed you?! She has not taken her eyes off of you. Keep in mind, her and her friends are in deep shit. She's probably a little tentative.

I can almost see Sam's wolf Jax's ears perk up and now Sam is trying so hard not to smile.

I look over at Mal. Her head is slightly tilted as she studies the kids. This whole situation sucks. These kids could have been seriously hurt or even fucking killed. And in the end, it would have looked like we openly attacked non rogues.

-Exactly what I was thinking. Mal says in my head. Shocked to hear her in my head, I look to where she is sitting. Perched in her chair, she is staring at me with a beautiful smile gracing her face.

-What babe?

-You had your link open. Since you marked me, I can hear when you link. But you are so right. This was a set up, and these kids were used as a pawn in someone else's game.

Fuck. This all has to be connected to whomever is trying to hurt Mal. This was made apparent when they had caught her scent and honed in on her. I pick up the phone to call the Alpha of Gold Moon.

"Hello, Alpha Tanner speaking."

"Hello Alpha, this is Alpha Landon from Full Moon."

"Alpha! Nice to hear from you. How is your Luna doing? Is she feeling better?"

"Thank you, she is doing much better. But I'm calling to discuss your son, future beta, and future gamma."

I start a tirade about everything that has happened today. To say he is pissed off is an understatement.

"Alpha Landon, I will be on my way to collect the kids. Thank you for not putting them in the cells."

"We understand it's not their fault. However, we do need to get to the bottom of this. Maybe we can work together on this and pull resources?"

"Of course, I will bring along a few warriors, and some of my top-level team."

A yelp of excitement interrupts my conversation. My eyes swing over to an excited Mal, bursting with elation. "Hold on Alpha." I put my hand over the phone and stare at Mal. "What's wrong?"

"Look," she whispers giddily.

I follow her finger and see the kid's eyes are glazed over, showing us their wolves have come back and they are mindlinking. Mal leans over to me "They just heard from the kids in the hospital, the boy is awake." I look at her like she has ten heads. How does she know this already? "Sahara told me." She smiles and winks at me and then jerks her head back to the kids.

Lara starts to sniff the air. Sam nearly launches himself out of his seat and pulls her to him. She looks up at him, wide eyed in surprised happiness.

"Mine," they say in sync.

This has my mate spinning around in her chair, doing a happy dance. She is squealing like a damn teenage girl. I see what Luna Stacy was describing when she said Mal really is a girly girl deep down, and she could not look any cuter.

Sam is looking at Lara like he is staring at the end of the rainbow. I'm so happy that he has finally found his mate. His finger has a slight tremble as he brushes a red strand of hair out of her face. "I can't believe that I almost had to fight you. What would have happened if I hurt you, I couldn't have lived with myself." He leans down and places a chaste kiss on her lips. The possibility that their relationship could have ended before it even started is a sobering realization that whatever is going on, the person behind this bull shit needs to be stopped.

"Alpha Landon are you there?"

"Ah yes sorry about that. My Beta just found his mate in Lara, and it caused a bit of excitement over here. So, we will see you as soon as you get here. I will let my border patrols know you will be here tonight or tomorrow. We will get rooms ready for you." We finish the conversation and I heave out a big sigh.

Lara's brother Tristian stands to shake Sam's hand. "Please take care of her, Lara is my twin sister."

Lara turns to face her brother. "Tris, you are going to find your mate really soon I can feel it. Don't give up hope."

I get up and go over to her. Wanting to be close to my mate, I place my hands on the back of her chair, spin her around and plant a kiss on her forehead. "Baby I need you to go and rest before dinner. You have had a crazy day."

She wrinkles her nose and looks like she is ready to argue but is promptly interrupted by a big yawn. "Fine." She says a bit miffed.

"If you go take a nap, I will finish up here and then you can have all of the apple crumble you can eat." I wink at her, and she blows her hair out of her face in defeat. "With ice cream" I tease.

"Stop. You had me at apple crumble." She leans in, kisses me and rolls out of my office.

MALINDA

Holy crap I slept for four hours. Stretching the sleepiness away, I jackknife off the pillow confused as to where I'm at. Quickly today's memories begin to seep back into my mind's eye, and even if I wanted to forget... now I know there's no going back to those few seconds of conflict free mindless thinking, but I can't. I realize where I am, what has happened and who I'm meant to become. Will the shock ever wear off that this is my life? I am going to be a luna again. This time though, this all feels so different. Is it because I'm now with my true mate? I hope I don't let this pack down, like I let Stone Mountain down. I left them after Stacy and John took over. I felt so broken and lost, but after all of this time guilt still weighs heavy on my heart... Like I turned my back on them.

A knock on the door brings me back from my thoughts. A deep voice follows immediately. "Luna, it's Ben. Just checking if you are up? Dinner will be ready in thirty minutes."

"Thank you, Ben. I will be down in twenty." I holler back as I get out of bed, get myself refreshed in the bathroom and put on a cute dress. A little makeup and a side braid, then I am all set to officially meet my new pack. I met a few of them earlier during the rogue scuffle, but I was a little preoccupied- trying to save their lives and all. I open the bedroom door to Ben sitting in the living room.

"You didn't have to wait for me."

"Luna, I think the Alpha is a little on edge after what happened earlier today. You are not just our Luna but our Queen. I think me waiting outside the door is the least of your worries."

He has a serious tone to his voice but there is a small smirk on his face. He is so right though. I need to be glad that Landon did not have Ben sitting at the end of the bed staring at me while I slept. I roll my eyes at the silliness of the thought, but I would not put it past Landon.

Ben holds the door open for me as we head out toward the elevator. "Hmmm." He sounds almost disappointed as I push the down button.

"Is there a problem with the elevator?" I question.

"Oh no Luna, I just figured you'd want to take the stairs again?" He tries to say straight-faced but fails.

"HA, ya got jokes Ben. Sorry to disappoint you but no. I will keep the stairs for emergency purposes only."

"Luna, I'm seriously impressed that you got down like you did! We watched it on the security cameras this afternoon. The guys could not decide if it was like watching *Fast and The Furious* or playing *GTA 5*." Oh, goddess I know I'm going to get an earful.

We get downstairs to the packed dining room, and I take a peek inside at the four huge, long tables. They must seat at least one hundred and fifty people each. Families are helping the omegas get the food on the tables. I love how everyone helps each other. Ben links Landon to let him know we were ready.

"Alpha is heading out of the office. He was just finishing up a phone call." I acknowledge the update and smile at Ben. The teens from the attack are sitting together with our top warriors at what I'm assuming is the alpha table. They're looking a lot more relaxed than they did before. Lara is leaning into Sam's embrace and the smile on his face is practically lighting up the room.

"Hey babe, sorry about that." I turn to see Landon jog up to me. "I had to make an important phone call and it took a little longer than anticipated." He reaches for my hand and intertwines our fingers. "Are you ready to meet the Pack?" I nod. Entering the room, the chatter dies almost immediately. Landon guides us to our table. Once we are all situated, he addresses the room.

"Full Moon! Thank you to everyone who came this evening and those families that helped with dinner. Thank you to all who are protecting our borders tonight so we can be here. Now, most importantly thank you to the Moon Goddess for blessing us with our Luna and future Queen. Full Moon, I give you my Mate and your Luna. Malinda." The room erupts into cheers and howling, and a strong feeling of pride overwhelms me.

I roll forward a bit and smile at everyone. "Please sit everyone, it will be a bit easier for me to see you all." Everyone settles down, their attention on me. "Thank you for your kind welcome. I also would like to thank the medical staff of Full Moon. I'm truly blessed to have been given a fated mate. I hope that I live up to the expectations you all have for a luna."

We all settle into our spots, eating and mingling. Everyone that has come up to introduce themselves is so lovely and I'm trying very hard to remember everyone's name. The food here is AMAZING. I have eaten way too much but I don't care because the scent of apples and cinnamon deliciousness assaults all of my senses. Dessert is finally hitting the tables and the spread that sits before us—wow. Mrs. Lane out did herself.

"Luna, I have your dessert." Mrs. Lane places, what I can only describe as, Heaven on A Plate, right in front of me. As I'm digging into one of the best apple crumbles I have ever eaten, the door to the dining room loudly bangs open.

"Oh, my bad. I guess I am a little stronger than I thought." A nasally giggle comes from the young woman that enters the room. I adjust myself to get a view. It's Jessica... ugh. Obviously reveling in the attention, she forced everyone to give her, she continues with her performance. "Since everyone is here and these things must be done in public..." I look over at Landon and he just shrugs. He also has no clue what she is going to do.

Taking a deep dramatic breath, she continues with her speech. "I am not sure if you are all aware, but our Alpha is still not marked. So, since this is the case, I would like to challenge our 'so called' Luna," Jessica uses finger quotes around *so called* and I debate breaking them off to use them as garnish for my pie in front of me... "for the position and her mate." She says with an evil smirk. There are audible gasps in the room.

Our top warriors who just pledged their lives to me a few short hours ago, all stand and growl. They slowly prowl over to Jessica, intimidation clear on their faces. They're stalking her like she is prey. There is a flash of fear in her eyes, but she schools her emotions quickly. Landon's grasp on me is tight, though he knows my strength, nobody wants their mate threatened. I look at him from the corner of my eye, give him a small smile and a wink.

I pierce a huge, plump piece of apple with my fork. I catch her snarky gaze through the sea of men and shrug, "Ok." And put the fruit in my mouth. Chewing, I made sure to get apple, crust and whipped cream on my fork. I was going to have to open wide if I wanted to get this all in my mouth. But I'm the Queen dammit, there's no way I'm going to shy away from a heaping fork full of goodness. The fork tines have just touched my lips when a shrill voice stops me from stuffing my face.

"Did you hear me?" She seethes, "I want to challenge you."

"Everyone heard you, and I said 'Ok'. Didn't you hear me?" I continue with my endeavor of stuffing my face. Usually, I would ask for ice cream with my dessert but I'm fairly certain Mrs. Lane hand whipped her cream and now all other toppings will pale in comparison. Maybe I should have some coffee. NO! Hot tea would be divine.

"...and you can't use your Luna command during the challenge."

I wave a hand in the air as if to shoo a fly, "Yeah, yeah, sure." Looking back down at my plate, I take inventory of my few remaining bites. I purse my lips and look over at Landon's plate. His slice is sitting there, completely untouched, his fork in hand, frozen above the plate. Maybe I can convince him to share, we are mates after all. I drag my gaze up to his and have to hold back my snicker from the priceless expression on his face. His eyes are wide, mouth open. Confusion, laughter, concern, and a multitude of other emotions fight for dominance in his eyes.

I'm about to smile, bat my eyelashes and seduce him into giving me his dessert. "...in twenty-four." Jessica strides over to me. Placing her hands on her knees and bending down as if she is going to speak to a toddler. "On the training grounds. And when I win, I'm going to make you watch me fuck him." She reaches her hand up and pats me on the head. She just fucking patted me on the head like a damn dog.

That's it.

I slam my fist on the table, nearby cutlery rattle with my rage. "And when *I* win, I will make you watch me fuck my mate. Then I'll kill you. Then I will sit on your grave and have another piece of god damn pie so I can eat in mother fucking peace!" My voice rises at the end, but when I'm done talking, the room is stunned silent. Now *everyone's* mouths are open, eyes on me. Even Jessica's. So, I pick my fork back up and calmly finish my meal.

"I accept the challenge from Jessica. Sunset tomorrow at the training grounds." I say with a roll of my eyes. This bitch thinks she can interrupt me when I'm getting my apple crumble on. I hear her walk out and slam the door. I don't even spare her a glance, she's not worth it.

"Luna." I'm pulled from my thoughts when a little girl no more than seven comes up to me, holding her plate of crumble. I grab my napkin and wipe my face.

"Hi sweetheart, how are you?" I ask as I push away from the table a bit.

"I'm good, Luna. Ummmm can I eat my dessewt with you and Alpha?"

How can I say no to a face like this? Plus, the way she says her r's are adorable. "Of course, you can." I say as I make Troy grab another chair for her. "What's your name?" Landon shifts his chair away from me to make room for her between us. She sits and Landon scootches her in. I look at Landon over her head and he is just watching her curiously.

"Eloise. But my fwiends call me Ellie. My mommy loved the Eloise books, so she named me after the little girl in the stowy." This girl is just adorable. I've only had a few seconds with her, but I can tell she is a three foot tall bundle of absolute spitfire. With red hair and sparkling blue eyes filled with light, I can tell that one day she will be a force to be reckoned with. She gives off a calming aura that makes you want to be in her presence.

"Where is your mom and dad?"

"Oh, ummm they're in heaven with the goddess." Her answer was matter of fact, like answering a question on a test.

My heart skips a beat as I look up from her beautiful face to Landon. I can tell he is getting the same feeling from Ellie, and that he doesn't know her story.

"Did they go to heaven during the Great War?" Landon asks and she just nods. While forking another piece of her dessert. I don't know what it is about this little girl, but I feel compelled to protect her.

"Luna, I just know that you will defeat your foe tomorrow. I can feel it in my toes." Ellie says with a mouth full of crumble. My heart warms at her declaration, then I inwardly wince when I realize she had heard the encounter... the whole encounter. Including the "fucking" portion.

"I promise that I will try my best but remember we should never underestimate our opponents." I tell her as she steals a bite of crumble off my plate.

"You love apple crumble, don't you?"

"Oh yes, I love all things, apple."

Chapter 14
LANDON

SERIOUSLY!!!! What in hell is going on today? I need a fucking drink. I nearly ripped Jessica's head off when she announced that she wanted to challenge Mal. Unfortunately, I know the rules to a mate or title challenge. In this case both.

The rule states that the mate who is being fought over cannot interfere in any way, shape or form. I also can't have contact with Malinda or Jessica until just before the fight. So as soon as Jessica announced her intentions, I had to keep my mouth shut. This also means that I can't do...other activities with her until after the fight.

I was extremely impressed with my little mate. As was the rest of everyone in the dining room. Mal handled herself like a true Luna. Especially when the whole "sex" thing was threatened. There's no way I could have sat by as someone threatened to have sex with Mal in front of me. Though I do not want anyone watching us together either. I could definitely see it as a perfect punishment if Jessica survives, fuck it maybe we just banish her.

Every ounce of my soul knows that Mal will come out of this fight a winner, but that doesn't mean she still might not get hurt. That thought is absolutely killing me. If she's going to do this, she'll need all the support available. It was that thought that has me reaching for the phone.

"Alpha John speaking."

"Hey John, it's Landon over at Full Moon."

"Landon, hey how is everything going? Is Malinda, okay?"

I then hear Stacy in the background...

"Is Malinda alright? John, what is going on? John GIVE ME THE PHONE!"

"Goddess, woman! Will you chill out and let me at least hear the response before you wolf out on me?"

"Mal is my best friend and if that is her mate calling then something must be wrong. I can feel it! Give me the phone you jackass."

I can hear a small struggle on the other end of the phone, and then a giggle from Stacy.

"Hi Landon, it's Stacy." I chuckle to myself, knowing John lost that battle.

"Hi Stacy, how are you?"

"Cut the shit. What's wrong with my girl?"

Her impatience is endearing. "Mal was challenged tonight for the title of Luna and for me and...."

"EXCUSE ME!!! Who is this slut, and does she really think that she can beat my girl!!! OH, HELL NO!"

"Stacy, will you let the man finish talking before you go on a rampage?"

"John... this close. You are this fucking close to not having sex for forty-eight hours."

You can hear John take a sharp breath. I can't help but shake my head.

"Stacy, I was wondering if you would like to come here, and surprise Mal. Help be a support system for her. She literally got out of the hospital today and you know the rules. I'm not allowed to have any contact with her till the fight."

She is all business as she rattles off her game plan and how many people, she is packing up to come here. There is no room to argue with her. "Okay great I will get that all set up and we will see you tonight. I will let it be a surprise for Mal, okay?" Then out of nowhere her whole attitude changes.

"Ohhhh this is going to be fun!" She squeals into the phone. "Oh, and by the way, it was so sweet of you to send us the fruit basket! It was delicious."

"You're most welcome Stacy."

We end the call and I link Sam and Troy to meet me in my office. "Hey boss, what's up?" Troy says as he plops on the couch in the corner.

"First, how is your mate, Sam? Is everything okay and are you getting along well?" Sam has the goofiest grin on his face.

"Yup and Yup." He says while popping the P on each word, his grin getting bigger by the second. I just shake my head and laugh at him.

"Okay, so I just got off the phone with John and Stacy at Stone Mountain. They are coming tonight and bringing a few people with them to support Mal. She really has no friends here yet and I want her to feel supported during this time. It's a surprise so . . ." I look them both directly in the eyes. "Do not spill the beans on this."

They both nod their heads in acceptance.

"Good, okay now Alpha Tanner should also be here around the same time that Stone Mountain does. Let's schedule a meeting with them for after breakfast tomorrow morning but let's keep it short and sweet. I don't know if I can keep a clear head with the challenge tomorrow."

They both nod at me. "To be honest, Alpha, I've got no clue how you're holding it together. I mean your mate is right down the hall crying her eyes out, smashing shit in your room and you're not even allowed to comfort—"

I don't wait around to hear the rest of what he's about to say. I'm out of my seat and running down the hall. I want to kill Jessica; she is a constant headache. And her bullshit that *I was in his bed before you* shit. We never fucking slept together! She snuck into my damn room one night.

As I approach Ben and Tim block the door. "Move," I growl.

"Alpha, you know that I can't." Ben shakes his head at me, but his eyes are looking past me. Sobbing spills out from behind the wooden barrier and seeps right into my soul. An icy wave threatening to destroy any self-restraint. It feels like my heart is being squeezed in a vice.

I knock on the door, searching for something to say. Something to make everything better. "I know the rules, but I have to tell you that I love you. It's you and me till the end."

I hear another gut-wrenching cry from the other side of the door. I lean my forehead on the door. I wait a minute, realizing that I don't hear her crying anymore. The tightness surrounding my heart slowly releases its hold.

Then Ben kicks the door with his heel and the sounds of smashing continue. Crap we're not going to have anything left in that room. Behind me, Ben clears his throat. "Keep moving, she-wolf," he growls.

"The name's Jessica, cutie. You better remember it because after tomorrow I'm going to be your Luna."

Tim wasn't able to cover up his laugh with a cough. "Warrior," she spits. "It sounds like your so-called Luna is weak. She can't even rein in her emotions for my challenge. Do you really think this is the kind of leadership we need? The kind of leadership our pack deserves? I am going to be stronger for *"my"* pack and be the Luna you deserve."

If looks could kill, between the three of us, Jessica would have spontaneously combusted on the spot. But Jessica was immune to reality as she places a long, red painted nail on my chest and trails it down my breastbone. Tim grips her wrist effectively removing me from her contact. "You know the rules. No touching."

With a scoff she walks off like she already owns the damn place. "Goodbye Mal, see you tomorrow." She sing-songs. As if competing in

122

a new Olympic event and have been practicing for years, we all roll our eyes in perfect synchronization, with Ben expertly landing it with an eloquent extension of his middle finger.

Behind me, the door cracks open and Mal pokes her head out. She does not look like she has been crying at all. In fact, she has a huge smile on her face. She high fives Ben, fist bumps Tim and blows me a kiss as she closes the door. There's no hiding the stupefied look on my face. "What just happened?"

The two of them share a look and smile. "Nothing Alpha, nothing at all."

SAM

Ugh, Jessica just waltzed her ass into the rec room, bitching about something to do with tomorrow. My sister Cammy and her used to be really good friends but now everyone barely tolerates her. Jessica thinks she is the ringleader, shit she thinks the world fucking revolves around her. No one has the time to even deal with her drama. Jessica was not always like this but war changes people. You know what I mean?

Now with this challenge tomorrow, I have no clue what she's thinking. Goddess, I hope Luna kicks her ass and knocks her down a peg or two. Maybe she will go back to the way she used to be, which was fun loving and really funny. Now she just channels all of her grief and creates drama. She refuses therapy, there's only so much one can do to help.

Tom walks in and every unmated female starts to drool. The triplets are twenty years old and some of the strongest warriors we've ever had. These bastards are walking gods around here. They've got the ladies falling all over them, my sister being one of them. She thinks she hides it—she needs to try harder. Thank god she has more self-respect for herself then some of these other she-wolves.

"Hey Tom," Cammy calls out from the other side of the room. I think she's one of the few people who can actually tell them apart. Tom crashes next to me as my mate says something to my sister before she grabs Cammy by the hand and drags her over to the couch. I pull Lara to sit on my lap and Tom pats the spot next to him for Cammy to sit. She nervously chooses to sit on the edge of the coffee table in front of us.

I can't help but notice the slight blush in her cheeks as Tom discreetly checks her out. Fuck, she turns eighteen in two days. I look between the two of them— shit.

"Hey Cammy, how is my baby sister?" I ask, trying to distract myself. "Are you excited for your birthday? The big 18!!!"

She just smiles and nods. Her cheeks are a permanent shade of pink at this point. "Wow that's right you're turning 18, in what two days right?" Tom questions as he gives her a megawatt smile. "The guys and I will be there." Fuck now he is even blushing. "Sam invited us. Is that okay?"

"Oh, ummm yeah, I think it's just Landon, Troy and the rest of the warriors. Oh, plus Malinda and Lara." She says as she reaches over for Lara's hand. I love that Cam is trying to make Lara feel included.

"Also, why would you not come to your unofficial little sister's party." Tom looks up at her and wrinkles his face when she says *sister*. I can read my sister like a fucking book, and she is taking his reaction all wrong. Cam abruptly stands, tripping over her words. "I'm—I'm going to run. I want to go meet the Luna. Well officially meet her. Yeah, I need to go check on her." We all just stare at her as she hustles out of the room.

"What just happened?" Tom asked as he stares after her retreating figure.

"Oh, I think you'll figure it out soon enough." Lara giggles.

Chapter 15
Malinda

That was a lot of fun. After Landon left I kind of felt bad that he thought I was really upset. Jessica's not the only one that can play mind games and the best position I can be in... is the one where Jessica thinks she is in the lead.

A quick knock precedes Ben's head peeking through the crack in my door, "Hey, want some company?" I smile and wave him in. A cute girl who carries a strong resemblance to Sam, follows him in. I wave at her as I finish chewing and take a sip of my tea.

"Hi Luna, I'm Cammy." I look between her and Ben, they look at me a bit confused.

"Ben, did you find your mate?" His eyes pop out of his head. Oh, I'm on the verge of an epic girly squeal and I sit my cup down on the table.

"What? No!" They both say in unison, laughing.

"Oh, no Luna, this is Sam's younger sister." Oh, that's right! I almost forgot he has a little sister.

"No, no, not mates." Cammy giggles at Ben. "I mean you're a nice guy Ben, but not my type."

Yup, I am going to love this chick. She is blunt. "I just wanted to formally introduce myself and be here for you for the fight. I cannot stand Jessica. So... yeah, just consider me your lady in waiting." She gives me this big smile.

"That makes two of us," I say.

"What are you up to in here? You're not crying again, are you?" he says with a sly smirk on his face. He knows damn well I was not crying.

"I hate Jessica even more for making you upset Luna."

Apparently, I am a better actress than I thought.

"Oh, Cammy, I promise you that I am fine." I give her a quick wink and turn back toward Ben. " I was just going through some old photos and videos from when I was in high school."

I look up at Ben and he is giving me a kind smile. It's almost as if I see a flash of Jared in his eyes. The thought warms my heart that Jared can hear this conversation.

"What did my wolf look like as a person and was he just as much a mature goof in person as he is in my head?"

"Ha! A mature goofball— oh gosh was he ever, this was taken just before our 17th birthdays." I lean over and show him a picture of us at the creek at Stone Mountain. It has an old bridge that crosses over it for good fishing, but really it was used for us to jump off of. In the picture Jared and I are sitting on the edge of the bridge. Stacy is looking down at the water and John is staring at her lovingly.

"He was a good-looking guy." Cammy says with a smile.

"He had a kind heart and was an amazing Alpha. Not going to lie, it was weird being mated to my best friend."

Cammy looks at the picture again. "Is it true that you guys never mated?" Her eyes go round, shocked by her own question...

"Oh, ha yeah no, that would've been gross. We did not feel the mate pull like everyone else."

After about ten minutes of going down memory lane came a loud knock on the door." Come in," I call out. Tim opens it and Stacy comes bursting through my jaw drops and my eyes nearly pop out of my head. And she's not alone, she's brought our crew!

"SURPRISE!" They all yell.

"Holy Shit! How, how are you all here? Why are you all here?"

"Your amazing man gave me a call today and let me know what is going on over here and I figured I would bring the gang and cheer you on." I give her the biggest hug ever. I introduce my girls to Cammy and Ben.

"So, who is the hottie outside your door?" Stacy asks, fanning herself off.

"That's Tim and he is a triplet," I say, causing the girls to swoon.

"Gosh yeah I can never think straight around them." Cammy says blushing.

My friend Erica looks at her with one eyebrow raised. "Have they met their mate yet?"

"No." Cammy and I answer in unison.

Erica slides over to Cammy's side and bumps hips with her. "So have you met your mate yet?" A blush takes hold of her face.

"Ummm no. I turn eighteen in two days. My brother Sam, our beta, is having a little party for me. It's basically all guys because I'm like the little sister to all of the warriors. Most of my friends are guys too, as a matter of fact. I only have one close girlfriend, but she is away visiting her aunt in another pack."

Another knock on the door gets my attention and Tim walks in. "Hey Tony." Cammy says and all of our heads snap to face her. "What? I can tell them apart."

All of the girls laugh because we have a feeling that her eighteenth birthday is going to be amazing. Tony walks over to Cammy. "First off, Luna, all of your guest rooms are ready, and second Alpha said that Alpha Tanner has just passed the entrance gate and he would like you to come down to greet him."

Tony puts his arm around Cammy's shoulder and looks down at her. "Your brother wants to see you down there too since his mate's dad is coming as well." He gives a sweet smile, and she nods. Then he puts his hand on her head and ruffles her hair. She swats his hand away and he busts into a fit of laughter as he walks out. Cammy is staring after him, cheeks still red as a tomato.

"Girl, you got it bad." Stacy states.

Cammy looks up at the rest of us, "Yeah but they only see me as a little sister, who can only sometimes kick their asses in training. To them I am just one of the guys," she says as she shrugs her shoulders.

"Alright ladies Tim or Tony... I'm not sure which will be showing you to your rooms. I will see you all in the morning." I wave goodnight to everyone as Ben, Cammy and I head downstairs to greet Alpha Tanner and his warriors.

We get outside just as the cars are pulling up. Landon, Sam, Lara and the rest of the Gold Moon crew are there waiting for us.

"Hey guys!" I greet as I roll up. Damn challenge, I can't even go in for a cuddle with Landon. Sam looks a little nervous. He is about to meet his mate's dad. Lara is holding on to Sam's hand and looking up at him lovingly.

"Alpha Landon, it's good to officially meet you." You hear Alpha Tanner say as he climbs out of the SUV. Everyone is shaking hands and I'm kind of just chilling in the back hidden from everyone.

"Also thank you again for listening to the kids and trying to find out the truth. This could have been disastrous."

"All the thanks goes to my Luna. She is the one who recognized that magic was involved."

Tanner looks around since I'm not next to Landon it looks like he is standing by himself.

"Where is she? I would like to personally thank her." I wave at him.

"That would be me sir, unfortunately I was challenged for my title and mate today soooo, yeah you know the rules." I say with a half-smile and shrug.

Tanner's shocked look doesn't go unnoticed, but he says nothing. I roll back to my spot away from Landon and give Landon a wink. "Alpha Tanner, this is my Beta, Sam, and you know his mate,

Lara. Troy, my Gamma and obviously the rest of your gang," Landon says as he slaps the back of Caden.

Tanner gives Lara a big hug. "Congratulations sweetheart!"

"Thanks Uncle Tanner, where is dad?" He will be here in an hour, one of the suv's has a flat tire." I look up to see Sam relax a bit.

"Would you mind if we have a quick debriefing and get everyone settled for tonight?" Landon proposes.

We are all in agreement since we are all tired and tomorrow is going to be a crazy day. Everyone heads inside and goes over a few details. Once we finish for the night, Cammy helps me get everyone off to their rooms and it is time to call it a night. I am beat.

LANDON

Twenty-four hours! So much has happened. Between the shit with Gold Moon and then the fucking challenge. AND now the icing on this fucking cake of the day, is I can't even sleep in the same room as my mate. I walk into the bathroom, staring at my reflection. Worry is evident all over my face.

"Landon, don't worry about our mate, she is going to be fine."

"I know man, I just don't want her in any danger." The thought of her ending up back in a hospital has my heart clenching. I reach into the on-suite shower and turn it on hot. The steam quickly fills the room with a heavy fog. Stepping in I let the heat of the water beat down on the tension in my neck and shoulders.

I just want to be with her. Closing my eyes, I can practically feel her touch lingering on my skin. The thought of her naked body on mine has my dick swelling and screaming for release. I slide my hand down my hard length, taking a firm grip of my shaft. With one hand on the shower wall, I let the spray and the thoughts of my mate wash away the day. Pre-cum mixes with water as it beads at the tip of my cock. I start to slowly pump, the memory of how she commanded me to make her come has me quickening my pace.

Visions of her breasts bouncing up and down while she rode my dick has it twitching in my hand. The way her nipples felt in my mouth as I rolled them with my tongue has got me chasing this high. I would give anything right now to be buried deep inside her tight pussy, but instead I'll have to settle for one more memory of me rubbing her clit. I can see her shaking from her climax. Her skin looked flushed as her eyes rolled in the back of her head. The memory of her screaming my name as I pierced her flesh marking her again. A shiver runs through me at the thought. "Mal," I moan. Tightening my hand pushing myself over the edge. I shoot my load all over the shower wall. My breath is shaky as my vision clears. Even masturbating is better now that I have my mate, though I much prefer doing it with her.

Once I have control over my dick, I take an actual shower and get ready for bed. I climb into the soft blankets and grab the pillow I snuck out of our bedroom earlier. It smells like her; nothing calms me down like her scent. My cock stirs at the thought of her in bed with me. Cursing Jessica, I can't help the growl that escapes my throat. Fuck this is going to be a long night.

Chapter 16
Malinda

Stacey's sing song voice wakes me in the morning, as does her gentle prodding of my shoulder to get me out of bed. It takes all my strength to not hit her with my pillow. I didn't get much sleep last night and it shows through my obvious irritation. Hoping a shower will change my disposition, I quickly get in and dress for the day.

Stacy talks my ear off as we meander to the dining hall, where Ben is standing stoically, waiting for me. With his hand on the door, he looks down at me. "Mal," a husky voice calls. Ben's eyes swirl with black letting me know Jared's talking to me now. "Own this whole day. Don't let that bitch get to you. Remember who you are." I nod my head with a smile. "Now get your ass in there and claim what's yours." His voice filled with emotion; I feel like I'm about to go to war.

Ben pushes the door open with such force the sound of it hitting the wall echoes through the room. All eyes turn to us. I roll in with my head high, instantly making eye contact with Landon. Damn he looks good today. He's leaning against a wall in worn out work jeans, well-loved cowboy boots, a blue t-shirt and a baseball cap. I unconsciously lick my lips and catch him laughing to himself as he sits down at a table.

Jessica strolls in a side door and saunters right to Landon and sits down. Sahara's trying to crawl her way to the surface, probably to scratch that bitch's eyes out. Just like I'm restraining myself from doing. Landon stiffens as Jessica brushes up against him. Sam is about to say something to Jessica, then a head full of red hair bobs its way next to Landon.

"Hey you!" Eloise shouts loud enough for me to hear from across the room. She gets on a chair and stares down at Jessica. Everyone's eyes bounce between the two.

"Yes, what can I do for you girl." Jessica's fake smile makes me want to slap it off her face.

"You touched the Alpha. You should know the wules of a challenge." Jessica narrows her eyes at the informative little girl.

"Listen here, orphan, I know the rules. I think you should mind your own business." She grits out. I look around the room. All of Stone Mountain, and Gold Moon are here. And they're watching this little girl handle herself like the warrior she is.

Eloise goes from her chair to on top of the table and starts walking on it to get a bit closer to Jessica. "I stand for our twue Luna." She places her tiny little hand over her heart. "Until my last bweath."

Jessica's mouth drops and she has nothing to say back to this brave little girl. What shocks the absolute shit out of me is almost everyone places their hands on their hearts and nods in solidarity.

Landon looks at Eloise, his head tilts to the side, like he's analyzing her. This little girl in a sundress and pigtails just got a pack of wolves to unite. He looks like he's having a conversation with Dex. Landon stands and walks over to her. Eloise has a moment of nervousness but holds her ground. Something a young pup should not be able to do.

He holds his hand out to her. It's now her turn to look at him curiously, she eyes his hand. Slowly, Eloise reaches for Landon. He helps her off the table and onto the chair. He places his hand that is holding hers on his heart. They are almost eye to eye. "Until our last breath." Landon whispers to her. He gives her a big hug and picks her up and carries her to his table. He has her sit across from him. Jessica is snarling at her and me... Oh I'm fucking losing it!!! This kid has got to have alpha blood in her, because that was mic drop worthy. The rest of breakfast goes along with minimal to no drama.

Before I know it, it's time to head down to the training yard and get this shit resolved. Stacy and the girls wait for me by the door. If they're trying to cover their shit eating grins— they failed. "You all know I haven't kicked her ass yet, right." As the words leave my lips Stacy holds up her hand as if to say *don't even go there*.

The sun warms my skin as we head outside. The light breeze that swirls around us carries an electric energy from the crowd that's building up down by the outdoor arena. I'm shocked to see my former fellow male warriors piling out of an SUV. They all bow their heads, then file in behind us. I feel like a boxer with their entourage but entering a fight this way is tradition for Stone Mountain and it's all I know.

My adrenaline pumping when Eminem's *"Lose Yourself"* blaring through the outdoor speakers. As we get closer to the ring you can see that the crowd is starting to get into it too.

My eyes land on Jessica as she prepares herself to get ready. She has no one to support her, not one friend. From the looks of it, the confidence she had before has disappeared.

My former warrior Zack helps me in the ring. I can hear Landon growl from the stands because Zack has his hands on me. I look at Landon and give him a, *what do you want me to do about it* look. He puts his hands up and runs them through his hair, clearly feeling defeated at this moment.

Zack pulls my chair into the ring and helps me into it. I see him sniff the air, then snap his head, looking at Jessica with what looks to be worry and anger in his eyes. You've got to be fucking kidding me.

"Zack, is she your mate?" I whisper in his ear. He looks hurt.

"Yeah, but she obviously does not feel the pull." He grits out

That must mean her mate died and Zack is her second chance mate. She won't feel the pull until they do something— intimate. I pat him on the back, "I promise I won't hurt her too much, but I can't stop this even if I wanted to." He nods his head in defeat and exits the ring. Jessica finally notices him as he is leaving, a confused look on her face.

"Shit," Sahara moans.

"Agreed."

Landon enters the ring to go over the rules. "Full Moon Pack and visitors. Today we are here to witness the challenge of title and mate. All challenges are a fight to the death unless agreed upon by the contenders. Ladies, what shall it be?"

I look over to Jessica "It is up to you." I make sure that my voice holds sincerity in it, because she doesn't know about her mate. I don't want this to be my choice either, I truly don't want to kill her. I see her tilt her head, something has caught her gaze. I look behind me— Zack. The look on his face is like he is willing her to hear him, and he wants her to choose life.

"I choose life Alpha." Jessica's whole tone changes. It's filled with respect as she addresses Landon as Alpha, but her eyes never leave Zack. The second chance mate pull is weird and it's throwing her for a loop. I give her a sad smile.

"Ladies shake hands, then enter your corners. Beta Sam, begin the fight when ready." Landon walks over to Jessica and shakes her hand. Then came to me to shake mine. "What's going on?" He whispers to me.

"My former warrior is Jessica's mate. I don't think she feels the pull though." I look over his shoulder at her. "I also have a theory as to why she did this."

I roll over to Jessica. "Listen, I think we got started on the wrong foot." She briefly gazes at me then nods her head.

"Luna, I'm sorry." she whispers for only me to hear.

I smile at her. "Then let's make this right. Tell them why you did this. If my gut feeling is correct... I do not think anyone will fault you." She looks at me speculatively. "Maybe after some time, that is."

"Everyone is expecting a show now. I really don't want to hurt you, Luna."

"No sunshine, we're giving them a show. I still need to kick your ass for the last twenty hours of aggravation you gave me."

She laughs and nods her head. "Yeah, I guess I do deserve it." I shake her hand and lead her to the center of the ring. Giving me a nervous smile, she begins to speak.

"Ladies and gentlemen. I need to apologize to you and our Alpha. This is not what I want. I.... I..." I give her a nod of encouragement. Releasing a deep breath, she continues.

"My reason for the challenge of the Luna position and her Mate was for selfish reasons. Like most of you I lost my whole family in the war. In a blink of an eye, it was just me." Tears roll down her face as the look of painful memories plague her mind. "Since I never found my mate... I just feel so alone all of the time. I don't know how to talk about my pain. So, I've been focused on finding a mate strong enough to protect me. Who better than our Alpha? I just wanted to feel safe and loved, and it's been so long since I have had either of those. So, in the midst of my grief, I became a bitch and treated you all horribly. I am sorry from the bottom of my heart."

Landon gazes upon me with pride. "What happens now?" A voice calls out from the crowd. I look out to everyone.

"Oh, we're still fighting. Jessica challenged me and our rules are absolute. There is no going back." I say with a smile and look at her.

"Are you ready to have fun?" I ask.

She chuckles while gliding to her side of the ring. "Why do I think you're the one who will be having all of the fun?"

I smile brightly. "Because I'm really good at this and I'm going to kick your ass." We both laugh. I can almost see the facade she has built start to fall. I don't know if we will ever be friends, but this will be a good start.

Sam looks at us from the middle of the ring. Then, loud and clear, he yells "Fight!" Jessica comes running at me, and swings first. I block the hit and move into my first combo. Two jabs and a right hook. Making contact with her nose, breaking it on the spot. I flip her onto the ground knocking the wind out of her. I won't hit her while she is down, so I wait a moment for her to get up. "Let's go Jess. Get up." I laugh looking down at her.

"Yeah, yeah Luna, I'm coming." Jessica gets up and I roll to the side of the ring. Now she's coming at me hard and fast. I turn and we start going punch for punch. Jessica is not a bad fighter, and she could make a fair warrior with a bit more training. She gets a good punch in, and my lip starts bleeding.

"Mal the crowd is looking for more, are you ready to give them more?" I hear Sahara say. I can hear everyone cheering but I'm too focused on the fight to care.

My lips smirk, the cut on my lips stinging even more. I hear my mate yell, "Let's go baby!!!" Pulling from his energy, my combo's get faster. Jessica is having a hard time keeping up as I land hit after hit. I feel a moment of anger come over me with everything that has happened lately.

Each swing gets more aggressive than the last. Out of nowhere Jess comes flying toward me, so I meet her stride for stride. I pick up speed as Jessica jumps to kick me in the face. I grab her leg and fling her onto the ring floor and in the process, I use that moment to use her leg as a pole vault and basically fling myself over her. Wheelchair and all. As I am flying over her, I hear her leg snap. "AHHHHHH". She screams, and the crowd goes crazy.

"Holy Shit."

"Did you see her jump in the chair!"

"What just happened? That was fucking insane."

To say the pack is shocked at how well I fight in my chair is an understatement. Landing with a skid, I roll over to her. A part of me feels terrible and the other part of me feels justified.

"Do you concede?" I growl.

"Yes"

"YES, WHO?" My voice booms with authority. I may have gone easy on her by letting her speak her peace, but I'm not fucking around about her submitting to me. I want her to know I mean business.

"YES, LUNA!" She screams from either the pain or the confession, either way... I win. I motion for someone to come help her and Zack comes running into the ring to grab her and get her to the pack doctor to have her leg set.

Sam walks into the ring "The winner of the challenge..." He holds my arm up in the air. "'Congratulations to our LUNA and our QUEEN." Sam's voice echoes loudly. He then kneels down and places his hand over his heart. As is everyone in the crowd, not just Full Moon. Stone Mountain and Gold Moon are all kneeling. Landon sprints over with the biggest smile on his face and scoops me up bridal style.

"Baby, I love you so much." He crashes his lips on mine, then puts me back in my chair causing me to whimper at the loss of contact. Then, my alpha mate gets down on his knees to join the rest. I look out at everyone and place my hand over my heart. Turning my gaze to Landon, I pull on his hand, so he is standing next to me. Showing everyone, we are a united front. Then I let my words carry in the breeze.

"Until our last breath we will protect you all."

Chapter 17
Landon

 Everyone is submitting to my mate. My Queen. I'm truly in awe of her. *"She's amazing."* Dex says as he curls up in the back of my mind. Exhausted from cheering on his mate. Then a warrior from Stone Mountain carries Jessica off.

 "That's Zack, Jess's mate, she just doesn't know it yet though." Mal says as she looks over to them off in the distance.

 "LUNA!!!!" Ellie's red hair is a red cloud of excitement as she jumps up and down outside the ring. The sound of Ellie's little voice causes Dex to stir again.

 "Pup."

 "She is adorable." I say as I watch her excited face.

 "She's our pup." I don't get a chance to question him because Mal rolls over to the edge of the ring.

 "Hey sweet girl."

 "Hey Alpha, can you help me up—peas?" Ellie asks but I'm already reaching over to pull her into the ring. She jumps right into Mals' outstretched arms. "Luna, I'm so proud of you." Ellie gushes.

 Mal brushes some hair from the little girl's face and smiles sweetly at her.

 "I'm proud of you, sweet pea! You were very brave earlier today."

Ellie looks between me and Mal. "I feel something funny when I am with you guys."

Mal and I look at each other. "What do you feel when you are with us?" Mal asks with a kind and warm smile.

"With you, I feel warm and cozy, but...." She stops talking and looks nervous. My mate places her hand under Ellie's chin pulling her attention back to Mal's face.

I come closer and kneel down, so we are all closer together. "It's okay El, you can tell us." I say to encourage her.

"Sometimes I hear a voice whispering in my head, and it calls you Mom and Dad. Which is weiwd because I had a mom and dad already and I love them, but I think my heawt needs more."

I see a tear form in Mal's eyes as she kisses the little girl's head. "What if I told you my wolf wants to claim you, as her pup?" Mal says with a smile as the tears roll down her cheeks.

I look at Mal with wide eyes, "My wolf calls you his pup too, Ellie." I say pulling both my girls into a hug.

"Wait! Does this mean you... you want me? You want me to be your pup, you want to be my mommy and daddy?" She sobs uncontrollably. Mal and I both have big smiles on our faces and even though we have not had one discussion about this I can tell we are one hundred percent on the same page. I reach for Mal's hand, sharing a meaningful glance, and I can tell from that look on her face she's all in.

"Do you want us to be your mommy and daddy?" I hold my breath because I don't want her to feel like we are pushing her. "YESSSSS. YES, YES, YES!!!! I want to be your daughter." Ellie jumps up and down screaming and clapping her hands. Behind us we hear a lot of people whooping and clapping.

We turn around to see not a dry eye as our close friends and warriors show their support. It's not like we were quiet about the conversation plus with our great hearing ability pretty much everyone heard what just took place.

Everyone comes up to Ellie telling her how strong she was today. Some even nickname her little alpha, because of how brave she is. "Oh, I can't wait to tell my best friend!!!" She squeals. Cammy makes her way over with the triplets. With the promises of ice cream and the boys helping to pack Ellie's things, we agree to meet back at our apartment. This will give us an hour or two to get her room ready. Cammy makes her way up and high fives Ellie. "Yeah girl, you did awesome today!

" Mal and I will go get your room ready. Then this week we will have someone come and help you make it all your own. How does that sound?"

"Ummm don't you mean, you and mommy will go get my room weady?" She says with a little pout.

"Yeah kiddo, mommy and I will go get your room ready." I say all choked up.

"Wait!!!!! Does that mean you all are my aunts and uncles?!!!" She yells with excitement. Everyone starts laughing and Ellie looks disappointed, but Cammy jumps right in there.

"Ellie we're not laughing at you sweetie; we're just laughing because you are so cute. I can promise we will all be your aunts and uncles." The warrior's give her a "hell yeah" cheer and the smile on her face is contagious.

We get back to our house and quickly clean out the largest spare bedroom for our little girl. We came up with a great plan to make this her own and I plan to call Rich our head contractor to set it all up.

"Landon I'm going to go jump in the shower real quick so that way we can get ready for dinner." She disappears into the bathroom, and I go to the closest to grab her some clothes. Reentering the bedroom, I pick up her scent and it's strong. Dex purrs in my head.

"Our mate is aroused."

I stroll into the bathroom and see her on the new bench I installed in the stall for her. She is leaning up against the wall massaging her legs. Her eyes close. I study how her hands rub her muscles. A moan escaping her lips. My dick twitches in my pants at the sounds coming from her mouth and there is no stopping me from walking fully clothed into the shower with her.

A startled gasp of surprise escapes those beautiful lips. Her eyes fill with lust and the sweet smell of her arousal fills my lungs as if it was life-giving air.

"Landon... you startled me," she playfully scolds.

I drop to my knees in front of her and reach my hand to her cheek. I gently slide my fingers into her hair and rub my thumb against her soft blush skin. She leans into my touch biting her lower lip as her eyes flutter close. This woman is my mate, my soul and I love everything about her. "Mal, I need you." I simply say. It's not a request nor is it a demand. It's just my truth.

A second later her lips are on mine as she slides her arms around my neck. This kiss is primal, and I'm desperate to be inside this woman. Pulling away Mal lifts my shirt over my head, throwing it across the bathroom. Lust fills her eyes as she licks her lips as she takes in the sight before her. Her fingers dance across my chest, leaving a trail of sparks in their wake. I stand as she brings her hands to the waistband of my jeans. I let her fumble with the button for only a moment before taking over and making quick work of the wet fabric. As soon as I step out of them her mouth is on my dick.

The feeling of my hard cock sliding down her throat is unworldly. I place my hand on the wall behind her head to brace myself. This woman does things with her mouth that should be illegal. She picks up the pace and moans, sending vibrations through me. I pull out of her mouth knowing exactly where I want my seed to land. I swiftly pick her up and sit down on the bench. Maneuvering her body so her legs straddle my hips. Her hands go right to my hair and her lips are on mine. I have one hand on her ass and the other is holding the back of her head as I deepen the kiss.

Passion and want swirl around us, as our tongues tangle together. Only pulling away to fill our lungs with much needed oxygen. I get lost staring into her beautiful eyes, but I'm snapped back to reality as I feel her wet slit slide along my cock. Without breaking eye contact, I lift her, so my tip is right at her entrance. Closing her eyes, her head falls back as I slowly slide into her. Inch by torturous inch I make her mine all over again. She places her hands on my shoulders to help herself move up and down my shaft.

"Harder," she rasps in my ear as she nips it.

A growl escapes my throat and I start to pump in and out of my mate, letting my unbridled need take the reins. She leans back, giving me a beautiful view of her breasts. I can't help but take a nipple into my mouth. Her breathing hitches as I suck, and then bite her nipple.

"Please!" She begs. She pulls herself closer to my chest and reaches her hand down and behind her to play with my balls. I groan as I pump in and out of her. This feeling is out of this world, and I can feel myself getting close.

"Faster."

"Fuck babe you're so tight. You're going to make me come."

As the words leave my lips, she reaches, grabbing a fist full of my hair and pulling my head to the side with a loud growl. Pain mixes with euphoria as the sting of her canines pierces my skin. Finally claiming me as her own. She moans as my blood drips from her mouth causing her pussy to tighten around my cock. Stars dance around my vision as a roar rips through my body. Throwing my head back, I lose absolute control. Thrusting into her draining every last drop of cum I've got. Her body begins to shake, chasing that last bit of her high and being the good mate I am, I throw her over the edge by biting her flesh.

She eventually releases her bite and licks the wound, allowing it to heal. I reluctantly release mine as well. We are both trying to catch our breath as I kiss her forehead. "That was incredible. I've never experienced anything like that. I am so glad the Moon Goddess gave you to me.... Mal, I love you." I say as I brush her wet hair from her face revealing her beautiful smile.

"Okay now let's get clean and get downstairs so we can be in the dining room before Ellie gets back." She says before placing a gentle kiss on my new mark.

After another round in the shower, we eventually get our asses down to the dining room. I want to make sure that Ellie is sitting with us from now on. Dinner goes great and we even planned out the luna and mating ceremony for this coming weekend. As we discussed everything, Mal came up with an idea for a bonding ceremony for us and Ellie. The idea is to make her ours as much as possible, also showing that she will be treated as if she was our own to other packs and even members of our pack.

During dinner, Ellie told us all of the ideas she and Cammy came up with, for decorating her bedroom. She wants a unicorn room and a mermaid bathroom. To say she was excited about getting her own bathroom is an understatement. But I have a feeling she'd be just as happy having a plain gray room, as long as she is ours.

"Can you wead me a book daddy?" she asks as we tuck her into her new bed. Mal and I both give her huge smiles. We can't help it.

"We don't have any books yet," I pause to collect my thoughts, "but I can tell you a story." Ellie quickly pulls the blankets up to her little chin and snuggles into her pillow. "Once upon a time an Alpha stumbled upon a beautiful, she-wolf. The second he saw her; he knew that she was someone special to him. That she was going to be his *Everything*."

"Oh, I think I am going to love this stowy! Is the beautiful she-wolf, Mommy?"

"Shhhh I can't give away the story." I scold and gently poke her on her little button nose. "Okay now where was I?"

"She was someone special." She gushes and Mal giggles.

I go on to tell the story of how I met Mal. Starting at the coffee shop. Granted I have to skip all of the inappropriate thoughts running through my mind the first time I saw her, but I think I did a pretty okay job. As I finish up, her little eyes are closed, and her breathing has evened out. We each sneak a kiss on her forehead, tuck her in tightly and quietly leave her room. Once in our own beds, Mal snuggles up next to me. "Goodnight, Daddy." She teases as she kisses me goodnight.

"Goodnight, Momma." I whisper, holding her tightly as we drift off to sleep.

Chapter 18
Cammy

What a day!

I spent the afternoon with Ellie. After the fight, she talked nonstop about her new mom and dad. It broke my heart when she said she "couldn't believe" that they wanted her. Anyone in their right mind would want this precious child. Even though I had a contact buzz from Ellie's high, I could NOT stay focused.

Why, you ask.

Three reasons. And they all start with a T.

The triplets came with us, making me more flustered than a nun in a sex shop. I really need to find my mate soon and work out these sexual frustrations, otherwise I'm doomed to spend the rest of my life in a sexual fog.

My chances of finding a mate in the rec room seem pretty high, since this is where unmated males my age go to hang out. So here I sit, watching a movie, lights slightly dimmed so the guys playing pool can still see the table. A few couples take advantage of the lowered lighting to make out in secluded corners of the room, hidden enough so younger, prying eyes wouldn't really be able to see what's going on.

These last fifteen minutes before I turn eighteen are really killing me. I want to wait for my mate, but my nerves are getting the best of me. My birthday present to myself arrived today and if I don't find my mate, I'm sure that will keep me occupied quite nicely.

I am stuffing popcorn in my mouth as Enola Holmes on Netflix plays on the big screen. The cushion sages as someone plops down next to me and without looking, I just pass the bowl of popcorn over.

"Thanks Cam." I freeze as the bowl leaves my hand. I'd know that voice anywhere.

"Tony," I say as I try not to choke on the kernels. He smiles his megawatt smile and passes the bowl to Tim and Tom who have slid on the floor in front of me.

Holy crap, I can't breathe when they are around. All three of them are gorgeous. Blonde hair, pale green blue eyes that I could get lost in for days that are even more vibrant set against their sun kissed skin. They have mountains of muscles, which somehow works perfectly with the beautiful wolf tattoo they each have on their backs. What I especially love about their tat is that it's in black and white scale of the wolf design. Everything is monotone, all except the wolf eyes. Those are painted to match their own.

I suddenly gasp from a sharp pain followed by a terrible throbbing headache. Quickly bring my hands up to rub my temples. I squeeze my eyes shut as a painful groan escapes my lips. "Ugh, fuck this hurts."

"Cam, you, okay?" A worried voice asks. My head falls to the side as someone's hand slides against my cheek. Running their fingers into my hair to help hold my head up.

"No," I manage to muster. "My head is pounding and I... I'm so dizzy." This is so weird. I fumble for my phone to peer at the time.

Tim leans over to check it as well. "It's midnight baby." He whispers in my ear.

"Happy Birthday!!!" Everyone in the room shouts. But I can't enjoy this, I'm in agony.

"Jesus guys, shut up! Can't you see she's in pain." Tom whisper yells. I'm starting to shake from the pain.

"Someone link the pack doctor." I hear someone demand as strong hands start rubbing my shoulders. Let me tell you, it's amazing and the pain starts to subside. Someone pulls my hair to the side and fingers graze my neck.

Then "It" happens. A whirlwind of feelings reverberates deep within me from a place I had yet to discover. Feelings that I have never had before. Feelings that I never even knew were possible. It's the most magical feeling in the world.

Sparks.

"*Cammy...*" a soft purr adds into the muddle of stuff happening with me. Then I realize it's coming from my head. I then hear a voice in my head. "*I'm Gwen, your wolf.*" I smile to myself. I am finally in contact with my wolf.

'*Hi Gwen. I am so happy to finally have you with me.*"

"*Oh Cam, I've always been with you and let me tell you I have the best birthday surprise ever for you.*"

THIRD PERSON POV

An anguished moan causes the triplets to pause in their popcorn eating endeavors. Cammy grabs her head, in obvious pain. The three brothers look at each other, not sure what is happening, or what they should do.

"Ugh. Fuck this hurts" She says in agony.

"Cam are you okay?" Tim asks, a mask of worry consuming his typically jovial expression.

"No, my head is pounding, and I am now dizzy." The comment barely leaves Cammy's lips when you can practically see all three of the boy's wolves' ears prick up in unison.

"It's midnight baby." Tim whispers just before their mindlink begins to wake up and immediately meld. All three wolves say the exact same thing.

"MATE."

Then a cacophony of comments flood the connections.

-Guys, Cammy is our mate.

-Why is she in so much pain?

-Why didn't we have a clue before now?

-She literally just turned eighteen.

-How can we help stop her pain?

Tom wants to lean in to tell her "Happy Birthday," but she's in so much pain, he knew that any sound would just add to it. So they all just smile at her but she is in agony and can't focus on the bond. She asks if anyone has felt this way before and everyone just shrugs and shakes their heads. Dean, one of Sam's friends, asks to link the pack doctor. This isn't normal for someone who is getting their wolf. A shift, maybe, but not for just awakening the connection between the human side and wolf side.

Tony slides behind Cammy and rubs her shoulders. She relaxes almost instantly. He pushes her long hair off to the side and as he does, he accidentally brushes up against her skin. Her skin prickles under his fingertips while the sparks tingle from the connection. That simple touch makes him bite his lip to stop from groaning in pleasure. More tension leaves her body, and she becomes visibly more relaxed. She snaps her eyes open and is looking at all three of the guys. Their hearts thump in their chests as her eyes dilate and glaze over.

"She is talking to her wolf for the first time." Tim says with a big smile on his face. Expectation heavy in his tone. The others just nod and lovingly stare at her. They watch her have this conversation knowing how special it truly is and then her eyes focus again. Her beautiful orbs grow wide and her jaw drops. Finally snapping out of her shock, a big smile on her face appears.

"Mates." She says in a breathy sigh, her cheeks turn bright red.

"Mate." all three guys confess.

Collective gasps surround us. Whispers of confusion grow throughout the room.

"Wait. Are all three of them mated to her?"

"How is that possible?"

"I think I heard of this before."

"Yes, this is how it works for multiples, jeez people. You can relax, there is nothing wrong with it." Dr. K says storming into the room and quickly shutting everyone up. K is the Alpha's cousin, and she is just as much a spitfire as Landon's mom was. She clears her throat in order to get everyone to stop whispering. She kneels down to Cammy.

"Happy Birthday Cammy. I'm sure you're a bit confused as to why you were in pain." Cammy seems to be in a bit of shock still, but she nods her head. "Your wolf came to you with your mates in front of you, she was trying to connect to you and took their wolves all at the same time. Since you have three mates it must have felt like you were hit by a truck." Cam just keeps nodding her head.

The doc looks up, leveling her stare to the triplets, "Boys please take your time with her, this is overwhelming." The guys unintentionally growl at the doctor.

"We would never hurt our mate," Tim shouts.

The doc rolls her eyes at them but smirks. "Listen, just be gentle with her and take your time with her. She needs to get used to the idea that she has three mates." The doc gets up and gives Cammy a birthday hug before she heads back to the hospital.

As if a switch was flipped everything clicks into place, and they understand what Dr. K was hinting at. She was telling them to not rush into mating. "We're all going to have to discuss this privately." Tony rushes out. He quickly turns, picks Cammy up and carries her to their little apartment.

"So much for taking it easy on her." Tom chuckles under his breath. Once inside, Tim goes straight to his bedroom, with the guys hot on his tail. He gently places her on the bed and the three of them sit down around her.

"Did you guys know that this was possible?" Her voice is quivering from ...fear? Or is that lust?

"Luna told us the other day that this was possible, we were just as shocked as you are now." Tony says a bit nervously.

"Umm, how is this supposed to work?" Cammy took a deep breath. "How are we supposed to mate? I have this urge to jump you all at the same time."

Her face turns bright red at her omission but they're her mates and she wants to be as clear as possible. The guys kind of laugh and all three rub the back of their necks at the same time. Cammy cannot help but think it's adorable.

"We've discussed this a bit since Luna let us know that sharing a mate was a possibility. We're very comfortable worshiping your body all at the same time." The way the words roll off of Tim's tongue sends a shiver down her body. "We only want you baby."

"At the same time?" Cammy asks with a glint in her eyes.

"Yes baby, we hope that soon you will be able to handle all of us at the same time. But there is no rush."

"At the same time—" Cammy repeats herself.

The triplets share a look of confusion. All of them wondering if they short circuited their little mate. "Yes."

"We're all going to mate each other?"

"Hold the phone— No. We will not be touching each other. We all get along well and good but not that well." Tony says, causing the guys to laugh and Cammy giggles.

As the conversation continues, the three of them inch closer and closer to her. It's as if an invisible force is pulling them to her. Tony brushes her hair from her face. Tim starts to rub her legs, while Tom moves behind her to rub her shoulders.

"Can we kiss you?" Tony asks.

"I.... ummm I've never been kissed before." Cammy says as she covers her face in embarrassment. He gently pulls her arms down to see her face. While one of the others gently rubs his hands up and down her arms to help calm her.

"We promise to take it slow." Cammy nods her head and Tony leans in and brushes his lips against hers. The sparks from the kiss ignite a fire deep within Cammy's soul, causing her to become overwhelmed with lust. She grabs Tony practically pulling him down on top of her, trapping Tom behind her. Her sudden enthusiasm has the other two chuckling.

Tony deepens the kiss by biting her bottom lip eliciting moans of pleasure to escape. This gives him the access he desperately needs to dominate her tongue, resulting in the most passionate kiss he's ever experienced.

Tony pulls away to kiss down her neck. Tom sits up a bit, and even though he is pinned under her; he turns her head so he can reach her mouth. His tongue slips right in claiming his part of her. Tom pours every ounce of love he can into his first kiss with his mate. Stroking one hand down the side of her ribs, his fingers gently grazing her breasts. He sensually moves down her body, enjoying the way he can practically hear her skin sizzle with the trail of sparks he leaves behind. Getting to her hips, he squeezes her waist, enjoying the way she reacts to their touch. The sensation causes her to buck her hips right before he plays with the waistband of her shorts.

Tim gently nips and bites his way up her legs, using all his restraint to keep himself from devouring her, from continuing his path to the juncture of her thighs. Cammy is more than aroused and her scent is driving the guys wild. The triplets desperately try holding onto their control as the doctor told them to take it easy. The guy's focus should be especially gentle, but the way her body is calling to them is making it difficult.

Tom breaks the kiss just as Tony starts to massage her breasts. "Finally," Tim moans. He moves his lips to hers, claiming their first kiss as mates. With gentle movements against hers, savoring the moment. Cammy could tell he is the more tender of the three, but she is not having any of that. She's over stimulated and 'tender' can't satisfy her any longer.

Tom seductively moves his hand into her shorts. He ghosts his fingers over her pussy and growls in her ear. "You're so wet for us." She eagerly bucks into his palm as he enters her. His two fingers barely fit between her tight walls, making her moan loudly into his brother's mouth. Then his thumb plays with her clit, her moan turns into a whimper of need. The sounds emanating from her has the three brothers harder than they have ever been in their lives and they're craving more. Hearing moans of pure pleasure coming from their mate far surpasses what they thought was possible.

Tony hastily removes her shirt and bra then throws them across the room. Once her beautiful mounds are freed, he takes the left into his mouth while he squeezes and teases the other. Tim pulls away, gasping as he catches his breath. Giving her a sexy smirk, he licks his lips as he leans down, moves Tony's hand out of the way and takes her right nipple into his mouth. Cammy becomes a writhing, passionate mess. She is making incoherent noises, which drives the triplets crazy. Tom, who is still behind her, grinds his massive cock against the globes of her ass as he continues to finger fuck her.

The other two can no longer take the pressure of their growing needs to be touched by their mate. Sensing their desperation as if it's her own Cammy reaches to carefully unzip their pants. Short lived relief is achieved when they both are finally free of the confines of their jeans. Their large hands each stroke up and down on their shafts as Cammy watches.

The visual stimulation of these two perfect specimens in front of her is almost enough to push her over the edge. Two extremely hot men, pleasing themselves while looking at only you…Eyes wide, Cammy cries out. "Oh, god. I'm so close."

"Just relax. Your body knows what it wants." Tom coaxes as he thrusts faster. Cammy has an iron grip on his arm as he pumps in and out of her. She can't help but move her hips to meet his every thrust.

This pushes her ass against Tom, rubbing against him in all the right spots.

"Please," Cammy pleads, her body tight with pleasure.

"Come for us baby."

Tony and Tim each take one of her hands and place them on their cocks, guiding her and showing her what to do. Their moans and grunts fill the air.

"Ahhhh oh goddess, yes, yes, yes," Cammy calls out as her walls tighten around Tom's fingers. Then he pinches her clit with his other. "YES!" She screams, coming hard. Watching their mate experience, her first given orgasm sends the guys over the edge. Her grip tightens as they jet long ropes of cum on her. One of the ways they will be marking her.

Cammy gasps for air as she slowly regains her senses. These damn men are too hot for their own good. And they are all hers. A small growl ripples from her chest as she reminds herself of this and she quickly turns over to straddle Tom. Their eyes meet. Swirls of black dance across their irises. Her core hovers over his bulge. He grabs her hips as he lowers her to his jean covered cock. She rocks her hips back and forth, internally praying that she is doing this right. She's desperate for him to feel pleasure caused by her.

Slowly losing her ability to think anymore, lost in the exquisite moment, Cammy picks up the pace. Needing more of his mate, Tom quickly sits up. Wrapping an arm around the back of her neck and one around her waist he stares deep into her eyes as she rolls her hips into him. Her arousal drips down her thighs with each grind against his cock. Wanting to taste her, Tom pulls her into a deep possessive kiss. Consumed by lust he begins to thrust against her fast and hard. Her body tightens as she is about to come again. Tom pulls at her shirt freeing her breasts. The sight of her rosy nipples pulls an animalistic noise from his throat. Without hesitation he takes one of them into his mouth, setting her ablaze. A tingle teases the base of Tom's spine as his balls tighten.

"It's your turn to come." She whispers into his ear, then nips it for good measure. Her sexy voice saying those dirty words is all he needs.

"Ah FUCK!" He shouts as he comes hard in his pants, completely saturating the material but he couldn't care less. His body shakes as he holds her tightly to him and she comes undone all over again.

Cammy looks over her shoulder to see her other two mates breathing heavily. Cum dripping from their hands. The sight before her causes a shiver to run through her body. She leans back to kiss both of them. It's soft and gentle.

Tony jumps up to get a warm towel to clean Cammy off with. While the others head to the bathroom, cleaning themselves up. Tony carefully picks up his sated mate, placing her on the couch. He makes quick work of the bedsheets.

Tom reappears in a pair of clean boxers. "Arms up baby." Without hesitation Cam lifts her arms and allows him to change her into one of his t-shirts. They all get back in bed and try their best to all snuggle next to their mate. Cammy is cocooned in their body heat.

"Cammy?"

"Hmmm?" She purrs, extremely tired and yet full of energy.

"We love you baby."

"I love you all too," she pauses then asks, "Guys?"

"Yeah?" They sit up a bit to look in her eyes.

"I...I want you to mate with me, mark me as yours." Her request has all of the men growling, unable to hold back the desire that her simple request has created. They slowly start to bring their hands to her soft skin. Tony crawls on top of her without breaking eye contact. He kisses his mate as he lines his manhood at her entrance. He may be the oldest by only five minutes, but this has given him opportunities afforded to only the eldest.

He pauses a moment. "Cammy, are you sure you want to do this right now? I told the doc that we'd take it easy on you and this might hurt."

She nods her head tentatively but gives them a wide smile. That's all the reassurance Tony needs. Gentle as possible, he pushes his thick head inside of her. Inch by exquisite inch until he is all the way in. The moans he pulls from her as he slowly plunges into her escalated the other two's burgeoning desire for their mate.

"Faster," Cammy croaks out, letting Tony know she is ready for him to start moving. The pain from his initial penetration is still there, but it eases and is quickly overpowered by pleasure as he plunges inside her. Her fingernails dig into his back as he tries desperately to hold onto his composure. He sets a rhythm all four of them can feel as it mirrors the beating of their hearts. "Tony, I'm not made of glass. I was made for the three of you, that means the moon goddess made me specifically to handle the three of you."

The guys' eyes nearly jump out of their heads.

"You... you want all three of us at the same time?" Tom's question was laced with undeniable excitement, while Tony freezes mid thrust at her declaration.

"Fuck yeah, I've been dreaming of this day for like two years." A big smile spreads across her face.

"I've got lube!" Tim shouts as he jumps off the bed, tripping on the scattered clothing across the floor. Falling to the ground but like a fucking ninja, he does a summersault and jumps back to his feet. He runs out of the room like a man on a mission.

"Well, he's excited." Cam giggles. In two seconds, he's running back with a bottle of lube. Sliding on a discarded t-shirt he crashes into the bed. You'd think he'd have learned his lesson when he left the room. All three of them are looking at him with smirks on their faces.

Indignant, Tim rolls his eyes. "What? I'm like a fucking boy scout. Always be prepared."

Not wanting to waste another moment Tony grabs Cammy's leg, rolling her onto her side. Tim squirts a little of the cold liquid on his hand and rubs it on her back button. Cammy rolls her eyes into the back of her head from the sensation.

"Cam, are you sure you want all three of us for your first time?"

"I want to fuck all of my mates. You're all MINE." Her eyes flash, showing them her wolf is present. This action causes the guys' wolves to surface. They want to play too. "I may be a virgin but that does not mean I have not used—other things." Cam says with a devilish grin on her face.

Tim rubs the lube onto his shaft then grips his heavy cock to position himself at her ass. He runs his hand up and down her spine in hopes of relaxing her. When she was right where he wanted her, he placed himself at her tight little hole. His entrance is slow but determined. She gasps at an apparent bit of pain. Tom, seizing the opportunity, lines his cock up with her lips. His dick twitches in his hands at the sight of her eyes locked on the bit of precum dripping his tip. She bites her lip as she reaches for him. Pulling him to her mouth, her tongue darts out to lick it off of his tip.

With a loud groan of impatience, she lets the guys know she is ready for them to start moving. The animalistic noises coming from the guy's spurs Cammy's lust even more. Taking Tom right down her throat, as he runs his fingers in her hair. Tony seems to be the one driving the flow with his deep plunges inside her wet folds. He's slow but deliberate with his deep thrusts. He wants to bathe in each new sensation, afraid if he went too fast, he would miss something vital. The last thing he wants is to miss one moment of this time with Cammy. She pulls Tom out from her mouth and glares at the guys, frustration evident on her features.

"I said *fuck me*." She growls.

"Yes ma'am," Tony says with his interpretation of a deep southern drawl. He throws her leg over his shoulder and holds on tightly. Pounding into her with all of the pent-up need of a twenty-year-old man. Tim has her waist in his strong grip and tries to pick up the pace, but her ass is so tight, making his pleasure too intense. Once he matches the rhythm of his brother, he knows he won't last much longer.

Cammy pulls Tom back into her mouth. Even with the erratic movements of her body, she's still able to lick and suck like a fucking pro. Her tongue glides along his shaft as he wraps her long brown hair around his hand, not wanting to lose her mouth. After an especially forceful thrust from one of his brothers, she uses her suction to stay attached to him, and now he knows he's past the point of no return. He adds his rhythm to the group and thrusts deeply down her throat.

"That's it, my good girl. Suck my cock. Oh, just like that."

"I could spend forever in this pussy. It's so tight for me."

"Fuck I am going to come. Cam your ass is...." This confession seems to flick a switch in Cammy because her whole body tightens.

Her rigidity turns into tremors, and the guys know she's about to explode. They've only been her mate for a few hours, but they can read her body like Braille. "That's it baby. Come with all three of us inside you. Just like it's supposed to be. Just like it's going to be—for forever."

Her moaning sends them over the edge. Tom finishes first, coming harder than he ever has before. He looks down upon his mate as she swallows it all. Growls now rumble through the chests of the others as Cammy screams for more.

"YES!!!!" She calls out as the three of them come together.

Their bodies are all frozen in position, heaving from exertion. Sweat trickles down chests, throats bob as they try to lubricate parched throats. Then they all collapse on the bed.

"Best. Birthday. Ever."

Chapter 19
MALINDA

  To say that the last few days have been crazy is an understatement. The challenge is over, we are adopting Ellie, and Cammy found out she is the mate of the triplets. Not going to lie I totally saw that coming. Sam was shocked as shit. He practically tackled the triplets the next day when he found out they spent the night together. He was pissed with them for not talking to him first before they touched her.

  Cammy went into full *mate mode*. She got up in Sam's face screaming to keep his nose out of their business. Lara was able to calm him down and after a lengthy conversation everyone seems to be doing well. Lara, Cammy and I may or may not have had some girl time and let. me. tell. you. Holy Shit! Cam's mating experience was insane. I was blushing as she recalled some details.

  Hot with a capital H.

  Oh, and let's not forget the small fact of being attacked by an army of rogues that were, in fact, not rogues, but another pack that was drugged by an unknown mystery person and one of those people from that pack was Sam's mate? Like I said, crazy.

  Lara was a bit shy around us at the beginning, but I think Cammy and I've successfully corrupted her. She should be talking like a sailor and bossing Sam around in no time. HA!

The Gold Moon crew left yesterday after we discussed that a stronger alliance was absolutely needed between packs. We contacted surrounding packs, asking them to keep an eye out for anything suspicious, and immediately let us know if anyone goes missing. I want to say what happened with Gold Moon was a fluke—a onetime thing. Ugh... but my gut? Yeah, my gut's telling me this thing isn't over and I hate that feeling. But I'm trying to focus on the positive.

Tomorrow is our mating, Luna, and bonding ceremony with Ellie. At first, I was extremely nervous as we rushed to plan everything as quickly as possible. When I was mated to Jared, my mom and Jared's mom planned everything. I wasn't really that into it but that was because it felt like I was being mated to my brother. Now.... this time around feels so different. I've got butterflies fluttering in my stomach, and I can't stop thinking about the future. I'm so excited to be officially mated to the love of my life.

Stacy stayed to help me get everything ready and Mrs. Lane has created a killer menu. We are having steak, ribs, and brisket, plus twice baked potatoes, baked beans and veggies. Yup we are having BBQ food!!! When I told Landon and the guys, they were so excited that it was not geared to overly fancy. I also asked for a Funfetti cake because I found out it is Ellie's favorite. I am so excited, I can't wait!!! PLUS, we are going to have tons of different apple desserts. I also did some digging and found out that Landon loves cinnamon rolls. So, Mrs. Lane is having a giant cinnamon roll made just for him for breakfast tomorrow. We invited all of the surrounding packs, and everyone seemed so excited.

Today we're going to pick up our dresses in town, grab some lunch and maybe some ice cream for El. We normally would have used the dress shop that is on pack territory but the family that owns it is away on vacation and does not come back till next week. They made a call to the shop in Paisley, it's human owned but they are used to rush orders and they have a few seamstresses on staff. We got super lucky.

"Mommy? Are you weady?" I pop my head out the bathroom door and I see Ellie twirling around in her new purple sundress. Her long pigtails flowing around her face as she spins. A smile tugs at the corner of my lips as I take her in. We've been so surprised how easy it has been for all of us to fall into our new roles. Becoming her mom has been such a blessing, the main reason. She is beyond beautiful and not just on the outside. Her soul shines brighter than the sun making being her new mom all that more special.

"Give me two minutes, sweet pea, and I'll be right there."

"Okay, mommy I'm going to get my new puwse Aunt Stacy got me. I'll be wight back." I totally forgot that Stacy has been spoiling her like crazy. She purchased a Disney Dooney and Burke crossbody bag for her and Chanel sunglasses. Not sure what seven-year-old needs name brands for but hey, it's good to have an awesome aunt.

I give myself a quick once over in the mirror. I'm not sure who is more excited about the Mommy and Me matching sundresses... it's me. I'm super excited about them. I paired mine with a simple sandal. My hair is in a half pony and has light wispy falling around my face. It's giving me bridal hair vibes and I love it.

I meet Ellie by the front door to our apartment. "Ready?" I ask her.

"I was bown weady." She says as she slips on her sunglasses and does an epic hair flip and marches to the elevator. *Bwahahaha* this kid is amazing. As we get to the main floor of the pack house, I notice Landon engrossed in a conversation with Sam, Troy and the triplets. He sniffs the air, catching my scent. He turns to meet my gaze with his perfect smile.

"Hi Daddy!" Ellie says as she runs up and gives him a big hug.

"Hey munchkin. Why don't you two look pretty in your matching dresses."

"Oh, and don't forget my fancy bag and sunglasses. Aunt Stacy weally gets my sense of style." She says, causing everyone in earshot to chuckle.

"That she does. Are you all headed out to the dress shop?"

I grin up at Landon. "Yes, we're going for the final fitting and then we will grab some lunch. Do you boys have everything for tomorrow?"

He puts Ellie down and bends to give me a quick kiss. "Yes, all the suits are with Cammy. We're going to get dressed in their apartment. Hurry home to me, I have a little surprise for you when you get back."

"Okay my love."

We head to the SUV's. Landon had a few cars converted to hand controls for me. I hated having to keep asking people to drive me around. Not that it would matter, because Ben and Tony are currently hopping into a matching one behind us. Landon wants us to bring a full security team, but I thought it was overkill. I told him that he could send two guys and that they had to drive in another car. Let's be honest, it's more for their benefit than ours.

We get to the dress shop and Ellie eagerly puts on a white, princess dress. It has sheer long sleeves, a cute square neckline, empire waist and so much tool it looks like a cloud ate my daughter. The dress is covered in embroidered flowers with a small little train in the back. She looks stunning. I have an overwhelming feeling of pride that this young lady is officially going to be my daughter tomorrow. I have always wanted to be a mother and I'm so excited that I get to love this little girl unconditionally.

"Malinda, are you ready to try your dress on?" The saleswoman asks.

I nod my head excitedly, Ellie and Stacy get comfy on the couch, as I roll into the dressing room. My dress is a silk organza, with a scoop neckline. Traditional sleeves with little buttons that go from my wrist up my forearm. The back is an embroidered see-through lace with buttons that go from the base of my neck to just above my butt. The dress is very fitted but the best part is the detachable train. It will look great in pictures but I can remove it so I can move about in my chair.

"Oh Mal," Stacy gasps as I come out of the room.

"You look stunning," the owner of the shop whispers.

"Mommy, you look like a goddess."

"Mallie... it's perfect." I look up to see Ben smiling as he speaks Jared's words.

I take them all in from the reflection in the mirror. "Girls don't cry it's just a dress," but even I'm having a hard time with my emotions.

"Tony, what no comment from the peanut gallery?" I say trying to lighten the mood.

"Mal, you make that dress... this look is the whole package." Stacy comes up behind me and pulls my hair up to see what it will look like tomorrow. "You have to wear your hair up because the back of this dress is FIRE!" We all laugh at her emphasis on the word fire.

"Landon is going to absolutely die when he sees you in this dress, plus the surprise you have for him." She says with a wink. "I think you're going to make the big bad Alpha mushy tomorrow."

The owner and sales lady helps us pack up all three dresses and by the time we are all done at the shop we are starving. At the restaurant Ellie had Ben and Tony in stitches the whole time. I love watching our family become a family. Once it was time for ice cream, I had to send the boys home ahead of us. Cammy needed help with something and apparently one of the staff members for the event company grabbed her ass. Which set Tim and Tom into a frenzy. Tony was practically crawling at the bit to get back, and I couldn't blame him at all.

"Okay, so promise me you won't tell Uncle Troy we ate ice cream in the car, okay Ellie?"

"Ha, totally not spilling these beans mommy, I pwomise."

We hit a bit of traffic on the way back to our territory. I sent a text to Landon, letting him know that we're going to be a little late for dinner. We're only fifteen minutes from the border but we haven't moved an inch in over twenty minutes.

Landon: Is traffic moving?

Me: No, it looks like a detour of some sort, there are cops ahead directing traffic, I think?

Landon: Maybe an accident?

Me: Not sure I will let you know later. I Love you

Landon: Love you too. Tell my little princess I love her too.

Me: (smiling like crazy) I will. xoxo

We roll down the windows and listen to some music as we slowly roll forward. A light breeze blows through the car and a rancid stench assaults my nose, setting me on edge.

"Rogues." Stacy and I whisper in unison. My eyes dart around quickly checking our surroundings. Trying to seek out where it's coming from. Squinting toward the woods, but I don't see anything hiding in the tree line. They must be in plain sight because there is no mistaking their rot.

"Do you see them?" I whisper. Stacy just shakes her head as she continues to scan the area. I take my phone out and text Landon. I would call but I don't want to scare Ellie.

Me: We are stuck in traffic still, but we smell rogues.

Landon: Okay, Babe stay calm. Where are you?

Me: I am calm, but I don't want Ellie to get scared. We're just south of the road that enters the border.

Landon: I'm on my way to you with Sam, Troy and Ben.

A sniffle catches my attention, Ellie has her nose up in the air. "Mommy I smell wogues." She calls out in a panicked voice from the back seat. "I... I'm weally scared."

I motion for her to come sit in the middle row of the car and stay low.

"Mal" Stacy whispers. "Look at the cops." She says with a jerk of her chin.

I focus my eyes ahead and try to get a good look at the men. The first thing I notice, they don't look put together. Their uniforms aren't the same and the cop cars are all different. The sinking feeling in my gut grows.

"It's a setup." I look at Stacy, whose eyes grow in fear. I hit Landon's number on the Apple Car Play. I have no time to be delicate, Ellie's already aware of their scent but if we don't get out of here now, I could be putting her in more danger, and she is the only one I care about right now.

"We are almost there—"

"Landon, listen to me, it's a setup. It's the cops. The cops up ahead are the rogues. There are too many humans around for us to cause a fuss and once we get close enough to them... I'm afraid they will make it look like we're doing something wrong. If we fight back, the humans might help the cops thinking they are doing a good deed." I take a deep breath because I know this is going to go over like a lead brick. "Now, I've got an idea but you're not going to like it."

I hear him grunt. "What are you planning?"

"If you keep heading towards us, just follow the sirens. I have a feeling they are looking for us. I need to steer them away from the humans and the pack."

"Mal, don't hang up, okay?"

"Okay."

I turn to face Ellie. "Sweetheart put your seatbelt on. Stacy, can you go sit back there with her?"

Stacy does not answer. She just jumps in the back and puts her seat belt on and holds onto Ellie. I grip the hand controls tightly with my left hand. The control is an automatic control. All I have to do is pull for gas and push it forward to break. My right hand is tight on the spin knob that is attached to the steering wheel. It helps you maneuver the steering wheel with one hand. I check my mirrors and make sure that no one is approaching from the opposite direction. I pull back a little on the hand control, reviving the engine.

"Ready?" I ask the girls and they just nod. I activate the emergency brake and pull the control all the way to me, causing the tires to do a burnout. I'm deliberately drawing attention to us.

"Mommy what's happening? What's that smell?" Ellie cries. As the smell of burning rubber fills the air and the look of terror on her face rips at my heart like nothing else has before.

I lock my eyes with hers in the rearview mirror. "Eloise. Sweetie. No, matter what happens, I won't let anything, or anyone hurt you. Do you trust me?"

The expression that takes hold on her face makes me believe her words. "I twust you."

I move my concentration forward, to the rogues that have taken an interest in the commotion I'm causing. They look at each other and I can see they're confused. Two of them start toward us on foot. I falter for a second but then Stacy breaks the silence.

"Do it." Two simple words, but her voice laced with anger, determination, and most noteworthy, her excitement at kicking rogue ass. I start a countdown in my head. 10, 9, 8, 7, 6, 5... Now I see six more walking in our direction. The closer they get the better this will work. 4, 3, 2, . . . "Hold on to Aunt Stacy!" I shout to Ellie.

1... I hit the emergency brake, turning it off and the SUV goes flying forward. I quickly change lanes and pull the gas control all the way toward me. We knock into one rogue and the others jump out of the way. Blowing past them as fast as we can. The bastards go running to their fake cop cars and throw on the sirens. I have a big lead on them and I'm now swerving in and out of traffic. I'm hyper focused on the task at hand, while Ellie and Stacy remain quiet in the back.

"Landon, is there another way into the territory?" I shout. "I don't want to lead them to the main access road."

"Mal, keep going straight. We can hear you coming and we're going to intercept. Drive passed for at least twenty minutes then turn around and come back."

"Okay baby be safe."

We're approaching where the main road leads to our pack. Within seconds, wolves are on either side of the road in the brush.

"Damn girl, where did you learn to drive?" Landon's voice bounces off the inside of the SUV as I zoom past another car.

"Just another one of my hidden talents. Okay listen there are eight of them and I think they doubled up. So, look out for at least four cars." I glance back again and see the first car with a flashing light gaining on me.

"Mal go faster, we got this."

I hit the gas again. That is when I hear it, glass shattering. "Landon, what was that?"

Silence...

"Landon?" I can't help the desperation in my voice.

"I'm here. It's all good. Just to be safe, drive another ten minutes ahead. We are following you in the woods."

I do as he says. After ten minutes, a bunch of our guy's wave at me to slow down. I start hitting the break. "Now pull off the road on your right. I will be right there."

Landon exits the woods in just a pair of basketball shorts. He runs over to the driver's side, whipping the door open. I barely get my seat belt off before he's pulling me into his arms. He is kissing me everywhere, "My little Luna, I know in like ten years we are going to look back at this crazy time and laugh... I'm just not laughing now."

"Why did you go silent? I panicked." I scold him.

"Listen, Mario Andretti. I had to shift to keep up with you. I had my phone in my mouth." He says with a laugh. All of a sudden, we both turn to the back seat and see Stacy breathing heavily, her hair is standing on end and she looks scared shitless, but all we can think about is Ellie.

"Ellie are you okay?" Landon moves behind me, fumbles with her seatbelt then pulls her out of the back seat and into his arms. He gives her a big hug and kiss on the forehead. She pulls back and just kind of blinks a couple of times. Then a smile brighter than the sun, cracks across her face.

"THAT WAS AMAZING! Did you see mom burn the rubber off the tires?! This was better than Mawio Kawt!!! We even knocked a wogue over! Holy crap!"

"Ellie! . . . Language!" We scold in unison.

"Amazing?! Ellie, are you crazy? Malinda, I swear I'm never... ever driving with you again."

Everyone starts laughing, and Ellie can't control her giggles. "I have the best family EVER!"

Chapter 20
Landon

  I have a bunch of warriors cleaning up the cars and dragging the rogues to the cells. I'm ready to kill them. All of them. They went after two Lunas and a pup... More specifically my Luna and my pup. I can't help the growl that ripples through me at the thought of my girls being scared.

  Damn it though... I need the fucking bastards alive. I need answers.

  "Landon, go back with the girls. We got this covered here." The look on Sam's face says it all, he was scared for his Luna. Even he didn't want to leave Mal alone.

  We had got the girls back on pack lands, Mal insisted that she was fine and that I should finish giving the guy's direction and head back when I was done. But something that she keeps forgetting is how possessive and protective I am over what is mine. I know damn well that Sam and Troy have everything under control. So, I shift and follow behind the girl's SUV in wolf form. Dex is just itching to kill who ever dares to fuck with his family.

  Mal parks the car and goes to grab Ellie from the back seat. Not needing to traumatize my daughter anymore, I throw on some shorts that are stored in one of the fake storage trees. They are weatherproof containers shaped to look like tree trunks. We have med kits, clean clothes, water and snacks inside them all. I thought it was a cool idea the triplets came up with. Troy being their older brother was more than happy to make this happen, it totally comes in handy, and nothing is ever weather beaten. But apparently this particular tree is out of t-shirts, and the new tattoo I had done this morning in honor of my mate and daughter is very much visible.

I already have a large tattoo that goes up my right arm, and spreads over my shoulder. It's a mixture of our pack's crest, along with images of my parents' wolves. My guy Sonny added some more detail that makes it look like it is transitioning into feathers and falling away. Representative of me letting go of the past hurt. The feathers become mixed with flower petals, and they are raining down on three crowned wolves. The piece takes up my whole back and took three guys to finish it today. I wanted it to be a surprise. Now it's on display to everyone. I just pray that she does not notice, but that's pretty much impossible.

I hear the concerned voices of our pack members that begin surrounding Mal as I jog up to them.

"Luna, are you and Ellie, okay?"

"Luna, can you teach me to drive with my hands?"

"Do you need anything Luna?"

I know everyone is worried, however they're bombarding her with questions. I don't know how she can handle the attention after the experience she just had. But Mal's handling it like the true Luna she is. Smiling at everyone, reassuring them she is perfectly fine. After the inquisition is over, she opens the SUV door to pull all the dresses out. Stacy tries to take them, but Mal insists that she has it under control.

"Baby, give me the dresses. You should take Stacy and Ellie to dinner. I think Mrs. Lane made you some crazy, amazing dessert." I know I'm playing dirty, but dirty gets it done... and I like it dirty. She smiles up at me and gives me a cute little wink. I throw the bags over my shoulder. Boom crisis averted! All thank you Mrs. Lane.

I run the dresses upstairs, then make my way to the dining room, Mal is in the buffet line with Ellie. What I see makes me love her even more. She's waiting in line like everyone else. She has every right as Luna to go to the front of the line but not my queen. I grab a plate and stand a few people behind them. Pack members offer for me to cut the line but that would defeat the purpose of showing the pack that we are one.

I can't help but think to myself that my grandmother would have loved Mal. After all it was her who started having the whole pack helping with kitchen chores. And in honor of that tradition the Alpha family and top warriors have volunteered for clean up tonight so everyone can get home and rest for the big day tomorrow.

The rest of dinner is filled with laughter and many toasts made by our beloved pack members. The sense of pride and love I feel for these people is beyond reproach. Mrs. Lane and the kitchen staff finish eating their meals, while dessert is being served. Tonight, the warrior families are bringing out dessert and their pups are so excited to be helping. Once Ellie's dessert is placed in front of her, she is practically screaming with joy.

"Ellie calm down sweet pea" Mal says with a laugh.

"I can't!!! This is my second favorite dessert ever!" She jumps up onto her chair looking for Mrs. Lane in the crowd. Once she makes eye contact with her Mrs. Lane can't control her smile or laughter.

"You WOCK Mrs. Lane!!! Ladies, gentlemen and pups! I give you what I call "home sweet home!" It's a chocolate mug cake with chopped up Weese's Peanut Butter Cups in the middle with cawamel pouwed on top!" Ellie dramatically waves her arms at her dessert concoction then bows. Everyone claps and giggles with her. She's such a ball of energy. Everyone digs in and the look of shock on their faces on how good it is makes Ellie giggle and scream with excitement even more!

"Ha, see I told you!!!" She shouts.

Mal is helping with Ellie's bath and nighttime routine. While I put on a pot of coffee and tea. I hear Mal call for me. "Be right there baby." Ellie's climbing into bed in her cute Chewbacca footie pj's. It even has a hoodie! I had told her how much I loved the Star Wars movies and said she was obsessed with Chewie! So, Mal ordered us matching Chewbacca pj's!

I kiss Ellie's damp hair. "You definitely had an interesting day sweetheart."

"Suwe did! Can I tell you a secwet if you pwomise to nevew tell anyone?"

Mal and I exchange a look of confusion, but nod our heads, letting her know that her secret is safe with us.

"I might have had a bwave face on today, but I was actually weally scared. I mean—you dwiving is so cool mom. But yeah, I was scawed the wogues were going to get you. Well, you and Aunt Stacy, I don't think she is scawed of wogues as she was your dwiving mommy."

"Oh Eloise, I'm so sorry that you had to be in that situation in the first place. I hope you know that I would never put you in danger on purpose." Mal's eyes glisten with unshed tears.

"Mommy, I did not think I was in dangew, I thought you were. You guys are mine now and I'm scawed to lose you."

We tuck her in, with big hugs, kisses and extra tickles. Mal starts to sing "You Are My Sunshine" to her, brushing her hair out of her eyes and pulling the comforter up to her chin. Ellie just stares at us with love in her eyes. Mal leans over and kisses the top of her head. "I love you to the moon, stars and back again."

Chapter 21
Landon

After we tuck Ellie into bed, Mal and I head to the kitchen. My original game plan for tonight consisted of candles and flowers being set up all over the back garden. I was going to get down on one knee and officially propose.

I know it seems crazy. Why propose if we're getting married tomorrow? The *why* is simply, I wanted her to have this special moment. Then the rest of my night was going to be spent in the triplet's apartment with the rest of the guys. I didn't want a bachelor party. I just wanted to watch a baseball game and enjoy a cold beer with my friends. And I can assure you that after this afternoon's adventure, I don't fucking care about the tradition. Fuck what people think... bad luck to see the bride on the day of the wedding, my ass. I'm not leaving her goddamn side.

I sip my coffee, just staring straight ahead. Not really focusing on anything in particular, just waiting for Mal to get out of the bathroom. Lost in thought, I begin milling over the day's events. I'm still in disbelief that these rogues were able to pull off the damn roadblock, the humans in this so-called traffic jam totally clueless.

One may wonder how we were able to have this earth-shattering war and how the humans remained none the wiser. It's true there were some humans who helped us fight the war, but they had already been exposed to our world. Whether it was by family members, mates, or friends. But if an area was decimated during the war, we had witches cast spells over the humans making them think that what happened to their towns was an act of mother nature. Whether it be tornado, earthquake, hurricane, you name it they believed it.

The City of Paisley is surrounded by several packs and covens but is still a human city so it's imperative that we blend in. What really bothers me about today is that these rogues were near the main road leading to our territory. It's like they knew Mal was going to be off of pack lands, but how.

"Ughhhh." I put down my coffee cup and rub my palms down my face. This night should be spent celebrating but instead, I've got to try and figure this shit out. First things first, we need to triple security for tomorrow.

"Baby, are you okay?"

I look up to see Mal already at the table in an old green and gold Stone Mountain High t-shirt, gray leggings and white fuzzy socks. She pours herself a cup of oolong tea and takes a sip while it is piping hot.

"How do you not burn your throat when you drink it that hot?"

She kind of giggles and shrugs her shoulders. "Are you headed to the office? I know you have to deal with what happened today." She says as the smile on her face begins to fade.

"Malinda, look at me." She lifts her gaze to mine. Those beautiful green eyes pierce my soul. Standing, I stride over to her. I pull out the chair next to her and sit so I'm facing her. "You and Ellie are my top priority." I swallow past the lump in my throat. "Today someone tried to take you away from me. They tried to take my woman and my pup." I can't stop the wave of possessiveness that overcomes me. "What pisses me off is I've got no clue as to who they are and how they knew you were going to be off pack lands."

"Landon, maybe they just got lucky today." She places her teacup on the table and grabs my large hand in her small one. "Or maybe this isn't the first time they did something like this. Maybe they've been doing this for a while. Thinking eventually, we would have to leave the territory."

"That's it!"

"What's it?" She asks with big eyes. I jump from my seat, grabbing Mal's face in my hands and kiss her on the head.

"Woman, you are a genius. But before I head to my office." I rush to my jacket. Retrieving the ring I stashed in the pocket earlier. I turn around, my hands behind my back so she can't see the blue velvet box. I prowl toward her, never breaking our gaze the sight before me causes my chest to tighten, she's so fucking beautiful. I think I will forever be ensnared in the web of her beautiful green orbs. I get down on my knees and turn her wheelchair, so I have her full attention. I reach and take her left hand in mine.

"This is absolutely not how I planned to do this, and if something would have happened to you today... and not being able to do this would have been my biggest regret." I say as I raise her hand to my lips. "I love you and I can't wait for all of the tomorrows that will come. Officially being connected in this life and the next." I wiggle my eyebrows playfully. "So, Malinda, will you do me the greatest honor in the world and become my wife?"

It takes a second for it to sink in, but soon Malinda is frantically nodding her head up and down. Throwing her arms around me and sobbing into the crook of my neck. I take a moment to revel in this feeling. That of being in the arms of the woman I love. Gently, I pull away and place the ring on her delicate finger. She barely looks at the ring before my face is pulled to hers and we share a passionate kiss.

"I love you." She breathes.

"I love you more." I whisper back.

Sam interrupts our moment with a mindlink.

-We are going to see if Dr. K will lend us Trinity for the interrogation but wanted to clear it with you first.

-Not a problem.

Turning my attention back to my woman, I give her another quick kiss. "I need to make some calls, check in with the guys who are interrogating the rogues tonight, and tighten security for tomorrow." I see her nod her head in understanding, but I can see the disappointment in her eyes.

"You know after my first mating ceremony to Jared; you could feel the tension in the air. We knew that the war was coming. Now..." She was facing me but looking past me as if remembering what happened all those years ago. "Ugh, Landon I don't think we can avoid a fight, but this time I think that is all this will be, just a fight. We need to be a united front, stick together and fight together. We are a strong pack; we will be fine."

I lean in and let my lips gently claim hers, holding them there a moment. Thoroughly enjoying the sparks that dance between us. Her scent invades my senses and calms my soul. I place my hand under her chin and guide her to look me in the eyes. At a loss for words, I palm her cheek with my hand. Knowing that is only one word I need her to hear.

"Mine."

"Yours."

I hold her eyes for a long moment, then I head out. As soon as the door closes behind me, I link Ben, telling him to get his ass to the apartment to protect Mal, Ellie and Stacy.

My office chair squeaks as I plop my tired body down. My quiet moment is shattered as Sam and Troy burst into my office,

Overflowing with energy, Sam immediately starts talking. "You will not believe who is in the cell right now!"

I respond with a bit of annoyance because I'm not in the mood for games right now. "Just tell me."

"Do you remember the guy that was standing outside the hotel in Paisley? My wolf kept telling me there was something off about him. Well, he's currently sitting in our cell." I sit straight up as I try to recall the memory. "I was staring at him because I could not place him, it was driving me crazy, because he looked so familiar. Then it hit me. I grabbed my phone and checked the picture you sent me. I'm a hundred percent sure this is the same guy."

Sam tosses me the phone and I look at the screen. The man in the image appears to be put together on the surface, but when I zoom in the telltale signs of being a rogue become more visible. "Is he talking?" I ask handing the phone back to him.

"No, are we going to have to go hard core in the interrogation tonight, or should we wait until tomorrow?"

"I want you and Troy to do whatever you feel is necessary. You need to get something out of one of them. Call Trinity in for this. I know it's not her usual setting, but she may prove to be vital." I start to feel a headache coming on. The first prisoner we had that attacked with the Gold Moon kids turned out to be a peaceful rogue that had a mate and kid. His pack was killed during the war and never found a new pack for his family. He fell on tough times and needed money desperately. So, when someone gave him a time and place to show up for "work," he did. He had no memory of anything after that until he woke up in our hospital. We had Trinity come and check to make sure that he was telling the truth and sure as shit there was no lie in his story. Mal ended up offering him and his family a place in our pack on a probationary period.

"Okay I am going to call all of our major allies and see if they can get here tonight, early tomorrow morning at the latest."

Sam and Troy nod. "We'll see what we can get out of these guys. Make your calls and then get to bed. Try not to worry too much, enjoy this moment with your mate." Troy says as he stands and heads for the door.

"Wow, Troy. Who knew you could be sooo sentimental?" I tease. "Listen I promise that I'm not going to be consumed by this till after tomorrow, I've just got this nagging feeling that today was just a preview of what's to come." I rub the back of my neck in frustration,

"Why can't Mal and I just catch a freaking break." I say to no one in particular.

"Sam and I got this okay, we promise to update you tomorrow morning."

I grab my phone to call the Alpha's. They should be getting ready to come to our territory for the wedding. Hopefully I'm able to convince them to bring more warriors. Maybe even strategize after the wedding, once I tell them of the possible threat, I don't think they'll argue. I start to dial the phone, take a deep breath and hit send. "Wish me Luck."

Chapter 22
Sam

Troy and I head for the cells after leaving Landon's office. When we get to the kitchen Trinity is sitting at the counter waiting for us. She stands from her chair and somehow loses the grip on her phone. The damn thing flies in the air and at the last second Troy reaches out to catch it.

"Hey, that was close." He says as he hands it back to her then turns to me. "Are we going easy on these guys or are we going hard core?"

"Alpha said to do whatever is necessary." I say as we reach the bottom of the stairs. I open the storage closet door, removing a large black duffle bag. I look over my shoulder to see a sick fucking grin on Troy's face.

"Hard core, nice choice." I roll my eyes at the asshole, but even I can't deny the man is fucking good at getting people to crack under pressure.

"First we need to figure out if these guys are affected by the same magic the kids from Gold Moon were. If they're under a spell, then Trinity will be able to figure it out. If they are not controlled by magic, then we need to figure out who they are working for, who is behind the attack on our Luna and little Ellie."

I stop in my tracks and turn. "Trinity, are you ready for this?" I eye her for any fear.

"Yeah Sam, I mean, yeah I'm a little scared but I will do anything for our Luna." I nod accepting her answer.

"Trin, I will be right there the whole time. I promise nothing will happen to you." Her face flushes at Troy's words, but she recovers quickly.

"You better not! I turn eighteen in two hours and if I die before I meet my mate I will come back and haunt your ass, Troy." Trinity sasses. She is going to fit right in.

Our goal is to have her listen in on the questioning so she can figure out if the captive is honest or not. She's about to walk into her first interrogation room, so I don't blame her for being a bit nervous.

Stepping inside the cell doors, I find the triplets with stoic expressions on their faces as they lean against the concrete block walls. In the center is a metal table and just one chair. There's a thick old wooden beam secured in the corners of the dark, damp room. At the top of each beam are security cameras, giving Landon the opportunity to check in on interrogations, when need be, and it looks like he has missed quite the show. The triplets have already done a number on this guy. I'm really proud of how strong they have become, more so now that they are mated. Even if it is with my sister.

A sweaty, bloody and dirty figure sits shackled to a cold metal chair. As I enter the room, he lunges for me bearing his canines, but is violently pulled back by the chain around his neck. He growls as Tom delivers a hard upper, throwing him back into the chair. He's either pretty stupid or very arrogant, however he has given Troy the impression that he's in some type of leadership position. I double check the picture on my phone. Yep, this is him. It would be quite a conundrum if we beat the shit out of the wrong person.

Quiet as a mouse, Trinity slides into the room behind us. The woman is pressed so hard against the wall that you can't tell where she ends, and the wall begins. I almost feel bad for her, but we are here to do a job. We are here to keep our queen safe.

I slam the duffel bag onto the table, and slowly unzip it. The sound of the zipper clicking open has the grin on Troy's face growing with each notch. It's been a while since I've had to open this bag. Peering inside, the tools have me finding it hard to hide my excitement. I drag my gaze up from my bag o' goodies and smile at the prisoner.

Revenge!

He just rolls his eyes at me as I dramatically remove things one by one. I may be putting on a show, but I'm definitely not playing any fucking games.

"Ohhh what do we have here? Hmmmm, wire cutters, pliers, tasers... oh and this here..." I say holding the blowtorch up. "...is a personal favorite of mine." Each time a new tool is set on the old, worn table, it makes a satisfying clunk, almost making me giddy. I typically don't take pleasure in having to torture someone, but this time is different. This time, it's extremely personal and this time, it's going to be very, very painful.

"Really? That's your favorite?" Troy saddles up next to me, reaches into the duffle and extracts a large vial of wolfsbane. "I like this."

The man barks out a snort mixed with a cough. "You think this is going to get me to talk?" He jerks his chin toward the objects in front of him. "Your *worst* is child's play to my boss."

"Who is your boss?" I rest my hand lightly on the blowtorch as if I'm contemplating using it. "Listen, you either tell us what we need to know, or we let our Alpha come at you." Everything is silent for a moment until I grab the knife at my waist and fling it with perfect precision past the rouges right ear into the wooden beam behind him.

"And I can assure you, he's fucking pissed that you went after his mate and pup." Tony chimes in. His words cause the rogue's brow to furrow.

"Did you not know that your target was our Luna?" Tony questions in exaggerated disbelief.

No answer... Troy grabs a syringe from the bag and begins to fill it.

"I'm only going to ask you this one more time. Did you know that your target was our Luna?"

Silence.

My patience is wearing thin with this guy. I'm thinking the only thing that will help with it, is fire.

After a few more seconds I spark the blowtorch. The whooshing noise it makes when the gas is ignited is the very balm, I needed to soothe my aggravations.

Apparently, Troy finds his serenity a different way. He grabs the guy's hair and yanks his head back, exposing the tanned and dark bristled column of his neck. With a steady hand he lines the syringe up to the struggling man's pulsating vein.

A loud slap of hands on a table pauses me on my trek to create a disgusting version of S'mores. The sharp noise has all three of us looking over to see Trinity standing at the opposite end table, her fists clenched.

"Listen asshole, these fine gentlemen are going to fuck you up, and I couldn't care less. But what I want to know is why are you so shocked that Luna has a pup."

She slowly stalks around the table then stops in front of the bastard. She casually leans her butt against its metal edge as she keeps eye contact with him. He licks his lips in an obvious ploy to unnerve her, but to Trinity's credit, all she does is lay her hands flat on the steel surface behind her and cross her legs.

"Answer her," Troy demands. His fist tightens in the man's grimy hair. If he pulls any harder the bastard may not have his head for long.

"It's not possible for her to be pregnant." He grits, gaining our full attention.

I bring the torch's blue flame to the flesh of his arm. The sound of his sizzling skin is dulled by his piercing screams.

"How would you know that our Luna can't get pregnant?" Troy demands.

"I know a lot about your so-called Luna." Although in pain, the man still tries to give off the impression that he's still in control of his faculties. I think we need to remind him—he's not.

Troy angrily jabs the syringe into his neck and harshly pushes the plunger down with his thumb. Wolfsbane rushes into the man's system, fast and hard. This is the type of pain that I wouldn't wish on my own enemy.

Well, except for this guy.

Just as the man screams from the shot's savagery, Trinity lifts her foot and kicks him in the balls. Hard. The noises coming from this man are nauseating.

"Trin, can you please leave the violence to us." Troy asks with a smirk as he steps back from the writhing man.

"Why should I let you guys have all the fun? Besides…" She crosses her arms in front of her and scrunches her nose at Troy. The syringe shatters on the ground as he drops it, his hands up "…he's keeping something from us. And I'll do whatever it takes to keep my Luna safe." She states with conviction as she pulls back a tiny fist aimed at the bastard's nose.

"Wait!" Troy bellows and she pauses mid punch. "Tuck in your thumb."

She gives him an impish smile and slides her little thumb in place. Not a second later Trinity right hooks the scumbag in the face. Even in agonizing pain the rogue still makes the futile move of trying to attack Trinity. However, Troy sees it coming and moves her behind him in one quick movement. The rage on the rogue's face tells me that we are going to have to get even dirtier.

After fifteen minutes half of my tools are covered in gunk and the rogue is drifting in and out of consciousness. By this point the three of us are saturated in his blood. Turns out Trinity is a great enforcer and I'm pretty sure we have found our new partner in crime. Trinity and Troy work in perfect tandem on a new technique.

Troy holds the rogue's hands down flat on the table as she stabs the knife between each of his fingers at a high rate of speed. "I'm starting to like this game." She says with a devilish smirk.

"FUCK!" He screams as she misses, and the tip of her blade penetrates his hand. I doubt this was an actual mistake though, because Trinity seems to have "accidentally" stabbed the only unmarried expanse of skin left on that body part.

"Oops." Her maniacal little giggle makes me thank the goddess and all of her creations that Trinity is on our side.

"Fine, I'll talk, but put her in a cage or something." He snarls out a mist of blood. "I thought male warriors were brutal. Fucking bitch." His words cause Troy to growl at the desperate man in front of us.

I laugh long and deep, "I can assure you; our female warriors are just as savage as our males. However, I have to admit, our females do have an advantage because of shit gobblers like you who underestimate them."

Trinity takes a big sigh, rips the knife from his hand and lets it clatter to the cement floor. "Whatever." Trin says with a flip of her hair as she makes her way to the corner of the dingy room. "Talk." She demands as she sits.

"Okay, it doesn't matter anyway, you'll kill me, or my boss does, either way I'm a dead man." Either my communication skills are lacking, or his hearing is because I'm fairly certain that statement was the theme of the night. "Somehow my boss found out about your Luna. He heard that she is the daughter of the Moon Goddess… he realized that when she mated, her powers would be unbeatable. We waited…but she never got powers." His breaths come out in harsh pants as the adrenaline from the last fifteen minutes begins to wear off. He gasps as a crimson trickle falls down his lip and joins the cornucopia of other bodily fluids contained within his beard.

"Doubt started to spread within our ranks that she was a goddess on earth. Here was this obnoxiously strong she-wolf. Practically untouchable, but no powers. There was supposed to be some prophecy that a powerful she-wolf would come to save the world and stop all evil. That her powers would be unmatched. And fuck was she strong-" he pauses as if remembering the time, he saw a demonstration of her incredible talents. "- but she had no magic. Some of us thought she was a distraction to the real savior of the supernatural's. We had to destroy her in order to draw out the real warrior. I was tasked with injecting her. I had no clue what it was, I just do as I'm told."

"Are you the one who broke her back?" Trinity asks, inching her way to her discarded knife.

He looks down at his bound hands. "Yeah." The fucker isn't looking down because he has remorse. He's looking down because he knows he's going to finally get his dose of karma.

Or should I say, his dose of Trinity.

It happens so quickly that I'm glad I didn't blink. Suddenly Trinity is standing there with her knife in hand, like an Avenging Angel of Death. She drives it into his arm with such force that I swear I heard the blade hitting bone.

"You mother fucking bitch!" The asshole shrieks and bucks his hips wildly. Troy lunges toward him and with a gloved hand he pulls the silver chains tight forcing him deep into the chair.

"Why are you only going after her now?" Troy demands as Trinity yanks the knife from his arm.

"SHIT.... okay, okay." He whines. "Listen, I don't know all of the details, but I believe that it's because she found her mate. Boss man wants to take over the four major packs of the area. We haven't killed her because we're trying to reveal the true goddess on earth. The boss figured if we got the bitch out of the way the goddess would've come to save her. But when she watched that asshole of a mate of hers die—

something happened that no one expected. She did magic." He finishes on a groan.

"Our chance to kill her was gone. Most of our soldiers were dead. We had to wait. She was injured. Her mate...dead. She wasn't a threat anymore. Somehow he kept p...p...poisoning her." He starts stuttering, fatigue and blood loss getting too overwhelming. "Then she met that guy...her mate. Somehow... somehow, he found out about the poison. She's gonna heal. Over... over time. Heal without poison. She may even get her powers...be stronger than before. She might even be able to take out my boss."

"How did he keep the drugs in her system?" I ask, clenching my fists, trying to restrain myself from punching him in the mouth lest he end his confessional. My blood is quickly reaching its boiling point. I want fucking answers.

He blinks his swollen eyes, trying to hold onto consciousness. "We have allies...everywhere. People keeping it in her system. She had no clue. It would...they would put it in her drinks...in her food. People she trusted... people she shouldn't have trusted. She can't have babies. It made her sterile. Having a pup is impossible."

Sick of his bullshit, I raise my fist.

"Hey!" Trinity cries out at me, making me pause midair. "Don't forget to tuck in your thumb." She quips, as she grins like a fool.

The metal door slamming against the cement wall is our only warning before Landon is standing in the broken doorway, chest heaving, and half shifted. Apparently, he has heard enough out of our captive. All knowing that our job is done, we back out of the room and gingerly close the door that's hanging on by only one hinge. We hear a loud roar from Dex, Landon's wolf, then the last scream the rogue will ever make.

Chapter 23
Troy

After Landon killed the first rogue, we went to interrogate the others. Trinity's ability really does come in handy. Not going to lie, she is freaking kick ass in the interrogation room. When the three of us entered the next room to question the rogue inside, we didn't need to do a thing to get information out of him. I like to think it's because I look intimidating, but it probably had something more to do with the fact that we had blood dripping from our clothing.

After questioning the rest of the prisoners, we realized quickly they knew nothing. Trinity was able to discern that they had no clue what the real job was. The rogues just followed instructions, basically free muscle for the guy in charge. Two hours passed by the time we returned to the kitchen. Making a beeline for the bathroom to wash up, Trinity hustles off. Sam heads straight for the whiskey. He pulls out three heavy, crystal glasses, placing them on the counter with a loud clanking noise. His bloody fingerprints smudge the pristine etching in the glass.

Landon's slumped form is already at the large island, sitting in a chair with an open bottle of bourbon and a full glass in front of him. He's just staring down into the gold liquid, absentmindedly tapping his index finger against it. The blood that he earned from destroying that asshole still speckles his body. Lost in thought, he almost misses it when Sam asks him how he's doing.

He lets out a big sigh. "I am getting married in the morning and I will officially become Ellie's father. I just killed the one lead we had in months... because I could not control my emotions. I am disappointed in myself."

"Alpha... Landon, dude you did what was needed to protect our Luna and your pup. No one faults you for it. Fuck, if you hadn't come in, I'm fairly certain one of us would have done the same exact thing to him. We have the interview on tape, and we will review it, commit it to memory. We will find who is behind all of this." Landon pauses his tapping while swirling around the words I had just spoken, in his head. Then his eyebrow raises at the loud, feminine voice that breaks the short silence.

"That smells wonderful!" Trinity yells, as she walks back to the kitchen. Her long blonde hair is still a little wet and she has taken off her saturated shirt and is now just wearing her tank top and jeans.

"What smells wonderful?" Sam calls out, while lifting his chin, nostrils flaring in a deep inhale.

"It kind of smells like hot chocolate, I thought you said after a good interrogation, whisky was the only acceptable drink?"

She walks through the doorway and stops dead in her tracks. "Holy Shit," she says as she looks at me with a big smile.

"Holy shit, what?" I say back to her. We are all looking at her now, we see her smile fall, then blinks rapidly. Is she blinking back...tears?

"Trinity what's wrong?" Landon asks with concern.

"N-nothing Alpha, I... um... apparently am just really tired and got emotional. Tonight, must have affected me more than I thought." She quickly wipes at her eyes.

"I'm not buying that line of bull shit that just came out of your mouth." Sam is now staring her down, but she is too busy fiddling with her hands. Her chest rises and falls very quickly. Landon swiftly steps to the fridge and pulls out an ice pack. He tenderly places it on the back of her neck. Maybe she is hyperventilating or overheating, or maybe shock has hit her.

Landon's full attention is on her now. "Trinity, obviously something just happened. I want you to tell me the truth, please do not make me use my Alpha command."

A sob rips through her, shaking her chest. A fist squeezes my lungs, making it hard to breathe. The sound of her crying is more painful than any of the screams I've heard tonight.

"I turned eighteen, two minutes ago Alpha, and I found my mate."

The three of us look at each other in confusion. Oh goddess, is it one of the rogues? Can she smell their scent from up here? Since Sam and Landon are mated males, it would be inappropriate for them to comfort her. They would end up going back to their mates tonight smelling like her and let's just say... not a smart decision.

I stride next to her and pull her in for a hug. She stiffens at first, but after a few hiccups, she quickly melts into me. I softly run my hand up and down her back, feeling calm slowly cover her like a blanket. After I'm confident she can talk, I pull back a little and look into her blue eyes. "Who is it... one of the rogues?"

She shakes her head back and forth almost in slow motion, her eyes never leaving mine.

"Trin, who?"

"Y-you," she says barely above a whisper.

I tilt my head at her confession. Obviously, I must have heard her wrong. I'm twenty-six years old and have already met my mate. Her name is- was Katie. She died in a car accident, with a few other teenagers, three days after she turned eighteen. I was devastated. Still am. The last eight years I've just been living day by day, my head barely staying above water.

Second chance mates just started to really make a comeback after the war. We could always choose a mate, but I wanted mine to be Fated. Survivors of the war who lost their mates in battle were starting to be blessed with second chance mates. I figured since my mate did not die in the great war, I was not getting another.

"Is this a mistake? I must have made the goddess mad. She has blessed me with a mate who has no bond to me." Her sobbing started up again and I squeezed her against me. "What could I have done to anger her?"

"Trinity, you did nothing wrong," Sam soothes from behind the counter. "You guys just have to do something... intimate."

Then Landon pipes up "Troy, a fated second chance mate, needs that intimacy to awaken that part of their wolf again. It was a kiss for Mal and me. For others it could need a little more."

"Troy, do you think it is possible that I am your second chance?"

I gaze back down into her eyes and nod.

What happens if I kiss her, and I don't feel anything? Will this poor girl be stuck with a one-sided relationship? Could I fall in love with her naturally? Fuck... I feel like I am losing my mind.

"I'm sorry that you lost your first mate, that must have been so hard."

I nod my head again, still a little too shocked to speak.

She has beautiful eyes.

"You are standing in front of me, and I feel like my heart is being ripped out because you don't feel the bond. Something tells me that this is just a very small percentage of how you must have felt over the years."

My eyes start to water. Damn it Troy, hold it together. In the typical world, I'm too old to be matched with this young woman. But if it was meant to be, then the eight years that separate us doesn't matter. Wolves consider age a moot point because the mate bond is so intense.

I lift my head toward my brothers, but they seem to have left the room. It is just the two of us. I return my gaze to the tear tracks on her cheeks. Ever so slowly, I lift my hand to her and wrap my fingers around her neck and let the pad of my thumb rest on her pink bottom lip.

Damn, she also has beautiful lips.

I stare at where flesh meets flesh and am mesmerized at how natural this feels. I rub the wet of her tears across her mouth. I have the urge to lick the salt off of them. She moves into my touch, her and her wolf desperate to wake the bond in me.

I slide my thumb down and gently lift her chin, so her eyes are upon mine once again. My heart is thumping so loudly, she has to hear it. Trinity's breathing becomes quicker and heavier. If she doesn't calm down, she may actually hyperventilate.

I lower my forehead to hers and take a moment, just breathing each other's air. I am trying to help Max, my wolf, he feels so confused. He is not coming forward to discuss this.

"Max, this is our chance at being happy and I am going to take it. I want us to feel whole again, we both deserve that."

...

"Max."

...

"Max, my friend, please."
"Okay, let's try."

With his small expression of consent, I rub my nose against hers. Her head tilts, the action causes our lips to graze each other. Trying to hold onto my self-control. My fingers tighten around the back of her neck, pulling her closer. The feel of her soft skin under my calloused hands, causing a hum to erupt from my throat at the contact. I wrap my other arm around her waist, not even a slip of paper can get between us now.

I must've been going too slow for her because in the next breath, her arms wind around my neck. Lips that taste like honey, press against mine with urgency. Lost in the moment, I find myself lifting her up as she wraps her legs around my waist. My hands slide under her plump ass to hold her up. I take a few steps toward the counter and slowly place her on it. Her teeth tug on my bottom lip. Throwing caution to the wind and give her access. The feel of her tongue in my mouth is exquisite.

Trinity pulls me tighter to her, not giving a shit that we're both covered in blood. I run my hands up her thighs, to her waist. My fingers play with the hem of her shirt desperately wanting to slide under the fabric and feel the warmth of her skin. She shivers in anticipation, and this little action makes my cock twitch. That's when it hits me, the smell of her arousal.

Her sweet scent of warm honey engulfs me all at once. A bolt of electricity shoots through my veins. The surge of energy has my heart beating erratically and for the first time in eight years I sense Max growl in pleasure. The sensation causes Trinity to grind her core against my now painfully hard erection. Making it even more painful, but this kind of pain I'd beg for. The intensity of our kiss has us both gasping for air. Her lips are a beautiful shade of pink, and I think it's my new favorite color. Our eyes connect and I move my hands to her cheeks, happy to discover her tears have turned to those of happiness.

"Mine." I growl with passion and excitement. Max is howling as he calls for Trinity's wolf.

I take her small hand in my and place it over my heart while she takes my other over hers. "Yours."

LANDON

Sam and I step out of the kitchen to give them a moment alone, but we stall outside the dining room door, guarding it from anyone that may try to grab a snack from the kitchen. Troy needs his moment, and I don't think Trinity, or her wolf can handle waiting. It must have been so confusing for her, for both of them.

After denying entrance to the kitchen for a few warriors, they took it upon themselves to start taking bets on how long it's going to take them to get their shit together and accept the bond. Ten minutes later, Troy bursts out of the kitchen at warp speed walking with Trinity's legs wrapped around his waist. His hands are on her ass and his tongue is in her mouth. They are practically swallowing each other. Sam and I can't help cheering at their happiness. It's always great to see two wolves find their mates.

Hoots and hollers fill the room, with a few looking pissed as they pass some cash to the apparent winner. Troy, without stopping, removes one hand from his mate's ass to flip us off. We all can't help but laugh, making Tory smirk against her lips. All of a sudden Trinity breaks the kiss and pulls Troy's hair, so he is focused on her again.

"Bedroom NOW!" She growls causing the room to go dead silent.

"Yes ma'am," he says before slamming his mouth back to hers as he sprints for the stairs.

A moment later, a door slams preceded by loud crashes. Everyone just stares at each other, wide eyed. Another loud bang breaks the silence as we all explode into laughter once again.

"He's going to be exhausted tomorrow." Sam laughs.

I nod my head in agreement.

"Okay Sam, why don't you head back to Lara and get a good night's sleep?"

"I will. I also linked the triplets; they're going to review the guest list and make sure no names or similar names for that matter come up from our list of potential suspects. You know, the one we made during Luna's big hospital stay." He says as he pushes off the wall. "I'll also have them review security footage to see if any of the rogues from the cells come up. Maybe we can catch one of them looking cozy with someone. Then we'll talk to Mal and see if she recognizes anyone."

"Thank you." I say with a nod. We hear another loud crash causing everyone to look toward the staircase.

"Harder, Troy!"

"FUCK Yes, Oh Goddess Yes!"

Clattering continues to echo from upstairs. Then we hear a very loud roar. I look around at everyone's knowing grin. Pretty sure Trinity just marked Troy.

"Holy Shit!" Comes a corresponding scream... annnnnnd now she is marked.

Our head of construction guy, Rich, walks in the front door, looking worse for the wear. In his right hand are several rolls of soundproofing tape and a hammer.

"On it guys, don't worry." He says as he heads up the stairs.

"Who linked you?" I ask with a chuckle.

That's when ten guys raise their hands, causing another bout of raucous laughter.

Chapter 24
MALINDA

Things didn't go as planned yesterday but nothing will stop me from making it great today. For this is the day I marry my best friend and my true mate. Also, today I will officially become a mother even though in my heart I feel like I've been her mother forever. Ellie just has a way about her, she takes you in with her whole heart.

I have dreamed of this day my whole life. When Jared and I had our ceremony, it wasn't like this at all. We knew it was wrong, it just didn't feel right, but today... Everything feels right. It's filled with love, passion, and an unyielding bond. Today I will become the official Luna of Full Moon, and Mrs. Landon Wright, as well.

I'm so freaking excited! A lot of packs are attending because word has spread that I'm the supposed daughter of the moon goddess, and I guess they want to get a look at me. I know that most are coming to show support and love, but I can't shake the feeling that a lot of people are coming to see if the whispers and rumors are true.

When word got around after the Annual Alpha Meeting, there was a lot of doubt. Trust me, I don't blame those people, but I just hope that they don't expect to come to my wedding and have me start turning water into wine here. Cause it ain't happening.

I honestly don't want to become a spectacle. I've been working so hard on my confidence for years now. You know, to not feel like such an outcast because of my disability. Please understand I'm not ashamed of my disability, and honestly it took a long time to get to that point. After the attack my life changed in the blink of an eye. I felt lost, but over time and with the help of a therapist I've come so far in my journey. During all of this... my path to healing, I never chased the prospect of a relationship.

Now that I've met my soulmate my biggest struggle is that I don't always feel so—sexy. There's nothing more that I want than to make Landon's jaw drop, and I just always had the vision of walking into a room and stopping him in his tracks. In my head I can't do that by rolling into the room. Crap I know I need to work on this but it's still a struggle.

The apartment door opens pulling me from my thoughts. Standing in the doorway is Stacy, Lara and Cammy. Their arms are overflowing with everything they will need to get ready for today.

"Morning beautiful bride." Stacy greets with a radiant smile on her face.

"Morning Stacy! Hey girls, how are you?"

"Good, Luna, how are you?" Lara answers, obviously still a little tentative about her new friends and environment.

"Excited, nervous... mostly excited."

"I brought some extra goodies from Mrs. Lane!" I lean over to see what Lara is placing on the table and can't stop the grumble my stomach makes. I help myself to a small plate of pastries and fruit while Stacy and Cam start taking the dresses out of the garment bags to see if they need steaming. I grab my phone and hit play on my favorite playlist as I settle on the couch with my snack and tea. The room is now filled with sweet smells and good tunes, and I find myself doing a little happy dance in my chair.

Ellie's bedroom door opens, and an exuberant flurry of red curls bursts out, all smiles as she skips out of her room. "It's Wedding and Gotcha Day!!!" Ellie yells as she runs into my arms for a big hug. I give her kisses all over her face, as she giggles away. I pull her up onto my lap and roll over to the table, helping her fill her plate with a hearty breakfast. Ben, who is eating eggs and drinking coffee in the corner of the room, looks up and gives me a cheesy grin.

"Knock, Knock!" a feminine voice sounds from the slightly opened apartment door. Ben jumps up to help whoever is at the door.

"Oh, hey Trinity!" Ben says as he opens the door wide for her to enter. I can't help but notice the blush spreading all over her face, as she scurries past everyone. Apparently, Cammy and Stacy saw it too because they are trying to suppress their laughter.

My brain is whirling. I need details, people. Too bad I'm not technically a pack member yet, so I can't link to ask what the heck is going on. Apparently, Ben feels my stare because he turns his head toward me. I'm giving him my best, *what in the world is that about,* look. I'm trying to will the info out of him, but the butt munch is just wiggling his eyebrows at me. Like I'm supposed to know what that freaking means. Ugh.

"Hi everyone!" Although she may be a lovely shade of red, Trinity's trying to disguise it with a big ass smile.

Cammy jumps up to hug her. "Girl oh my gosh, congratulations! Can you believe we are mated to the Blaney Brothers."

"Wait! Trinity you're mated to Troy?! How am I just finding out about this?" I gasp, dropping the strawberry I was about to devour.

Cammy looks at me confused.

"Couldn't you hear them last night?" Cammy asks, making Trinity cover her face with her hands.

Ben chokes and spit his coffee across the table. Not being able to control himself, he jumps up and leaves the room.

"Goddess Cammy! I had no idea that his room wasn't soundproof! He's freaking twenty-six years old!"

I look wide eyed at the girls, remembering the noises from last night.

"Holy shit that was you guys?" Trinity's eyes grow at my admission to hearing their sexcapades. "Yeah girl, get it." I say bumping into her with a smile.

"Okay, okay this is Luna and Ellie's day, enough about me." Trinity says while biting her bottom lip and smirking.

Ellie looks up at me from her demolished breakfast. "Soooooo can I wear a bwaid crown mommy?"

"You are our princess, so a crown is fitting, don't you think?"

She smiles wide and spins around to jump from the table, glasses clank together from her bumping the table. "Aunt Stacy glam me up!" We just shake our heads at her antics.

After a little more pleasantries, and a few more apple turnovers, it's time to get ready. Lara does all of our makeup and let me tell you she's a freaking artist. She must be, to be able to use all of these colors and make everyone look so elegant.

Stacy is busy putting the finishing touches on my hair. I just sit in awe of everyone. Gazing at my reflection and for the first time in such a long time I recognize myself.

I haven't seen this woman staring back at me through the mirror since before the war. This woman was a warrior, she had big dreams. How did I lose myself—let my disability take over my life? I've always tried to not focus on the fact that I was in a wheelchair. The only problem with doing that was I never allowed myself to embrace this new side of me. I should've offered up my suffering to the Moon Goddess. I should've known she would have a plan for me. I've allowed myself to get lost in the sea of my hidden emotions and in turn hiding myself from the world. Now in front of me sits the woman I thought was gone forever. Here I am, ready to start anew. No longer hiding or running from my past.

"Oh Luna! Don't cry, you will smudge my hard work." Lara teases.

The day flies by as we chat and reminisce about the past. Stacy tells Ellie G-rated stories of our childhood and she's eating every moment up.

I help Ellie into her dress and put a few flowers in her hair. Stacy applies glitter spray in it as well so it truly looks like it sparkles.

"Ellie, we got you a small gift for today." I pull out the locket that Landon and I bought. Inside is a picture of her original parents on one side and a picture of Landon and me on the other. The back is simply engraved: "*To the moon, stars, and back again.*" We also got her a charm bracelet with a little wolf on it. She stares at the locket, then looks up at me.

"I wuv you mommy."

I give her the biggest hug I can. "I love you too."

"Alright chicka, let's get you dressed." Stacy carries my dress over and the girls help me slide in and button me up. It is even more gorgeous than it was yesterday. I position myself in front of the mirror as Stacy puts the veil on. I am absolutely speechless.

"Wow," says a gruff, emotional voice. I look up to see Ben's reflection but it's Jared talking.

"Hey, so what do you think?" I ask, suddenly shy.

"I think I'm beyond lucky that I get to walk you down the aisle to your true mate."

I swallow past the lump in my throat and try to hold back the tears, but I fail.

"Don't cry Mal, I'm just so happy for you."

I smile and realize that this is the best gift ever, all of my best friends are here for me. How did I get so blessed?

Once downstairs everyone is given their bouquets and I'm in awe of the beauty before me. The back garden is glimmering with gorgeous hanging lights. A beautiful array of different colored flowers cover everything. At each aisle chair there are shepherd hooks that have beautiful lanterns hanging with real candles. The cut outs in the lanterns create the effect of a million fireflies twinkling about. It's absolutely breathtaking.

We're lined up in the living room of the pack house, and when the music starts the girls head out the french doors one by one. There's a symphony of *Awww's* as Ellie steals the show. I'm so glad that we ended up hiring a videographer. I'm going to want to relive this moment all the time.

A change in the music signals that it's now my turn. I adjust my chair as Ben leans down to my ear, "Ready Luna?" All I can muster is a small nod. I hold on to my bouquet as Ben begins to push me out into the crowd. Hundreds of people turn in their chairs and smile. Everyone has been asked to stay seated, allowing me to see everything that's going on.

The aisle is long and at its center is a small curve, not allowing me to see Landon just yet. As we approach the curve, Ben stops. Looking down at me, he gives me an encouraging nod. I take a deep breath. *It's now or never.* Ben gets eye level with me, and I wrap my arms around his neck. "One, two... three." He whispers as he pulls me up to stand. I hold on tight to keep my balance and once I'm at my full height, I release the breath I've been holding. Someone passes Ben the set of forearm crutches he stashed away here earlier.

I slowly release my hold on his neck and take a firm grip on each crutch. Once he feels that I'm secure and that I'm not going to fall, Ben moves to stand next to me. I slowly bring my eyes up from the petal covered ground and finally get my first glimpse of my mate. Even with the shocked look on his face, he looks amazing in his navy-blue tux.

I can't help but giggle at the fact I was able to pull this surprise off. Unable to contain his emotions any longer, Landon leans his head back in an attempt to stop the tears from flowing but it's a useless task. Sam places his hand on Landon's shoulder, even he looks choked up. Pulling himself together, Landon's eyes meet mine, bathing me in a sense of calm. His lips move, "I'm so proud of you."

Keeping my eyes locked on his, I move the left crutch ahead. I take in a deep breath and with all the courage I can muster, I begin to slowly drag my right leg forward. One step after the other I move closer to my goal— my future. Ben follows along helping me keep my balance as I make it down the aisle. Stacy has tears rolling down her cheeks as she stands up front in her matron of honor position.

I'm not sure why I never thought that this small action would be so impactful. I just want Landon to know that I will always push myself for him, our daughter, and our pack. Ben and I had been practicing secretly for the past couple of days.

I can't stop looking at my handsome mate, and before I reach the platform Landon runs down the steps and sweeps me up in his arms, bridal style. The love he shows me at this moment is overwhelming. He places his forehead to mine and breathes me in deeply. I wipe the tears away from his beautiful face as he whispers, "Babe, don't worry I got you the rest of the way."

Chapter 25
LANDON

I'm standing on the platform in my tux along with Sam, Troy and the triplets. There easily has to be over a thousand people here. Whimsical music fills the air to accompany the bridesmaids as they begin to proceed down the aisle. Sam's mate Lara makes her way down the aisle, followed by Trinity and Cammy. Stacy, as the matron of honor, comes down just before little Ellie.

Oh, Ellie. This little ball of sass strolls down the aisle as if she owns it. I swear this kid has alpha blood running through her veins. She's tossing flower petals everywhere, winking at people and blowing kisses. It is hysterical. Then she runs up the platform stairs to stand next to the ladies but not before giving me a big hug.

"Love you daddy."

"Love you too pumpkin."

The pianist effortlessly transitions to *A Thousand Years* by *Christina Perri*. The anticipation is killing me. It's hard for me to stay still in my assigned spot.

Then, I see her.

My chest almost hurts from how violently my heart is pounding, as if trying to escape. Ben pulls Mal up and hands her crutches. She slides her arms into them and lets her dress fall to the ground. She looks stunning. She swings one leg forward and then the other. I can't breathe past this lump in my throat. We lock eyes... ugh my heart. My head falls back as I try to keep the tears in but damn, she is a fucking angel.

And she is all mine.

Not being able to take it anymore, I race down the stairs and sweep her up into my arms. I put my forehead to hers, so close that our breaths intermingle, and tell her, "Babe, I got you the rest of the way."

Ben follows us with her chair and places it on the platform, then I gently place her on it. Stacy scurries up and smooths Mal's dress, making the gown the focal point and not her chair.

Needing a better angle, I adjust my chair that I had placed here before the ceremony. This way I'm eye level with Mal. She smiles her million-dollar smile as I sit down next to her. I reach for her hand and gently run my thumb over her fingers. Her green eyes sparkle back at me. Lost in her gaze I find it hard to pay attention to what the elder is saying.

Malinda's laughter pulls me from my daydreams, making me take notice that the elder is motioning for us to take each other's hands. I squeeze her with excitement. This is the moment I pledge my love and undying faith to my mate.

"I, Alpha Landon Wright, promise to love, cherish, protect and honor you, Malinda Smalls as my wife and Luna. I promise to be your partner in crime, your ride or die, your first and last love. I will go to the ends of this earth to make you happy, and I will kill anyone to protect you. You are my everything."

"Alpha Landon, do you take Malinda Smalls as your wife and mate?"

"I do."

"Do you accept her as your Luna?"

"I do."

I don't think Malinda has stopped smiling yet. I place the white gold band on her left ring finger, and whisper. "With all that I have."

Malinda says her vows and her I Do's and as she slides the ring on to my finger the leaves begin to rustle on the trees. The string lights above our heads start to sway as a huge gust of wind comes out of nowhere, picking up the scattered flower petals causing them to swirl around us. I shift in my seat to look into the crowd. My eyes grow large with confusion when I see that we're all alone. Everyone has disappeared. I quickly turn back to see where the elder once stood, but in his place is the moon goddess, herself. I've never been in her presence before. Overcome with gratitude, I get down on one knee and submit. Mal's squeezing my hand so hard, and I finally look up when the goddess places her hand on my head.

"Oh Landon, get up," she sasses. "I'm your mother-in-law now. No need for submitting... I know where your loyalty is." I see where Malinda gets her feistiness from. I glance back up at the goddess and she's no longer alone. There is a man holding her hand, looking at her lovingly. Another couple who I believe is Mal's adoptive parents, appear next to them. They match the family picture we have hanging up in the living room. My breath catches in my throat when the four of them step aside, revealing my parents.

I'm in utter shock. *How is this happening?* Mal squeezes my hand again and smiles at me. "Go hug them silly." She whispers, and once my brain finally processes what she just said I jump to my feet. I grab both of my parents and pull them into a hug. I don't know how long this moment is going to last or if I will ever get it again... so I hold on tight.

"Alpha Wright, you say you don't do mushy but I'm calling BS on that sir." Mal says to my father, and he just laughs at her, then reaches toward her for a hug.

"How is this possible?" I manage to eventually stutter out.

"My dear Landon, your wife is my daughter, and though there are things I cannot control in this world... I promise that when I can, I will always make a little magic happen. Although you will not see us, know that we are always here. However, this moment now, is fleeting, your guests have no clue anything is going on. But we wanted to let you know that there is a big surprise about to happen."

All of the parents came in for one more hug. Then, in a blink of an eye, they disappear and the elder reappears, speaking mid-sentence, "I introduce to you Mr. and Mrs. Landon Wright. You may kiss your bride." It doesn't take me but a second for the shock to wear off. We are back at our ceremony. Happier than I ever thought possible, I wrap her in my arms and kiss her deeply. The crowd erupts in cheers and howling from every direction.

I pull away from the kiss to ask Mal if she is ready to become Luna. She nods with excitement. Turning us around to face our pack, I begin the next phase of our ceremony.

"I, Alpha Landon Wright have accepted my fated mate Malinda Wright as my Luna. Do you Malinda Wright accept Full Moon as your one and only pack, do you promise to support your Alpha?"

"I do."

"Do you promise to put Full Moon's needs above your own?"

"I do."

"Do you promise to love and protect Full Moon to the best of your ability?"

"I do."

"Lastly, Full Moon, do you accept Malinda Wright as your Luna and the promises she has made today?"

"We do!" The voices cheer loudly.

With a small gust of wind coming down from the heavens, the transfer of power from my mother, the last luna of Full Moon to Malinda occurs. The wind swirls around her. You can see it practically dance across her skin and through her hair. A small tear forms in Mal's eye as her aura shifts and the strength, she had just moments ago doubles.

I look at my mate, my Luna, and I am in such awe of her. I know that this is her doing, she somehow made this all happen. She takes a deep breath and motions for Ellie to join us.

The elder smiles at us and whispers to Ellie. "Are you ready, little pup?"

She just jumps up and down clapping her hands. The laughter around us grows at her excitement. Everyone is already in love with Ellie and her personality. I know she is going to be accepted throughout the whole pack as our daughter. This thought alone fills me with pride.

"Eloise, the Alpha and Luna have chosen you. Their wolves have chosen you. Today they want to make the adoption official. Do you accept?"

"YES!" She screams with delight, her energy infectious. The crowd is cheering along with her.

The elder asks us all to join our left hands and he ties a red ribbon around our wrists. Ellie watches as he twists the satin fabric around again and again. She is taking this all in, and when she realizes the significance of this moment, she stands a bit taller.

"You good, princess?" I whisper in her ear.

"I'm going to make you pwoud that you chose me daddy."

"Eloise, you make me proud just by being you." I extend my hand to her, and she grabs it with delight.

"Daddy is right, just be the best "you" you can be. Love with all your heart and always be kind and fair."

"And kick ass when necessawy, wight?"

"Ellie- language!" Mal and I scold, causing all of the warriors to laugh.

"Eloise, you have accepted The Alpha and Luna, do you accept their name as well?"

Shit, I didn't think that was going to be a question. I don't want her to feel pressured and by the look on Mal's face she is thinking the same thing.

"Ellie, do you want to think about this? You don't need to decide now?"

"No. I'm weady." She whispers. Turning to the Elder with her eyes locked on him, "I choose to be Eloise Wight." She announces loudly for all to hear.

"So, it shall be." He declares.

The elder unties our wrists and the room erupts into applause once again. Ellie jumps into our arms shouting, "I'm so happy, I love you guys so much." I'm overwhelmed with emotion from the feel of our bonds connecting. It feels strong—dare I say-unbreakable. The last of our invisible cord snaps into place, signifying we are officially a family.

"What is this?" Ellie asks, raising her arm. I grab it and am shocked to see that she has the mark of the moon goddess. There, tattooed to her delicate little wrist, is an image of the full moon with a crown on it and two tiny stars. "Look," she gasps, pointing at mine and Malinda's wrists. There upon our skin sits the same mark.

"How can this be, is this what she meant by surprise?" I whisper to Mal. The elder comes forward, examining our new marks. Gasping, the elder links Mal and me.

-This bond between you and the child has been blessed by the Moon Goddess herself along with the girl's birth parents. The moon and crown are the symbols of the goddess, but the stars represent Eloise's parents' blessing. She was destined to you, and to our pack.

Mal and I exchange a look between us. The elder continues, -If she so chooses, she can be our next alpha.

Holy Shit! Mal and I smile with excitement, our union and bond has been blessed by the goddess. We turn to face the crowd and we hold up our wrists to show the marks. What we hear next is almost indescribable. Everyone howls in unison, the sound of it shakes the ground. Then every single person present kneels before us. Ellie is the only one to come up with a word to describe the site before us....
"Wow."

Chapter 26
MALINDA

Married, we're married! I'm so happy I could burst. Landon carries Ellie down the aisle and holds my hand as I wheel back toward the pack house.

After the ceremony we have a receiving line of all our allies. Everyone wishes us well and hands us a card, a small token of congratulations. It will take a long time to greet every one of them, but I don't care. I'm so thankful for the friendship and loyalty these people are giving us.

After an hour we return to our apartment with our close friends, while the event staff switches the back yard over for dinner. Our guests are enjoying a nice cocktail hour that is spread throughout the other gardens and everyone seems to really be enjoying themselves. We've all changed into our reception clothes and are having some snacks and relaxing before the main party.

I look around the room at everyone and I feel so happy. Landon has started to open the cards and begins reading a few to us. At mating ceremonies people do not bring gifts, they bring cards and well wishes. With so many people attending, by the time we finish opening them it will be next year.

"Congratulations Luna and Alpha and Eloise, we love you! Mrs. Trey's 2nd grade class." Landon holds up the drawing the class made and shows Ellie how they all signed it.

"Awww that is so sweet!" Stacy says as she props herself on the back of the couch. The ones from families I find to be the sweetest. The pups decorate the envelopes, they are filled with love, warm wishes and they simply stand out to me. The ones from allies are wonderful, as well. However, they are very professional just not the same as the ones from our pack families.

Landon hands me a small pile of cards to dig into. One after the other my heart fills with pride on how welcoming they've been to me as their Luna and Ellie as our daughter.

The sound of glass exploding as it meets the floor makes my heart jump into my throat. All of us quickly turn to see an upset Ellie standing in the middle of the shards.

"I'm so sorry Mommy," she whispers.

"It's okay sweetie! We have plenty of glasses." I try to ease her sadness. "It's not a problem. Just do me a favor and run downstairs and grab the broom and dustpan."

With a slight smile, she nods and dashes out of the apartment. I grab the next card and notice the envelope is already opened. That's odd, I think as I slide the card out, revealing the blank white cover of a card. I open it revealing a handwritten message that had been crossed out, then a new one written underneath it.

'Luna,

I am no longer going to be a patient man. I have allowed you to live your life freely. Now that you have taken a mate, you interfere with my plan. You can either join me or I will have you and your mate killed.'

The last sentence is crossed out and now reads...

'You can either join me or we will kill your daughter. She is such a pretty little thing too, isn't she? You will meet us by the side entrance of the territory after the midnight run. If I have to, I will take you by force. If your mate reads this, know you are to come alone. I am not a stupid man. I have eyes everywhere.'

My whole-body freezes as I read it over, and over again. *Eyes everywhere...* Does this mean we have a breach in our pack? Without as much of a thought I quickly transfer off the couch to my wheelchair and start to head over to my office.

What the hell is this shit? Do I show Landon? Do I try to handle this on my own? Dear goddess, they want to harm Ellie. She is just a pup.

Ellie.

I stop mid roll and look around to where the shards of glass lay on the floor. *She's not back yet.* The pit in my stomach grows and not telling Landon just went right out the fucking window. Everyone's chatter comes to a crescendo and panic swallows me up in an instant. Landon jumps up and comes to me quickly. He is feeling my stress level rise through our bond.

"Baby what's wrong? Your emotions are everywhere." He whispers and he guides my face toward his.

I don't answer him, I just send a massive mindlink because at this moment a psychopath is on our land and threatening our family.

-Attention all available warriors and trackers. Locate Ellie immediately.

No one in the apartment had a clue that something was wrong up until this point. So when they hear my link, everyone goes silent, turning toward me. I throw the card on the table totally ignoring the fact that I just mindlinked more than just my pack...

Landon and Sam are the first ones to the crumpled paper. Landon reads it twice, then passes it to Sam. As I watch Sam process what it says I grab him by the jacket and pull him down to my level and I do it hard. We're eye to eye, not aware that I'm basically choking him.

"FIND MY FUCKING DAUGHTER!" I scream, practically throwing Sam across the room. He lands on the coffee table as I fly out of the front door.

LANDON

Sam recovers fast and catches up to the guys. We run down the stairs. I can't wait for the fucking elevator. I'm sick to my stomach with worry. How the fuck did this happen? I turn my head to shoot my team a death look.

"I thought you said you had security under control?! I thought you said you triple checked the guests list?! How the FUCK DID HE GET IN?!"

"We will run prints on the card and envelope. We will find the bastard who took her!" Sam growls in aggravation. Ellie has become family to all of them, to her they are all her uncles. This is beyond personal to them. This faceless coward has taken our Future Alpha... they have taken MY PUP!

We get down the stairs and Mal is already directing our warriors. John has linked his warriors from Stone Mountain and Sam is getting Lara to call her dad and Alpha Tanner. Before I know it, I have a hundred guys standing in front of me. I fill them in on what is going on and they scatter into groups. Each group has a member of each pack to make linking easier for when we find her or the suspect.

Mrs. Lane and the omegas are checking every nook and cranny of the house.

-Landon it's been thirty minutes. Mal's fear-laced voice spears my thoughts. I look around for her and notice she is no longer in the house.

-Where are you so we can look together?
-Front of the house by the tree line.

I run out the front door and look to the tree line and see Mal frantically searching everywhere. She's trying to hold it together. Then her body freezes and she release a soul splintering scream. I'm at Mal's side in a flash and try to see what she is looking at. Fucking shit... a white scrap of Ellie's dress is snagged on a branch, and it's speckled with blood.

I let out a massive howl that attracts all of the wolves helping us search, plus every top official that attended the wedding. Everyone quickly meets us in the front yard.

"Someone has taken our pup. Know now that no one leaves these lands without a thorough investigation." Every word out of my mouth is dripping with violence. Those not aiding us in the search are asked to go back to the garden, which is now heavily guarded.

I turn to see Mal staring out into the forest. Her eyes dart back and forth through the trees, waiting for another clue to make itself present. I get down on my haunches.

"Baby... look at me."

Her head barely turns toward me, her eyes refuse to miss anything.

"Mal, we will find her."

She does not answer me.

"Baby."

I can't fight this anymore; I need her in my arms. I pull her in and hug her with everything I have. Finally, she melts into me and places her face in the crook of my neck. She takes a deep breath in an attempt to calm herself, but as soon as she releases it I can feel her begin to sob. It rips through her, and I hold her as tightly as I can. After a few minutes her breathing changes and I can feel her start to calm down. I pull back, taking in her features. Gently brushing the hair from her face. Her eyes are void of all emotion. It's at this moment, the way she looks at me, I know whoever is responsible for this is not going to make it out alive.

UNKNOWN

She couldn't have just stayed single, could she? No, no, no...she had to go and get fucking mated. Then she had to go and adopt a fucking pup. MAL SHOULD HAVE BEEN MINE. It should have been my mark on her neck and NOW... I have to fucking deal with all of this bull shit. I should have taken her when she moved to Paisley. But I couldn't, nothing had been ready. But now I have to deal with this shit show!

Damn it!

These fucking rogues can't do anything right. It shouldn't have been this hard to overthrow my brother. Once I take over his pack, it shouldn't be a problem to overthrow the remaining three I need for my plan to be effective. But I have to complete the takeover before my nephew takes over for his father. I don't want to have to kill my nephew, but I will if necessary. Ugh, this is spiraling out of control and fast. I need to regain command of this plan before something else decides to pop up.

"Sir, your Gamma that was placed with the event staff just kidnapped their pup. It was spur of the moment, but he saw the opportunity and he took it." I sit up in my seat trying to process what the dipshit just said to me. *He kidnapped her.* Oh, this could work out. I will trade the child for the Luna.

"Tell him to go to the meeting place, do not harm the child. The Luna will definitely show up. We will take her and leave the girl."

Malinda... I'm coming for you.

Chapter 27
MALINDA

It's been an hour and there is no sign of her. I feel like I'm losing my mind at this point. How... How does something like this happen? We are currently sitting in Landon's office with a top warrior from each pack. There are several alphas and a few betas that are filing in. The sense of power that is flowing throughout this room can only be described as suffocating.

"Okay gentleman, thank you for wanting to help find our pup. Most of you know what happened at the annual Alpha's meeting with my Luna." Everyone just nods in understanding, allowing Landon to continue.

"About a month ago we experienced a rogue attack. Yesterday my Luna, along with our pup and the Luna of Stone Mountain were in a car chase with rogues as they tried to get back home, to our territory." Landon goes into more detail about what happened with the first attack and how we've been working with Gold Moon. Even though there are no hard feelings you can see the look of disappointment on Alpha Tanner and Beta Jim's faces. Landon continues sharing what info they got from the interrogation and the card we received today. He is going into more detail on his plan, as I try to reach out to Sahara.

I've been trying to reach her all afternoon. I don't know where she is and I'm starting to feel empty without her. You see, Dex and

Sahara accepted Ellie as their pup. They felt a pull from her little dormant wolf. Then today the goddess marked all of us with her bond. This doesn't happen often. Shit, I don't think it's ever happened. But it means that our bond is so strong that we might as well have conceived Ellie ourselves. What's even more incredible about it is that her parents loved her so much they allowed this to happen. It truly is an overwhelming feeling, but now my gut is wrenching not knowing where she is.

    I keep staring at the mark on my wrist, tracing it with my finger over and over again. Thinking about what our little girl is going through. Is she scared and frightened? Is she driving her captor crazy? Or is she paying attention to what is going on around her, taking it all in? As soon as this is over and she is home safe, her alpha training will begin right away. She needs to be able to think like an alpha and protect herself.

    "Mal."

    "Sahara, where the hell have you been, are you okay?"

    "Mal, we don't have time for questions. I need you to try something..."

    "Try... try what?"

    "This might sound crazy, but I need you to focus solely on Ellie. Picture her face, in great detail. Picture yourself holding her."

    "Okay, is something supposed to happen?" I'm desperate to try anything at this moment.

    "I think that since we are the daughter of the goddess, if we can focus enough on her we might be able to pinpoint where she is. We are supposed to be blessed and have powers... let's see if we can get them to work."

    "Sold, you don't have to ask me twice."

    I focus as hard as I can on her beautiful face. I envision every detail... her eyes, her freckles, her button nose. I'm overcome with so much emotion from just thinking about her. So much so that my chest tightens, and my skin begins to tingle. I gasp at the sensation that's now taking over my whole body. It almost feels like I can't breathe. But I don't care. I'm not going to stop. I close my eyes and I see a perfect image of Ellie. The vision of her brings my soul peace, helping me to regulate my breathing. In and out, in and out. That's when I notice how quiet it has become in the room. I slowly open my eyes. Confusion clouds my vision, as I'm no longer in the office.

HOLY SHIT! I'm no longer in the office! I look around trying to get my bearings. I'm in the middle of the woods. How in Goddess's name did I get here?

"WE CAN FREAKING TELEPORT!" Sahara screams in my head.

"Say what now?!"

"Okay we can get into the details later, look for Ellie first. It should have brought us right to her."

I peruse my surroundings as calmly as I can. The only sounds I can hear are my ragged breaths, and the tires of my wheelchair rolling over dry leaves and twigs. I'm on the damn edge and it feels like an hour has gone by when it really has just been moments.

I push forward, noticing a small clump of disturbed bushes in the distance. I don't smell Ellie's scent, just rogue stench. If she was taken by this asshole most likely it was by one of his minions. So, I go with my gut and follow the scent. As it gets stronger, my stress level rises. The sweat is pouring down my face and my heart is beating in my throat.

As I get closer to the brush, the foulness has become so much stronger. The overgrowth is out of control, and I'm now stuck in vines and other detritus created by nature. I can't really get my chair any closer to the area I want to inspect. Taking a deep breath, I slide down and into the dirt, then army crawl into the brush. Reaching out trying to feel for anything through the debris, but nothing.

"DAMN IT!" I shout into the night air. The sound of rustling leaves has me snapping my head around. I move closer to the indistinguishable noise that is now coming from under the leaves a yard away from me. "Hello... Ellie?" I call out.

"Mmm...mmmm."

My attention is drawn to the small pile of leaves that are moving ahead of me. Frantically getting to the pile I begin to dig. Pushing leaves off a small lump, revealing a dirty brown blanket. My heart's beating a mile a minute and with a shaky hand I reach for the blanket and pull it up.

Lying underneath is my beautiful daughter. Her mouth and hands are taped up but I can tell she is smiling at me. I yank her into my arms and hug her like I have never hugged anyone before. I gently pull the tape off her mouth and undo her hands. I keep hugging and kissing her all over her face, making her giggle.

"Mommy! I knew you would find me; I just knew it!"

"I will always find you." I stop and pull back to look at her, "But right now let's get the hell out of here."

We get back to my chair and Ellie climbs up on my lap. "Wait." She jumps off and runs back to the bush and grabs the blanket.

"What do we need this for?"

"The twackers from our pack, mommy, duh."

Goddess, I love this kid! She climbs back onto my lap, and I hold her tightly. I tell her to close her eyes and think of daddy in his office and only of daddy. I do the same and just like before I feel the sharp pain in my chest. When I open my eyes, we are outside Landon's office door. I look down at Ellie and she is looking up at me like I am the coolest person in the world.

"Are you good baby girl?"

"Pewfect."

I can hear Landon screaming at someone through the door. "She was fucking right here and then she disappeared! Find her now!" He roars. He sounds more like a lion than a wolf. Ellie jumps off my lap with the blanket in hand and opens the door.

"DADDY!"

Landon stops mid pace and turns to face her. The look on his face would make me laugh if I wasn't so relieved.

"ELLIE! Oh, my goddess Ellie!"

Landon runs over to her and sweeps her up in his arms. He hugs her like his life depends on it. I slowly roll into the room and watch the heartwarming scene unfold. Every man and woman in that room sits down at the conference table and quietly watches as Landon, the big bad wolf and mighty alpha, falls to his knees, cradling the pup who stole his heart.

As I get closer to them, he reaches up and swiftly pulls me out of my chair and onto his lap and he holds us both, breathing in our scents.

A crash sounds from outside the office, followed by what seems like a herd of elephants running down the hall. The office door slams open and Sam, Troy, and the triplets come flying in almost tripping over each other.

"ELLIE!" They all yell in unison, the relief in their voices is palpable. They all run in for a group hug. She just giggles as she enjoys the moment with her uncles.

Landon reclaims his daughter. He stands her up. "Let me look at you." He studies her body, then his eyes widen in disbelief when he finds nothing wrong. "How is it possible that you're not hurt? We found a piece of your dress with blood on it!"

"When the bad man took me, he was puwlling me by the arm weally hard..."

A growl rips through Landon and the guys. Not going to lie, I love how much they love her.

Ellie rolls her eyes at them, then smiles in mischief. "Soooo, when he bent over to pick me up, I kneed him in the face!!! It...Was... AWESOME!" Her little girl giggle tinkles like bells all over the room and the men can't help but chuckle along with her. "I tink I bwoke his nose, because it stawted bleeding. Some of it got on my dwess. I think I got him angwy. That's when he picked me up and put tape on my mouf and hands. My pwetty dress got caught on the twees. Can you believe that, ugh now what am I going to wear to dinner!"

"You really kneed him in the face?" Sam asks, pride taking over his features.

"Yeah! Should I have kneed him in his twig and beerwes? Would that have been better? Anyway, Uncle Twoy I twied to do the thumb thingy... you know how you taught me to poke someone's eyes?" Troy nodded his head, "Yeah, I got close, but he just swatted me away like I was an annoying fly. I got to work on that move."

Everyone has a smile on their face, Ellie is infectious with her happiness. "Oh, and one more thing", she runs over to the blanket and hands it to the triplets. "This is what the other guy hid me under. Can we twack his scent?"

Silence muted everyone's reactions. I don't think there is one person in this room that isn't impressed by my little cub.

"You bet your ass we—" Tony exclaimes but I catch the glare Landon gives him so he tries to correct himself, "I mean, yes, we can sweet pea. Yes, we can."

"Gweat, so when's dinner?" Ellie asks, like it's just any other day.

Chapter 28
LANDON

When's dinner? I repeat Ellie's question in my head.

I can't help but laugh at my spitfire as she talks to the triplets. They are telling her how proud they are, and she is acting as if what just happened is no big deal. I can't get over how she seems so calm and collected. I mindlink my cousin, Dr. K. She comes quickly and takes Ellie to the bedroom to give her a full head to toe examination. I just want to be one hundred percent sure she is fine.

Once they both leave the room, I give voice to the question I have been dying to ask. "Okay Mal, how in the freaking world did you find her?"

Mal dives into the explanation of how Sahara talked her through it. Everyone is kind of jonesing over her teleportation ability. Can you blame them though? My girl is awesome.

I straighten my back. "What we need to figure out first is: was the person who is behind all of this here tonight? Or did the rogue act alone and pose as one of the event staff or something?" I stare over the table at my team.

"Tim and Tom had a chance to look over the letter. The card was written by two different people... look." Tony slides the paper across the conference table.

"Here, the original note is in very neat handwriting, but the added part is rushed and definitely not written by the same person. My gut is telling me the person behind this was not here, just wanted us to think that they were." Tony is rocking back and forth on his heels; his adrenaline is still pumping.

"We also have drones in the air, we need to see if this guy shows up tonight. This way if he does, we get a good look at him and we can narrow down the search." Tim says looking hopeful.

Mal is quietly taking it all in, deep in thought. Then the rhythmic drumming of her fingers on the table stops. "Last night you said the rogue you interrogated mentioned that his boss tried to get close to me. I'm going to assume this is when I lived in Paisley. I have been wracking my brain as to who I was close to that would stand out to me as an evil villain. There was my physical therapist Austin, the café owner Jake... oh, and the gym owner. If anything, the gym owner is the only guy who ever rubbed me the wrong way."

Alpha Tanner stands from his place on the brown leather couch to pace back and forth. "Luna, what gym did you attend when you were in the city?" Tanner asks almost cautiously. As if he's afraid of the answer.

"Tone Your Inner Wolf." I answer and the look on Tanner's face has the hair on the back of my neck standing straight up.

"Jim, do you think Scott is behind this?" Tanner asks his beta.

Tanner's beta sits forward and leans his elbows on the table. Leveling his alpha with a serious stare. "Alpha, it wouldn't surprise me but..." He takes a deep breath, calming his nerves. "That means that he involved our kids. They could've been killed."

I look between Tanner and his beta, and their worried expressions piss me off. "Okay gentleman, fill us in."

"Alpha Landon, my brother Scott is a few years younger than me. He was going to be my beta when I took over, but an injury... among other things, rendered him unable to fulfill the beta duties. Jim had to formally challenge him for the position. Scott lost obviously, and he became very angry with me. He kept going on and on about how I could have just appointed him to Beta, but I refused because I respect our laws. The moon goddess has a reason for everything. He ended up leaving the pack with a few others. Last I heard he had opened up a few gyms and seemed to be happy in the business."

"Do you have a picture of him?" Mal asks.

"Yes Luna." Tanner scrolls through his phone and hands it to Mal. "Here, this was a few years ago but I don't think he has changed that much." Mal takes the phone and examines it closely.

"Austin was part of your pack as well?" She asks, a little dumbfounded by what she sees on the image. Tanner peers over her shoulder to see who she is looking at.

"Yes, Austin and Scott were best friends growing up. Though my brother manipulated their relationship to the point that Austin became more of an errand boy for him and less of a friend."

"I was played." Mal whispers softly. "I remember the day I met Austin. I was supposed to have another therapist, but Austin said that I was reassigned to him. Every now and then Scott would visit with me while I was working out. He was always over the top in trying to be my friend. It was a little creepy, but I trusted Austin. Scott would always have a protein drink waiting for me with my name on it." She flicks away a tear from her face. "Our friendship was a lie. I trusted Austin... with so much." The room falls silent as we watch her process this information.

But the silence is short lived. "Fuck. It was the drink, wasn't it. That's how the poison was always in my system." Her eyes find mine. "I could never figure out how I always had elevated numbers. This is the only thing that makes sense, he kept me sick. They kept me sick!" She shouts, but it quickly turns to a sob. "I may never be able to have a pup because of what they did to me." She chokes out, causing a growl to erupt from my soul. Many of the people in the room were unable to contain their growls, as well. "This guy didn't want my powers to come out because it would interfere with his plans. Now that they will, he wan...wants me." A fire lights the emerald in her eyes as a calmness cloaks her movements like a blanket. "Let me make one thing perfectly clear. I belong to Landon, and that's not going to fucking change. Plus, he took my child. Now, let's come up with a game plan. I'm going to kill this motherfucker and I want it to be as bloody as possible."

I haul my mate into a big hug. "Letting you go was never an option." I say just above a whisper. I hold tight as that cloak of calm slowly ebbs away and is replaced with anger. So much anger her body is shaking with it. I move my hands to hold her face, cupping her cheeks. I try to calm her and Sahara down.

Dex responds to Mal and Sahara, "*Mine.*"

Mal nuzzles her face into my hand and the slightest of smiles plays with her pink, full lips. "*Yours...forever.*" Sahara answers back.

John abruptly stands. "What four packs is Scott after? You were telling me the rogue mentioned he was after four packs. There has to be a reason it's specifically those packs."

Jim looks at Tanner, "I think Scott attempted to challenge a few pack Beta's back in the day, but failed at each fight. If that's the reason, it has to be those packs. He must feel slighted."

Mal pulls from me a bit, "Wait a second, you said that he suffered an injury... so you overlooked your own brother because he had developed a disability?" The look on Mal's face is that of pure disgust.

"Luna, though his disability hindered him from a lot of normal beta duties, he still would have made a fine Beta. The reason for not wanting him was his already shitty temperament. He has always been a huge asshole. His attitude and behavior towards others was cringeworthy. When you treat your best friend like shit, how will you treat your pack? I held him to a higher standard, especially when you are from Alpha blood, but he never rose to the occasion. He never had the pack's interests at heart. He lost the challenge fair and square, he just could not get out of his own way."

Mal seems to take this information in and really digest it. All of a sudden, her eyes get big and she looks at me.

"Landon, didn't you say that the rogue last night was the one who injected me at the battle?"

"Yes, that is what he said."

"Guys, we have a bigger problem now. I'm not sure what side Scott fought on during the war, but we know what side he is on now. If he is after four packs- that means that he is after those packs that he lost the fight for the Beta title in. If he is now coming after us then he must have raised an army, no? Who in their right mind would come up against a pack this large without an army?"

"How do you do that under the radar though?" Troy asks, frustration clear in his voice.

"The gyms," Ben interjects from the corner of the room.

"Yes! I trained at the gym three nights a week. The other nights Austin said they held free classes. What if they had a way of masking the rogue smell so they could train at night totally under the radar!"

I lean over and kiss Mal's forehead. "You, my mate, are an absolute genius. Tanner, please call all of the packs surrounding yours. We need to see if there was anyone who challenged their beta's. If so, send a photo of Scott for confirmation. If it was him that made the challenge, I want details of when the challenge happened as well as the details of the fight."

"Landon, tell me all of the measures in place for pups and non-warrior pack members. If a fight is to come here, I want to make sure that we have our most vulnerable members safe and protected." Mal states as she reaches for a pen and paper.

"Sam, review everything with Mal. I'm going to talk to all of our other guests and let them know we will be celebrating on a different day."

Everyone turns their heads to the door when it rattles with a knock. I can't help but be shocked when my cousin Sean strolls in.

"Hey man," I get up and move over toward him. "What is going on? I thought you guys couldn't make it?" I say as I slap him on the back before I give him a big hug. Sean's pack is on the east coast, and I have not seen him in a few years. He is supposed to be leaving for a study abroad program any day now and the fact that he's here means the world to me.

"My parents couldn't make it because Becca is sick. So, I hitched a ride with my Alpha. We had a layover and just got here. Something tells me though this is not a normal mating ceremony." He says as he sweeps his arm around the room acknowledging the war meeting, we are conducting. I quickly fill him in so we can get back to business. "Jesus Christ," he says after taking a moment to digest the information. This is crazy, but you are in luck because I don't leave for Ireland for two more weeks, so you got me till then."

Chapter 29
Trinity

I can't believe what little Eloise has been through. She is such a trooper. When we got to the Alpha's apartment, we headed for her overstuffed, comfy couch then sat there while Dr. K asked Ellie some tough questions. K grabs a doll and asks Ellie if the bad guy touched her, and if so, could she show us where on the doll.

"He gwabbed my awm hewe." She says as she holds the doll by the whole arm up by the armpit. "This is how he dwagged me. Then he taped my mouf and my hands, he threw me over his shoulder. One hand was on my butt and the other was awound my legs to stop me from wiggling."

"Okay, then can you tell me what happened next?" K asks as she moves the doll to the side.

"Another man came. He told the fiwst guy that he was going to take over. He seemed weally weally mad at him. Once the fiwst guy left, the second guy hid me under the blanket and leaves. He told me not to be scared and that my mommy would find me."

"Ellie, do you think you could give a description of the two men later today?" I ask.

"Yup! Can I shower now?"

"Yes, sweet pea."

Her hair bounces as she skips off to the bathroom and I let out a sigh of relief. "This could have been so much worse." K nods her head in agreement.

"Link Troy, have him set up a meeting with the security team so she can describe the guys. Hopefully the camera system picked them up at some point."

-Troy, are you guys still busy?

-What's up sweetheart?

-I think Ellie will be able to give you a good description of the suspect. Could you send a guy up to do a composite sketch?

-Of course! I will send Nick up and meet you guys there in a couple of minutes. We are almost done here.

Ellie comes bouncing out of the bathroom all clean and dressed in a cute little sweatsuit. I let her know that Uncle Troy is going to bring Mr. Nick from security and what we are going to do.

"Hmmm, I can totally do that. Do you think daddy and mommy will give me my own office for meetings? I mean it should be pwofessional wight? Can you link daddy if we can do the meeting in his office?"

"Of course, sweetie."

-Ummm Troy, is the Alpha busy?

-Kinda why?

-Ellie would like this to be a professional meeting and since she does not have her own office she would like to meet with Nick in Alpha's office.

... Silence

Then I hear a loud roaring belly laugh. Troy is wheezing because he is laughing so hard.

-Goddess, I hope our pup is half as funny as Ellie because she is a freaking pistol.

-Oh yeah? You're thinking about our pups already?

-You have no idea. I would be surprised if I haven't put a pup in you yet.' I can hear the smirk on his freaking face.

-Alpha said of course she can have the meeting here.

-Okay great we will head down, love you.
-I love you too.

I head to the kitchen to grab a snack. No one has had dinner because of what happened, and not going to lie I am super hungry, and super distracted. As I am walking through the door, I almost knock over a couple walking hand in hand.

"Oh my gosh, I'm so sorry I was not paying attention." I look to see who it is and I'm shocked to see Jessica and her mate, ummm… Zack I believe.

"Hey Jess, how are you? Are you guys here for the wedding?"

"Hi Trinity! Trin this is my mate, Zack! Yes, Luna invited us." She says with a shy smile.

"Nice to meet you, Zack." He shakes my hand in a polite greeting. "I'm happy to hear that. Will you be staying long?" Not that I mind, she seems to have changed now that she is mated.

"We are here for a few weeks to help out. Zack is a top warrior at Stone Mountain. He grew up with the Luna, and he really wanted to help."

"That's great! I will see you guys around."
"Bye Trinity."
"Bye."

SCOTT

"Austin how the fuck did she get away? How did all of my fucking plans go to shit? Why is everyone so incompetent?"

"Listen, I put her in a secluded area so that way she would not be found. The goal was to sneak off the property to get you and then you could meet Mal at midnight. Unfortunately, security is out of control now. We might need to wait until they relax a little, then make a move. At this rate we will both lose our lives if we try today."

"I do not care how this happens, she either joins me or she dies. Because if she is against me, she will try to stop me." I turn from Austin and start to pace. "We might need a witch to help out here. I don't know if Nora will keep helping me. Especially since I haven't asked her to marry me." Pausing, I twirl around and spear Austin with my eyes. "I really don't want to kill Malinda. What if we try to erase her memory, or something?"

"Scott, this is crazy. Do you hear yourself? This crusade you are on is a fucking suicide mission. You are going to get yourself killed. You are no longer after Beta's... you are going after fucking Alpha's. I don't know if I am ready to die for your damn revenge." Austin storms out of my office and slams the door behind him.

I can't take it anymore. That fucker is pissing me off. I am a fucking Alpha by blood! The Gold Moon Pack should be mine. I want to take everyone out that has said "no" to me, everyone that fucking beat me in those fights. I'm fucking ready. I am stronger than I've ever been. I will finally have my god damn moment. It is finally my fucking time to be Top Alpha!

AUSTIN

He has lost his damn mind. I mean he has always been a bit off his rocker, but this is out of control. I can't believe he approved of the kid being taken. I almost had a heart attack when Tyler, Scott's so-called "Gamma" of his pretend pack, called and said he took her. I interceded as quickly as I could. I know how much Malinda wants to be a mother, then this asshole steals her kid. I tried to hide her in a spot that would be patrolled and easily discovered. It killed me, having to leave her tied up and alone but if I didn't do it, Tyler would have done way worse. I shiver at the thought of leaving her in his hands. Not trying to make myself feel better or anything but seeing the look of determination and perseverance in the little pup's eyes granted me a little relief when I had to walk away from her.

I was invited to the wedding because I'm the 'Luna Queen's' supposed friend. The problem is we aren't... or we weren't meant to be. But we became friends. God, I'm such a fucking pussy. I have spent my life afraid of Scott, I can't even remember why at this point. What I do know is that she fucking trusted me. The more I got to know her, the more I realized that Scott's vendetta was crazy. That Scott was crazy. Like seriously nuts. It's a damn death sentence. For him and for me. And I'm not so sure I wouldn't welcome it for both of us.

I watched as the woman tried to walk down the aisle; she was able to do that because I was always pushing her to do better. She looked over at me with this look that said *"I did it. Thank you."* Now it is my turn to do fucking better. I need to be the person she believes I am— a true friend.

My goal today is to seek out Alpha Tanner. Scott needs to be stopped and I'm hoping his brother can help. I know that I will face death no matter what I do, I deserve it. My involvement put a target on my back long ago. I'm the one who's kept the poison in her system. After a while I started to dilute it so that way it would not affect her as badly, because the more time we spent together the closer we got and the more of an asshole I realized I was. I couldn't just stop giving it to her, if she started recovering while Scott had his watchful eye on her, who knows what he would have done to keep her under his thumb. She is an amazing person and does not deserve the shit we have put her through. I know death is around the corner for me and I need to die with my conscience clear.

Shit, how the fuck do I get to Tanner now without being killed on the spot? The girl saw my face, but I need to warn him.

Goddess help me.

Chapter 30
MALINDA

It has been a week since the ceremony. We are reviewing all security tapes, over and over. I wish I had figured out the Austin angle earlier because I was the one who had invited him to the wedding. But hell, if I knew then what I know now, I would have hunted him down and introduced his ballsack to my kung fu grip. Being in a wheelchair, you gain a lot of strength in your hands and fingers. And I really would have liked to have shown his twig and berries, as Ellie says, just how strong they have become.

I've spent the past several days reflecting on my relationship with Austin, and I can't pinpoint any moment during that time when I thought something was off. Was I just so consumed in my own world at that time? Had I really lowered my guard that much, that I didn't even notice what was happening around me? As the days went by, I couldn't stop beating myself up about this.

We had to meet with Dr. K after she talked to Ellie. We got Ellie tucked into bed, then we all headed back to Landon's office. When K described how she got Ellie to talk, I thought Landon and the guys were going to explode. He nearly went on a killing spree when K said the rogue manhandled her. This feeling of absolute need to protect her is still so overwhelming. I wonder if this is what it truly feels like to be a parent, or is it the fact that the three of us are orphans? Is it my overprotective nature and deep desire to be a mother that makes me want to put my tiny firecracker into a bubble, so she never gets hurt?

What's really putting everyone on edge is the uncertainty of when the next attack is going to happen. The days have been ticking away and so has everyone's sanity. Everyone is on edge. Everyone is training extra hard, and patrols have been doubled. The only downfall is that we have no clue what the next move is, what exactly we are training for. Landon has trackers out, but we still haven't found Scott.

I'm currently looking at the two chicken Caesar salads on my desk. Landon was supposed to eat with me about fifteen minutes ago. There's so much to do that I have been eating in my office more often than not. I'm about to mindlink him to ask his ETA, when my office door swings open, and he strolls in. Exhaustion is etched into his face; his eyes look sunken and his usual happy- go -lucky self seems like a memory. All of this is a result of the search for Scott. It's wearing on him and my heart breaks just a little more each day when he still gains no reprieve.

"Hey Mal, you didn't have to wait for me to eat." He leans over and gives me a sweet gentle kiss.

"I will always wait for you." I respond as I examine him closely.

Landon sits down on the couch. He's covered in sweat and dirt and looks like he could sleep for a week straight. However, I can't help but drool over him. He's wearing black sweatpants and a white t-shirt that is way too damn tight for his own good. Well, too damn tight to be seen by anyone other than me that is. I can't help but lick my lips at the sight. A smirk grows on his face, and I just shrug off the fact that I've been caught ogling him. He quickly and smoothly snatches me from my chair and places me on his lap.

"Mmmm much better," he says as he inhales my scent deeply, while he buries his head in the crook of my neck. I slowly brush my fingers through his hair, in hopes of bringing him some comfort. He lifts his head and tenderly rests his lips against mine. It's so light it's as if the kiss didn't even happen, but the action instantly sends a shiver down my spine and a pool of moisture between my legs.

His arms tighten on his guttural groan. "Baby."

With that one word that slips past his lips, I become putty in his hands. I know he will catch the scent of my arousal at any moment. He turns my body so I'm now straddling him, then runs his calloused hands up my legs and under my skirt. Even though his hands are rough, at this moment they feel like silk against my skin. As they inch closer to their target... I wait. I bite my lip as his eyes grow large when he realizes that I'm not wearing any panties.

"Mal." The sound of my name rolling off his tongue is dangerous, and I want more. I slide my hands down to free him from his pants. I wrap my small hand around his length and run it from bottom to top. He's already hard and I'm overcome with need. I can feel Sahara wake, pushing herself to the surface, she wants her mate. She shoves me back into my mind and I'm more than happy to take a back seat so she can play a little.

"Alpha, take me." She purrs in a sultry voice.

Landon looks at me with a cocked brow as the change in my voice registers. Black swirls through his breathtakingly blue eyes letting me know at this moment Dex is fighting for control. He desperately craves his mate, and I always feel guilty that I can't shift for him. Even though our bond is strong, we have not given Sahara and Dex their moment.

"My Luna." Dex growls.

Sahara rubs my wet slit against his cock and revels in the feeling. With Dex in full control, she can't stop the excitement that shoots through us as he lines himself up at my entrance. She fists his hair, yanking his head back roughly. She wants his full attention as we lower ourselves onto him. Her movements are slow and deliberate. His eyes roll into the back of his head as we bottom out, basking in the sensation of being full. Then, ever so slowly, she grinds down on him. Just a little bit, then pull us up, leaving only the tip of his cock inside.

My pussy tightens around the head just before she slams us back down onto his shaft.

Hard.

And she's rewarded with a growl. I can't stop the smirk from growing on my face as he grabs my hips, holding us still.

"Love, I'm going to take you hard and quick."

"As long as you take me high baby."

Dex uses his hands to lift my hips and begins to pump in and out of me relentlessly. The pain is deliciously welcomed. Reaching up he claims our mouth, diving his tongue inside. The feeling is exquisite.

She gasps at a sharp sting that burns the flesh on my hips. Little droplets of blood run down my sides as his extended claws dig deeper into my skin. "Dex," she moans loudly.

He leans forward and flattens his wet tongue on my marks, licking the sweat that has formed there, causing a delicious shiver to run down my spine. Dex pistons his cock in and out of me, pure need to connect with his mate dominating every thrust. I can tell he is chasing his high, he needs this, and Sahara wants to give it to him.

"Sahara, fuck you feel so fucking good. Mmmmmm your pussy's so tight."

As he slams up into me, I try to match him by pushing myself down harder onto him. I can feel he is getting close. I lean in and return the favor by licking over my mark. He shivers under my touch. A bead of sweat rolls down his face and I want nothing more than to taste this sweet man. The drop rolls onto my tongue and I humming in pleasure at the taste.

Dragging my lips back down and feather kisses on his neck. When I think he can't take anymore, Sahara bites his mark hard. "Fuck, yes!" He growls loudly as his cock twitches inside of me. My pussy milks his dick for every drop it can give me. My head falls back, and I roll my hips a couple of more times. Applying pressure with his thumb to my clit, my body begins to shake and his grip on me tightens as I reach my own end and collapse on his chest.

"Now that I have had you, I don't think I will ever get enough of you baby. I do not know if I can ever sit in the background again." Dex says.

I look up at him through my lashes. "I'm just grateful." I smile and kiss his nose. Landon's eyes fade back to their human color as he lays us down on the couch. He pulls me tight against his chest, both of us not caring one bit that we are half naked. Before we know it, sleep comes for us.

LANDON

I wake up on the couch in Mal's office. She is snuggled in my arms, her hot breath fans my skin. Looking down at my little luna, I'm always in awe of her. Her beautiful skin still looks flushed from our love making. Her locks are sprawled all over, but her mark is visible to me. I lean in and brush the hair from her shoulder, placing sweet kisses on her mark. She nuzzles deeper into me but does not wake up. I continue my gentle assault on her mark, causing a growl to come from her.

"Mmmmm Mate..."

The sound that comes from her is sweet and sultry, but does not exactly sound like Mal.

"Sahara?"

"Yes." She purrs and snuggles in closer. Once Sahara surfaces, there's usually no stopping Dex from coming forward. He feels that he is missing the connection and one on one time with his mate. So how can I deny him? And if he wasn't currently snoring in my head, I know that he would be front and center ready for one-on-one time. But he's snoring so loud he sated ass can't even sense her calling to him.

"Mate, you seem worried?" Sahara asks as she runs her fingers across my forehead.

"I am worried." I prop myself up on my elbow to look into her green glowing eyes. "I don't want anything to happen to you or Mal.

You girls are mine and Dex's whole world, we would die without you." I reach in and kiss her on her nose.

"Landon, you cannot stop fate. We are the daughter of the goddess, and we must fight. We love that you try to protect us but remember that the four of us are a team. If you fight the process, you're just making it harder to do what we know must be done."

I look at my mate and smile. I don't think I have ever had a long conversation with Sahara before. I must admit that I sometimes forget that she's there since Mal can't shift. I really need to let Dex take over a little more and I'll have to talk to her and get to know her better. It really is the only way they can communicate.

"I'm sorry that I don't give Dex control as often as you probably need. I'm sorry I have not put your needs on the pedestal that they belong on. I really would have loved to have run my fingers through your fur. I bet you are the most beautiful wolf too." I see a gentle blush creep onto her face as she chews on her bottom lip.

"I would have loved that…" Tears fill the corners of her eyes. She looks lost in thought, then shakes her head like she is trying to regain her composure. I stare into her beautiful eyes and notice that there is no trace of the green glow that is normally there when Sahara's in control.

"Mal?"

"Yeah, sorry about that. Sahara feels left out sometimes." She fumbles with her fingers. Like she is recalling a bad memory. "I haven't shifted in years, and she just wants Dex, we can hear him howling at us, begging us to shift. She wants nothing more than to shift for him, to chase him in the woods… to be whole again. You know what I mean?"

She sits up, adjusts her clothes and gets that sweet little ass of hers back into her chair.

"I promise to let Dex have control more often. We want to keep our girls happy and content." I start to wiggle my eyebrows at her. I cannot stop the warm feeling that consumes me as I hear her giggle.

"You're beautiful, baby." Mal stops and looks at me with the sweetest smile.

"I'm going to head downstairs to my office to meet with the guys. We have a call with Alpha Tanner today."

"No worries, just make sure to meet Ellie and me in the dining hall for dinner."

"Of course." I walk over, give her a kiss and head out.

I mindlink everyone to meet in my office and I send Sean a text as well. When I get there, everyone is chatting and stuffing their faces. "What are you guys eating?" I ask as I sit behind my desk.

Sam has his mouth stuffed to the brim with what appears to be cake and Sean walks in carrying two plates.

"Ellie made cake with Mrs. Lane." Sam mumbles.

"It's a freaking funfetti cake!!" Sean says with a big smile. "I haven't had funfetti cake in years." Sean hands me a plate and we dig in. Holy crap this is so good. A light knock sounds on the door and I try to say come in, but it comes out garbled.

"Ome N."

Ellie pokes her head in with a questioning look on her face, then comes around the door. Rocking on her heels, she looks around to see the guys are smiling at her.

"Do you like it?"

Troy is the first to answer her. "Princess it is awesome."

"Weally?! YES!" She jumps up and down in excitement and then runs out the door. A moment later she is back pushing a serving cart. She has a whole other cake on it and three gallons of milk with cups.

"Hell, yeah little Alpha!" The triplets say in unison. She beams at them while on her way to give me a big hug. "I got to go daddy; I got a play day with Twevor fwom school."

"Have fun sweetie." She skips out the door, we're all kind of in a sugar daze as the door closes behind her... wait. "Who's Trevor?" We all ask at the same time.

"I'm already linking Trinity to ask." Troy says.

"We just linked Cammy too." The triplets add.

"Lara has been substituting at the school so… I might have linked her as well." Sam finishes.

Sean looks at all of us. "Do you want me to get his fingerprints? Run a background check on his family? Jesus Christ guys, she is going on a playdate, not the damn prom."

We all growl at him.

"Okay, okay I'll run a background check." He says with a huff quickly scrolling through his phone for his contact. We have all become so preoccupied with "Operation Playdate" that I almost don't hear the phone when it rings. I sprint back to my desk and nearly trip over Tim who has a map of the territory on the floor. He is scoping out where this kid Trevor's house is located. I can hear him mumble that we should add extra patrols in the woods when she is on a playdate. I realize at that moment that we all may be borderline overprotective, but I don't care.

"Hello?!" I say a little more aggressively than I planned.

"Uh, Alpha Landon?" I look down at the caller id and see that it is Alpha Tanner's office.

"Ah shit, sorry Alpha Tanner."

"Everything okay?" I hit the speaker button so the guys can hear the call.

"Ha yeah," I rub the back of my neck. "Ellie informed us that she was going on a playdate with a kid named Trevor…" I cough a little more dramatically than necessary. "The guys and I may or may not be doing a background check." As the words leave my mouth all the guys look up from the tasks they had been assigned. I can hear Tanner and Jim belly laughing in the background. Tim gives the phone the evil eye and the guys go back to work.

"I will never forget when Lara had her first playdate with a boy." Jim says right before a growl comes from Sam, causing everyone to start laughing. "My wife didn't inform me so when I opened the front door, this little shit was standing there. Calm as can be, saying *I'm here to play with Lara*... Like hell, you are kid. I turned him around and sent him home. I might have gone off the deep end as well. It gets easier the more girls you have." Jim chuckles, then releases a deep breath, taking a moment to gather his senses.

"Okay, okay... Let's get back to business. There was a reason I wanted to contact you, Landon. I received a letter that was left at the border this afternoon. It's from Austin, he is asking for a secret meeting. He wants to meet at midnight tonight in the same spot."

"What else does the letter say?"

"He said it is a matter of life and death."

I scan the room at everyone and they all nod, there is no way they are missing this. I wrap up the call with Tanner and tell everyone to meet downstairs in twenty minutes.

On my way to meet Mal in our apartment, I link the kitchen staff to pack some coolers for the ride. We won't have time to stop at all.

"Landon?"

"I'm in the bathroom."

Mal rolls to the door. "You, okay? What's going on?"

I explain what happened at Gold Moon. Her eyes grow big, but she gets a faraway look about her. She seems lost in thought. "I wonder what Austin could want?" Saying more to herself than to me. She rolls into the hallway, and I quickly grab my bag off the bed and run after her. Mal stops in front of the window. I come up behind her and follow her line of sight. She's watching the SUV get loaded up. She exhales deeply then gazes up at me. "Sorry, I'm just frustrated, Landon."

All I know is that I'm not going to let anything happen to her. I'm going to follow every lead possible, and I will not rest until my girl feels safe...until my girl*s* feel safe. I had Sam set up extra patrols while we're gone, and the surrounding packs sent extra patrols to where our borders touch. I feel confident leaving Mal for the day.

We get outside, everyone is saying goodbye to their mates and slowly getting into the Suburban. Omegas are loading the last cooler into the back. I turn to Mal, the look on her face has not changed. I get down on my knees and pull her to me. I place a gentle kiss on her lips, she wraps her arms around my neck and holds me tightly.

"Come back to me safely, please."

"Always baby." I give her one more kiss then jog off to the car. If I wait one more moment, I won't be able to leave her. The suv has barely traveled two feet when I hear a little high-pitched squeal.

"DADDYYYYY WAIT!!!"

Sam peers at the rearview mirror and sees Ellie chasing after us.

"Stop Sam!" I yell as he slams on the breaks. I make quick work of my seatbelt and swiftly jump out.

"Daddy! You were leaving without saying goodbye." She scolds, her hands on her hips and full of attitude. She's putting on a show, but I can see the sadness she is trying to hide.

"I'm so sorry, I didn't want to bother you on your playdate with Trevor." At the mention of the little boy, a growl seeps out from the vehicle. I can't help but smile as Ellie glares over my shoulder at the men, then she rolls her eyes and shakes her head.

Dragging her attention back to me, she closes the small distance between us and throws her little arms around my neck. "Oh daddy, come home safe." When she pulls away, she dashes over to the SUV. "Bye to my favowite uncles!" She waves, blows kisses, then turns, sprinting back toward the pack house. She turns around one last time and smiles big. I wave as I climb back into the car and see all the guys are looking back at her. They are all just mush in her hands.

"I'm her favorite, you know." Tony boasts with a smug look on his face.

We get back on the road when a ding sounds from Sean's phone. After a brief exchange, Sean relays the information. "Trevor passed the background check. Apparently, he is top of his 1st grade class and his dream is to be a warrior when he grows up just like his dad

Michael. He even stood up for Ellie when she got picked on for being an orphan. They have been friends for years. His mother and her mother were friends." We all look at each. Damn this is a good kid. Everyone seems to be nodding in approval. Shit, I think I'm going to end up liking this Trevor kid.

The rest of the ride is quiet and smooth. We finally get to Gold Moon's gates just before midnight. The guards let us through. We pull over and get out to walk the rest of the way. We head a mile northeast into the woods. It took five minutes to trek to the meeting location. We spot Tanner, Jim, Caden, Tristan and I believe his name is Liam, Caden's Gamma. After everyone gets reacquainted, everyone finds a defensive hiding spot.

Jim greets Sam with a friendly slap on the back. "Cutting it a bit close, hmm?"

"We hit traffic." Sam replies, returning Jim's smack.

Troy links me... -**Someone is approaching one hundred yards to your right.** I turn to see if it's only Austin or is someone with him. I nod my head in the direction of Austin and everyone turns as he appears out of the shadows.

"Alpha Tanner?"

"Austin."

Austin bows to the Alpha, which shocks us all. This is the man that has been poisoning my mate and queen. I'm desperately trying to keep Dex in the back of my mind, because if this guy makes one wrong move, I might kill him.

"Fuck, if he breathes wrong, I might tear him limb from limb." Dex growls in my head.

"You better start talking because if we don't find this information credible you will be killed on the spot." Alpha Tanner states coldly.

"I deserve to be killed sir; I know that is my fate. I just want the opportunity to die with a clear conscience." He looks around and takes a deep breath. His movements are sluggish, he seems extremely tired and looks like fucking shit. I'm beginning to think that this meeting will be very beneficial. "I know that I willingly went along with this plan for Scott to take over. In the beginning... Listen I can't even justify why I choose to follow him all of these years. But the further into this we got, the crazier he became. He wasn't always this way." He slumps down on a tree stump, rubbing his face in frustration. He takes another deep breath, and as he exhales, he looks up to the moon. Seemingly directing his next word toward it.

"Ever since we fought together during the Great War... he had this whole plan to expose the chosen one. He thought Malinda was a decoy. He laid in wait... wanting to witness the descendants' powers emerge. Scott was ecstatic with what happened to her mate. Then when the bright light swept through and killed the rogues, he swore it came from Malinda. Proving she is the goddess on earth. Since then, he has become obsessed with her. At first Scott just watched her and studied her from afar. He then got this idea to send her advertisements about physical therapy at a local gym to her pack- some subliminal messaging type shit. Even sample protein drinks... trying to feed on her emotion of wanting to be whole again. But it actually fucking worked. She started going to a small gym just outside her pack territory. It was some friend of Scott; he had the asshole there feedin her daily drinks and fillin her head with bullshit that if she got to Paisley she could work with *Scott and his up and coming trainer/physical therapist he knew*. He made it sound as if Scott could help her get to the next level of the healing process. I was shocked when it fell into place for the bastard. Because she really moved to Paisley. He thought if he just kept her secluded and drugged, she would remain wolfless and mateless. By doing this she could never get her powers and interfere with his grand plan."

Wolfless and mateless? That asshole is more of a piece of shit than I could have imagined. I try to clear my mind so I can concentrate on the rest of what Austin is saying.

"Scott has been training rogues in the gym at night. He has an on again, off again witch girlfriend and she helps mask their scents. It worked because none of his customers were able to smell their disgusting asses after they left. Without me knowing, he set me up as Malinda's physical therapist. It didn't take much time for me to get to like her."

Hearing that causes Dex to growl dangerously low. Austin throws his hands up in a protective manner.

"I mean, like a friend Alpha, I swear. I have never had feelings for Mal. Scott on the other hand I'm not sure. She always intrigued him. Scott would visit her at our training and always offer her "a protein drink," but as you can guess it was laced with the poison. I had no clue that he had been poisoning her, until he asked me to start making the drinks for her when he was not there. I had to think quickly and come up with a plan because I wanted no part in that. So, I started to dilute the poison given to her. I will never forget how proud he was of himself for coming up with the idea. That's when he told me that the samples, he had mailed her at Stone Mountain were all laced with it. He had been doing this for years."

"Why did you dilute them? Why would you do that?" I ask as calmly as I can.

"Because she does not deserve this. She's a good person, all she wanted to do was walk again, find a mate who could love her like she is, and become a mother. This poison would eventually prevent all of those things from happening. When she met you and I told you not to give up on her, I was totally serious. You would save her from that hell. I was hoping that Scott would back off with his plan and just let it go. Instead, he flipped the fuck out. He got her at breakfast before your annual meeting. He had room service send her a drink, and as you know that dose almost killed her..."

"What do you want now?" Tanner asks, obviously pissed.

"Like I said, I know I'll be killed for my actions. I just want Mal to know I tried to right my wrongs. Let me keep you apprised of what

Scott is doing. Let me be your eyes and ears and when you get the opening to kill him… you kill me too."

Chapter 31
Landon

    I'm hearing Austin talk and he does not sound like a criminal mastermind, and on the other hand it seems like Scott doesn't either. I'm still trying to figure out how he is putting this together. Seriously, how has this plan lasted this long?

    Tanner glances at me, "Landon, she may be our future Queen, but she is your mate and Luna. What do you want to do here? It's your decision."

    "Listen Alpha Landon, I know I have no right to ask this but let me try to fix this. If anything, let me be a spy. I have to make this right."

    I examine him, trying to gauge if he is telling the truth. The look in Austin's eyes gives him away. He lights up when he talks about helping her, he cares for her. You can see by his body language that he is riddled with guilt. I'm so deep in thought that I'm startled when a buzz of an incoming mindlink penetrates my head...

    -So, what does your gut tell you?

    -Sam, my gut says trust him; I do not think he is lying to us. He is not trying to bargain for his life. He knows death is coming for him. I say we make this work.

    "Austin, if you double cross me and I find out that this is a trick to get to my Luna or my pup I will rip your heart out and shove it down your throat. Do you understand what I am saying to you?"

He straightens his back and looks me straight in the eye with absolutely no fear.

"Yes, Alpha Landon."

A cacophony of phones simultaneously ringing breaks the silence of the night. We all grab for our phones while looking at each other. Our mates are calling us. I answer quickly as do the others.

"Mal what's wrong?" I demand, my heart in my throat.

I pull the phone from my ear when a blood curdling scream comes from the other end of the line.

"Mal!!!" I yell into the receiver.

"Landon, we are under attack." She sounds out of breath. "Rogues have breached the western border. The alarm never went off, it never went off!"

I can hear her frustration as she tries to describe what is happening. That they are trying to keep it under control. Then a scuffle interrupts her.

"LUNA! GET BACK IN THE HOUSE NOW!" A warrior shouts at her.

"YOU GET IN THE HOUSE AND FUCKING GUARD THOSE PUPS!!!" She roars back. Then in a rushed, yet normal tone, she addresses me. "Landon... Get home."

Those were her last words before her phone disconnects. I don't even blink. I have Austin by the throat and up against a tree before I had even thought about doing it. "Did you set us up?" I demand. He is pawing at my hand trying to get me to loosen my grip. "Did you set us up?" I repeat, growling louder. He shakes his head adamantly, and I throw him across the field.

"No." Austin coughs out, desperate to get air in his lungs. "Alpha Landon, Alpha Tanner." *cough* "I swear, this couldn't be Scott...but," after taking a few seconds to regain some composure, he rubs at his throat and stares off into the woods.

"But what, Austin? What aren't you telling us?" I snarl, flexing my fingers.

"But his Gamma, Scott's Gamma. Tyler. He's the guy that took your little girl. I didn't know that Scott sent him in as part of the event staff. I saw him the day of the wedding when he snatched her. I'm the one who took her from him. I made sure that she was not hurt and put her in the path of patrols. I didn't want her with him. Tyler is on a power trip; he seems to have something to prove with Scott."

Sam's loud gasp draws my attention to him, he is still on the phone with Lara.

"Lara, it's okay.... No, don't talk like that...." He jabs at the speaker button on the phone, so he won't have to relay any information.

"Sam, I love you."

"I love you too."

"Please know I tried to protect the pups, the warriors were all on patrol and couldn't get here fast enough." Her breath is extremely ragged, each one more laborious than the previous. This makes my feet hit the gravel even faster. Tanner screams into his phone to *get the plane ready* as he and Jim jump into the car with us.

"Lara, it's dad. Hold on sweetheart we're coming."

"Daddy..." She can barely say his name through all of her sobs.

"Baby...what happened to you? How are you hurt?" Sam asks, desperation heavy in his voice.

Nothing... no response.

"Lara!" Sam lurches forward in his seat and grabs his chest. The best way to describe the sound that comes out of his mouth is agony and despair and torture all thrown together in the most painful howl I have ever heard.

A commotion of unidentifiable noises emanate out from the other end, Lara must have dropped the phone. All we can do is listen.

Then a commanding female voice breaks through, clear as day. "Lara, look at me.... Lara, it's Mal. Look at me damn it.... Cammy start breathing for her, and I will do chest compressions." There's more clattering and shuffling, then Mal calmly starts counting. "1, 2, 3, 4, 5… now pinch her nose, tilt her head back a bit and breathe in her mouth."

You would never know the extent of the mayhem going on back home, by listening to Mal's voice. She is calm as can be, which is exactly what is needed in a time like this. Her counting turns into a low mumble and she must be concentrating on her work. Then she interrupts herself, "Now Trinity, how bad is your injury?" Mal asks gently.

"I will live Luna."

"Good. Hold this and apply pressure to help with her bleeding."

"Absolutely," Trinity states, then adds, "Cammy you're going to need stitches."

"I know, the triplets are going to be pissed." All of the men in the car are in a constant growl.

Then a shock sounding Trinity shouts, "Jesus Mal, you're going to need stitches too!"

"Shit, I can't see it. Is the wound bad?"

"Yes, Luna very. Mal you're actually losing a lot of blood."

"I can't focus on that right now. Cammy are you sure you're, okay?"

"I'm, uh, I'm…" Cammy starts, then her voice breaks. "No," She sobs. "I have never killed anyone before, but I saw those assholes hurt Lara and then try to take Ellie." She hiccups as she tries to breathe, "What if these rogues are like the Gold Moon kids? What if I killed an innocent person." You can almost hear her struggling with this potential issue.

"Listen to me now. All of you fought well and you did not hesitate… You made me proud; your mates will be proud, I can personally guarantee that your Alpha will be proud… Damn it Lara, fucking breathe!"

"I GOT A PULSE!" Trinity screams "I linked the docs."

Then the phone goes silent.

It fucking died.

I stare open mouthed at Sam. He is physically shaking; silent tears are pouring down his face. Jim is trying to comfort Sam... but Sam has nothing to give Jim in return. Tanner pulls our vehicle up next to a small, luxury looking jet and then yells at everyone to get on.

"I don't care how you got this but just tell me it can get us there fast." I pant as my shoes clang up the portable metal staircase to the plane's door.

Right behind me, Tanner answers, his voice full of certainty. "It will."

We pull up to the pack house to see my warriors dragging the dead rogues into a pile. I open the car door and the anger that's rolling off of me seems to heat up the atmosphere as I stare at the destruction in front of us. It takes me a half a heartbeat to take all of this in. Cars are flipped upside down, small trees knocked over. There is a gaping hole on the side of someone's house. "How the hell did this happen?" I angrily demand of no one in particular.

I try to link Mal, but I get nothing. "Landon, they are all in the hospital." Troy yells as we all break into a full sprint to get there. I fling the doors open and Dr. K is in front of me almost instantly.

"Stop right there." She yells, causing growls from everyone. "If you want to see your mates then you must stop and listen to me. If not, you need to wait outside. Do you agree to my terms." I go to walk around her, and she puts her hand on my chest and pushes me back with all her might. "I am not fucking kidding Landon!"

"Kara, watch your tone," I snarl at her.

"Yes, you are my Alpha, but this is my hospital and if you do not agree to my terms, you will wait outside. Do you all hear me?"

It takes a few seconds, but we all end up nodding in defeat. My cousin turns to my Beta. "Now Sam, Lara is still in surgery. She will end up in room 225. Her wounds are severe. Her right lung was even punctured." Sam is breathing very heavily but he is listening to every word that K says. I place my hand on his stiff shoulder, hoping it brings him at least a little comfort.

Dr. K continues. "When she comes out of surgery, I am going to keep her in a drug induced coma. This will give her and her wolf a chance to heal." Through his distress, Sam nods in understanding. Jim pulls Sam into a big hug.

K turns to Tony, Tim, and Tom. "Cammy needed thirty stitches for a deep claw gash on her arm. She is patched up, but she is with a counselor in room two-twenty. I am not sure if you know but Cammy had her first kill today. She is only eighteen. If you remember your first kill, it doesn't matter the circumstance as to why you had to do it, it is still traumatic. Lara had been severely injured, and we found Cammy standing over her, protecting Lara and pack pups Lara had been protecting. I linked the therapist to let him know you are here, he asked for 5 more minutes then you three can go in." Tony seems to be holding it together. Tim and Tom not so much.

"Troy, Trinity needed ten stitches on the back of her head." Relief slowly claims his features as he realizes she is going to be okay. "Troy, there is one more thing you need to know. She also sustained a deep claw wound over her mating mark. She noticed it after I took over Lara's care, when she had time to take care of herself. She is now terrified you will no longer want her. The mark is visible, but it is distorted." Troy's eyes nearly pop out of his head. "I put her in room 221 which is connected to Cammy's."

"Alpha, Luna is in her room 215. She needed over one hundred stitches..." K coughs into her fist as if she is apprehensive about revealing the next part. "She lost a lot of blood and needed a transfusion. She is currently resting with Ellie. Our little alpha needed a cast on her left arm because she has a small fracture. She also received a few stitches from a claw scratch when a rogue tried to take her. Luckily a little boy pulled Ellie out of the way, so Cammy was able to snap its neck."

Scanning over the furious faces of all the men in front of her, she continues. "I'm begging you to reign in your anger. Your mates have been through a lot. I know your wolves may not agree with them trying to help, but just know that without the top female leaders of this pack those pups would have died tonight. Those women are selfless heroes." She says as she stares us down. "Now go to your mates."

Not needing any other encouragement, the guys run off to see their women. All I want is to see Malinda, but I am the Alpha and I need a quick debriefing. "K, can you give me a run down on the rest of the pack? How many more injured and how many losses??"

"Landon... we have twenty-five injured and no loss of life yet. Some of our allies did lose a few."

I stare off at nothing as I take all of this information in. Down the hall is Dr. Taylor with John, Stacy and one of his warriors. I'm too far away and it's too loud in here for me to hear what they are saying. But then my attention is grabbed by a warrior that crumbles to the floor. A pain filled roar explodes from his throat. It's raw and completely heartbreaking.

"His mate?" I ask K.

"That is Zack... yeah his mate did not make it." I nod my head in understanding, grief and guilt. I can relate with what he is going through from my short time with Tara, "Alpha, his mate was Jessica..."

Oh goddess... Today has been a nightmare. That information has me excusing myself to find Mal and Ellie. It's almost a tangible need to be with them.

I tiptoe into room 215 and find my girls sleeping, snuggled up close in the same bed. Mal has tubes coming from her left arm and leg, draining the infection. They are both bundled up under the sheet, so I'm not able to see much of her body. However little skin that is exposed, is bruised. Her healing ability is just not what it used to be. I think the doctors are using the method of: Better to be safe than sorry, when it comes to her treatment. I know that they are doing all that they can.

Gingerly placed on top of the sheet is Ellie's arm, encased in a bright pink, sparkly cast. A direct hit with a sledgehammer to my heart couldn't have hurt more than the sight of my girls in this hospital. I quietly amble over to the bed and pull up a chair. I sit and just stare at them, glad they are alive, glad they could defend themselves, but damn I would fucking do anything to trade places with them right now.

A faint knock on the door sounds before a nurse is wheeling in another bed. She places her finger to her lips to make a shhhh warning then shoos me out of the way. Without making an ounce of noise, she has connected both beds, almost making it a queen size. I barely wait for the door to close after her before I crawl into the bed and carefully pull my girls into me. Having their slumbering forms in my arms while inhaling their scents calms me enough to finally meet up with my own long-lost friend, Sleep.

Chapter 32
Sam

The hard plastic chair that I have been sitting in creaks as I shift my weight, yet again. Trying to get comfortable. Trying to keep myself calm. My ass has been in the waiting room of the pack hospital for three hours. I am fucking losing my mind. Jim called Tristian and he is on his way to us. At this moment I wish my parents were here, I wish I had someone to comfort me. When I lost them, it felt as if my whole world was ending… but now losing my parents doesn't even come close to knowing how close I was to losing my mate.

My wolf Jax and I are going insane. When we were leaving Gold Moon I thought I felt our mate bond break. Now I don't know if it was the bond or just my heart, all I know is that I was in so much pain listening to her scream. For the first time in my life, I feel helpless, lost and alone. The doors leading to the surgery wing open with a loud bang, pulling me from my thoughts. Dr. Taylor appears with Dr. K following.

Jim and I jump to our feet, bombarding her with questions at the same time. "How is she?" "Did she wake up?" "Is she going to be, okay?"

K puts her hands up to stop us from rambling. She exchanges a look with Dr. Taylor. "Beta Sam, Beta Jim please try and keep your composure." She gives us both a stern glare, compassion mixed with a little scolding resides there. I look at Jim, he's looking back at me. We are both just so worried that it seems we can't control our emotions. We both face her and nod in understanding, there really is no arguing with her. I mean, I get where she is coming from, but she has no clue how hard this is for us... for me.

"Lara is stable and her wolf has already started to heal her. Like I said before I have her in a drug induced coma. This is only to help her heal faster. She's still in recovery but soon we will be moving her into a room where we have added another bed for you. Please just be careful of the wires and tubes. It will be just a few more moments. The pup seems to be doing completely fine, however just as an extra precaution we are going to keep monitoring it."

"Oh, thank goddess." Jim says as he pulls me into a big hug. I hug him back as hard as I can. He has taken a liking to me, and it is nice to have that father figure in my life again. Especially since he is a Beta, he feels like home, and I realize I am not alone anymore.

Pup.

Wait a second...did she say 'pup'?

What pup?

Her words barge through the fog in my head... I pull away from the hug slowly, my jaw is on the floor and my heart is beating in my throat.

"Did you just say, 'the pup'?! We are having a PUP?!"

"Sam, you're squeezing me." I have a death grip K's shoulders, I quickly let go and smooth out her white jacket. Holy crap, I don't think I can handle any more emotional surprises today.

"Thank you. Yes, Lara and the pup will recover. Now go be with your mate, Daddy."

She doesn't need to tell me twice. I sprint down the hall, Lara's smiling face is all that my mind's eye sees. I want it tattooed on the back of my eyelids. I rush into her room and almost double over from a pain that I can only compare to being punched in the stomach by a bear. Seeing her like this... rocks my whole world. All of the wires, tubes and monitors are confusing, as someone who never has had to spend time in the hospital.

I pull a chair up next to her. The bruises that mare her perfect skin are slowly healing. The faint outline of a hand on her throat and the subsequent bruising in the pattern of fingerprints is forcing Jax to the surface.

'Jax, I need you to relax please. I need full control in order to take care of our mate. I can't have you going off the deep end buddy.'

'Make her better Sam, I don't want to lose my mate or pup.'

'I promise they will be okay.'

He grunts then moves to the back of my mind. He can be so stubborn sometimes. Jax needs to realize that I would do everything in my power to keep my little mate safe. I reach for her hand and place sweet kisses on each finger. Not knowing what else to do, I began to talk to her.

"Lara, I am here baby girl. I just want you to know that you were so brave tonight. I am so proud of how strong you are. I hope you can hear me, I just wanted to tell you how much I love you."

THIRD PERSON

As soon as K dismisses everyone Tony, Tim and Tom go flying down the hallway to their mate. They slide to a stop crashing into each other. Tony pushes his brothers off of him and rolls his eyes. "Chill, you two."

They all take a deep breath trying to compose themselves. Slowly opening the door, they stick their heads into the room just to see their mate sitting in a chair staring out the window. She is silently wiping her tears; her face is all blotchy and her hair is all over the place. But to them she has never looked more beautiful. Cammy turns her head slowly to the sound of the door's heavy squeak. The way her smile does not reach her eyes tells the boys just how much she is hurting.

Slowly they approach, trying not to startle her. Tony brushes the hair from her face and gently tilts her chin up so she is looking in his eyes.

"Are you okay?"

She slowly nods her head, the tears not letting up.

"Will you let us, see?"

She nods her head again then carefully lifts her shirt a bit to show the eight-inch gash on her side. Stitches now grace her beautiful skin. Tom reaches out as if to touch them, his fingers hovering over the black thread.

"It's okay. I barely feel it." Cammy says with a sniffle. "I don't even know why they gave them to me." Tim's face scrunches at the sound of her voice breaking off.

Stitches are only needed when the wounds are deep. Even for a wolf, a deep gash can take over a week to heal, but with the help of stitches it will be reduced to a day or two.

"Cam, we are so proud of you. You are going to make a great warrior, taking on an adult male rogue. That is badass."

"But what if he was like the kids from Gold Moon... What if he had a family and did not know this was happening?" She sobs. "What if I killed an innocent man?"

"Cam, look at us." Tony gets to his knees pulling her chair closer to him. He places his left hand on her knee and his right hand on her cheek. His thumb wiping away the tears that are now running in a constant stream. "From what we have gathered this was not related to those who are after Luna."

Tom sits next to her. "You did what you are trained to do. You protected Mal and we are beyond proud of you." He leans in and kisses her forehead. She nods her head and takes another deep breath.

"Jessica... Jessica is the one that alerted us. The siren never went off. That is why we were caught off guard. The rogue attacked and started for Mal. Jessica... She just dived in front of Mal. This gave Mal a chance to get the rest of the pups in the house. But Jessica was in human form because we could not link each other now that she is part of Stone Mountain... so she took some hard hits. She was never a warrior."

"Cammy, we know that your relationship with Jessica was difficult at times but today she showed that it is all in the past. She put the Luna Queen first above her own life, she may not have been a warrior, but she definitely died as one." Cammy cries into Tim's side and they all just hold onto their mate.

TROY

I softly open Trinity's door and peek in to see her curled up in a ball on the hospital bed. Although the doctor said her injury wasn't severe, being a top female in the pack requires her to stay for twenty-four hours for any kind of injury.

"My love."

She turns her beautiful face to me, our eyes meet. Then she bursts into tears. For an unbelievably strong woman, at this moment she seems to be a shell of her former self. I try to hug her, but she resists. Not letting that deter me, I wrap my arms around her, and pull her in, holding her tightly to my chest. Within moments she melts into me. I lean my head back a little, brushing the hair from her face.

"Trin, you fought bravely today. What has you so upset? You saved Lara, you protected the pack pups, and you defended our Luna!"

The tears are flowing freely as she sits up and pulls the collar of her hospital gown down to expose her mark. There are three large claw marks across her mating mark.

"I failed you, the one thing other than my life I should have protected was my mark. I am not a warrior. Through the whole thing I was going on adrenaline." She quickly pulls herself up onto her knees, her hands grasp my face and stares deep into my eyes. "Can you still feel the mate bond?" She delves into my eyes, hers pleading silently for hope. The expression on her face is absolutely killing me. I place a hand on each side of her face and rest my forehead to hers.

"Yes, I feel the bond. I can feel it running through my blood."

With that she smashes her lips to mine. This kiss is filled with raw passion and need. Apparently, her wounds are bothering her because Trinity rips my shirt off, then glides her hands down my chest to my jeans.

"Trinity, you are in the hospital and my brothers are right next door." I say breathlessly.

"You are going to mark me again and there is no way in hell I am leaving here without it."

"Baby, your mark is still beautiful, those cuts will heal." "I do not care." She snarls as she extends a claw and rips my pants off, coming dangerously close to my cock. Yeah, she means business.

Pushing me to my back, Trinity climbs on top, straddling me. She grabs my now painfully hard cock and starts to stroke. Don't judge me, she is my mate, and she is hot as fuck. A moan escapes my lips. She smirks as she leans in and kisses down my jaw. Down my chest and now she is wiggling herself to line up that lush mouth of hers with my dick.

"No... you have just been through something traumatic. This can wait."

"I want you, Troy." I half-heartedly try to pull her back into my arms, but she smacks my hand out of the way. She licks the whole length of my cock before taking every inch of me in her mouth. I can't help the groan that comes from me. From her reaction, she loves knowing what she does to me. I love to watch her especially when she wants control. She is doing things with her tongue that are making my toes curl.

A growl reverberates from my chest as she releases me and crawls back up to my lips. "Take me," she whispers as she puts her mouth on mine. My mate doesn't have to ask twice, I'll give her whatever she needs to feel better in this moment. I pull us off the bed and turn her so she's standing with her back against my front. I push her front down to the bed and she extends her arms to catch herself. I slowly kick her feet apart, with mine, then open her legs up even more with my knee between her legs. I run my hands down her back, over her ass and run my fingers over her delicate flower that is dripping with want and need.

I take my wet finger and run it around the crown of my dick, then I line the head up at her entrance. She whimpers as I insert just a very little bit of myself into her.

"Please." I know what she is begging for, so I swiftly enter her from behind and her pussy quickly clenches around my dick. Her thighs slam against the side of the mattress. The feeling of being inside my mate is exquisite.

"Harder!" she breathes out. I tighten my grip on her hips. I'm sure I'll add to her bruises but at least these ones will have a happy memory attached to them. I pump in and out of her mercilessly. Tremors start taking over her body, so I grab her hair and pull. The force brings her hands off the bed, her back makes contact with my chest. I wrap one arm around her waist to keep her cemented to me. I slide my other hand out of her hair and move it to the base of her jaw, holding her chin high...exposing the long column of her throat so I can access the delectable flesh of her neck. I am fucking my mate just how she craves it. Just how I crave it.

"Yes, goddess... Ahhh yes Troy."

"Fuck... you like it like this, my love?"

"Goddess yes Troy."

My arm tightens around her as she is now shaking uncontrollably. My canines extend. I am going to mark her; I am going to make her come like she has never come before. She will know that I will always feel the bond and she is my goddamn world. I start to rub her clit. She screams my name and as I sink my teeth into her sexy neck. Claiming her all over again.

"Mine." Max and I growl.

"Yours. Always and forever."

Chapter 33
Landon

I wake with a start... I swivel my head around the room and remember I am in the hospital with my girls. It takes me a moment to register the voices and sounds that are coming from outside our room.

Wait... are people...mating? Those Blaney brothers are very vocal. "Ah fuck that's loud." I whisper to myself. I tell Dax to remind me to talk to Rich to see if there is a safe way to soundproof these hospital rooms.

Our door opens and a nurse pokes her head in then shakes a little package at me. "What are those?" I ask.

She walks over to open it. "Ear plugs," she whispers as she puts them in Ellie's ears while she sleeps. Hmmm, I nod my head at her smart thinking. I am thoroughly impressed... the nurse giggles at my response. Apparently, this is a common thing. I snuggle back into Mal as the nurse's footsteps disappear once the door is shut, only to have Mal stir in my arms.

"Landon?" She questions in her sleepy voice.

"Shhh, baby I am here, please rest." She stretches her arms, then winces a bit. I can't help but reach over to help her get comfortable.

"Oh, I am fine, I promise. I have been hurt much worse before."

"That is not the point Malinda Marie Wright, you have over a hundred stitches in your body... you take longer to heal... I just..."

"You just what?" She tries to sit up in anger but can't because of the little girl in her arms. So, she chooses to give me the death stare instead and if looks could kill, yeah, I would be six feet under.

"First of all.... did you just Full Name me?! I can't believe you want to pull that shit with me Landon Hunter Wright. You are not my parent, you sir are my mate." She whisper-yells at me. I scrunch my eyebrows up; shit I am an adult and this woman just stripped me bare by using my full name.

"Second of all... do I need to remind you that I am a warrior... chair or no chair. I am going to get hurt, it's part of the job."

My eyes are now bulging out of my head. Why is it that every time I bring up her safety, she automatically thinks I am attacking her skills.

"You are my mate first and seeing you in pain is fucking killing me right now. My mate and my pup are in the fucking hospital. I was not here to protect you. My job is to fucking protect my god damn family. Why do you always think I am attacking you? Why can't I just be scared for just one moment that your lives were in danger, and everything was totally out of my control. Even though I had enough warriors here to protect you properly... it still was not enough. I have no clue why the alarm did not go off. All of my preparations were in place, and they did not work. It was about an hour to get back to you but that hour lasted years for me. It was eating me alive, how could I have left my Luna and pup defenseless."

I yell a little louder than I intend, and Ellie starts to stir. At this point I am kind of glad for the ear plugs the nurse gave her. This woman, my mate, ugh she is going to be the fucking death of me.

"Mal, I love you with everything I have in me... why do you always seem to doubt me and my intentions?"

Malinda is now looking down at her hands as she fiddles with the blanket. I tilt my head to catch her gaze.

"Landon, you did not leave us defenseless. You had so many warriors here from our surrounding allies. The alarm not going off, I think that is how it got so out of hand... but you are right, and I am sorry."

"Say what now..."

A small smile appears on her face as she coughs nervously." Ahhhh, I said you are right." She mumbles but it turns into a sweet laugh that fills me with such joy. She reaches up to my face and brushes her thumb over my lips. "I'm sorry sweetie, but none of this is your fault." I reach for her hand and kiss it.

We eventually get to discuss everything that happened with Austin. He said that this could not be Scott because he was with Scott just two hours before he met with us. That if he was going to attack, he knew that Scott would be there. He would need to be there in person to formally declare a challenge.

"It has to be tied together though, all of the high ranked wolves are gone for the night, and the alarm just mysteriously stops working. We would have had no injuries if the alarm was working and that frustrates the shit out of me. Was it this Tyler guy?" She scrunches her nose as she thinks hard and that is when I realize she said injuries...not deaths. Oh no, she has no clue that Jessica died.

"Mal, I need to let you know that at this time we do have one reported death." Sadness immediately darkens her beautiful features.

"Who...?" Tears well up in her eyes. As a Luna, she is connected to her pack, and Mal... as the daughter of the goddess, she is connected to all.

"Mal, it was Jessica... apparently you were trying to get the pups into the pack house, she jumped in front of the rogue that was after you. They fought and when he tossed her, she hit her head really hard. They could not stop the bleeding on her brain."

Tears fall freely down her face... Mal spared Jessica's life. She wanted her to live a happy long life with her mate, but in times of war no one is safe from cheating death. She sniffles then reaches for more tissues. "Poor Zack."

"It will be okay; the goddess will bless him. I just know it. Jessica was not a warrior, she could have called for help, but she chose to help save you, like you saved her. If that is not a change of heart, then I don't know what one is."

Mal gives me a half smile and snuggles deeper into my side as K walks in. She goes right to the monitors to triple check everything is good and then leans over to see how Ellie is healing. Once she seems happy with her round and sure that Mal is healing nicely, a nurse comes in and removes Mal's drains.

Mal tries to get comfortable again, I help her with her pillow and a thought crosses my mind. "Babe, who was the pup that helped Ellie escape?"

"Trevor."

"I knew I liked that kid from the moment I saw him."

It has now been thirty-six hours since the attack, the alarm has been fixed with a backup system added. Apparently, someone had removed the fuse for the alarm, thus inspiring me to have more cameras installed around the border. Everything is being double, and triple checked. The files on my desk are piling up and with each meeting we have the more frustrated I get.

When Tanner got back to Gold Moon he interrogated Austin again. We realized he truly was clueless concerning the breach and we all agreed that we needed him on the inside. I may regret letting him go but Malinda was certain that Austin was going to stay true to his word.

"I don't know why Landon; I just have a gut feeling." The look on her face was so sure, that she could now trust him. After speaking with Tanner, we did come up with a few theories about the attack.

Theory one: Scott's so-called Gamma was here as part of the event staff. He could have figured out how to deactivate the alarm to allow Scott to cross the border the night of our wedding. Since they never came back... the alarm went unnoticed. Then a group of rogues saw the male ranked wolves leave the territory and thought they would take a shot. Without the alarm they got far onto the property. Even with all of the extra security, sometimes shit happens.

The other theory is that Scott is responsible or maybe his Gamma is. Maybe they're onto Austin and wanted to take advantage of the window of opportunity. Either way a battle is brewing, and we need to have our defenses strong. With the upgrades to our security systems, we should be all set. Everyone is training harder than ever before. We are holding training sessions several times a day, most importantly we are trying to train our Omega members. I need to make sure that even they are prepared for this battle.

"Alpha?" Sam and Troy call out as they enter my office. I am just finishing up a call with Gold Moon, I wave them in to have a seat.

"Thank you, Tanner, I will call you back later." I hang up the phone and rub my hands over my face. Fuck I am so tired. I look at the guys and they look beat as well. Sam's mate Lara woke up and was crestfallen that she did not get to tell Sam about the pup. She had found out that morning and had planned a surprise for later that night. You could see the disappointment all over her face and it broke Sam. So, Mal promised Lara that she would come up with a fun gender reveal party for them, this news made Lara screech with joy.

"Okay, Sam and I have a bet going on, what did Gold Moon have to say?"

"No, we do not... ignore him would ya." Sam says as he shoves Troy and rolls his eyes.

"Guys seriously grow up." Troy tries to feign hurt. "Like I was saying, Tanner has been in contact with Austin. He is saying that Scott is planning an attack on one of the packs in the next month-ish. He's not one hundred percent sure on the exact date though, but it will definitely be soon." The guys exchange a look with each other.

"With this being said, I want the pups shipped out to Harvest Moon and New moon. I have already talked to their Alpha's, and they are more than happy to help us. We need to make sure that the territory is prepared for battle. Training needs to double and even triple for those at certain levels. I know we started training the Omega's, but we really need to push everyone in human and wolf form." Now here is where I bury myself. "Also, something else to consider and help give me ideas on how to accomplish my next ridiculously hard task…" Everyone's eyes are on me and as the words start to roll off my tongue, I know I have just signed my own death cert. "How do I get Mal to go with the pups and leave the fighting to us?"

They rapidly blink at me before these bastards burst out laughing. They are practically rolling on the fucking floor. "That's a funny one. You think she is going to leave you behind and miss this fight? Apparently, you need to get a checkup from Dr. K because you are losing it my friend." Sam says as he wipes his tears from his face.

"I think it's cute that you think she will go without a fuss. I mean, you have met your mate before, correct?" I roll my eyes at Troy for his very childish comment.

"Yes, smart ass." I needlessly answer.

"Oh good, just checking, because she would never leave you… ever. You are going to even have a hard time convincing Ellie to leave you, too. That little pup is a whole other ball of wax." Troy continues.

"You know, the only way I think you could get her out of here is to have Trevor ask her to follow him. She is a smitten kitten with that boy whether she admits it or not." Sam laughs.

"Okay, Okay… I get it! Can we stop trying to mate my daughter off to the little fucker? Yes, he saved her, but I am not ready for her to be *smitten anything* yet! They are freaking seven years old. Now let's come up with some game plans so we are ready for any scenario."

Chapter 34
Malinda

Ellie is fully healed now she has her sparkly cast sitting on her shelf in her bedroom and since K used dissolvable stitches, we don't have to worry about another appointment to have them removed. She is currently on a playdate with a few kids from her class. She asked Trinity and Cammy to come with them, so they could help with dress-up clothes. It was super cute, and it seemed to help Cammy.

Cammy was struggling, thinking she possibly killed an innocent man. K did some tests but what we really need is someone who knows and understands magic. K let me know that she has a good friend, Serina, who is a witch. We brought her in to make sure that these rogues were actually rogues. Serina did several "tests" to detect any kind of magic and they all came back, saying the same thing. These were actual Rogues, and no magic was detected. The relief that overcame Cammy was unmistakable when she found this out. She is still going to keep meeting with her therapist and increase her training. The guys were not overly thrilled that she now wants to be one of our top female warriors, but they are not going to stop her. One, because I will beat their asses if they try to stop her from pursuing her goal. Two, because they love her. And three, I will beat their asses....

I am heading to Landon's office when tendrils of his stress reach for me, swirling around me before absorbing into my skin. Then his link opens to me, and I'm basically eavesdropping on his thoughts.

-How do I get Mal to go with the pups and leave the fighting to us?

Oh, sweet baby moon goddess, is he looking to never have sex again?! I swear his overprotective possessiveness is getting out of control. My hands pump my wheels faster down the hallway, I cannot believe he is thinking this way.

I reach his office door and I'm stunned that all I can hear is uncontrollable laughter. I lean my head closer to try and hear what they are saying.

"You think she is going to leave you behind and miss the fight? Apparently, you need to get a checkup from Dr. K because you are losing it my friend." I think I can hear Sam wheezing as he is laughing so hard. Then I hear Troy try to get words out, but he is laughing so hard. At least I know they got my back.

"I think it's cute that you think she will go without a fight. I mean, you have met your mate before, correct?"

Seriously, Landon! I feel like I am about to rip his head off. That is when I feel more worry pass through our bond. That is when I can hear his thoughts,

-These fuckers, I just want her safe, I would die without her. I instantly feel guilt. His love for me is unconditional, it's overwhelming and I have to try to remember that he is not a male chauvinist pig. He doesn't want me here because he thinks I am weak... He knows I am strong.

The door swings to reveal a very handsome, yet very annoyed man. "How could I ever think you are weak?" He grabs me and hugs me so close.

Ugh. The freaking link was open both ways. I really have to work on that. I take a deep breath, enjoying his scent of fresh rain. I nuzzle my face a little deeper, and just for fun I quickly lick over his mark. A low growl emanates from his chest, and he smiles.

"BWAHAHAHAHAH!"

This sends Sam and Troy into another fit laughter. "Dude you are so whipped."

"I wouldn't have it any other way," he says with a wink. "Come on in Mal we're trying to come up with a game plan on how to handle the next move." Landon goes back to his desk pulling me along with him linking our hands together he quickly lifts me up and sits with me on his lap. He nuzzles his head into me this time, I feel him lick my mark and it sends a shiver down my spine.

I pull myself away from my mate. "As for you two…" I say, staring these two numb-nuts down. "You're just as whipped. If I have to, I will just send a link to your mates to prove my point." They both raise their eyebrows in surprise that I would throw them under the bus. Landon is now the one laughing his ass off at their facial expressions. I lean in and place my mouth on his for a sweet kiss. As he bites my bottom lip, I can't help the moan that escapes.

"Alright enough you two. How are you feeling Luna?" Sam asks.

"I feel much better thank you," I respond as I reluctantly pull away from Landon. "So, are we officially abandoning the 'Get Mal Out of The Pack' plan?" I ask sarcastically. Troy snorts at this and tries very hard to hold it together, but he fails. I can't help the smile that claims my face and I don't miss the one on Landon's.

"Yeah, babe we will let that go, as long as you promise to help us with strategy." He says then kisses the tip of my nose. My eyebrows shoot up with excitement, he wants me to help with the planning of the attack!

"Are you serious right now?!" He looks into my eyes and nods his head. I can't stop the girlie squeal that escapes my mouth. I throw my hands in the air and wrap them dramatically around Landon's neck and squeeze with excitement! I plant kisses all over his face to add to the overdramatic display of affection.

"Ha, okay we get it you are excited." Landon says as he pretends to not enjoy every minute of this. I compose myself with some deep breaths.

"Boys, let's do this the right way. I want all of the top warriors here in ten minutes. Also link Mrs. Lane for lunch to be sent up. Make sure Sean is here as well, I like that Irish kid. Though it's such a bummer he does not have an accent."

"What is it with girls and accents…" Sean comments as he walks into the office. "My dad's accent is thick and the ladies always swoon. My mom is a little less possessive as she has gotten older but it's still funny when she loses her shit on, she-wolves who drool a little too much for her liking."

"Ha, I can't wait to meet them!" I say at the thought of meeting them.

After everyone gets to the office, we have a nice lunch before we get down to business. I look around the room and everyone seems eager for this nightmare to end.

"Okay the report we received from our intel team states that Scott's army is spread out around three different packs. In between all of this is Forage Woods. It's located an hour from here and with over 300 acres in the center of all of the thick woods, this could be the best place to fight. It will allow us to fight safely away from any humans.

My goal is to draw him out. He may want to challenge Landon for his title, but I am tired of waiting around for his sorry ass to show up. I want to make him come to us, and my hope is this will confuse the shit out of him. What we have learned about Scott is that he is too cocky to back down… So, I say let's set him up!" Everyone is listening, excitement is almost a tangible thing between them all.

"Luna, how do we draw him out?"

"I am not going to lie; this was something I have thought about long and hard. The only thing I can come up with… We need to go after the one thing he values above all things, his ego. So, we issue him a challenge to draw him out."

"Who is the challenger?" Sean asks.

"Whelp... Me."

The room is filled with a bunch of gasps, growls, "fuck no's", "Dear moon goddess" and I think I even hear a "she's got a death wish."

"Hear me out, please guys." After some coaxing, the room quiets down. I take a deep breath because I know that this is not going to be easy for them. "Scott either wanted me out of the way or wanted me as a mate. Since I am already marked and mated, he can't challenge our Alpha for that. Also, no sitting Alpha just randomly challenges a wolf for his pack. That has red flags written all over it." You can see the weight of what I just said hitting them like a ton of bricks.

"Guys, enough with the faces, please. Now, since we all know neither of those things will happen, our only option is for me to challenge him for the right to the throne. We have not had my coronation yet, so the spot is vacant. We can have all of our allied packs bring their warriors a few days early. We can set up security cameras, create blind spots, we could set it up assassins' fucking creed style for all I care. All I know is that we are going to end this on our terms. Full Moon is going to be the home of the royal family and I refuse to let this douche canoe come into our home and mess with our family!"

Everyone is just kind of staring at me. I just had a Braveheart moment and all I got was crickets. I start to panic a little that everything I just said fell on deaf ears. Then everyone cheers loudly and laughs their asses off. Not going to lie... I am sooo confused.

"Holy shit Luna, you just called him a what!"

"I am sorry but how can we not stand behind our Luna, Alpha we support the plan." The men start cheering louder.

"Luna, what in the hell is a douche canoe?" Hee Hee.

"Listen, calling him a twatwaffle just did not fit." This causes the guys to go another round of uncontrollable laughter.

Landon's office phone rings, he goes to grab it while wiping the tears from his face from laughing so hard.

"It's Alpha Tanner," he says before placing it on speaker phone. He smiles at me but the second we make eye contact he starts freaking laughing again.

"Babe get a grip, it was not that funny." This just causes him to laugh harder.

"Malinda that was fucking hysterical." He clears his throat before answering to try and regain some composure.

"Alpha Tanner, how are you? Please know that you are on speaker phone, we have our top warriors in a strategy meeting."

"No, worries Alpha Landon. I wanted you to know that Austin made contact with us about an hour ago. He overheard a conversation that Scotts Gamma Tyler is the one who planned the attack to see if he could get to Malinda. Apparently, he wanted to be Scott's Beta when he finally gets his own pack. He thought this attack would show how ready for it. He failed obviously but the kid is not stupid and knew what to look for in a good attack. So, Scott is training everyone for an attack in two weeks."

I look at Landon and nod. He goes on to explain the situation and the battle plan and Tanner LOVED IT! He is not thrilled it's me fighting but hey I'm not going to be able to make everyone happy. Tanner also agreed to help us call other packs to set up the challenge. Today is Sunday so I want this to happen on Friday. This will cut off one week of training for Scott's men, and it gives me a week to figure out what the fuck I just got myself into.

Everyone chips in on making calls and now we have a team heading out to Forage Woods. The plan is to have cameras going up in the trees and we will have the feeds going back to a hidden base we are building. The goal is that as soon as the fight starts the other wolves come out and flank the enemy. People have been coming and going while the preparations are made. The pack house feels like a revolving door. It is a bit overwhelming, and I have been training so hard the last couple of days. I need to be at the top of my game. I need to be smart because I have never been to a challenge that included a rogue that followed the rules.

It's now Wednesday and today I make the call to challenge Scott. I am a little nervous, but I will not tell anyone that. According to Austin their numbers are around twelve hundred, that's a huge number. What I was surprised to hear is that Austin is trying to recruit these guys for our side. So, they are going into this with twelve hundred but really only seven hundred wolves are fighting for them. The other four hundred will turn on Scott, and I am hoping more will join us. Knowing this makes me feel a bit better, just a little though.

I am now sitting in my office and Landon, Ben, and Sean are with me for support. Austin offers to give us Scott's cell number, but I really want to protect Austin's identity as long as I can. So, my crazy ass is just going to call the Paisley gym location and hope he is there.

"Ready baby?" Landon asks as he kisses my hand.

"I was born ready." I answer with a wink.

Landon smiles and sits back in the chair and nods to me to signal everyone is ready. Goddess, he looks so sexy right now. He is wearing a blue button-down shirt with the sleeves rolled up and a pair of jeans. My body gets warm in all of the right places. -**Mal if you do not focus, everyone in this room is going to catch the scent of your arousal.** It is at this moment that I am beyond grateful for the ability to mindlink, but that does not stop the blush that takes over my face. I can't help but bite my bottom lip causing a small growl to come from Landon.

"Focus, you two!" Ben scolds us. I clear my throat and hit the speaker button on the phone and start dialing the number. On the second ring the voice of a very chipper young woman answers.

"Tone Your Inner Wolf, Alyssa speaking how can I help you?"

I roll my eyes at the name of the gym. I always thought it was silly.

"Oh, hi Alyssa, could I speak with Scott please?"

"Sure, may I ask what this is in reference to?"

"Oh yes, we have an upcoming meeting and I want to let him know of a location change."

"Oh, sure hold one second please, ohhh what is your name?"

"Sara."

"Okay great, hold one second please Sara."

I exhale some of my anxiety. The guys are staying as calm as possible, and I can feel Landon through our bond. It is giving me peace.

"Hello Scott speaking"

I take a deep breath and pull my big girl panties up.

"Hello Scott, how are you?" I sound overly sweet at this point.

"Good and you?" He hesitates... I can tell he recognizes my voice. "Ummm, Sara, right?"

Ah shit I am just going to jump in with both feet here. I don't want to waste time playing games.

"Nope this is Luna Malinda Wright. I hear that you are looking to take a pack or two. So, I was wondering if you were up for a little challenge?"

.... Silence on his end.

"Scott, cat got your tongue?"

"Ummm."

"Scott, this does not sound like a man who wants to be in charge or is ready to take over a pack. Maybe I have the wrong man or maybe you're just not man enough?"

We hear him growl through the phone. BINGO, I hit the right nerve.

"You think that you can just challenge me, little girl? What is in it for me?"

"Well, I am to ascend the throne soon..."

"Your point little girl?"

"My point is you fight me... if you win, you become king... if I win, I kill you."

"When and where?"

Chapter 35
LANDON

I just finished up two hours of training and am rushing to get in my office for a quick call with several Alpha's that will be participating in this fight. We have forty-eight hours and there have been teams working out in the field to get everything ready. Everything's coming together, as I look over the plans that are scattered all over my desk. I hear the phone ding and quickly check my text messages. It's from Tanner.

The meeting has been pushed back fifteen minutes. Call you soon.

Thank goddess, I need a minute to think. I walk over to the little fridge and grab a beer. "Ah Fuck," I am fucking beat.

"You got this!" I hear from outside. I walk over to the window looking out on the training center. I can see everything from this angle, "Yes, just like that." I hear Mal yell. She has been training everyone hard. We even have a pup training going. Ellie was adamant that the pups should start with the basics before the age of twelve. I shake my head thinking back to the discussion we had in my office the other day.

Ellie and a few of her little friends knocked on the door. She came in so confident, like she owned the place. She did not care that we were in the middle of a meeting. She had three little she-wolf pups and two wolf pups with her. Everyone looked nervous except Ellie and Trevor.

Freaking Trevor.

"Alpha, may I ask a question?" I cocked my eyebrow at my daughter. She is going the professional route, she means business.

"Why, yes, Miss Wright you may."

"Thank you, oh, ummm." You can see Trevor lean in and whisper in her ear.

"Oh, wight Thank you Twevor. Can we please stawt a twaining class for pups under twelve. I think it is super important that we know how to defend ouwselves or help ouwselves if we ever get kidnapped." Her little face scrunches up at the memory as Trevor reaches to hold her hand.

"Ahem," Sam coughs while staring this kid down. These kids are freaking seven years old… stop with the touching… dude. Ellie shot her uncle a look and held his hand tighter.

I can see that all of the guys are now eyeing Trevor, but he is just staring at Ellie with a smile. I hear Troy link everyone in the office.

-You are so screwed Landon.

The guy's cackle, but Ellie and the kids think we are laughing at them. They popped their heads up and looked at us with an attitude.

"Don't laugh at us! I don't want to be Cindewella and wait for someone to wescue me. I don't need a boy or mate to save me. Oh no! I want to save myself!" She yelled and slammed her tiny fist on the table. The little girls are all nodding their heads in agreement, but Trevor looked at her with hurt on his face.

"You awen't always going to be thewe daddy. Neither will all of you. Look what happened to us when you guys were gone. If we knew mowe stuff, maybe mommy and all of my aunts would have been safe. We would not have had to hide. We could be like a little pup Army."

"Eloise Ann Wright, first of all I'm so proud of you and your friends for coming to us. We do not have a problem with you all training. I think we should teach our pack pups the basics, but I am against you all going into a fight at your age."

"But what if we get supew stwong?"

"Ellie, how about you and the pups start training, and we see how it goes first. Also, it is okay to ask for help, never feel like you are not strong if you have to ask for help. Always know that a mate does not make you weak, they make you stronger." Trevor puffs out his chest at this information. I am giving this kid way too much hope. Ellie is not allowed to date till she's thirty.

"REALLY? Thank you, daddy... ummm" She clears her throat. "Thank you, Alpha!" All the pups came to shake my hand and then they ran out of the office excited. You could hear them cheering in the hallway.

"I knew you could do it Ellie, I just knew it."

"Ewwww you let him kiss your cheek Ellie."

I heard some cheering that brought me back to the present. I squint my eyes at the ladies training, and it looks like Trinity just pinned another warrior and everyone is going crazy for her. Troy runs over, picking her up and swinging her around then gives her a passionate kiss in front of everyone. Trinity has been training with the warriors after her rounds in the hospital and has come very far in her training. She was adamant on learning to fight better after the last attack.

The phone rings and I quickly get to my desk. I hit the speakerphone. "Alpha Landon speaking." A thud followed by a girly squeal sound from in front of my desk. Mal is doing a happy dance; she is getting this teleporting thing down pretty good.

"Ha, sorry did I scare you?" She whispers as she rolls closer to my desk. I shake my head and smile at her.

"Landon, it's Tanner. I just spoke to the other pack Alpha's, and we are all set. Is the plan for Mal to actually fight Scott?"

Malinda is exuberantly nodding her head in the affirmative.

"Yes, she insists that we stick to were-law, but the second something fishy happens we take everyone out. Her protection is top priority."

"Agreed."

We spoke for a bit longer finalizing a few more details before we all head out tonight. Several pack leaders and their warriors are already there getting themselves situated. Mrs. Lane and her staff along with several families made food to literally feed an army. It has all been loaded into the cars that are in the convoy. I think we are all set to head out in a few hours. Dr. Taylor and Dr. K had sent medical supplies up yesterday so that way we could help the injured easily.

"Landon let's go spend some time with Ellie."

We head back to the apartment and have some nice family time. We talk, laugh, and snuggle. Eventually when it is time for us to go Ellie begs to walk us out. As we get outside the entire pack is there to see us all off. To see all of the love our pack has for its warriors is so overwhelming. Mal looks out to our pack and waves to quiet everyone down.

"Thank you all for the sacrifices you make every day for our pack. I am sorry that we have to go forward with this plan, a plan that will put the lives of our loved ones at risk. Most importantly, I promise to end this threat tonight. I can't promise that this is the last threat we will face but I truly believe as long as we keep working together, we will always be unstoppable.

You have all come so far in your training and I can't even describe how proud I am as your Luna. To see the growth and confidence that has come from each and every one of you is amazing. To those that are staying behind to protect our pups, and land, know that we value your courage, and hard work. Thank you... all of you."

Everyone claps and cheers. Those that are staying behind have special moments with their mates before we start to load into the cars. It is heartwarming but also very difficult to see. You never know who is not coming back, though you hope everyone does.

We hit the road with over one hundred cars in our convoy. We don't need to worry about sleeping or who is driving because the location is only an hour from our pack so it's not too bad. We will have to park far from where we plan on having the battle. The goal is to carry everything to the location and finish our set up.

I pull off the exit and look over to Mal and notice she is deep in thought. Since there are six wolves in the SUV with us, I link her to make sure she is okay.

-Yes, babe I am fine, don't worry. To be honest I am just a bit nervous but please keep that to yourself.

She looks over with her cute serious face.

-You got this. I have seen you fight, and I know you can take him.

-What I know is, I can take Austin any day of the week. The last time I checked I have never taken on a psychopath that had Alpha blood.

I reach for her hand and give it a squeeze.

-Love you.

-Love you more, Lan.

Chapter 36
Malinda

We get to the site, and everyone is setting things up and putting the finishing touches here and there. I study where the challenge will take place and realize that overgrowth is very difficult to move the wheelchair around in.

"Landon, this is a problem."

He calls a couple of guys over and they get to work clearing the weeds, branches and larger rocks. This is still going to be difficult, but it is better than before. I am lost in thought when I'm lifted out of my chair. I raise my eyebrow at Landon.

"What, I can't carry my wife and mate?" I snake my arms around his neck and kiss his cheek. The beautiful smile on his face makes my heart race, and I can't help the warm feeling that rushes to my abdomen. "I can smell your arousal baby." I can't help the giggle that comes from my lips.

"Can you blame me; it is not every day a sexy beast of a man carries me through a beautiful forest."

He strides into the woods and for some time all I could hear were the dry leaves crunching under Landon's feet. It seems so peaceful here in the woods, it is almost hard to believe that in a few hours all hell is going to break loose. I almost wish we could warn all of the animals of the forest.

Now my goal is just to relax for a moment. Landon's scent of freshly falling rain tickles my nose and brings me a sense of calm and peace. Sparks cover my body as I realize that one of his hands has slid under my shirt. I am not sure if his hands are keeping me calm or getting me hot and bothered...despite his intentions, it's working.

The deeper into the woods we go, the more people I see. It's like they built a little city here in between the trees. A not so little tent city was set up. There are wolves cooking some meals and some are sharing stories. It's the random bits of laughter that get to me, because everyone here is just spending time together. In the world of the supernatural, battles, wars, and fights are so common that we try not to take little things in life for granted. We try to make every moment count and as I spin my head around to take in the environment, a few raise their glasses to us as we walk past. All I can do is nod my head in acknowledgement.

Once at the tent, Landon kicks the flap open. We get inside and he has a little lunch set up for us. He catches my eyes, and that is when I see it... fear. I have seen concern before and I know he has talked about being afraid for me, but I have never seen it in his eyes before. I know right now that he is scared that this could be our last moment and he did this, so we have some alone time together. During the Great War we each lost our mates, and it does not matter how strong you are or how much confidence you have... you can still be afraid for your loved ones.

Landon fidgets with the containers to open the food. His hands shake, it breaks my heart. I reach for him, placing my hand on his thigh. He cups my face with his hands.

"If this was me fighting, I would not be a mess. Please... I know you can do this; I know you are strong, but you are my whole world and I know that one scratch on your perfect body is going to send me crazy. I tried so hard to hold it together while you and Ellie were in the hospital. As Alpha, I need to remain levelheaded, and I think you bring the right amount of crazy to balance us out. I know you will come out on top, but that doesn't mean I'm not worried."

I just stare into his eyes; this is one of the most intense experiences of my life. My breaths become ragged, and I am overwhelmed by this man's love for me. The rise and fall of his chest increases and I can't hear his heart beating out of control.

Then in the blink of an eye his lips are on mine. This kiss conveys our unspoken words, our tongues pledging endless promises of our love for each other. His lips are like silk against mine. I am savoring every moment. He slowly lowers us onto the blanket, then glides my shirt off. He pulls back to look at me as I lay under him. I reach up to pull his shirt off and am treated with a body that makes my core ache. I slowly run my fingers down the curves of his abs and stop just above the rim of his jeans. He is watching me so intently; the heat is overwhelming. I am overcome with love and lust; it feels like my heart is going to beat out of my chest. I want him, I want this, and I want him to know that this is not goodbye. This won't be the last time we are together. I let my fingers glide to the button, and I pull ever so slightly. My fingers make efficient work of undoing his jeans, then move to his extremely hard cock. I can't help but lick my lips. "Please let me take you in my mouth," I say with a small pout.

Abruptly, Landon gets up and quickly removes the rest of our clothes. I give him an odd look until I realize what he is doing when he positions himself above me. He gets down onto his knees, his long shaft hangs above my face, and I can't stop myself from licking the bead of pre-cum off his tip. He crawls down my body, licks and kisses as he goes. I can feel my sweet arousal drip from my pussy as his lips hover over me. His hot breath fans my flesh. I have never done this position before, but I can't wait any longer to have him. I open my mouth and take every inch down my throat. Landon rocks his hips as I suck his cock as if my life depends on it.

"You're so wet for me." He gently runs his nose between my lips and darts his tongue inside me. I cannot help the moan that escapes my lips. He is now eating my pussy like it is his last meal. He is twisting and curling his tongue and bringing me close to my edge. The harder he goes the deeper I take him.

I Want him to feel just as good. I take my fingers, reaching down to play with my clit just a bit, I need it wet for what I am about to do. I bring my hands up and grasp his ass cheeks hard pulling him as deep as I can get him. The moan that rumbles through his chest just spurs me on. Slowly, I run my finger to his tight hole to push his threshold just a bit. I slide my finger inside, earning myself a growl. "Baby," he calls out into my pussy. I continue my little assault on his ass as his hip thrusts become more demanding. "Two can play this game." With that Landon pushes three fingers inside me and begins to pump in and out of me mercilessly, while still sucking on my clit. I'm now meeting his hand thrust for thrust. He does not stop, and I am right on the precipice, ready to fall. He begins to shake and with one twist of my tongue he comes undone. His warm seed spills down my throat and I swallow every drop.

Landon curls his fingers and bites down on my clit causing my pussy to clench onto him for dear life. We're both desperately trying to get air in our lungs as we come down from this high. "I hope I didn't wear you out?" I shake my head and give him a crooked smile. "Good because I'm so not done with you yet." We spend the next hour wrapped in each other's arms making love and not caring who hears.

Everyone is where they need to be, and I have never felt more on edge. Things have been falling into place a little too perfectly and that makes me feel so uncomfortable. You know what I mean? I feel like I am just waiting for the other shoe to drop.

We are currently standing in the middle of the field waiting for Scott and his army to appear. Let me tell you the suspense is fucking killing me. What feels like hours, is probably only a moment or two. I give Landon a gentle smile and when he returns it, the look on his face warms my soul.

Sam cuts into my thoughts.

-Luna they are twelve minutes from the clearing, be prepared.

-Thank you, Sam. How many wolves do you see?

-The cameras are picking up around twelve hundred. Some are very close to our hiding spots but since Dr. K's friend hid our scents, they can't detect us.

-Good, be safe.

As the minutes pass, wolves pour out of the trees and into the clearing. Landon is standing next to me, and his Alpha aura is rippling off of him. It is so intense that it would make anyone shake into submission... *'almost anyone.'* Saraha smirks as she says it. Typically, his aura sends a bolt of electricity through me, but today it feels a hundred times more powerful, somehow making me stronger. I stretch out my neck, take a deep breath and put on my best resting bitch face. Now, at this moment... I am ready for war.

Scott pushes through the front line of guys like he is already a goddamn king. Arrogant fuck. I try very hard not to roll my eyes at him. I forgot what a big guy he is. He has to be close to 6'2" - 6'3" and pure muscle. Though I didn't expect less coming from someone who owns a gym. He is now fifty yards from me with Austin and, who I believe is Tyler by his side.

"Well, well, well. I see you have brought yourself a little army, Malinda."

"Hello Scott. You can't blame me; I have never known a rogue to play by the rules. I see that you are extremely protected too." I extend my hand to point out the obvious.

"These men are going to be in my high court and army once I am King, so of course they are here to help protect me. Now enough of the chit chat let's get this over with, the quicker I kill you... the quicker I take my place on the throne."

He advances farther into the clearing and Landon squeezes my hand.

"No matter what happens, please know I love you. If this all goes to shit and he kills me... you kill him. Do not let him take the crown."

Although I know it goes against every fiber in his being, he gives me a quick kiss then pushes me to the clearing.

"Seriously, how are you meant to fight me if you can't even get to the clearing? This is almost unfair." He laughs and the crowd behind him begins to snicker.

"How about you mind your own damn business." Landon yells, barely able to contain his fury. Once we reach our designated sides, he jumps around, stretching his muscles.

Ben stalks to the center of the clearing and goes over the rules...

"And lastly... Let me stress that if there is any outside interference, this challenge will go from a one-on-one fight to a free for all. Do you both understand?"

"Yeah." Scott snaps sarcastically.

"Yes."

"Okay..." Sam straightens his shoulders, clears his throat then yells: "FIGHT!"

With that, Scott flies at me and I block what I can. His fists are a blur of motion.

Shit he is really fucking fast.

I am able to throw some good combos at him, making contact most of the time but he is getting in just as many. He is a blur of movement, it's almost impossible. It's almost as if...

MAGIC!

This mother fucker is using magic!

Damn it! I totally forgot that his girlfriend is a freaking witch. Five minutes of this back and forth and he finally gets a good punch to my left cheek. Landon's growl can be heard across the field, as can other comments from my pack.

"Come on Luna!" Troy yells.

"Let's go girl!" Screams Stacy.

Everyone is cheering for me, but I am having a hard time moving on the dirt. This has always been my biggest fear, the fear of not being able to fight on dirt. I can barely move my chair, and an overwhelming feeling that I'm in over my head is fogging my brain.

I catch movement out of the corner of my eye as Scott's leg comes up to kick me. I push myself forward in my chair as fast as I can and duck under his kick. As I pass under his leg, I grab the leg he is standing on. I pull with my momentum, and he spins, falling to the ground, leaving him gasping from the air getting knocked out of him.

I launch out of my chair and start landing blow after blow to his face and body. He twists and turns his head, trying to evade my assault but my knuckles keep making contact with my target. He is trying to fight me off, but I refuse to give up. His blocks are getting sloppier and sloppier. I finally feel like I have the upper hand now.

"That's it Luna!"

"Take him out!!!!"

As I land a particularly well-placed punch to Scott's left eye, a gunshot cracks through the air. This is followed shortly by Landon's roar of pain. My eyes are drawn to the sound and my heart is being ripped out when I see bright red blood seeping down his arm. "LANDON!" I scream. Our pack is immediately at his side, assessing the damage.

"Luna behind you!" Ben yells with pure fear laced into his voice. My attention is redirected to Scott- who is no longer in human form. They did this to distract me.

"Fuck me," and in a split second he is on top of me in wolf form. Both of my hands are on his jaw, pushing his mouth away from my neck. Landon is screaming for me, mingling with my warriors growling. I can hear their anger.

I can't see a way out of this. I think through all of my options desperately trying to come up with an idea. However, my mind is completely blank. I close my eyes and try as hard as I can to push him back. Now would be a great time for my legs to fucking work so I can also kick him off.

As if not getting to my blood quick enough, Scott changes tactics as his wolf pulls his face back and directs his destruction toward my waist. He quickly takes me in his mouth and throws me across the field. My body hits the ground hard and slides a few feet.

Pain.

Immense and debilitating pain is radiating throughout my body. Breathing is a struggle, each inhale an excruciating chore, each exhale, ragged and excruciating. My energy level seemed to have just evaporated into thin air. Scott prowls toward me. His gray wolf slowly and methodically stalks toward me and the look in his eyes lets me know my end is here.

"Mal, Shift!"

"Sahara what!! How?"

"Forget about how- just do it! Do it for Landon, for Ellie, for the were-world! Just fucking shift NOW!"

A fever begins to slice through me, and quickly morphs into an inferno that rapidly ravages my body. A distant memory of a feeling claws at me, trying to surface. Each laceration releases more and more of this memory...of this feeling. Then whatever is trying to surface gets ignited from the fire coursing through my veins. Magic is what erupts from the gashes, infecting every cell, saturating every drop of blood that is coursing through every cell within me. And as if I never stopped, I shift. One moment I'm lying on the ground, ready to die, then the next I'm in wolf form, standing on all fours. I am STANDING on all fucking fours!!!!

"Focus Malinda" she says before she howls so loud it shakes the leaves off of the trees. Scott skids to a stop, staring at me in shock. Looking down on him, I realize I'm much bigger than I remember. The look on Scotts wolf's face says it all.

Ha that's right asshole... I'm the daughter of the fucking moon goddess.

"You're fucked now Scott!" Austin yells at him. The young guy that had taken Ellie is standing next to Austin. At this outburst, he raises his arm to punch Austin in the face. Austin ducks and nails him so hard with a 1,2 combo he goes flying. The guy goes down faster than a drunk guy walking on ice.

"It's on now Mother Fuckers!" The triplets yell.

Sahara slams her front paws into the dirt as her goddess aura rolls off of her. She wants Scott to submit, but we know he's never going to do that. So, she is ready to kill him. Scott recovers from his shock and lunges for her neck. As he flies through the air Sahara jumps up at the right moment grabbing his throat. She bites down as hard as she can. His claws frantically bat at the air, trying to make contact with her in hopes she will loosen her jaws. With one might shake, a loud snap pierces the air. Scott's neck was snapped.

She drops his limp form on the ground. She sits back on her hind legs and howls loudly, signaling the end of the challenge. Our supporters howl back in acknowledgement. It is an overwhelming feeling. The rogues growl in challenge, they aren't ready for this to be done. This does nothing to calm down Sahara, she is now pissed off that they want to continue this. Turning her body to face them, her growl reverberates loudly. Game on.

The gentle push of a wolf's nudge against our side reveals Dex next to us. He licks my face letting me know he is good.

-You okay babe? I mindlink my question to him.

-Yeah, it was a through and through shot. Once I shifted Dex healed us super-fast. He was not missing this.

More growling than the rogues start positioning themselves to fight. One after the other they start to shift into their wolves. Ha! They have no clue what is in store for them. However, their expressions start to change when our pack, in wolf form, slink out of the woods from all directions. Then they nearly shit themselves when several hundred of their own turn on them. My warriors are snapping their jaws and growling at them, but the rogues are ready for a fight, and they break the line first. I give the signal and the fight is on.

It is a mess of fur and blood. I am going from rogue to rogue, Sahara has not been out in 3 years and the blood lust is strong. I tense my back leg muscles, getting ready to lunge for another wolf when I am hit on my side and knocked to the ground. I scramble up as quickly as I can, but someone jumps on my back. In a flash I am taken back to the last battle of the Great War. I am struggling to get the wolf off of me, fighting against the current moment and the past. Panic seizes my movements and they become more frantic. He is snapping at the back of my neck and ears.

-Mal, where are you?

-Landon, no stay where you are! Ah fuck this guy is driving me nuts, I can't shake him off. In my struggle, I see Dex run to me at full speed and my panic shoots through the roof. In a flash I no longer see Dex but I see Jared- Jared is running to me and then being attacked. I am frozen in fear as I watch Jared die in front of me all over again.

-*MALLIE! Snap out of it.* Jared's voice yells at me in my head. That's enough to knock me out of my fog. I am knocked over and brought back to the present. Dex throws the rogue off of me, with Jared leaping over him and landing on the rogue. The rogue's neck snapped on impact. -**I will never not get to you again, okay?** I nod my head and Jared jumps back into the fight.

Dex licks my face… -**Babe NEVER tell me to stay away again. I will always come to you.** He nudges me with his big head. -**You good?**

-Yeah, I'm good.

-Promise?

-Promise. Now go kick some ass.

Landon bounds back into the fight, making me aware that my warriors have me shielded from an attack. This allows me a moment to catch my bearings. I scan out over the battlefield and the overwhelming pride I have for my pack as they fight to protect the ones that they love is tremendous. I'm observing two wolves fight when I realize it is Austin, and he is losing. I break out into a sprint to get to him. At this moment I do not care what he did in the past, He is helping us now. I ram the wolf in the ribs and knock him away from Austin, giving Austin the opportunity to get at its neck. He is quick and in an instant the wolf is dead.

The dead wolf shifts back to its human form. Tyler... He is so young and yet so misguided, but this bastard took my daughter and now I kind of wish I was the one to kill him.

The fight lasts for thirty minutes. That is all it took for us to come out on top. The rogues lay dead on the field of battle, Sahara and Dex walk to the center clearing. Howling in victory. Dex rubs his fur against Sahara showing his love to her. She nudges her head into him and with that we shift back into human form.

I am looking at Landon standing there in all of his glory, and I run into his arms. He picks me up and swings around.

"Baby *kiss* I *kiss* am *kiss* so *kiss* proud *kiss* of *kiss* you."

"Landon, I shifted" I sob into his chest. "I shifted!!!!"

"Mal you just fucking ran into my arms! You just ran into my arms!"

He puts me down and he holds me carefully. Ben throws Landon a t-shirt and shorts. He helps me into the shirt and Ben supports me while Landon gets dressed. It's been a while since I have shifted, and it's really drained my energy. Then with my mates help, I take another step and then another. Landon and I are now in front of everyone, and the amount of howling is emotional. Pride rolls off of everyone here, as they start to take a knee and place their hand over their hearts. Every Alpha, Beta, and warrior here is submitting to us, and it feels fucking good.

Chapter 37
MALINDA

Life has been crazy the last couple of weeks. As soon as we got back from the fight Dr. K and Dr. Taylor had me in their office to run tests on me in human and wolf form. After I shifted back to human form my legs were stronger, but the loss of feeling is back within 30 minutes. So, I still have to use my wheelchair all of the time, but I get to shift into my wolf again so I will take it.

I have started to experience new abilities as time goes on too. I can now project my memories onto anyone. Which by the way is really cool. I used this ability to show Landon that Austin's really not an asshole, misguided yes but not an asshole who deserved to die. I was able to show him our private talks when Austin must have known we were truly alone. That is when he opened up to me, and in return got me to open up to him.

With this information Landon decided to present Austin to the Elders. I was called in as a witness and said my peace. What surprised me was when Austin had the opportunity to speak, he begged for death. He said that his actions were unforgivable, but to me they weren't. Without him I would have had full doses of poison in my system. I would have been brainwashed into believing that I was useless, it is because of Austin that I kept my fighting spirit. Austin was sentenced to ten years in our cells. He truly begged for the death penalty, but I felt that his actions of trying to right his wrongs proved himself worthy to live.

Sean left for Ireland a few days after the battle. He was excited to do his study abroad there, also he wanted to look into the Great Rogue Wars that happened while his parents were still young. I think knowing you come from a line of Alphas, but not really knowing what happened after everyone fled to the US has him intrigued. We had a going away party for him, I was kind of hoping he would find his mate while here, but alas he did not. Ohhh maybe when he goes to Ireland.

Last week we celebrated the mating ceremonies of Sam, Lara, Troy, Trinity, then finally the triplets and Cammy. They each had separate ceremonies and they were all so beautiful. For the reception we had one huge party! Since our reception was interrupted by Ellie's kidnapping everyone decided this was the best way, plus who doesn't love a good party?

Today is our coronation and all of the girls are in my bedroom getting ready. Ellie is dancing around the room eating a donut, Stacy is laughing at something that John just texted her. Lara is steaming her dress, but her baby bump keeps knocking into the counter and let me tell you, she has the cutest baby bump you ever did see. Cammy is by the door and currently making out with one of her mates... Tim... hmmm no it is Tony. Definitely Tony... Crap I have no clue. It is aggravating that I still can't tell those boys apart.

"Cammy go fix your makeup." Lara yells over to her. Cammy pulls away from him and he slaps her on the ass as she walks toward me. "That was Tom by the way." She says with a snicker as she leans down and gives me a big hug. "Damn it! Ugh one day I will figure it out."

We all are now dressed to the nines, and it is such an odd feeling that in fifteen minutes we are going to be crowned into royalty. I feel like Mia from the movie Princess Diaries. The big poofy dress and the big red furry cape, but I do feel beautiful. I don't think just because we are royalty now that much will change, I mean other than extra security, but hey, as long as we maintain peace, I am a happy little wolf.

We get to the great hall; it has been turned into a throne room and almost every pack has sent representatives. The place is packed and the only one of us that does not seem even a bit nervous is Ellie. The high ranked males and their mates walk in first taking their spots on each side of the two centered thrones, men on one side and ladies on the other.

Next Eloise walks in, her dress is a gold and cream color. It has long satin sleeves with beautiful embroidery. She looks every part of the princess she truly is. She holds her head high as she walks down the long aisle and takes her spot on the stage next to her little chair. Landon comes up to me and holds my hand.

"Ready baby?"

"As ready as I will ever be." I say smiling up at him.

We enter the room to a string quartet playing. Everyone is standing as we pass them and for the first time in my life, I feel like I am where I am meant to be. The closer we get to the stage, power surges through me. My eyes are drawn to Landon's.

-Do you feel that?

-Yes, I'm glad I am not the only one,' he says with a smile.

We arrive at the steps of the platform, Landon bends down to pick me up and carries me to the top. He places me on my feet and Ben hands me one of the crutches I used from the wedding. I am supporting myself with Landon on the other side of me. I am taking deep breaths as I look out over everyone. This is such a surreal feeling. I look over to Ellie, she is smiling at me with such pride on her face. She blows me a kiss and Landon catches it for me.

Then the four high elders come in. They are dressed in long black robes that look like they are hundreds of years old. In three of their hands are pillows with crowns on them, I had no clue we even had these.

The elders stop at the base of the steps and turn to face the crowd. That is when a female elder who I believe is named Millie walks halfway up the stairs as she begins to talk.

"Today we crown our next royal family. As elders it is our job to pray to the Moon Goddess for guidance. Slowly whispers reached our ears of a she-wolf warrior. Her skills were unmatched. We continued to ask the Goddess if this is the chosen one, we have been waiting for. Her answer was simple and required no words. You see when each werewolf dynasty ends the Goddess takes back the crowns of the kings and queens.

So, it should only be fitting that when we prayed to her, three crowns appeared in the council's artifact room. At the time, Malinda had no mate and no pup, so it is amazing how the Goddess just knows. Over time Luna Malinda's spirit began to heal from her past and with the most recent events she has proved herself true."

The elders walk up to the platform and place the crowns on a small table off to the side. She turns to face us with a big smile and then looks like she forgot something. Millie giggles to herself as she checks her pockets and finds the paper she is looking for.

"I was so nervous that I wrote everything down but forgot where I put it. I apologize." I look at her with a big smile on my face. She is like the grandmother you always wanted, simply adorable.

"Do you, Alpha, Luna, and Eloise promise to do everything in your power to protect the Were community?"

"We do."

"Do you promise to rule fairly and justly?"

"We do."

"Do you promise to communicate with the council?"

"We do."

"Lastly, do you promise to rule as the Moon Goddess sees fit with light and love."

"We do."

Elder Millie and Ben walk over to the crowns, she hands them all to Ben who places them on a large try. They first walk over to Landon placing the crown on his head. "I hereby declare that you, Alpha Landon Wright will rule as our King. You will rule beside your Queen and protect her until death."

Then she turns to Ellie. The Elder places the most beautiful crown on her head and looks her straight in the eye. "Eloise Wright the Moon Goddess has blessed you with her mark, you are destined for greatness. Remember to always honor our world in return it will honor you. I hereby declare you Eloise Wright Princess of our world."

The elder walks behind me lifting the crown above my head for all to see.

"Luna Malinda Wright, today we crown you, our ruler. Never doubt that this was always meant to be your journey. There are times we wish we could have walked this path for you, but your suffering and your strength are what has gotten you this far. I now call upon the Moon Goddess to bless her daughter with her true gifts… It is time for you, our Luna Queen, to Awaken."

She places the crown on my head, and I can feel my eyes glow green. A warm breeze blows through the hall and dances around everyone. It's almost sparkling the way it twirls around. A feeling even stronger than before runs all over my body. It's as if my aura is growing stronger. My skin tingles all over, I know that Landon and Ellie feel it too. Confidence evident in their features as they look out to the crowd. Gasps from the onlookers let me know that my eyes are not the only ones glowing.

The wind dies down and the room erupts into cheers and it's the best feeling in the world. In the back of the room unbeknownst to anyone else but us three, appear several figures: the goddess, her mate, my parents, Landon's parents, and Ellie's parents. Her little fingers squeeze my arm tight. Tears roll down my face as they wave and cheer for us. Ellie is waving and blowing kisses, to everyone she is just being Ellie, but we know who they are for.

I raise my hand to thank everyone, and the room instantly quiets. I take a deep breath ready to address the room when the goddesses voice fills my family's ears. "I have one last gift." She whispers... The room is now so quiet that you can hear a pin drop.

"Mommy do you hear that?"

"Hear what baby?"

Her eyes get huge, and she gets even closer to me. She puts her head against my stomach.

"That... can you hear that.... mama, it's a heartbeat."

I whip my head around to look at Landon and I see tears in his eyes. Through the now deafening silence we hear the faintest heartbeat. Ellie gasps, sitting up straight and points to the little table with the silver tray on it. There on the tray is a white glowing orb. All eyes are on this and as the light begins to fade away, we are shocked to see a sparkling little crown.

Landon places his hand on my belly and the room erupts into cheers again. Our families slowly fade away back to the heavens. "Thank you," it came out more as a whisper, but I gather myself and scan the crowd.

One by one everyone takes a knee, and Alpha Tanner's voice rings out through the hall. "We will protect you, until our last breath." I can't help the smile that graces my face at his words, and I can't stop the pride that beams through me as the whole room responds.

"Until our last breath."

Epilogue
LANDON

It has been 8 months since we had our coronation and life has been a little crazy. Our lives have been filled with meetings, pack visits and so much more. We vowed to make sure we treated the werewolf community fairly and we are trying our best.

We are currently at Cammy's baby shower; she is expecting triplets and they are waiting to find out the genders. It's so cool to watch our closest friends grow their families. Though, I know we are all in for it when they get older. The guys and I were always getting into trouble as kids, and something tells me that our pups will be no different.

Mal is sitting at the table with Lara and Trinity. Lara and Sam had a little boy five months ago. They named him Allen after Sam's dad. I will never forget the look on our Beta's face.

We were all in the hospital room visiting the new addition to our pack. The ladies were going crazy over how cute he was, and I asked, "Have we come up with a name yet?"

Sam shook his head and said something like "We are still narrowing it down."

That is when Lara said "I have a name, but it was not on our list... I want to name him Allen." The look on Sam's face was priceless, I don't think he could love Lara any more than he already did but if he could love her more, he does now.

Allen is adorable, he looks just like Lara. Sam is going to be an amazing dad; he wants to be involved with everything. He is even trying to explain baseball to him already, his first mitt was ordered two days after he was born and I'm not going to even lie... it's fucking cute. I had to get him his first baseball jersey. Sean even had a personalized baseball bat made and sent over before he left. We're all huge baseball fans in this pack and since my family is originally from the east coast, I've been able to convert a lot to my favorite team The NY Mets. So, the jersey I got was of course a David Wright one!

Mal and I welcomed another little girl into our family. We named her Summer, and we are all smitten with her. She had Malinda's hair and my eyes. Summers' closet is stuffed to the brim with dresses and cute outfits, mostly from Aunt Stacy. Oh, and don't get me started about big sister Ellie! Summer is the apple of Ellie's eye.

Ellie just celebrated her eighth birthday and yes freaking Trevor was there. I'm not trying to give the kid a hard time but seriously dude, slow down. Ugh, all of Ellie's little friends think Trevor is her mate. Ellie says "how am I supposed to know who the moon goddess blessed me with... She is just grandma to me." We could not argue with her logic.

I even asked Mal one night when we were getting into bed, "Do you think you could just ask your mom if they are mates? That way I can start training the kid now... you know." Malinda just laughed at me, kissed me on the cheek and rolled over. The next morning, she said to me that maybe I should just train all of the little pups to be Alpha Strong so that way we don't have to worry about it. I just rolled my eyes and sipped my coffee.

After the battle before you knew it pregnancy announcements exploded from the pack like wildfire. I am pretty sure that all if not most of our warriors announced they were expecting a pup. Dr. K was crazy busy over the next five months with prenatal appointments and births, but it's so nice to see how much our pack is growing.

I am eating cake as my mate talks to a few pack members. She is laughing and enjoying herself. She looks over her shoulder and winks at me. I give her a big smile and she returns it with a little wink. There are so many people here to celebrate with Cammy and the Triplets.

The side door opens and in storms Ben with an envelope. The look on his face tells me he is not here to party.

"Hey man, have a seat... cake?"

"No thank you Alpha, I am here on official business." He slides the letter across the table with **Urgent** scribbled in black ink. Raising an eyebrow at him, I open and read it.

Dear Alpha Landon,

We have an issue here on the east coast in Silver Moon. Since you are related to our Beta's family, we thought we should inform you sooner rather than later. As you know Sean went to Ireland to study abroad, while he was there, he wanted to do some research on his family's old pack. We have been informed from the school he is studying with... that he is missing.

The next day there was a mysterious package delivered to the Beta family. The package exploded and Rebecca, their daughter, took most of the blast. She is currently in a coma, and we hope that when she turns 18 in a few days that her wolf will heal her.

Please let me know if you can help us out in any way. We would be very grateful.

Sincerely,

Alpha Aaron - Silver Moon Pack

"Here read this." I pass the letter over to Ben to read. My head is swimming, with what could've happened. I'm shocked to hear about Sean. Him and I are pretty close. I talked to him just a few weeks ago before he left for his trip. I can feel Malinda staring a whole into the side of my head from across the room. I look at her through my peripheral vision and concern's written all over her face. The downfall to the bond is that she can feel my emotions.

"Holy crap." Ben says as he passes it back to me. I nod my head in agreement and look around the room. Then I'm hit with a great idea.

"Hey, Troy... Trinity..." They make their way over to me.

"What's up?"

"I have a job for you. Pack your bags, you're going to Silver Moon."

BOOKS BY THIS AUTHOR

The Queen's Court Series

What Once Was Mine – Book 2
The Full Moon Pack is at it again. When the daughter of the Silver Moon Pack's Beta is injured in a horrible explosion, Trinity and Troy must travel across the country to the east coast to investigate the attack. When astonishing new information comes to light, buried memories of Trinity's past come back to haunt her. Can Troy help his mate face her fears or will the road to healing take a deadly turn?

The Claiming Curse – Book 3
Becca O'Reilly
Three years ago, days before my eighteenth birthday, my world was turned upside down after an attack on my pack left me in coma. My family hoped that once my birthday came I would gain my wolf and be able to heal from my injuries, except that did not happen. Now, I'm days away from my twenty-first birthday and adjusting to life in the human world. Everything has been going well until one phone call changed my life forever. I no longer know who to trust or believe— about myself or my pack.

Connor Shaw
As the future Alpha of Blue Moon, I have spent my whole life preparing to take over for my father. What I was not prepared for was running into my mate in the human world. She is everything I ever wanted in a mate and more. But now a decades old curse hangs over our heads, and if we don't figure out how to break it I could lose my mate before we get a chance to live. The more we learn, the more dangerous things become. Secrets new and old begin to surface that threaten my mate, our packs, and our future. I will stop at nothing. I will find a way to keep her safe, before it's too late.

Made in the USA
Columbia, SC
14 February 2025

d409388c-1ff3-410e-842e-f5d37edf3abfR01